COLLABORATION

DAVID L. GURNEE
&
DIANE C. GURNEE

COLLABORATION

by David L. Gurnee & Diane C. Gurnee
©2003 David L. Gurnee & Diane C. Gurnee

This story is a work of fiction.
Characters and incidents are fictitious, and
are products of the authors' imaginations.

Printed in the United States of America by:

WindTime Publications
PO Box 1934
Mackinac Island, MI 49757
www.windtime.com

ISBN 0-9719244-6-5
First Printing: June 2003

WORKS BY DAVID L. GURNEE:

Books:
Memoirs of Elise
A Love of Time
Collaboration
Add Cinema and Stir

Music CDs:
The Winds of Time
Coming Home
Themes

ACKNOWLEDGMENTS

Many thanks to all that were so helpful and supportive in this project. To Kristen Diehl, Scott Strait, Carl Ter Haar, Jim Patrick, and Jessie Hadley for answering our endless questions while we were doing research for this novel. Special thanks and love to our daughter Autumn for holding down the fort while we clicked away on the keyboard. We couldn't have done it without you!

FOREWORD

I NEVER WANTED TO BE A WRITER. I wrote *Memoirs of Elise* only out of necessity, to outline my ideas for a sequel movie to *Somewhere in Time*. I fully expected someone else would take those ideas and make a movie out of them. I would go back to computer consulting, and that would be that. However, life had other plans.

Besides bringing me to Mackinac Island, writing *Memoirs of Elise* did two major things for me. First, it indirectly got me back into doing something I had always loved – composing music. Second, it helped me to realize, that though I didn't enjoy *all* aspects of writing, I *did* enjoy crafting scenes, plots, and dialog – processes of screenwriting and filmmaking. This realization helped me enormously when writing my second novel, *A Love of Time*. And just as with *Memoirs of Elise*, I felt *A Love of Time* was a movie that I had condensed into a novel, rather than a novel that I hoped to turn into a movie.

As I began hatching the story you hold in your hands, I realized that I wanted to collaborate with a capable writer who enjoyed the process of descriptive writing, while I focused on scenes, plot, and dialog. My good friend Christopher Knight and I had discussed doing just that for a couple of years. In the summer of 2001, I laid out the plot of *Collaboration* to Chris, and we were prepared to begin writing. But again, life had other plans. Chris' *Michigan Chillers* series exploded, and Chris found it all he could do to keep up with personal appearances, new books, and a new book series, *American Chillers*.

Though disappointed, I never gave up the idea of having *Collaboration* be a collaboration. I found my collaborator, however, in the most unexpected place – under my own roof. My partner in crime on this novel is also my editor – my *wife!* And I must say, not only do I love Diane's descriptive writing, but well, I love *her!*

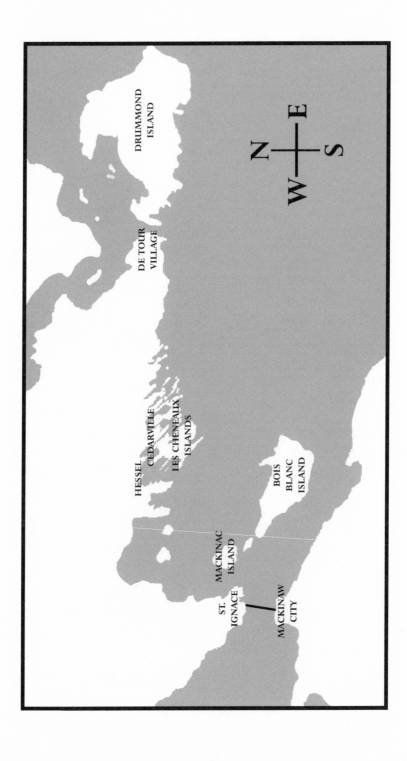

SHATTERED
DREAMS

FRIDAY, MAY 23ʳᵈ

JOHN HARRISON OPENED his living room window and breathed in the fresh, Northern Michigan air.

It had been a long, cold, winter. So cold, in fact, that for the first time in six years, Little Traverse Bay had frozen over. Ice shanties had dotted the bay for months, and a great deal of Northern Michigan's male population had been ensconced in those shanties; cozy and warm with propane heaters blasting; well stocked with the necessities to weather the long, empty months ahead.

John had seen them in the grocery store. Grown men standing in the checkout line with grocery carts filled to overflowing with so-called supplies: vodka, orange juice, beer, loaves of white bread, and a stab at nutrition — some lunch meat from the deli. They all had that gleam in their eye — part childish glee, part convict just released from prison. They were escaping the confines of home and family, roughing it (with all the comforts of home) with their buddies out on the ice, in their home away from home.

John would just smile to himself and shake his head. Occasionally he would join his next-door neighbor, Jim, and his buddies for an afternoon of poker and ice fishing. But most of his time was spent either pounding away at his keyboard, working on his fifth novel, or hanging out with Amy, his eleven-year-old daughter, the true joy of his life.

They'd had a blast this past winter – sledding, ice skating, building snowmen in the yard – and their pièce de résistance – an igloo. It had taken them two months; Amy had packed the snow in rectangular plastic tupperware containers, and carried them over to John. John had slowly formed the walls with the blocks, packing in wet snow like mortar to seal the cracks. When it was finished, they'd christened it Fort Bubbleskeeb (a nonsensical name that Amy made up) and planted a homemade flag at the top.

It was times like those that John lived for. They'd taken tons of pictures of each other standing on top of the fort, beside the fort, and inside the fort. He'd tried to get his wife Betsy to take some pictures of the two of them together in front of their creation, but as usual, she couldn't be bothered.

"John," she'd snapped, "I'm really busy right now. I have three appointments today to show the Carson house, and I haven't even gotten in the shower yet. Can't you set up the tripod or something?"

"Never mind," John had said. He should have known better. Since Betsy had received her real estate license, she'd spent less and less time with her family. John knew she felt left out of their *little club*, as she called it. After Amy was born, Betsy had decided to *do something with her life* and went to school to get her real estate license. Being a writer, John worked at home and had done most of the parenting for Amy.

As time passed, Betsy had grown distant, pulling farther and farther away. John and Amy had grown closer, clinging to each other for the love and comfort they sorely needed and missed from Betsy. Many times, John had tried to bridge the widening gap between them and include her in their lives. But it was not to be. Betsy was only interested in her real estate business and the hob-knobbing with the rich and infamous that went with it.

When they'd married, twenty years before, Betsy was a sweet, tenderhearted girl with a promising future as an artist. But that fair-skinned girl with the emerald green eyes and long, auburn hair, was gone now. In her place was a cool beauty in her late thirties, who decked herself out in Ferragamo stiletto pumps and Adrienne Vittadini skirt suits, with pearls at her ears and throat.

John sighed and reached for the door handle. *Enough with the melancholy*, he thought. *It's Memorial Weekend, buddy! You know what that means!* Summertime was around the corner. He and Amy would have all summer together at the cabin. He smiled and stepped out onto the front porch.

John was in his early forties, about six feet tall, with a muscular, athletic frame. He had mischievous, blue eyes, and tawny gold hair that feathered back from his face in layers and fell to his shoulders. Dressed in a plain white t-shirt with a plaid flannel shirt thrown over it, a pair of faded jeans and scuffed hiking boots, he looked more like a lumberjack than a successful writer.

He pulled the door shut behind him, and drank in the sunshine and fresh air. The ice shanties and snow were long gone. It was a gorgeous day. John had checked the weather on the internet earlier that morning. It was supposed to get up to seventy degrees in Petoskey, which meant probably sixty degrees up at their cabin in the Snows.

What a perfect day, he thought. Today was the day he would traditionally go up to the cabin to open it up and get it ready for summer. He turned and looked toward the driveway. His smile widened into a face-splitting grin. There in the driveway sat his newly reconditioned pride and joy – a 1934, twenty-six-foot triple cockpit, Chris-Craft Runabout – all that a wooden boat should be.

He and Amy had spent every summer since she was four years old, cruising through the Les Cheneaux Islands in that boat. Amy's favorite pastime was to sit in her daddy's lap as they cruised slowly through the sparkling blue channels. Light breezes would cool their faces as they threaded in and out of the islands. Amy would cry out in delight at the wildflowers that nodded and winked at them from the tree-lined shores. Birds chirped and chattered in the branches above, and an occasional deer would flash its white tail at them as it bounded away into the woods.

Amy was totally enchanted by the Snows – the local nickname of the Les Cheneaux Islands. Nestled against the northern shore of Lake Huron, the archipelago was a hidden treasure for the angler, boater, and nature lover. Amy loved learning the names of each new flower, bird, or animal they encountered in their explorations. John kept tattered, thumb-worn copies of wildflower and bird guides in the boat, plus duplicate copies at the cabin. Amy's thirst for knowledge and her enjoyment of the natural wonders around her thrilled him. Seeing life through her eyes was to see a miracle in a snowflake, the handiwork of the Creator in a pebble.

John felt a lump in his throat. *Today's the day,* he thought. *Amy will be so excited!*

John had always gone by himself to prepare the cabin for the season. Then Betsy and Amy would always join him there the next morning. For the last two years, however, Amy had been bugging him to go along. This year he would take her with him. She'd get the biggest kick out of it, helping him get the dock into the water, taking down the shutters and storm boards, sweeping the cabin out. It would be fun.

He smiled again and patted the side of his boat. Suddenly, a voice shattered his reverie.

"John! Need a hand there?"

John turned to see his neighbor, Jim cutting across the lawn toward him.

"Yeah, thanks, Jim."

John walked over to his black, Ford Explorer, whipped his keys out of his pocket, and jumped into the driver's seat. He adjusted his rearview mirror and stuck his head out of the window. Slowly he started backing the SUV toward the boat, as Jim coached him from behind.

"Keep coming, keep coming. Ho! Stop. Okay, perfect."

John slammed the gear into park and hopped out of the vehicle. He walked toward the rear of the boat, and removed the chocks from in front of the trailer wheels. They squatted down, grabbed the trailer hitch, and lifted. Grunting in unison, they struggled a few minutes until the boat hitch was securely hooked onto the car.

"Thanks again, Jim."

"Don't mention it," Jim replied. "So, you heading up to the cabin for the weekend?"

John smiled. "Where else?"

The sound of a ringing phone filtered through the living room window.

"Hey, your phone's ringin' buddy."

"You know, I don't think I can hear it," John smirked. "I do hear something though," he said as he cupped his hand to his ear. "Sounds like the roar of this boat motor up on Lake Huron."

They grinned at each other conspiratorially.

"Catch a few muskies for me, will ya?" Jim said as he reached over and clapped John on the back.

"Sure thing, buddy. See ya around," he called, as Jim headed back across the lawn to his house.

3:11 P.M.

BETSY HARRISON CURSED. "Damn! Why doesn't he pick up the phone?" She held her cell phone to one ear and she beat out an impatient tattoo on the steering wheel with her long, manicured nails. The answering machine at the Harrison home clicked on. The bubbly voice of her daughter Amy started to speak.

Hi! You've reached the Harrison home. We're not here right now. Please leave a message and we'll call you back. Thanks!

Betsy tried using the phone as a loudspeaker. "John! John! Are you home? John! Pick up the phone if you're there! Well, I'm stuck in traffic on the bridge. I was hoping to talk to you before you left for the cabin. Anyway, Amy and I will meet you there tomorrow. Bye."

Betsy jabbed the end call button with her fingernail. She looked at the phone for a moment, then tried to make another call. Now all she heard was a maddening Beep! Beep! Beep! sound. "Damn! All circuits busy! Not much of a phone service if you can't make a phone call when you need to!" Disgusted, she threw the phone down on the passenger seat.

She was mad at everything and everyone. *Stuck in a traffic jam on the Mackinac Bridge of all places!*

"I can't even get out and have a smoke!" she raved. "This is just the icing on the cake."

Betsy was already furious at John about last Friday night. She'd been invited by friends to a huge party down in Detroit. Everyone who was anyone was going to be there. Lots of potential for new clients. She'd even heard a rumor that Madonna and her husband-of-the-month were planning on dropping by. *Wow! What a client she would have been!* Betsy salivated at the thought. Madonna already owned a palatial mansion in Bay Harbor. She'd heard that the material girl was looking for a cozy cabin in the U.P. for when she *really* wanted to get away from it all. But John had insisted that Betsy attend the school play that Amy was in.

The blast of a car horn startled Betsy back to reality. Apparently she hadn't noticed that the car in front of her had moved ahead a half-foot. She hesitated for a few moments just to further irritate the guy in the red Cavalier behind her. Another blast of his horn told her she'd succeeded. With a self-satisfied smile, she moved her taupe convertible Mercedes forward to close the gap. Then, catching the eye of the driver in her rearview mirror, she gave him a combination half-smile, dirty look, as if to say, *There! Happy now, asshole?* Betsy returned to her thoughts.

"John," she'd said, "I'd *love* to go to Amy's play. But this is a *big* deal. I can't afford to miss this party. My business depends on contacts that I make. A major potential client is supposed to be attending the party, and Todd promised he'd make introductions." (Todd was her hairdresser friend in Detroit who ran a salon that catered to the wealthy and the *who's who* in the music world.) "This could be a major coup for me."

John had blown a gasket. "A coup, Betsy? Are you starting a war or something? Is that all you care about, the next big kill? The next notch on your belt? What about Amy, for God's sake? She's your daughter, your family. She craves your love and attention so desperately. She may be a child, but she's not stupid. She sees by your actions, or rather *lack* of them, that you care more about spending time pursuing your next kill, than spending time with her. Sure, I'm always there to cheer her on, but damn it, Betsy, she wants you there too. You're her mother. Why don't you act like it?"

Betsy was so immersed in her thoughts that at first she didn't hear the honking horns. The man in the red Cavalier behind her had been laying on his horn for a good ten seconds before Betsy reacted. "What the . . . ?" she yelped. She looked ahead and saw that the traffic had cleared. Here she was holding up a line of cars behind her. Quickly she threw the car into first gear and stomped on the gas pedal. Without warning, a semi-truck veered over from the left lane right into her path. Betsy screamed and slammed on her brakes.

3:25 P.M.

JOHN PULLED UP in front of Marquette Elementary and waited for the school bell to ring. He realized that with the boat hitched behind him, he was hogging half the driveway, but it couldn't be helped.

He turned the engine off and waited for Amy. *She's going to be so surprised!* He smiled at the thought. He sat there enjoying the momentary peace and quiet. He looked out through the passenger's window and watched a squirrel as it scampered across the grassy lawn in front of the school. It ran up a nearby tree and paused long enough to scold him, whipping its tail back and forth to show its irritation. A blue jay landed on a branch just above and to the right of the squirrel, and let out a rattling Caaaank! to claim his territory. This was more than the squirrel bargained for, and it bolted.

John chuckled. "Gee, reminds me of a quarrelsome couple I know. You did the sensible thing, Mr. Squirrel. Run for your life!"

Abruptly, the loud, shrill school bell shattered the afternoon calm. Noisy kids poured out of the front double doors of the school, laughing and running, pushing, shoving, and yelling. Teachers positioned themselves along the sidewalk, vainly attempting to corral the excited children until they were loaded onto buses, or safely delivered over to parents waiting patiently in cars.

John scanned the throng. He spotted Amy and her best friend Kali Morgan walking toward their school bus. His heart swelled as he watched his little girl walk down the sidewalk.

"She's the spitting image of her mother," he breathed. Amy had the same creamy white skin, long auburn hair, and delicate, heart-shaped face. The only difference between them was that Amy had big brown eyes. Where she'd gotten them from mystified John. Everyone in his family had blue eyes. Everyone in Betsy's family had either hazel, or emerald green, like Betsy. "I'd better check and see what color the milkman's eyes are," he'd teased after Amy was born. Betsy, in full blown, post-partum depression, hadn't been amused.

John tooted his horn twice, then once, and Amy looked up. He leaned over and opened the passenger side door for her.

"Daddy!" Amy cried as she ran up to the car.

"Hello, sunshine," John grinned.

"What are you doing here?" Amy asked.

"Well, you've always wanted to go with me to get the cabin ready for the season . . . "

"You said I wasn't old enough."

"You're eleven years old. I think that's old enough, don't you?" John and Amy smiled at each other in agreement.

Amy looked back at her friend Kali and shouted, "I'm going with my dad to the cabin! See ya Tuesday!"

"Here, let me help you with that." He leaned over and grabbed the bookbag that Amy was struggling with, then swung it over the front seat and plopped it neatly onto the seat behind them.

"We'd better give mommy a call and let her know you're going with me, or she'll kill me," he warned.

Amy buckled her seat belt as John reached into his jacket pocket for his cell phone. He flipped open the phone and hit the speed dial for Betsy's cell phone. All he heard was a Beep! Beep! Beep! sound. "Darn! All circuits busy! I guess we'll have to try again later." He started the car, pulled out onto the street, and turned left. "Don't let me forget, okay, Punkin?"

"Daddy! How many times do I have to tell you my name's not Punkin' anymore? I'm almost twelve years old!" Amy pointed out.

John took a right onto US-31 toward Mackinaw City. "Okay, okay. You're right. I keep forgetting how grown up you are. I suppose you'll always be my little girl, even when you're married and have kids of your own," John sighed. "Hey, what do you want to have for supper tonight?" he said, changing the subject.

"I don't know," said Amy. "What do *you* want?"

"Well, since it's a very special occasion tonight, what do you say we *really* celebrate. Why don't we order pizza with all your favorite toppings?"

"You mean sausage, pepperoni, and double cheese?" Amy gasped.

"Why not?" he replied.

"Daddy! You're supposed to be watching your cholesterol!"

"I *am* watching my cholesterol," he teased. "It's going up and up and up!"

"Daddy! You've got to take care of yourself!"

"Oh no, here it comes," he groaned, as Amy burst into song.

"Take good care of yourself," she chirped, "you belong to me!"

"Do you have to sing that every time I want to eat something fun?" he teased. "So it's settled, then. Pizza it is!"

Amy caved. "Well, I guess so. Just this once, Daddy. But *promise* me we'll eat really good for the rest of the summer. Okay?"

"Okay," John promised. "How does S'mores sound for dessert?"

"*Daddy!*" Amy protested. John laughed heartily, grabbed Amy's hand and kissed it.

"What in the world would I do without you?" he said gently.

3:40 P.M.

NATALIE HEBERT LOOKED at herself in the bathroom mirror. Her olive skin looked pale and sallow, the dark-brown tan she'd sported last summer a distant memory. Her hazel eyes looked a little bleary from lack of sleep. She'd just switched over from day shift to night duty and her body hadn't adjusted yet. She brushed her long, brown-black hair, pulled it back, and with a flick of her wrist, wound it into a French twist. She grabbed two large bobby pins, pried them open with her teeth, then stuck them in at strategic places to anchor her hair. She stuck a few more bobby pins in for good measure, then peered into the mirror to check her work.

Not bad for a girl from the bayou, she thought. She was thirty-three years old, but people usually guessed her to be in her early twenties.

She fastened her modest silver stud earrings in her ears. Her only other adornments were a silver sports watch, and a simple, hammered-silver ring she'd fallen in love with at a pricey boutique in New Orleans one summer.

Except for chapstick, Natalie didn't wear makeup on the job because she didn't want to call attention to herself. She was very conscious (almost to the point of being self-conscious) about being the only female deputy sheriff in a fifty-mile radius. She fit in okay, but this part of the country had a rugged breed of people, and was still in many ways a *man's* world. The other officers were polite, even kind, but she could sense that they were somewhat uncomfortable with a *girl* in their midst. They liked having a woman around, but even after five and a half years, they still weren't sure how to act around her, not wanting to offend her with their normal bawdy humor.

Natalie straightened her tie, then stuck her tongue out at herself in disgust. "Khaki! A khaki tie!" she said aloud. "Why couldn't our uniforms be a nice, elegant, midnight blue like my N.O.P.D. uniform? No, they have to be brown and khaki! It totally washes me out and makes my skin look green! Oh well," she sighed, "can't be helped, I suppose."

She turned and flipped off the bathroom light, then padded over to the kitchen in her socks, pausing to look out the window over the sink. She took a deep breath, inhaling the cool, fresh air coming in through the open window. A delightful cacophony of birdsong assaulted her ears. During the winter she'd had only the chickadees, jays, juncos, and the occasional cardinal to keep her company at her cabin. Now, robins whinnied, sparrows chirped, and warblers whistled and trilled. Of course, those annoying starlings were also back – their jumble of squeaks, rattles, wheezes and chuckles, competing with all comers for turf, letting all their lady friends know that the unattached males were back in town.

Reluctantly, Natalie closed the window and latched it. On her next day off, she vowed to take her kayak out, paddle over to the marsh, and check on the Great Blue Herons that nested there.

The coffee finished brewing. Natalie switched off the coffee pot and unplugged it for good measure. She had a tendency to forget whether she'd turned it off or not. Usually, right about the time she reached for her thermos to take a swig, she'd start second-guessing herself. Rather than having to drive all the way home to check it, she had simply started unplugging the coffee pot after it had finished brewing.

She grabbed the carafe by its handle, flipped up the lid, stuck her nose next to it, and inhaled deeply. "Aaaah! Nectar of the gods," she said. Carefully, she poured the coffee into her thermos. It smelled rich and strong and expensive. It *was*. It was a special blend of chicory roast coffee that she'd special-ordered from Café du Monde in New Orleans. She poured in the usual half-ton of sugar and added about a half cup of heavy cream. She popped the lid on, spun it with a flick of her thumb, then twisted it a couple of times to make sure it was securely sealed.

There was plenty of coffee to be had at the station in Hessel, she knew. But Natalie was a self-confessed coffee snob. She wouldn't drink that nasty-smelling, burnt-tire-tasting swill, even if she was desperate.

Natalie glanced down at her watch. "Geez!"

She bent over and checked the dog dishes. Their food bowls looked pretty good, but the water bowls definitely needed filling. She ran the tap for a few moments to make sure the temperature was right, then filled both water bowls, and set them on the floor. Natalie glanced over to the sofa where her two dogs, Abby and Salty, lay sulking.

"Come on kids, you know the drill. I have to go to work now. I promise when I get home, we'll go for a late night walk, okay?"

Abby's ears perked up at the word *walk*. She lifted her head in anticipation. She was a malamute with blue eyes and a beautiful, thick coat with soft black and grey markings.

Salty lay there without moving. He was the more sensitive of the two dogs. His feelings were easily wounded. The big German shepherd languished there on the couch, his head resting on a red throw-pillow, his sorrowful brown eyes accusing her of neglect.

"Oh, all right, all right!" Natalie said, exasperated. She walked over to them and squatted down beside the sofa. She petted Salty gently, and then nuzzled her face in his soft fur. He licked her face a few times, signaling that she was forgiven, for now. Abby watched intently.

Natalie gave Salty a big hug and turned to Abby. "Yeah, I know, equal time." She petted Abby for a few moments, cooing and praising her as she stroked her fur. "I love you guys, you know that. I promise we'll go for more walks now that it's warm. You can chase as many squirrels as you want, okay?" Abby's ears perked up again, and her tail thumped in excitement on the sofa, recognizing yet another familiar word. "Later, Abby. Later," Natalie admonished. Abby's tail stopped and she put her head down on the sofa. Natalie smiled and shook her head. "Gotta go, kids. I'll check on you later."

Natalie grabbed her thermos and water bottle and headed toward the front door, flipping lights off as she went. She walked over to her designated shoe mat lying just inside the door. From the collection of shoes that had accumulated there, she picked out the appropriate pair. While tugging on her standard-issue, black leather police shoes, she glanced at her watch. Then she grabbed her hat off the side table in the hall, flung the front screen door open, crossed the porch in two strides, and flew down the steps.

She whipped open the door of her cruiser, and with a flick of her wrist, sent her hat sailing frisbee-style onto the front seat. Then she ducked her head and knelt on the front seat. Leaning over the radio tower, she carefully placed her thermos and water bottle in the holder on the floorboard of the passenger side.

She scooted back out of the car and ran back into the house to grab her brown sheriff's department jacket. "It'll probably get cool tonight," she said aloud. "Better be prepared." She scanned the cabin again just to make sure no lights had been left on, then closed the door and locked it. The screen door banged shut behind her. She stood on the front porch, closed her eyes, and forced herself to pause for a moment before rushing off to work. Mentally, she ticked off her *to do* list, prioritizing her evening ahead. She decided to do the most unpleasant task first. Paperwork. She'd go to the station, attack the stack of papers on her desk while she was full of energy, and then later that evening, she'd cruise around the area, especially the trouble spots. The next two days would be pretty busy.

Today was the Friday before Memorial Day Weekend. Lots of summer people would be heading up to the Snows to open up their cabins, and do a little boating and fishing. Today was also payday for Port Dolomite, and that meant the local bars would be hopping tonight. The younger, twenty-something crowd that hung out at one of the local bars, was still in that brash, posturing, *young buck* stage. She figured she'd have to break up at least one fight that evening. And to top it all off, tonight was a full moon. "What is it with men?" she groused to herself aloud. "Can't live *with* them, can't shoot 'em." With that remark, she sighed heavily, opened her eyes, and jogged down the steps to her car.

3:55 P.M.

AMY CHATTERED non-stop as they drove north on US-31. If it weren't for the seatbelt holding her in place, John mused, she would be ricocheting around the car, she was so excited. Visions of Speedy Gonzales bouncing off the doors and the windows of the car made John laugh.

Amy stopped in mid-sentence. "What's so funny, Daddy?"

"Nothing Punkin', er, Amy," he corrected himself before Amy had the chance.

Amy picked up where she left off and continued her story about the new teacher at school, oblivious to John's inattention. Normally, John listened attentively when Amy talked, but today he was distracted. Part of it was the excitement of going to the cabin to open it up for the summer. The night before, John barely got any sleep. His anticipation of the summer ahead was as great as that of any child awaiting Christmas morning.

He'd planned all kinds of new adventures for the two of them. Betsy, he knew, wouldn't be a part of those adventures. She would come up for the obligatory

Memorial Day weekend, but by Tuesday morning she'd be chomping at the bit to get back to work. "Darling," she'd say to Amy, "I'd love to stay, but I have so many business meetings this summer. Maybe next summer I'll stay longer." She'd plant a kiss, leaving her signature mark of red Chanel lipstick on Amy's cheek. Then she might give John a peck. Despite protests from both John and Amy that she would miss all the fun, she'd climb into her sleek Mercedes sports coup, slip on her Chanel sunglasses, and secure a silk scarf over her hair. The car would roar to life, and with a wave of her hand, she'd be gone. Every year it was the same. Why would it be any different this year?

John sighed.

"What's the matter, Daddy?" Amy finally noticed that her daddy wasn't his normal, attentive self.

"Oh, nothing, sweetie," he covered. "I just wish Mommy could spend more time with us this summer."

"Me too," Amy said sadly. Then abruptly, her tone changed. "Daddy! You were supposed to call Mommy!"

"That's right! Thanks for reminding me, honey." John hit the speed dial for Betsy's cell phone. Again, all he heard was a frustrating Beep! Beep! Beep! sound. "Darn! Now what?" he said. "I can't get through at all."

They were just passing through Alanson when John spied a pay phone on the wall outside of a convenience store. John pulled in the driveway and parked in front of the phone. "I'm going to have to use the pay phone to call mommy."

John opened the door and said, "Wait right here, okay?"

"Okay," Amy replied.

John walked over to the pay phone and picked up the hand set. He dialed his card number, then Betsy's cell number. After a few rings, he heard a recorded message: *I'm sorry, the person you have called is out of the service area.* He put the phone back on its cradle for a moment, then picked it back up, and dialed home. The phone rang the usual umpteen times before the answering machine clicked on. When he heard the beep, he started speaking. "Betsy, it's me. I can't reach your cell phone. I picked up Amy at school and we're on our way to the cabin. We'll see you tomorrow, okay? Bye." John hung the phone on its cradle and walked back to the car.

Twenty-five minutes later, they were crossing the Mackinac Bridge. The view was breathtaking. Amy sucked in her breath in awe, and for a moment was speechless.

Huge strands of green steel cable arced gracefully up to the two, tall, cream towers in front of them. On either side, a vast panorama of sparkling blue waters met their eyes. To the right, Mackinac Island floated serenely on calm waters. A large, white building sat halfway up the hillside, nestled snugly amid the dark green pines and cedars. "There's Grand Hotel!" Amy called out. The palatial hotel glowed in the afternoon sun. "And there's the lighthouse!" she pointed to the right of Mackinac Island.

Last July, one of their biggest adventures had been to motor over to Round Island in their Chris-Craft runabout, *Almost Paradise*, for the day. "Can we hike around Round Island again this summer?" Amy begged.

"Again?" John asked. "Don't you want to have *new* adventures this summer?"

"Well . . . what did you have in mind?" Amy said, as they pulled up to the toll booth on the other side of the bridge.

"You'll have to wait and see," John teased. "Excuse me, honey, can you open the ashtray and get me eighteen quarters?"

"Sure, Daddy." Amy opened the ashtray they used for loose change. She picked eighteen quarters out of the mass of coins and carefully handed them over to John. "Here ya go."

"Thanks, sweetie."

The toll booth operator leaned over to take the fare. "Have a good day, sir," he said, and smiled at them through the car window.

"Thanks, you too," John replied, and drove away.

"Daddy, I'm cold. Can we roll up the windows?"

"Sure." John held his left thumb on the window switches until both windows were shut.

"So, munchkin, what are you going to do first when we get there?"

"Well," Amy thought for a moment. "I'm going to go check on Bullwinkle to make sure he's okay, and then I'm going to say hi to Rocky."

"Rocky? Did you get another stuffed toy to keep Bullwinkle company?"

"No, Daddy," Amy replied. "Rocky is a *real* squirrel. Mr. W. tamed him last summer. He lets me feed him if I'm real quiet and stand real still so I don't scare Rocky."

"That's really cool," John said. "I'll bring my camera over and we can take pictures of you feeding him."

Mr. 'W' was John's neighbor, Ted Wolenchenski, who lived a few cabins down from them. He was a tall, robust man in his mid-sixties, who had been a world-class photo journalist in his youth. He and his wife had lived in Minneapolis, and had summered at their cabin in the Snows every year for twenty-seven years. His wife had died a little over five years before, and to the consternation of his only son, Ted moved to the cabin permanently.

"The memories Rachel and I made together in this little cabin are my most cherished possessions," he'd once confided to John. "I intend to live among them until the day I die." Those words were etched indelibly in John's mind. They'd touched him deeply, but had saddened him at the same time. Many times over the last several years, Ted's words would come to mind and painfully remind John of what he was missing in his own life.

Stop it! John said to himself. *You have so much to be thankful for, buddy. Why don't you pay attention to what you do have, Harrison?!* John swam up out of his dark, murky thoughts, and turned to look at his daughter. Amy was looking out of her window at the shimmering, diamond-spangled waters of Lake Huron. Suddenly she shouted, "Daddy, look!"

John glanced over and saw three bald eagles standing on a spit of land. "Wow!" he exclaimed. "Aren't they beautiful?" The proud, majestic birds were oblivious to their admirers passing by. He made a mental note of the spot — right at Nunn's Creek, not ten minutes away from Hessel. He would return with Amy some day soon to see if they could spot the magnificent birds again.

The afternoon sun cast a warm glow over the scenery. "God, this place is incredible," John whispered to himself.

5:00 P.M.

GREG REYNOLDS SAT DOWN in the rickety lawn chair on his deck. It wobbled a bit, then stabilized. He took a swig of Jack Daniels and then popped the cap on the last bottle of Strohs.

"Where the hell is Tyler?" he asked. "We're out of beer chasers."

His cousin, Mike, sat next to him in a lawnchair that rivaled Greg's in decrepitude.

"He sh–, he'll be back any minute, cuz." Mike's speech was a little slurred, and he was having trouble forming certain consonants. He'd already polished off a half bottle of Southern Comfort and four beer chasers.

"Well, he better hurry up," Greg complained. "I've had just about enough of his crap, I tell ya." His speech was no less garbled than Mike's, due to the vast quantity of Jack Daniels he'd polished off in an alarmingly short period of time.

Today had been payday at Port Dolomite, and after work, the three of them had met up at Greg's place for their weekly binge on bullets and booze. They'd all get roaring drunk and practice target shooting in the field behind Greg's dilapidated trailer.

They had sent Tyler out on a beer run over a half-hour ago, and he hadn't returned yet. "What in the hell is takin' him so long?" Greg snarled. "Did that little pissant get lost or something? The store is only five miles from here."

Greg was in a black mood. "I've had just about enough of him, I tell ya. A couple a weeks ago, he started buggin' me about the money I owe him." Greg shifted his weight to get comfortable. His chair groaned and squeaked in protest. "He said, 'when you gonna start payin' me back the five grand you owe me?' as if I'd forgotten all about it or somethin'. Then he said, 'you always seem to have plenty of money to buy booze and cigarettes, but you never seem to have any left over to pay *me*.' Right in front of the other guys at work! Do you believe the nerve of that little shit?" Greg raved on. "I coulda killed him right then and there."

"What'd you do?" Mike asked.

"I grabbed him by the neck and started squeezin'. His eyes popped out and he turned three shades of red before I let go."

Mike grinned wickedly. Greg continued.

"He backed off real quick, then. I told him to quit buggin' me."

Greg waved his beer in the air. "Don't he realize how much money it takes to keep up a place like this?" He gestured to his trailer behind him.

Mike looked around him. The yard was littered with old, threadbare tires and car parts in various stages of decay. A couple of ancient snowmobiles sat rusting in the weeds off to his left, waiting to be cannibalized. The trailer house behind them was an unattractive combination of baby blue and rusty metal.

For the life of him, Mike couldn't figure out what Greg meant by *keeping up the place*. But Mike knew better than to contradict his cousin. Greg had a nasty temper, especially when he'd been drinking. He'd seen Greg more than once come out on top in a bar fight with men twice his size.

Greg was on a roll. "Then, there's the crap Tyler pulled last week. A buddy of mine told me he saw Tyler gettin' cozy with Jenny, up at a bar in the Soo. I was pissed, let me tell you, cuz. What the hell does she want with him? Lazy dirtbag. He don't have nothin' I don't have." Greg lapsed into silence.

Greg Reynolds was in his thirties, with coal black hair and blue eyes. Many women had commented on his baby blues, calling them *bedroom eyes*. It was an accurate assessment, since those enticing eyes had been the reason he was so successful in getting plenty of female visitors to that particular room.

Why Jenny had preferred Tyler's bedroom to his, was a mystery to Greg. It never entered his mind that Jenny might have grown tired of Greg's tomcatting around, and found someone who would really care for her and be faithful. When Greg had heard about Jenny's betrayal, he'd decided right then on his revenge. Tyler would never see one cent of that five grand. He'd just keep stringing him along, forever.

As for Jenny, he'd already fixed *her* little wagon. He'd shown up at her house the next day and had beaten the hell out of her. She'd lain on the kitchen floor, curled into a fetal position, sobbing and pleading for mercy. He'd leaned over and whispered in her ear, "If you tell anyone about this, you're gonna wake up dead one morning." Then he'd grinned at his own humor, stepped over her bruised and battered body, and walked out the door.

Greg grinned to himself and then looked over at Mike. "Cuz," he said, "why don't we get started on our target practice while we're waiting on pissant?"

Mike was relieved to see that Greg's dark mood had lifted. "Sure."

Greg rose from his chair and stretched to get the kinks out of his back. He walked across the weathered deck and disappeared into the dark recesses of the trailer. A few minutes later he reappeared, juggling two guns and a box of ammo.

Mike had stepped off the porch and was headed toward the makeshift target area – a few cedar posts sunk in the ground at irregular intervals across the field behind the trailer. He had the nearly empty bottle of Southern Comfort in his left hand, and juggled three empty beer bottles in the crook of his right arm.

"Hey Mike!" Greg yelled. "Bet I can shoot that bottle of Southern Comfort off your head from fifty yards!"

Mike took another swig from his bottle and looked at Greg for a second. "You're full a shit. You'll end up shooting my dick off."

Greg grinned at Mike. "Nobody but you would miss it anyway."

Mike thought about it for a second or two, then guffawed. "Good one!" At that moment, he heard Tyler's truck pull in the driveway. "Hey, why don't we use Tyler for target practice instead?" He grinned wickedly at Greg and winked.

Greg smiled back. "Not a bad idea, Mike! Not bad at all."

Tyler turned off the engine and just sat there for a moment, wondering what in the hell was he doing there. He used to enjoy their Friday night ritual. But not anymore. Not after what Greg did to Jenny.

Jenny never said a word to Tyler about the beating. She didn't have to. Tyler had taken one look at her bruised, swollen face and bloody lip, and had flown into a rage. He told Jenny he was going to give Greg a taste of his own medicine.

"Don't," Jenny had begged him. "Please don't go after him. He'll kill me if you do. He's done with me. Let's just put it behind us and move on, okay, honey?"

After much coaxing, Tyler had grudgingly agreed. He hated Greg for what he'd done to Jenny, but he knew for Jenny's sake, he'd have to let it lie. At least for now, anyway.

Tyler gritted his teeth and opened the truck door. He grabbed the grocery bag from the front seat, and carefully made his way through the minefield of rusty car parts. Greg rarely mowed the yard, so more than once, Tyler had stumbled over a piece of junk hidden in the tall weeds. Today he managed to make it around the side of the trailer and into the backyard, unscathed.

"There you are, Tyler! We thought you'd run off with our beer money with some blonde floozy," Greg cracked. Jenny was blonde. Tyler of course, knew that Greg was needling him. He stared blankly at Greg. He knew better than to let Greg pick a fight with him.

Greg looked at Tyler and then pointed toward the back of the field. "Tyler, why don't you go down about a hun'erd yards and put that bottle of Southern Comfort on your head?" Greg pointed at the bottle Mike was waving around in the air.

Tyler gave Greg a dirty look. "Are you outta your mind, Greg? Why would I do that?"

Greg looked at him suspiciously. "What's the matter, Tyler? Don't you trust me?"

Tyler eyed Greg for a moment. "I trust you," Tyler said slowly. "I just don't trust your aim, right about now."

Greg suddenly whipped his 30.06 up to his shoulder, aimed at a dark-brown beer bottle sitting on a tree stump about eighty yards away, and fired. The bullet found its mark and the bottle shattered.

Mike cheered. "Yahoo! Way to go, cuz!"

Greg looked back at Tyler. "Well, Tyler, what are you waiting for?"

Tyler weighed his options. Greg wasn't crazy enough to try and kill him right here in broad daylight. If he refused however . . . Tyler decided that it would be safer for Jenny's sake to play along.

"Okay, Greg." Tyler pasted a smile on his face, grabbed the bottle of Southern Comfort out of Mike's hand, and started to walk toward the end of the field.

"Where the hell you think you're goin'?" Greg yelled.

Tyler was getting tired of Greg's games. "Where the hell you *think* I'm goin'?"

Greg gave him a dirty look. "Come er'!" he commanded.

Tyler trudged back over to Greg. Greg grabbed the whiskey bottle from him and polished it off.

"Ain't gonna waste good whiskey," Greg said. Then he handed the empty bottle back to Tyler. Tyler turned and started walking toward the edge of the field.

5:24 P.M.

AMY UNBUCKLED her seatbelt and leaned over the seat. She rummaged through a pink canvas tote bag, then plopped back down in her seat looking perplexed.

"What are you doing, Amy? You know you're supposed to be buckled in your seatbelt while the car is moving."

"Daddy, where's Rebecca?"

"Rebecca? Who's Rebecca?" he asked in mock innocence.

"*You* know, Daddy, my favorite doll."

"Oh, that's right. Rebecca," he teased. "You have so many dolls, I can't keep track of all of them. Well, I thought since you were too old for hugs and nicknames, you wouldn't want to be seen carrying a doll around," he taunted.

"Daddy!" she huffed indignantly, "it's *tradition*. I *always* take her with me to the cabin every summer. It wouldn't feel right without her there." Amy was angry now.

"Whoa there! Hold on darlin'! I was just teasin'! She's right there in the blue backpack at your feet. You can take her out, but be sure you get buckled back in real fast, okay, honey?"

Amy's smile lit up her face. She bent over and unzipped the backpack and pulled Rebecca out. John turned his attention back to the road as Amy straightened back in her seat. He heard a curious plink sound, and felt something wet on his face. Immediately he felt Amy fall hard against his leg. He looked down and saw blood everywhere.

5:30 P.M.

NATALIE WALKED ACROSS the parking lot to her car. The late afternoon sun warmed her face and soothed her nerves. She'd just transported an exceptionally obnoxious prisoner from the Mackinac county jail, up to Kinross Correctional. The man had hurled obscenities at her the entire trip, and she was more than happy to get him out of her car when they reached the prison.

A low rumbling sound informed her that the two pieces of toast she'd eaten for lunch were not going to hold her until supper time.

"Hmmm. Maybe I should eat early tonight. Some fried perch would be nice." She didn't realize she'd been talking to herself until she looked up and saw a fellow officer give her a curious smile as he walked past her in the parking lot. Natalie flushed with embarrassment.

It wasn't the first time someone had caught her talking to herself. With the police force being as small as it was in the county, she didn't have a partner to keep her company during the long, tedious hours between calls. She'd started talking to herself to keep from going crazy from the silence. It helped her organize her thoughts, too. But Natalie had been teased many times by friends and co-workers about her one-sided conversations.

Natalie unlocked the door of her cruiser. Before she'd even climbed in, the agitated chatter from her car radio arrested her attention.

"We have an accidental shooting near the corner of Hennepin and Blanchard roads. Request medical and officer assistance immediately. Over."

Natalie's breath caught in her chest. Was it her imagination, or did the dispatcher's voice tremble just then? She started the car and quickly backed out of the parking slot. She heard Charlie Tanner's response to Dispatch.

"Roger that, Dispatch, this is Deputy Tanner. I'm three minutes from that location. I'll be there in a heartbeat. We might need Advanced Life Support Intercept from Kinross if it looks bad. Over."

"Way ahead of you, Charlie," Dispatch responded. "We'll notify Kinross and have a paramedic ready to go if needed. Over."

Natalie's heart beat faster. She reached over to the radio tower next to her and flipped on her siren and light. She threw the car into gear and shot out of the parking lot.

"Dear God, I hope it's not bad," Natalie said. She was a good thirty minutes away. Everyone in the area would be responding to this call. She turned onto I-75 and headed south, the siren screaming its insistent warning as she flew down the highway. The traffic parted before her, as cars obediently pulled over to the side of the road to let her pass. Natalie checked the time. Only a few more minutes before her M134 turnoff. Another twenty-five minutes after that and she'd be there.

Two cars just ahead of her, however, didn't seem to notice the flashing lights atop her cruiser. "Get out of the way, you idiots!"

The red Jeep in the left lane ahead of Natalie contained two college-aged girls. They were attempting to flirt with a carload of the opposite sex in the silver Trans Am in the right lane in front of Natalie. The girl on the passenger side of the red Jeep was leaning out of her window, trying to talk to the driver of the Trans Am. "Flirting is dicey enough when standing still," Natalie fumed. "This is downright precarious!"

Natalie honked her horn and flipped the siren to a different tone, trying to get their attention. Finally, the girl aborted her gymnastics and settled back into her seat. The Jeep shot forward and passed the Trans Am, giving Natalie room to pass.

"You'd better be glad I'm in a hurry, kiddos." She floored the gas pedal, and within a few minutes, had left the pack of raging hormones behind her.

Natalie continued down I-75. Normally she was able to tune out the sound of her siren, but today was different. Today its urgent wail set her on edge. She remembered the communication she'd heard minutes before. *Something* in the dispatcher's voice. A ripple of fear went through her body.

In the five and a half years she'd lived in the area, Natalie had grown close to many of the local people. Cedarville and Hessel were small, tightly-knit communities. Everyone looked out for each other, to the extreme annoyance of the local school kids.

"It's like living in a fish bowl," Christina, one of the Jr. Girl Scouts, had bellyached to Natalie last summer. Natalie had taken the troop out to Government Island for a hike and a picnic. "Can't get away with nuthin' around here," Christina had complained.

"Can't get away with *anything*," Natalie had gently corrected her.

"See what I mean!" Christina had retorted. Natalie just smiled in response.

Through her involvement with the local Girl Scouts and the D.A.R.E. program at school, Natalie knew most of the local kids and their parents by name. It made for warm and friendly relationships, for the most part. The sticky side of it was when the call from Dispatch would involve someone she knew from the community. Natalie had endured a crash course in diplomacy when she'd first moved here. Things were not done here the way they were in New Orleans Sixth District, that was for sure.

Charlie Tanner's voice interrupted her thoughts. "Dispatch, cancel that Advanced Life Support Intercept. Over." His voice had a flat, dead quality to it.

Natalie went cold. Her grip tightened on the steering wheel.

About ten minutes later, she arrived at the accident scene. Cruisers were scattered everywhere, as if a giant toy box had been dumped over, its contents spilling out onto the roadway and nearby field. Natalie pulled in behind a State Police cruiser and turned off her engine. She noted more than a half dozen cars – the Chippewa County Sheriff's Department, State Police cruisers from both St. Ignace and Detour, Charlie Tanner's cruiser, an ambulance, and even a Tribal car. She noticed a black hearse about three car lengths away. It slipped out of the gnarl of vehicles and silently pulled away. Her mouth went dry.

Then she noticed the silence. *It's so quiet*, she thought. The scene before her seemed surreal. The sirens had been silenced, but the emergency vehicle lights still flashed blue and red – a bizarre, dream-like disco scene with the sound cut out. Even the birds were silent.

Natalie got out of her car and started walking toward the knot of uniforms standing in a field off to one side. Every face was set in a grim line. As law enforcement officers, they'd all seen their share of tragedy, but even Charlie Tanner, the hard-boiled veteran of the group, looked rattled. He nodded hello as Natalie walked up to them.

One of the officers broke the silence. He began recapping the events for the officers who had arrived late on the scene. "The kid didn't stand a chance," he began. "The shot blew off the side of her head. She was killed instantly."

"For Pete's sake, will you bring it down a bit, Brad?" Charlie hissed. "Her father is right over there," he nodded toward the ambulance.

Natalie turned and looked. Her hand flew to her mouth. "Oh, my God." She instantly recognized the man sitting on the back bumper of the ambulance.

John Harrison. She didn't know him personally, but her friend, Ted Wolenchenski, lived just down the road from the Harrison's cabin. His daughter Amy had come by Ted's cabin once, when Natalie had been visiting him.

Amy.

Oh, my God. Amy. Natalie's stomach flip-flopped. She quickly turned away, her mind reeling. For a moment she thought she was going to be sick. She balled her hands into fists and willed her mind into subjection.

"Get a grip, girl," she whispered to herself. She turned and looked at John again. He had a blanket over his shoulders, and an EMT specialist stood next to him, holding the IV bag he'd hooked up to sedate him.

Charlie leaned toward Natalie. "The EMT had to pry him away from her body. He tried to get him to lie down on the gurney, but he put up such a fight, the EMT finally gave up."

Natalie's heart went out to John. He sat there silently, a glazed look in his eyes, no doubt caused by the potent cocktail of shock and sedatives. He had a shattered, fragile look about him.

"Poor guy. I'm gonna see what I can do for him," Natalie said. She walked over to the back of the ambulance.

"Mr. Harrison," she said gently, "I'm Officer Hebert. Is there anything I can do for you?"

John looked up at her and suddenly, the catatonic look on his face dissolved into raw, palpable pain. He squeezed his eyes shut, as if somehow he could will away the nightmare he was living. His chest heaved and his shoulders shook as sobs racked his body. He rocked back and forth hugging himself, wailing in anguish like a wounded animal.

Natalie bit her lip so hard it drew blood, as she fought back the tears that stung her eyes.

"Oh, God!" he wailed. His agony was painful to watch. Natalie sat next to him and put her arm around his shoulder.

"I'm so sorry," she whispered. He leaned his head on her chest and cried. Her gentleness had unleashed the torrent within him, and the tears continued to gush as she held him close, rocking back and forth with him.

Abruptly, John stopped rocking and sat up. He looked into Natalie's eyes. The look on his face broke her heart. He wailed, "Oh God! Has anyone told my wife?"

6:15 P.M.

BETSY ARRIVED at the Harrison home. She unlocked the front door and walked through the hallway. Reaching the kitchen, she tossed her keys and purse on the counter, kicked off her shoes, and picked up the phone. Without warning, her knees buckled and her legs gave way. She collapsed into a kitchen chair. She put her head down on the kitchen table and closed her eyes.

"Good Lord!" Betsy sighed deeply. "What a crappy day it's been." She thought of how she'd almost ended up under the wheels of that semi on the bridge. Her quick reflexes had saved her life. The after-effects of shock and adrenaline had left her shaking and crying. She'd been so unnerved, she'd had to stop at Lester's on the way home. After the two glasses of merlot had sufficiently calmed her nerves, she managed to drive the rest of the way home.

Betsy lifted her head. "Another glass of merlot sounds good right about now," she said, and glanced over at the wine rack on the counter. She realized that she still had the phone in her hand, and sighed heavily. "First things first, I guess." She dialed the Morgan's number.

"Hi Elaine. Sorry I'm late picking up Amy. I'll . . . "
Betsy paused for a moment, her facial muscles working to
contain her feelings.

"He *what*?!"

She slammed the phone down. She thought for a
moment, then picked up the phone and quickly dialed
another number. The line rang several times, but no one
answered. Betsy slammed the phone down in its cradle
again. Her face was flushed and her pulse raced. She
glanced over and noticed the light on the answering
machine blinking insistently. She pressed the button. The
machine droned the day and time:

Friday, Three-Eleven P.M.

John! John! Are you home? John! Pick up . . .

Recognizing her own voice, she skipped to the next
message.

Friday, Four-O-Two P.M.

*Betsy, it's me. I can't reach your cell phone. I picked up
Amy at school and we're on our way to the cabin.*

"Shit! Damn him!"

We'll see you tomorrow, okay? Bye.

Beep.

Betsy shoe-horned her feet back into her shoes,
grabbed her purse and keys, and headed for the front door.
As she reached for the door handle, there was a knock at
the door. Without thinking, she flung the door open and
found herself face to face with two Petoskey police officers.

6:25 P.M.

NATALIE HELD John in her arms until he finally succumbed to the sedative. She nodded to the EMT specialist and then motioned to a nearby officer. He walked over and the three of them gently lifted John and laid him on the gurney. The EMT strapped him down, then the three of them positioned themselves around the gurney.

"Okay, are you ready?" The EMT glanced at the two officers. They nodded. "One, two, three, lift."

They lifted the gurney and carefully maneuvered John into the ambulance. Natalie took one last look at him and shut the doors. The ambulance pulled onto the road, turned around, and headed away.

Natalie looked around and saw several officers engaged in collecting evidence. Charlie Tanner was standing on the road taking pictures and measurements of the scene.

"That's odd," she said. Normally, Russell would be right in the thick of things. "Does anyone know where Townsend is?" she called out.

"He's checking out our good ole' boys over off Portman Road," Charlie answered. "You'd better go give him a hand, Natalie."

Natalie sprinted toward her car, jumped in, and fired up the engine. Charlie stepped out of the way and the car leaped forward. She drove to the corner of Hennepin, then hooked a right onto Blanchard Road, sliding and spitting gravel as she cornered the turn.

Barely two minutes later, she turned right onto Portman Road, pulled up to Greg Reynold's trailer, and cut the engine. Two disheveled men stood handcuffed by the back of Russell's cruiser. Russell was on top of the third man, savagely beating him into submission.

"Damn!" Natalie swore loudly and jumped out of her cruiser.

Russell Townsend was an extremely powerful man in his mid-thirties. He wasn't tall — five-foot-ten — but he was solid muscle. His fists were like blocks of cement — deadly weapons fashioned from years of boxing in college. Russell pinned Greg's arms behind him and snapped the handcuffs around his wrists. He stood up, and started kicking Greg in the ribs.

Natalie strode over to Russell, grabbed his arm, and pulled him away from Greg. "Gee Townsend, sure glad to see you're in control here," said Natalie, her voice dripping with sarcasm.

Russell glared at Natalie and wrenched his arm free of her grasp. He was still red-faced, and she noticed his hand trembled as he wiped the sweat from his face with the back of his hand. His brown hair was tousled, and he had grass stains on his tan pants. Other than that, he was no worse for the wear.

Greg, on the other hand, was a different story. Natalie grabbed him by the shoulder and turned him over. He had a split lip, and blood gushed from his nose. His right eye was beginning to swell. He'd have a nice shiner pretty soon, and judging from the grimace on his face when he took a breath, he probably had a few broken ribs to boot.

As she helped Greg to his feet, he shot Russell a look of pure hate, then he turned to Natalie.

"What the fuck's his problem? We're just doin' a little target practice. It's not like we killed somebody or somethin'."

Natalie resisted the urge to give him a matching shiner. "Well actually, Greg, it *is* like you killed somebody," she said through clenched teeth. "You really screwed up this time, guys."

"What in the hell are you talkin' about?" he asked.

"A little girl just took a stray bullet at the end of your field," Natalie informed him.

Greg's jaw dropped, and he sobered instantly. Mike blanched, then sat down suddenly on the ground. Tyler just stood there, his face frozen in horror.

Natalie opened the back door of her cruiser. "Help me get these idiots in the car, Russell." Russell did not respond. "Russell! Get a grip!"

Russell turned and walked back over to Natalie. She could see he was still visibly upset. He grabbed Tyler by the arm. With one smooth motion, he pushed Tyler into the back seat of the car with one hand, and ducked Tyler's head with the other hand to keep him from bumping his head as he entered the car. Russell jockeyed Mike into position next to Tyler in the same manner. When he helped Greg into the car, however, Russell conveniently forgot his manners, and slammed Greg's head against the door jamb.

"Ow!" Greg yelled.

"Oops! Sorry!" Russell retorted. Natalie shot Russell a withering glance. Russell slammed the door shut and turned to Natalie. His face was twisted in anger.

"I knew it! I knew as soon as I heard on the radio what happened. These assholes do this every Friday night after they get off work. Get drunk as hell, and then come out here and target practice."

Natalie had never seen Russell like this before. She'd seen him angry, but she had never seen his anger erupt into such excessive violence. She shuddered inwardly to think of what might have happened had she not arrived when she did.

Natalie upbraided him. "You should have called for backup!"

Russell ignored her reproof. "I've dealt with these yahoos a hundred times. I knew something like this was going to happen someday!" He was upset all over again. His face was red and blotchy, and the veins in his temple bulged. For a moment, Natalie thought he was going to give himself a stroke.

She grabbed his trembling hands and gripped them firmly in hers. She looked into his eyes and saw the pain. "Russell," she commanded, "stop it." He looked away. She spoke his name again, this time more gently. "Russell, come on, buddy, get it together. I need you with me."

He looked at her again and saw the compassion in her eyes. His labored breathing grew quieter and he managed a weak smile. She smiled back at him and squeezed his hands. "Let's try and get this wrapped up here, okay? What do you need?"

Russell sighed deeply and ran his hands through his hair. "I need someone out here to help collect the evidence. I'll hang here, if you want to take them to St. Ignace." He jerked his thumb toward Natalie's cruiser.

"No problem. I'll see you in St. Ignace. You gonna be okay?"

Russell nodded wearily. "Yeah, I'll be all right." He propped his foot on the back bumper of his cruiser. He shoved his hands in his back pockets and looked away.

Natalie climbed in her cruiser and buckled her seatbelt. She glanced in her rearview mirror, assessing the men sitting silently in her back seat. Greg met her gaze and held it. His eyes held no sympathy or regret, only defiance. She stared back at him, studying him, trying to figure out if somewhere in that soul, there was a real human being. Finally, she looked away. She started the car, backed out onto the gravel road, and began to drive away. Glancing in the rearview mirror again, she saw Russell, still leaning against his cruiser. He looked crushed, devastated. She shook her head sadly. This had been a terrible day for everyone.

FROM
ASHES

SATURDAY, MAY 31ST

A SOFT, STEADY RAIN drummed solemnly on the black umbrellas gathered near the dock. The air was cool and damp. Forget-me-nots, Amy's favorite flower, grew in profusion near the shore, their bright colors seemingly muted for the occasion.

John stood there silently, clutching the urn to his chest. Alice Harrison, a widower in her early sixties, held the umbrella over both of them. Her eyes were wet, her heart heavy. It was just the two of them again. John's father, Charles, had died two years before Amy was born. Amy's birth had been a welcome, healing addition to her life.

She remembered the look on John's face as he held the tiny bundle of life in his arms for the first time. She'd been sitting in the waiting room of the hospital. John walked through the double doors with Amy wrapped in a small, pink blanket. The joy and pride that lit up his face overflowed and ran down his cheeks – great, big tears of happiness. She remembered feeling whole again as she gazed at the two of them together.

John stared out over leaden waters, as the rain made small pockmarks in the surface. The islands beyond were cloaked in mist. He looked down at the weathered boards beneath his feet. Amy had counted them. *Eighty-eight boards*, she'd announced proudly. They'd spent so much time here. So many summer evenings spent sitting on the end of the dock, holding hands, watching the fish jump as the sun disappeared behind the islands.

John walked out to the end of the dock. His heart squeezed within his chest. Tears flowed freely and mingled with the rain that soaked his face. He closed his eyes. The pain was more than he could bear. He opened them again and then knelt on one knee. He opened the urn and gently poured the ashes out onto the waters below. The wind rippled across the water, causing small waves. The waves moved outward, carrying their precious cargo toward the open waters of Lake Huron. John felt as if his heart would burst.

Betsy watched from the shore, her face set in stone. When it was over, she turned and left without a word.

John stayed there at the end of the dock, watching the waves for a long time. His mother walked over to where he was kneeling and put her hand on his shoulder. She stood there silently for a moment. Then she bent over and kissed the top of his rain-soaked head, turned, and left.

The rest of the mourners left a few at a time, until only Ted and Natalie remained. John stood up and walked back down the dock to the shore where they were standing.

Natalie looked at John. He looked forlorn and wretched, his wet hair plastered to his face. He had a black trench coat on, pulled close around him with the collar up, as if trying to ward off the chilling loneliness.

Ted gave John a fierce hug, almost crushing him with his bear-like arms. "John, I'm so sorry."

"Thanks for being here," John said. He looked at Natalie. "You'd better fry the bastards that did this."

Natalie looked into John's tortured face. "We'll do everything we can, Mr. Harrison. The judge has set the date for the preliminary examination for next Friday. The trial date will be set then."

"If there's anything you need from me . . . " John paused.

"I'd like to be able to talk to you Monday, if that's available, I mean, if you think you'd be up to it," she said.

"I'll be at our home in Petoskey. Anytime. Unless you want me to come here . . . "

"No, Petoskey is fine," she said.

John looked at Natalie. He read the care and compassion in her hazel eyes. "Thanks for coming," he said softly.

She grasped his hands in hers and held them for a few moments, then let go. She turned and walked away, joining Ted as he walked toward his cabin.

John walked back to the end of the dock and resumed his vigil, watching the waves as they moved out toward the open waters of Lake Huron.

MONDAY, JUNE 2ND

BRIGHT SUNSHINE blinded her as she stepped out of the cruiser. Natalie shaded her eyes. She saw Russell coming out of the station, probably on his way to breakfast at, where else, Ang-gio's.

It was the local breakfast hangout of the *Coffee Gang*. The unofficial roster included the Fire Department Chief, Charlie Tanner, Russell, a few of the ambulance corps, and various members of the local road and construction crews. Every morning, from about eight to nine-thirty, the group would sit around a long table drinking coffee and swapping stories.

Russell walked over to Natalie's cruiser. "Isn't this your day off?" he asked. Natalie was in full uniform.

"I'm going over to Petoskey to see the Harrisons."

"I've got the investigation covered, Natalie."

"Yeah, well, to be honest with you, I just want to see how they're doing. I've been through this, and I know . . . "

Russell cut her off. "Nat, you can't get personally involved with cases."

"I can still care, Russell," Natalie retorted, then walked toward the station.

"You're making a mistake."

"Yeah, well, my mistake, okay?" Natalie said over her shoulder.

She walked into the station and saw Charlie sitting at his desk. Standing next to him was a young police officer. He was of average build, had sandy-blond hair and friendly, brown eyes.

"Natalie. This is Eric Jones," Charlie said. "He's our new Marine Officer. Eric, this is Natalie . . . "

"Ā-bear," Eric said, visibly proud of himself for pronouncing her name correctly. He extended his hand. Natalie grinned. She reached over and shook his hand.

"Charlie's told me all about you," he said. "Hear you're from Louisiana. Got a good Cajun joke for you."

Natalie flashed Charlie a look. Charlie raised his eyebrows.

"Okay. Boudreaux and Thibodeaux are driving downtown one night, and they come to a red light. Boudreaux doesn't even slow down, he just runs right through it. Thibodeaux says, *Boudreaux, you gotta be careful! You jus ran dat red light!* Boudreaux tells him, *Don't you worry, Hebert does it all de time, and nutin ever happens.* They come to another red light, and again, Boudreaux runs through it. Thibodeaux yells at him, *Boudreaux, you gonna get us dead, you keep running dose red lights!* Boudreaux tells him, *Mais I done tol you, don't to worry. Hebert does it all de time wid no problem.* When they get to the next intersection, the light is green, Boudreaux slams on the brakes, and comes to a complete stop. Thibodeaux yells, *Damn Boudreaux, why you stop for de green light?!* Boudreaux looks both ways cautiously, then tells him, *If I gots de green light, I gots to be careful, 'cause Hebert might be passing de other way.*"

Eric cracked up laughing at his own joke, but Charlie and Natalie were silent. Charlie glanced over at Natalie. The smile on her face had disappeared. Natalie turned and walked out of the station without saying a word.

Eric stood there with his mouth hanging open. "What? Wha'd I say?"

They heard the sound of her car as she pulled out of the parking lot and drove away.

* * *

Natalie turned onto the highway and headed west. It was a gorgeous day. The trees were decked out in their summer finery, and the sun shimmied and danced on the surface of the water, instantly lifting her spirits.

As she drove, she glanced upward through the windshield from time to time. She knew birdwatching at sixty miles an hour wasn't exactly safe, but she couldn't help herself. She loved spotting the large dark shapes in the sky. By their wing shape, span, and flight pattern, she could identify them correctly, for the most part. Turkey vultures, hawks, kestrels, and her favorite raptor, bald eagles. It never ceased to thrill her when she sighted one. They looked so fierce, so powerful – a defiant symbol of the vanishing wilderness.

She looked over at Lake Huron again. The play of light on water was mesmerizing. Her hands itched for the feel of her paddle. She couldn't wait to get her kayak out on the water again. It was a beauty, her pride and joy – a seventeen foot, Betsie Bay Valkyrie. It wasn't cheap, that was for sure. It had taken her two years to save the money. Each kayak made by the small company was custom built. The company only built about two dozen a year. The Okume beauty had set her back thirty-five hundred dollars for the kayak alone. The paddle had cost another two hundred and fifty dollars.

Natalie took the I-75 exit and headed south. She was so deep in thought that before she knew it, she was crossing the Mackinac Bridge. She gazed out over the Straits of Mackinac. "Wow! You couldn't pay me a million dollars to give this place up," she said. "Why would anyone want to live in Mallville, USA after they'd had a taste of paradise?"

She shuddered involuntarily. The thought of living in a big city again was repulsive. The crime, the crowds, the pollution, the stress – "No thanks!" she said as she took the Petoskey exit.

Forty minutes later, she turned onto Lake View Road, and drove slowly, scanning for the correct address. "Let's see, 499 Lake View Road. There it is." She slowed even further, turned on her blinker signal, and turned left. She drove up the long, u-shaped driveway, and parked behind Betsy Harrison's taupe Mercedes. Natalie let out a low whistle. "Wow! Nice place!"

It was a white, two-story Georgian with a high ridge roof. Square-topped, triple windows were set just above the doorway, which was topped by a pillared portico. On either side of the door stood globe-shaped topiaries in elaborately carved urns. Neatly trimmed ivy climbed the walls, giving the house a cozy, yet elegant appeal. A huge oak growing in the front yard partially shaded the house from the noonday sun.

The most impressive part, however, was not the house itself, but its location. Natalie turned her back to the house for a moment and took in the sweeping view below her. The house sat on a high hill overlooking Little Traverse Bay. Sailboats hovered on the gentle swells of the bay — colorful butterflies on a shimmering blue meadow. The huge cerulean sky had a soft, watercolor wash of clouds painted across part of it, softening the brilliant blue of the top half of the sky to a gentle robin's egg hue.

Natalie forced herself away. She turned and walked up to the front door of the Harrison home. As she reached out to ring the doorbell, she heard loud voices emanating from inside the house.

"I want you out of this house by the time I get back!" the female voice said. That instant, Betsy came storming out of the house, dressed in a stunningly-short, navy blue skirt suit, with matching high-heeled pumps. She nearly ran smack into Natalie. Just in time, Natalie avoided the collision, quickly stepping to the side. Betsy looked shocked and embarrassed to see her standing there. Betsy stared at her for a few awkward moments. Then, without a word, she pushed past Natalie and stalked over to her Mercedes. She got in the car and drove off, tires squealing, announcing to the neighbors her anger and irritation.

As Natalie stood there bewildered, John appeared at the front door. When he saw her standing there, he gestured to her.

"Please come in, Officer . . . ?"

She recovered quickly. "Hebert. Natalie Hebert."

"I'm sorry you had to hear that," John apologized.

"No problem, I've heard a lot worse," she quickly countered as she stepped into the foyer.

"Would you like some coffee, Officer Hebert?"

"Please call me Natalie. Sure, that would be great. Three sugars, lots of cream, please."

"Make yourself at home," he told her.

Natalie sat down on a chocolate leather sofa. John walked into the kitchen to make her a cup of coffee.

She could see he was still terribly upset from the confrontation with Betsy. She also saw the grief that weighed heavily upon him; the way his shoulders sagged; the strain in his voice as he struggled to function. She knew how hard it was. Right now, even getting out of bed in the morning would be a Herculean task for him.

Natalie felt a crushing pain in her chest. She knew it wasn't physical, but unconsciously rubbed the spot anyway. Restless, she got up from the sofa and walked around the living room looking at pictures – snapshots of the past. She picked up a frame from a carved mahogany bookshelf. It was a school picture of Amy. She looked like she was around five years old. Amy had long pigtails tied with emerald green ribbons, and a radiant smile, marred only by a single gap where a baby tooth was missing. She gently returned the picture to its resting place.

She noticed another framed picture on the bookshelf, but did not recognize the beautiful, demure, young woman.

"Who is this picture of?" she asked.

John looked in from the kitchen. "That's the woman you just saw storm out of here like a bat out of hell."

Natalie couldn't hide her amazement. "She looks so different!"

John walked into the living room and handed Natalie her coffee. He laughed a small, unamused laugh. "That was when she was still a human being."

Natalie looked at him sympathetically. "Hey, I'm sure you'll work things out. You're both going through a lot."

"It was over between us a long time ago," he said flatly.

"I'm sorry."

John motioned for her to sit. Natalie sat back down on the couch, and he chose a scarlet, wing-backed chair across from her. A black cat strolled into the room. It walked over to Natalie and started rubbing against her, purring loudly.

"His motor is running," she joked, trying to lift John's spirits.

"That was Amy's cat, Felix," John said gently. "He normally hides when people come over."

Natalie reached down and scratched Felix behind the ears. "Hello, Felix."

"Amy liked the old cartoons. She named him after Felix the Cat."

"Yeah, I like that one, too." She sensed John's pain and looked up. His eyes were moist.

John spoke, and his voice quivered. "You know, I've already answered all the questions the other officer asked me. Do I really have to go through this again?" His eyes searched hers.

"I . . . you know, I think we have pretty much concluded our investigation. To be honest, I was just really concerned about you. I know you're going through so much and . . . "

John interrupted. "You have no idea what I'm going through. No one does."

"Mr. Harrison," Natalie paused. "My little brother was killed when he was sixteen. A drunk driver ran a red light. We were really close, and I thought I'd never be able to go on. I remember what it was like. I *do* know what you're going through."

John looked away from her and teared up, but said nothing.

Natalie continued. "I know it's a really hard time for you, right now. I know that it feels like you'll never get through this. I just want you to know that I've been where you are, and I understand, and if there's anything I can do to help . . . "

John did not respond. He sat there, his head averted.

"Mr. Harrison, this isn't a good time for you to be alone. Is there anyone, a friend or relative . . . ?" Again, no response.

Natalie stood up. She pulled a business card out of her wallet and tried to hand it to John. "My number is on here and . . . "

He didn't take the card. She took out her pen and wrote something on the back of the card.

"I'm putting my home phone on the back here. If you just need someone to talk to . . . " She laid the business card on the coffee table between them.

John looked up at her and tried to muster a smile.

Natalie looked directly into his eyes. "Okay, well, you take care now." Natalie walked to the door. Felix followed her, meowing plaintively.

She put her hand on the door knob and pulled the front door open.

"Officer?"

Natalie stopped and turned toward John.

"Thanks," he said.

Natalie looked into his eyes again and saw a flicker of life. She smiled warmly at him. "You're welcome," she said and softly closed the door behind her.

FRIDAY, JUNE 13TH

THE WIND blew cold and damp. The sky had a gloomy, gray cast to it, as clouds scudded hurriedly across its surface. The trees moaned and swayed in the wind, and a flock of dry leaves left over from last fall, took flight and swooped over Natalie's windshield before landing on the side of the road. Natalie felt chilled and rolled up her window.

After two hours of trudging through the pile of tedious paperwork on her desk, she needed a break. She decided to patrol the area in her cruiser for a while, then around seven, stop at Hessel Bay Inn for a Hawaiian Chicken dinner.

It was going to be a long night. Today was Friday the thirteenth, a perfect excuse for adolescent miscreants of all ages to think up ways to get into trouble. She immediately thought of Greg Reynolds. He and his cousin Mike were still cooling their heels at the county jail in St. Ignace, where they'd stay until the trial at the end of August.

She took a right and drove down the country road. On either side was a dense forest of evergreen and hardwood. She felt a magnetic pull, drawing her toward the intersection of Hennepin and Blanchard. She came to a field where clear-cut logging had denuded it of large, old-growth trees many years before. Young white pines and birches had sprung up since then, taking the place of their fallen comrades, slowly filling the gaps left behind.

Natalie pulled over and stopped. The grass just beyond the berm of the road was still flattened from the feet that had trampled it exactly three weeks ago today. There were skid marks on the pavement in front of her car. Other than that, there was no trace of the tragedy that had taken place. John thought it cruel to mark the spot of the tragedy with a makeshift cross and flowers, forcing everyone who passed by to relive the horrible events that had taken place there.

John.

Natalie closed her eyes and was haunted by the memory of his anguished cries and the sight of the black hearse as it silently drove away. She quickly opened her eyes again, but it was too late. She couldn't stop her mind from making the inevitable connection. The black hearse. Just like the one that she'd seen on July 17th, seven years ago.

Natalie's kid brother Joey had griped and complained to her about how boring it was in the little town of Milton, Louisiana. Natalie had invited him to stay with her for the summer at her two bedroom apartment in the Garden District of New Orleans, if their parents consented. Her mother hadn't been crazy about the idea at first.

"What will he do all day long when you're at work?" her mother worried.

"Don't worry, mom," Natalie assured her. "He can hang out with Tim."

Tim Broussard was Natalie's next-door neighbor's son. He was fifteen, only a year younger than Joey. Natalie had introduced the two teenagers on a previous visit, and they'd bonded immediately. She had checked Tim out thoroughly, and could find no glaring faults in the freckle-faced red-head. He was a good kid — no drugs, no record, played the trumpet in his high school band, and made decent grades.

She gave her mom the thumbs-up sign. "He's a great kid. I checked him out myself."

Her mother acquiesced, but still had a troubled look in her eyes. "Joey is a good kid, but the Garden District is only a streetcar-ride away from the French Quarter," she said. "I'm not sure if all the parent-child talks we've had, would be a match for 'Sin City'. They have such a cavalier attitude toward drinking. There's a bar every three feet, and if that's not enough, they give you a go-cup when you leave the bar!"

"Look mom, if you don't want him to go, just say so."

"No, no. I guess he can go if his father says yes. He's a good kid. I know you won't let anything happen to him."

It happened on a hot, muggy night in July.

A business man from out of town had decided that after dinner and six vodka martinis at a four-star restaurant in the French Quarter, he was capable of driving back to his hotel room. He stumbled out of the restaurant, go-cup in hand, and somehow managed to find his car that was parked a couple of blocks away.

He started the white Lexus and drove slowly down the street, not wanting to attract attention from the local law enforcement. As he neared the intersection of St. Charles and Napoleon, he was doing fifty. He told the police that he'd hit a bump, and his drink sloshed over the side of his cup and into his lap. He didn't see the light had changed to red.

Joey and Tim had caught the streetcar earlier that evening and had gone down to Copeland's for dinner. Afterward, they'd decided to go down a few blocks to a local café and get a cappuccino before heading back home.

They stood patiently at the corner, just outside Copeland's, waiting for the light to change so they could cross the street. The light changed. Joey stepped off the curb and into the street ahead of Tim. At that moment, the white Lexus flew through the red light and struck Joey in the side. Joey flew through the air, and his head hit the concrete curb of the sidewalk. Tim started screaming for help.

Natalie had been on duty that night. She got the heads-up call from Dispatch, and had raced across town, sirens blaring. But it had still taken her twenty minutes to get there. Joey was already dead. Tim was sitting on the ground crying and shaking uncontrollably. The paramedic on the scene was treating him for shock.

The guilt and grief had been unbearable. She took an extended leave from the police force. She couldn't work, she couldn't sleep, she couldn't eat. She would just lie in bed, staring at the ceiling, watching the shadows change as the sun moved across the sky.

Gradually, Natalie came out of her depression with the love and support of her parents and friends. A month later she went back to work. But it was no use. Every place she went reminded her of Joey. The Audubon Zoo where they'd watched the apes clown around in their cages. The Jazz Festival, where they'd roamed from stage to stage together, listening to the Cajun, Zydeco, and Jazz bands, soaking up the warm April sunshine. The streetcars. The French Quarter, with its narrow cobbled streets, where they'd spent many afternoons exploring the myriad shops and restaurants, sampling the incredible cuisine New Orleans was famous for.

A month later, she moved away. She thought if she left Louisiana and started over somewhere far away from her homeland, she could escape the horrible pain.

She was wrong. It followed her all the way from the swamps of the south, to the boreal forests of the U.P. She felt it would be her companion for life. She had learned to live with it, even push it far enough away to be able to function again and lead a quasi-normal life.

Natalie put her head down on the steering wheel of her cruiser and cried hot, angry tears. The overwhelming grief and guilt surfaced again and washed over her in waves. Everyone had assured her over and over that it wasn't her fault. Deep down she knew they were right, but she couldn't seem to totally break free of the agonizing guilt.

It is my fault Joey died, she thought. *If I hadn't invited him to stay with me for the summer, he'd still be alive. He'd be twenty-three years old, already graduated from college, his whole life ahead of him.* The tears continued to fall.

She thought of the school picture she carried of him in her wallet. He had the same dark, brown-black hair, hazel eyes, and olive skin that she did. Though she was ten years older than he, people had often thought they were twins.

"Oh, God!" she cried. "It hurts! I miss him so much!" She sat there for a long time, sobs racking her body as she wallowed in her grief and guilt. After awhile, the storm subsided. She sighed heavily and lifted up her head. She took a deep breath and straightened her shoulders.

"Pull yourself together, girl. You can't help anybody if you're a mess."

Natalie looked over at the trampled grass again. She started the car, pulled out onto the road, and hooked a right onto Blanchard. She felt drained, exhausted. She needed a shot in the arm if she was going to make it through her shift.

Ted. She hoped he was home.

Natalie pulled up to the stop sign at the corner of Blanchard and Portman Road. To her left was Gower Lane, a gravel, crescent-shaped road that skirted the lake and gave access to the cluster of cabins that cozied up to the lakeshore. She turned left and drove slowly down the road.

She passed the Harrison cabin and saw a blue car she didn't recognize parked in the gravel drive next to the cabin. She assumed it was John's new vehicle. John's SUV had been at the station for several days, and when it was finally released, Ted had picked it up, and had taken it straight to the car dealer. John couldn't bear even *seeing* it again. She wondered how he was doing.

Ted's place was four more cabins down. She pulled up in front of his cabin and got out of her car.

The wind had increased. Natalie dubiously eyed the black, ominous storm clouds that were gathering in the north. It was supposed to blow over, the weatherman had predicted. Natalie prayed that was the case. She didn't relish the idea of wrestling with deluges and degenerates on the same night.

She walked up to the door and knocked loudly. It was a small log cabin with only two tiny bedrooms (one of which had been converted into a darkroom), a cramped living room, and a pocket-sized kitchen. Ted and his brother-in-law had built it by hand more than thirty years ago. It had a wonderful rough-hewn, carved-from-the-woods feel to it.

Ted opened the door. He stood there in the doorway; his hair mussed, his clothes rumpled. He blinked several times, trying to adjust to the light. His thick-lensed, horn-rimmed glasses sat slightly cockeyed on his face. He reminded Natalie of an owl just disturbed from his sleep.

"Well," he said, finally awake enough to find his tongue, "you look like hell. Get in a scuffle with those 'North of Hessel' boys again?"

"Gee, thanks, Ted. You don't look so good yourself."

"You woke me up from a nap. What's your excuse?"

"Are you gonna invite me in or what?"

Ted smiled and waved her in. "Coffee?"

"Got any of the good stuff?"

"What else? Ordered it off the Internet from Café Du Monde."

Natalie walked over to a narrow table sitting against the living room wall. She saw a stack of photos laying on the table and picked them up.

"Hey, these are new," she said.

"Na, not really. Took them about three weeks ago. Just got around to developing them yesterday. Wait until you see the roll I took the day after these."

Natalie's ears perked up. "What?"

"I got a picture of that cougar everyone tells me doesn't exist. Great shot with a telephoto."

"Yeah, right. Get out of here. Where is it?"

"Haven't developed it yet. I'm *so* far behind in my lab work."

"How convenient."

"You're going to eat your words."

Natalie had the last word on the subject. "I'll believe it when I see it," she smirked.

She walked over to the living room window and looked out. From where she was standing, she could see the back of the Harrison cabin. John was sitting there in an old, weather-beaten chair. He was alone.

Ted walked into the tiny living room and handed Natalie her coffee. "He just sits there. All day long." He fell silent for a few moments. "How's the investigation going?"

"The good news?" she said.

Ted lifted his eyebrows in anticipation.

"We've got our case together. The prelim was Friday, and the judge set the trial date for August twenty-ninth."

"And the bad?"

"Greg Reynolds was charged with involuntary manslaughter. He *might* get two years."

"Sure don't want to be around when John finds out he's only gonna get two years."

Natalie and Ted stood there silently, looking at John. A few minutes later, John got up and went into his cabin.

"He really shouldn't be alone," Natalie said.

"Maybe you should pay him a visit."

* * *

The rain began to fall softly on the deck of the Harrison cabin. Just the way it had at Amy's funeral, almost two weeks before. John stood by the living room window of the cabin and looked out on the water where Amy's ashes had been spread. He walked over to his desk and opened the top drawer. Until a few weeks ago, he'd always kept it locked. Now there was no need to. He took out his Taurus 9mm pistol. Its sleek, stainless-steel barrel glinted in the dim afternoon light – a tempting remedy for the excruciating pain that squeezed his heart in its merciless, vise-like grip.

He opened the drawer a little further and took the lid off the box of shells sitting near the back of the drawer. Taking out a single bullet, he loaded it directly into the chamber. He snapped the chamber closed with a smooth, reassuring metallic click, and savored the feel of the cool metal in his hand.

A knock at the door made him jump. He shoved the weapon back in the drawer and closed it. He walked through the hallway leading toward the side door of the cabin and saw Natalie peering in through the screen door.

"Is anyone home?" she called.

John walked to the door, surprised and a little upset to see her there. He hoped she hadn't seen him with the gun. He colored.

"Officer Hebert?"

"I was just visiting my friend Ted, and I thought I'd stop by and see how you're doing. Do you mind if I come in?"

John opened the screen door for her without saying a word. As she walked into the hallway, he avoided her eyes.

"How *are* you doing?" she asked him.

John let out a deep sigh. "I put one foot in front of the other. I do my best to remember how to breathe." He raised his head and looked at her.

His eyes had a shattered, desperate look in them that alarmed her.

"John, come sit down," she said as she took his arm. She walked him over to the couch, sat him down at one end, then she sat down at the other. "I wanted to let you know that a trial date has been set for August 29th."

John looked up for a moment, then picked up a small chocolate brown stuffed moose that sat between them on the couch. He held it in his hands for a few moments and then hugged it close to his chest. Tears slid down his cheeks. "How could God do this to my little girl?"

"Oh, John." Moved with compassion, she slid next to him and put her arms around him. Tears stung her eyes and her throat tightened.

"God didn't do this, John. Some out-of-control bastard did. He's gonna pay. I promise you."

He continued to cry. "It won't bring my Amy back."

Natalie held John, trying to comfort him. She heard the back door slam shut and looked up.

"How cozy," said a voice, cold and dispassionate.

Natalie looked up to see Betsy standing there, and she flushed with embarrassment. She knew her motives were pure, but still, it was awkward. She wanted to say something, but she sensed that nothing she could say would satisfy Betsy. Natalie stood up and headed for the side door.

"Glad to see your investigation is progressing so nicely," Betsy said coldly. She had a nasty smile on her face.

Natalie stopped. She searched for the right words, but still, none came. She pushed the screen door open and left.

John was angry. "She was just trying to be helpful, Betsy."

"Just how helpful *was* she, John?"

"Come on, Betsy. What do you want?"

"I want everything, John. The house, the cars, the rights to your works. Everything."

"Take it. It doesn't mean anything any more."

"The grieving father," she said bitterly. "She was my daughter, too. I'm the one who gave birth to her."

"Who in the hell raised her? You were too damned busy working on your next deal and fawning over the rich and famous."

John walked to the window, and looked out on the water. "Amy loved this place. I want the cabin. And I'm keeping *From Hell to Paradise*. It was Amy's favorite story. She inspired it. You can have all the rest."

"I said I want it *all*, John."

"Why, so you can get Tom to make some commercial piece-of-crap movie out of it? You are not gonna get your hands on it, Betsy. Hollywood is never gonna get their hands on it. I owe that much to Amy."

"You owe me, John. I left my art. I left everything behind to support your god-damned writing, and follow your dream to Hollywood. And then when I made friends there, we had to move back here to Michigan because you couldn't hack it with the big boys. You owe me everything."

"Parties, snobs, and coke. *Some friends!*" John retorted.

"You're a loser, John. That's all you'll ever be."

"God, Betsy, what happened to us? What happened to you? You used to be so . . ."

Betsy cut him off. "Used to be. That's the world you live in. That's what your little romance stories are all about, John. You can't hack it in the real world, so you climb inside the past."

"I'd rather live in the past, than in your sick present."

"I want it all. And I'm going to have it."

Betsy shot John a venomous look, then turned and walked out the door.

MONDAY, JUNE 30TH

MACKINAC ISLAND was visible in the distance. The bright morning sunlight almost blinded Natalie as she looked out over the glittering waters of the lake. Today was her day off. She'd just finished running errands in St. Ignace, and was on her way back to Hessel to spend some time with Ted.

The skies had finally cleared after several days of foggy, gloomy weather. She'd worked the St. Ignace car show that weekend, and it had been a rough time. The bad weather hadn't helped the mood of those attending the car show. It hadn't helped Natalie's mood much, either. But tomorrow she'd be back on day shift for the next two months. That was some consolation. Now all she needed was some coffee, and Ted had the good stuff.

Natalie had the top down on her classic 1962 candy-apple red Volkswagen convertible, with a black top, and white leather interior. She had her hair pulled back into a ponytail, the way she always wore it when she was off duty. On the seat behind her was an eclectic assortment of music CDs. Everything from Wayne Toups to Vivaldi. The music du jour was a digitally re-mastered album from the

60's – Mike Bloomfield, Al Kooper, and Steven Stills – *Super Session*.

She loved the summers in Northern Michigan, cruising with the top down, listening to music. Next to kayaking, it was the only thing that would help pull her out of a funk. But after recent events, even the music failed to cheer her. She turned off the CD player. She couldn't get John out of her head.

And Amy.

Natalie had seen some horrific things in her eleven years as a police officer. Some of those things still gave her nightmares. For the most part, she had learned to push those images out of her mind. She was glad that she'd arrived late on the scene, and hadn't seen Amy's body.

*　*　*

Natalie stopped by her cabin to walk Abby and Salty, then headed over to Ted's. When she arrived there around eleven, Ted was standing at the front door. He waved her in, then disappeared. She knew he was headed for the coffee. She entered and he greeted her.

"Didn't bring the children over to visit grandpa?" he asked jokingly, referring to Abby and Salty.

Natalie noticed that all the cabin windows were open, letting in the fresh, cedar-scented air. A soft breeze blew in. The white cotton curtains filled with air and billowed out like sails.

"No, just felt like I should leave them at home today."

"Bet they're not too happy."

"No, but we went on a road trip last week. So that ought to hold them for a while."

"So what's new in the photo department?" she asked him.

It was a tradition that whenever Natalie entered Ted's door, he would head straight to the kitchen to get the coffee, and she would head straight for the narrow table that sat against the living room wall, to look at his newest photos.

"I'll be darned!" Natalie said dumbfounded.

"Told ya," Ted smirked as he handed her a cup of coffee.

She stood there in amazement, gazing at a magnificent photo of an adult cougar.

"Uhum!" Ted was waiting for her to take the cup. She was too engrossed in the photo to respond. Ted finally had to set the cup down on an end table next to the couch.

"This is unbelievable. This is right over on Blanchard!" Natalie was animated, and for a brief moment, forgot about her troubles. But the next photo in the pile brought it all back. In the background was Russell's cruiser. The photos had been taken the day of the accident.

"That's a day I want to forget," she sighed. She put the photos down on the table, then walked over and sat down on the couch.

She sat there quietly, sipping on her coffee. Ted could see she was upset. He walked over and sat in a chair adjacent to the couch. He knew Natalie well enough to know that she'd talk when she was good and ready.

Finally, she broke the silence. "I was just starting to enjoy my life again. I moved up here to get away from all the death and destruction. I thought I'd moved to a nice, sleepy town where nothing ever happens."

"You love police work, Natalie. You know you do. If you didn't, you'd have gotten out of it a long time ago."

"You think I *like* this crap?"

"No, but I know you live and breathe to help others. Like Salty. You're a softy, Natalie."

"What was I supposed to do, let them take him to the pound? I took Salty in because he's a good dog. He's just not a good *police* dog. Besides, Salty takes care of me."

"Yeah, right. If someone broke into your cabin, he'd probably *lick* them to death."

Natalie smiled in agreement.

"And John?" Ted asked.

"John Harrison? What *about* him?"

"You gonna take him in, too?"

Natalie sighed deeply. "I don't think he's gonna make it, Ted. I've seen this before."

"I know you well enough to know that there's a lot more going on in your heart than stray puppy syndrome."

"What in the hell are you talking about? The man's hurting." Natalie was visibly upset by Ted's comment. "I just want to help him. Somebody's got to help him. I just don't know what to do."

"To start with, *someone* needs to get him out of that house. God knows *I've* tried."

"Wait a minute," Natalie said, realizing what Ted was suggesting.

"Why not?"

"The guy's married, for God's sake!"

"You mean the wicked witch of the west?" he quipped.

"Yeah, well, no comment. Anyway, how would *you* have felt if someone said you needed to get out of this cabin after Rachel died?"

"Someone *did* say that to me. My own son said it to me."

"Didn't do any good," she retorted.

"Natalie, Rachel and I had thirty-seven wonderful years together. Twenty-seven of them right here at this cabin. I'm thankful for every day we had."

Natalie smiled at Ted. She reached over and grabbed his hand. "You amaze me. I hope I can find what you and Rachel had."

"You can't *find* a love like Rachel's and mine. It finds you."

Natalie looked in the direction of John's cabin. "I know what you're thinking, but circumstances like these, sure in hell didn't come from heaven."

"No, they didn't, but I don't believe that it was coincidence that you moved up here around the same time that Rachel died. Your visits helped me through so much."

Ted walked over to a tall, pine bookshelf, and pulled a book down. He walked back over to Natalie. "Remember what brought you up here?"

"Lots of things brought me up here."

Ted handed her the book. She read the title.

"*From Hell to Paradise*. Yeah, this was the cap on the bottle, all right."

"It's an autographed copy," Ted pointed out.

"Wow! Mark Emerson signed it for you?"

"Read the inscription."

Natalie read the inscription:

To my good friends Ted and Rachel,

Best Wishes,

John Harrison.

She looked up at Ted. "John *gave* this to you? I don't understand."

"John autographed it. Mark Emerson is John's pen name."

*   *   *

Natalie strode purposefully up to John's cabin. She walked across the deck and banged loudly on his back screen door. No answer. She knocked again, and a soft meow came from inside. She peered inside to see Felix stretching up on the door.

"Hello, Felix."

He meowed back.

She banged on the door again and yelled. "John! John! You home?" Again, no answer.

"John! I know you're in there. I need to talk to you." She heard some noise in the recesses of the house. After a few moments John came to the screen door. He looked no better than the last time she'd seen him.

"Hello?" he said. Natalie could tell that John didn't recognize her without her uniform on.

She smiled uncomfortably. "Officer Hebert. Natalie."

"Oh, yes. What can I do for you . . . do I call you officer?"

"Call me Natalie, please." She paused. "I just stopped to see how you're doing."

By this time Felix's non-stop complaints had earned John's attention. He cracked the door a bit to let Felix out. Felix rubbed against Natalie for a moment, purring his approval, then quickly disappeared around one side of the house, apparently having more pressing business to attend to.

"This really isn't a very good time for me . . . "

"This isn't really a good time for you to be alone. Ted told me he tried to get you out of the house. You *need* to get out. Just for a little while," she said, practically pleading with him.

"Can't you just leave me alone? Can't everyone just leave me alone?"

John walked away from the door. Natalie turned, and started to walk away, but she stopped abruptly. She was almost angry. But more than that, she realized this might be her last chance, her only chance, to help him. With that thought, she quickly turned, swung open the door, and walked right into the cabin.

"John. Come on. Let's go. You're coming with me." She had a look of dogged determination on her face. She walked up to him and grabbed his wrist. "I'm not taking *no* for an answer."

Her directness caught him completely off-guard.

"Are you arresting me, officer?" he said dryly. He had no fight left in him.

"It's Natalie. And, yes, I will, if you don't shut up and get in the car."

"On what charge?"

"I'll make one up. You need to get out of this place for a while." Her face softened. "Come on, John, it'll do you good."

John said nothing, but the stubborn look on his face told her she hadn't fully persuaded him yet. "Please, John? Just for a few hours?"

He looked at her dubiously. "If it will get you to shut up and leave me alone after this, I'll go. For a few hours."

"I promise I'll leave you alone if you come with me today," Natalie fibbed.

John started to walk away from her.

"Where are you going?" she asked.

"Can I get my shoes on, officer?"

Natalie looked down and realized his feet were bare. "Yes, you can," she replied. "On one condition."

"What's that?" he eyed her suspiciously.

"You start calling me Natalie."

"I promise. Now can I *please* go get my shoes on, Natalie?" He managed a small smile.

"Okay," Natalie smiled back, "but if you don't come out in five minutes, I'm coming in after you."

He turned and walked into the bedroom. A few minutes later, he reappeared. They walked out the door.

"Let's take my car, okay?" Natalie said.

John offered no resistance.

Natalie hopped in the driver's side and closed the door. John was still standing on the passenger side of the car.

"Oh, what about Felix?" Natalie asked.

"Felix is exploring," John answered. "When he's ready to return to base, he has his own secret entrance to the house."

She leaned over and pulled a baseball hat out from under the back of the passenger seat. It was navy blue, with a kelly green Peace Frogs logo on the crown. She tossed it to John.

"Well, are you coming or what?" she smiled at him.

John climbed in the car without comment. She backed out of the driveway and headed down the gravel road. She took a right onto Blanchard Road, and a few minutes later, came to the end of Hennepin. If there had been any alternative, she would have driven some other way. But there wasn't. Turning right went to the water. She could only turn left.

She glanced at John. He kept his face turned to the right as they drove down the road. She knew he was avoiding having to see that place again. Natalie, on the other hand, couldn't help herself. Her eyes were drawn to the spot where it had happened.

How does he do it? she thought. *I couldn't do it. I couldn't handle living so close to where she died.* She felt that maybe people dealt with grief in their own way. Some, like her, had to get away from any connection, any physical reminders of their loss. Natalie kept several photo albums filled to the brim with family pictures in her closet, and from time to time, she would take them out and look at them. But she couldn't handle having pictures of Joey on display in her cabin. It was just too painful.

At both John's house and cabin, she saw pictures of Amy everywhere – on the fireplace mantel, on the walls, on the end tables. Natalie wondered if maybe he wasn't dealing with the grief at all. She wondered if he was trying to drown in it.

The warm sunshine baked their faces as the wind whipped over their heads. Talking over the rumble of the engine and the roar of the wind was impossible. It was just as well. John had slipped back into his funk. She could see the dark clouds forming over him. She wasn't sure if he was really up to this trip. Maybe Mackinac Island was a little *too* cheerful for him. She glanced over at him again. His face was impassive.

* * *

They arrived at the St. Ignace ferry dock about forty-five minutes later. She parked in the lot off to the left of the dock. John helped her put the top up on the car, in case of rain. The sky was a gorgeous blue, not a cloud in sight, but then again, you never knew. Michigan weather could, and did, change in a heartbeat.

Natalie walked up to the white ticket booth and purchased two ferry tickets. She returned to where John stood near the entrance of the ramp and handed the dock porter their tickets.

"Watch your step, ma'am," the dock porter cautioned.

The ramp before them was slanted at a steep angle. For the past few years, the water level in the lake had dropped dramatically, causing the boat to sit lower than the dock. They walked carefully down the steep ramp and onto the boat.

"Let's sit on top, want to?" Natalie suggested. John nodded his consent and she led the way to the top deck of the catamaran. Ten minutes later, all the passengers and cargo were on board, and the boat slowly backed away from the dock. Once far enough away to maneuver properly, the large craft swung around easily and headed toward the island, picking up speed as it left the harbor.

The summer sun beat down upon their heads as the boat sped across the glass surface of the lake. The wind roared in their ears making it necessary to shout to be heard.

Natalie leaned over and shouted in John's ear. "I lived on Mackinac Island the first summer I moved up here."

John felt the need to be polite, so he responded. "What was it like living there?"

"It was a unique adventure, that's for sure. A little too much like Disneyland for me, though."

John nodded. Natalie sat back in her seat, realizing that trying to carry on a conversation at the moment was futile.

They passed in front of the island and she looked up at the mansions on the West Bluff. She smiled to herself. It never ceased to amuse her that they were referred to by everyone as cottages. She picked out her favorite, the White Pines cottage. It was a tall, white, Queen Anne with two balconies. Beautiful stained glass inserts bordered some of the windows. Its varied architectural features gave the house an intriguing, waiting-to-be-explored look. She'd often thought that it must be an exciting place for children to spend the summer in. She imagined all sorts of adventures to be had in it. It probably had a large attic filled with old clothes and costume jewelry to play dress-up, and secret passageways enabling impish children to sneak unseen from room to room, and play pranks on their unsuspecting siblings. The balconies of course, begged for damsels in distress and knights in shining armor.

The thought of those laughing, mischievous children made her sad for a moment. She wondered if she would ever have any children of her own. She'd always imagined that she would enjoy motherhood, sewing costumes for Halloween, making quarts of lemonade for her industrious little munchkins to sell at their lemonade stand.

She started to feel sorry for herself and then remembered the man sitting beside her, and his loss. She looked over at him. He was staring out over the water at Round Island, and the red and white lighthouse that stood on the edge of its tiny peninsula. He looked so sad. She wondered what he was thinking. She tried to put herself in his shoes and then the thought struck her. He'd probably brought Amy here to the island before. Probably more than once. Surely he had memories attached to this place, too.

She reached over and gently squeezed his shoulder in understanding. The gesture must have telegraphed its meaning, because John looked back at her. His eyes expressed his gratitude. Then they clouded up again, becoming unreadable. He turned away.

The boat slowed as they neared the harbor. Gulls wheeled and dipped overhead, crying their welcome. One of them landed on a large piling, and greeted the tourists as they departed the ferry.

John followed Natalie down the stairs, up the ramp of the boat, and onto the dock. It was a zoo. Literally and figuratively. Horses stood patiently waiting as an odd assortment of cargo was loaded from the boat to the dray behind them. Excited dogs strained at their leashes, barking at one another, and at the large workhorses in front of them. Distressed cries from a frightened cat in a carrier sitting on a bench nearby, mingled into the din. An elderly woman sat next to the carrier, cooing and reassuring the poor animal.

Behind them on the boat, dock porters yelled out warnings to the crowd that blocked their way. "Coming through, please! Move to the side!" Natalie and John quickly stepped out of their way. Pulling, pushing and groaning under the strain, the dock porters maneuvered the heavily stacked luggage carts up the steep ramp from the boat and onto the dock.

A Japanese tour guide stood off to the side of them calling to his tour group in Japanese, clucking over them like a mother hen, counting heads and motioning to them to stay together.

Natalie grabbed John's arm. "Let's go." She expertly threaded through the crowd with John in tow, dodging the dock porters on their bikes with their towering stacks of luggage, and steering him away from the crowd of tourists that had started spilling out from the newly-arrived Mackinaw City ferry. They reached Main Street and she finally let go of his arm.

He looked at her questioningly. "Where to?"

She pointed to her right and they headed for the nearest haven from all the bedlam. Minutes later they arrived at Marquette Park. She pointed out a secluded bench up toward the back of the park, near some lilac bushes. They walked to the bench and sat down.

They sat silently for a while, looking out over the park and marina, watching the hustle and bustle before them. To the right and front of them, a flock of gulls squabbled over the tidbits thrown to them by a family sitting on a blanket. Directly in front of the Father Marquette statue, four college-aged kids threw a frisbee back and forth. Down below them, pedestrians strolled along the sidewalks, as bicycles wove and zipped around the yellow, horse-drawn taxis that clip-clopped down the street. Other, more elaborate private carriages sat patiently along the side of the street, waiting for customers. Sailboats and yachts bobbed gently in the silver-blue waters of the marina.

Natalie breathed in the sweet-scented air and smiled. She turned and looked at John. "So, you're a writer."

"*Was* a writer." His face was unreadable again.

"Don't say that, John," Natalie admonished gently. "Your book *From Hell to Paradise* changed my life. It's the reason I moved up here. I went to Hell to see the places you talked about in your book."

John raised an eyebrow.

"Hell, Michigan," she smiled.

He smiled wryly and shook his head.

"Then I drove up to the U.P. to Paradise and spent a week there. I loved that book. You have a wonderful ability to touch people's hearts."

John didn't respond. Natalie was determined to get him to talk. She knew she'd have to ask questions that didn't have *yes* or *no* answers.

"How did you get into writing?"

John took the hook.

"Got interested in it in college. I thought I wanted to write for movies. My first book was pretty commercial, *Calm Violence*. The book did well. A studio in Hollywood bought the rights, then asked me to move out and work for them. I wrote the screenplay, and the movie was released as *The Killing Calm*."

"You wrote that?" Natalie asked excitedly. "It was horrible!" she said with an identical amount of enthusiasm.

John couldn't help but smile at Natalie's honesty.

"Yes, it was," John said in agreement. "The book was much better," he added in apology.

"So how'd you end up back in Michigan?"

"I hated Hollywood. For some reason, Betsy loved it. That place really changed her. She loved rubbing shoulders with the stars. I tried to weather it out for her sake. I mean, she gave up her art for my career. I thought it was the least I could do. Anyway, Betsy got pregnant with Amy."

John became silent. Natalie pressed on.

"Your wife? You said she changed?"

"If you'd known her twenty years before . . . she was amazing. We met in college. I took an art class, just to round out my education. She was a sophomore. She was so beautiful, so kind. Her art was indescribable."

"I'm sorry things aren't working for the two of you."

"Yeah. There's a lot of things I wish we'd done differently. Except for Amy. She's the only thing I don't regret." His face darkened. "You said you lost your little brother."

Natalie nodded.

"How do you go on? How do you even *want* to go on?" he asked.

"It's tough, John. It was seven years ago, and it's still tough, to this day. But I think about all the time we got to spend together. And I believe with all my heart that I'll see him again someday. That's the thing that really keeps me going."

"Do you believe they are with us right now? Your brother? Amy?"

"Some people believe that. A lot of people believe that. I don't. But I do believe that someday, everything that humanity has broken will be fixed, in spite of humans."

"Why would God allow things like this to happen?"

"I think God gets a real bad rap from people. People have freedom of will, and some use that freedom of will irresponsibly."

"Like Greg Reynolds."

"Yeah, Greg Reynolds. And the guy that killed my little brother. Each person makes their own choices, and their choices, good or bad, affect everyone else. I had a really tough upbringing. But I made up my mind that I was going to get out of my circumstances, and that I was going to make a difference with my life. Each day I make that decision."

"I miss her so much," John said with tears in his eyes.

Natalie opened her purse, and took out a small day-planner.

"John, I only met Amy once, but I'll never forget it." She opened the day-planner, and turned to one of the pages. Pressed between the pages were a few Forget-me-nots. "I was visiting Ted, and Amy came over. She gave me these." Natalie looked into his eyes and felt a spasm of pain in her chest. Her emotions overflowed and she began to cry.

John smiled understandingly at her. "She loved those flowers. She loved giving them to people."

Natalie laughed through her tears as she wiped her eyes. "Yeah. She gave me several Dwarf Irises along with the forget-me-nots. I didn't have the heart to tell her there was a five-hundred-dollar fine for picking them."

They smiled at each other warmly. Natalie reached in her purse for a tissue, mopped up her tears, and blew her nose.

"Let's go for a walk," she said. She stood up and he followed her lead. "Have you ever been to Grand Hotel?"

"Yeah, I've been there."

"Why don't we go up there and grab a bite? I love the apple pie they serve at Carlton's Tea Room."

Natalie started walking across the grass toward Market Street, not giving him an opportunity to say no.

*   *   *

They sat at a small café table and looked out the window. Red geraniums bloomed in window boxes outside. One of the stately Grand Hotel carriages trotted past briskly. Natalie caught a glimpse of the towheaded driver that sat on top, nattily dressed in a red jacket and white breeches, his black top hat and black, knee-high boots completing the outfit.

Natalie finished her pie long before John. He swallowed his last bite, and washed it down with a swig of coffee. The Jamaican waiter promptly removed his plate.

"Reminds me of my *mom's* apple pie," John said.

"You said you've been here before?"

"I used to come up a lot with my parents when I was a kid," John answered.

Natalie could tell he was warmed by the memory.

John became reflective. "When I was young, I thought all the answers to my problems were in the future. When you get older, you start thinking the answers are in the past."

Natalie smiled in agreement. "People a hundred years ago probably thought that same way, and they'll still think that way a hundred years from now. The sad thing is, by the time we finally get wise enough to live life in the present, we usually don't have much time left."

"This place hasn't changed much." John looked around at their elegantly appointed surroundings. "Hmm. The front desk used to be upstairs, though."

"I've seen old pictures. It basically looks the same," Natalie said.

"I came here once with Betsy, for a real estate convention. That was *loads* of fun," he said sarcastically, then quickly asked, "What's the date?"

"It's June 30th. Monday. Why?"

"Oh, just curious. Betsy had a convention up here this past weekend."

Natalie felt an unexpected twinge of jealousy go through her. She quickly reminded herself of her intentions, to befriend John, and that he was still married. "Oh, that's nice," she managed to squeak out.

"Are you ready to go?" John asked. "Looks like it's starting to cloud up outside."

Huge, dark clouds started to stack up in the east.

"Sure."

John paid the bill, as Natalie looked around. She noticed the displays on the wall of the three movies that had been made on Mackinac Island. John walked up behind her.

"I need to hit the boys' room."

"I'm just gonna run to the gift shop," she replied. "I'll meet you there."

She smiled in response, and John disappeared into the restroom.

Natalie headed for the gift shop, but paused when she saw a display case with photos taken over the weekend. She casually walked over and scanned the photos of the convention attendees. Mixed in with photos of group shots, were a few of couples, dressed in elegant evening attire, smiling and holding drinks. For a brief moment, Natalie entertained the idea of her and John in some similar event in the future, dressed to the nines with bright, happy smiles on their faces. She continued to scan the photos, when suddenly her eyes locked on one in particular. Natalie gasped as the shock of recognition hit her. It was Betsy with her arm around a man. A man that Natalie knew.

She turned and saw John walking toward her. She walked briskly toward him and grabbed him by the arm, whisking him away so he wouldn't see the photo.

"Don't you want to go to the gift shop?" John asked.

"It looks like it's going to rain. We'd better go."

* * *

The air was pungent with the smell of wet clothes. Fifty-some-odd people huddled together under the roof eaves of the dock building. John and Natalie had just about made it to the docks when the heavens had opened up. Natalie shivered, her wet jacket clinging to her skin. She hoped the rain would stop before the boat came in. It was coming down in torrents.

Ten minutes before the boat docked, it started raining even harder than before. In unison, the crowd groaned, "Whoa!" A few seconds later, the downpour again increased in fury and again the crowd went, "Whoa!" Unbelievably, seconds later, the rain increased its strength yet again, and the crowd cried out "Whoa!" for a third time. This time, sprinkled throughout were a couple of laughs and extra groans; the hapless crowd knew their fate was sealed.

Right in the middle of the downpour the ferry pulled in and docked. The incoming tourists on the boat raced from the boat to the shelter of the waiting area, getting soaked in the process.

Natalie grinned at John. "Our turn, now!" she said.

They hung back a bit and watched as everyone else plunged into the sheets of rain and raced to the boat ramp. John started to go, but Natalie held him back. "Wait," she instructed. "We have five minutes until the boat leaves. They're all going to bottleneck at the ramp and get even wetter before they can get on the boat." Sure enough, they did. Natalie reached down and slipped off her Birkenstocks and shoved them in her purse.

"What are you doing?" John asked.

"These shoes have cork soles. They don't take kindly to getting soaked," she replied. "Okay, let's go!"

They ran for the boat and stopped suddenly at the steep ramp, then gingerly made their way down and onto the boat. Natalie found a couple of empty seats in the upstairs cabin and they plopped down into the red theater-style chairs.

John looked at Natalie and laughed. "You look like a drowned rat!" he said.

"Thanks a lot! You don't look much better!" she retorted with a grin. Then her voice softened. "That's the first time I've ever heard you laugh."

John gave her a meaningful look and smiled gently. "Thanks, Natalie. Thank you."

*　*　*

Natalie put the heat on full as they exited the parking lot, but it wasn't until they hit I-75 that the air-cooled VW engine finally started supplying heat. By the time they'd reached Hessel, they were almost dry again and the rain had ceased.

"Do you mind if I stop by my cabin for a second? I just want to check on my dogs."

"No problem."

Natalie turned right on Island View Road and headed toward Hessel Point. They arrived at her cabin on Mackinac Bay a few minutes later.

"Come on in. I want you to meet Abby and Salty."

"Sure. Why not."

John walked up the steps of the quaint log cabin and onto the porch. Two rattan chairs and a wooden bench with a pot of impatiens sat off to his left, arranged in an inviting, outdoor-living-room manner. Natalie opened the wood-framed screen door. Before she could even fit the key in the lock, John heard excited barking and pawing sounds on the other side of the door. Natalie turned the key in the lock and pushed open the door. The two excited dogs leaped at her. Abby jumped up on her hind legs, put her front paws on Natalie's shoulders, and licked her face repeatedly. Natalie turned her head to the side trying to avoid the slobber.

"Whoa there, kids!" she protested laughingly. "Come on now. Mind your manners. We have company!"

Abby and Salty settled down immediately, as if they'd understood every word. John squatted on his heels and gently offered his hand for them to sniff. They obliged him and began wagging their tails in friendship.

"You've passed the test," Natalie grinned. "They approve of you."

She walked over to their empty water bowls, picked them up and walked over to the sink to wash and refill them.

"Make yourself at home, John. I'll only be a minute."

John looked around at the compact, tidy cabin. The log walls were stained a mellow shade of honey. Several rectangular windows were set at well-placed intervals. He looked outside. The late afternoon sky was still overcast. The lake waters that peeked through openings between the trees were gray and choppy.

John admired the cheerful living area, noting the bright colored quilts draped on the sofa and side chairs. A collection of plants sprouted from the tops of the armoire, the entertainment center, and every other level surface available. He saw fat, popsicle-orange candles on the coffee table with stacks of books sitting next to them. A wicker basket near the sofa was piled with magazines. Yet another basket held music CD's and record albums. John recognized various pieces of hand-made pottery and an emerald green vase made from hand-blown glass, as the work of talented locals. They were nestled in another collection of books on a bookshelf on the far wall. He had the distinctive impression, however, that something was missing, but couldn't put his finger on what it was. Then it hit him. There were no pictures of Joey.

On the boat ride home earlier that day, Natalie had shown him a picture of Joey she kept in her wallet. He scanned the room again, but could not see a single picture of her little brother, anywhere. It struck him as being a little strange, but he said nothing to Natalie about it.

Natalie finished her task and smiled at John.

"I'm done. Ready to go?"

"Yup."

They said their goodbyes to the dogs, and left.

They drove east down M134. Natalie pointed toward 4 Mile Block Road as they passed it. "You've met Officer Townsend. He lives down toward Connor's Point in the old Weymouth Cottage."

"Oh, sure, I know the place. Betsy sold it to his parents."

A little later, they arrived at John's cabin and she let him out. She looked up at him as he stood by the side of the car. "Fourth of July is in a few days. Want to go see the fireworks together?"

He politely declined. "No. No thanks."

Natalie wasn't ready to give up yet. "Come on. It will be good for you to get some fresh air."

John shook his head no.

"What, you don't like my company?" she joked.

He was silent for a moment. "Yes, I *do* like your company." He paused again, longer this time. Natalie gave him a sweet, pleading look. Finally he spoke. "Okay, all right, I'll go."

Natalie smiled triumphantly.

FRIDAY, JULY 4TH

CEDARVILLE, MICHIGAN was where the locals all gathered for the annual fireworks celebration. The fireworks were staged on Islington Point, and the best place in town to watch them was from Taylor Lumber. It had become the standing joke, that the high point of the celebration was watching the fire department put out the fire in the marsh nearby; which to the locals' delight, and to the fire department's chagrin, always seemed to catch fire every year.

Natalie was so glad she had the night off. She could just be a spectator. She wouldn't have to work the crowds tonight, and doing traffic control was probably her least favorite job in the world. But most of all, she was excited about seeing John.

She pulled into the station a little after 5:00 p.m. She was done for the day, thank God! And yes, it was Friday.

When she walked into the station, she saw Eric with his feet up on the desk, watching the small, wall-mounted TV in the upper corner of the room. He was totally engrossed in a news program, and apparently thought it was Charlie who had entered the station. He was yelling at the gun-control advocates that were on the screen.

"You stupid idiots. I suppose if someone gets killed by a car, you wanna outlaw cars, *too*. Why don't you deal with the nut *behind* the wheel?"

Eric looked around to see Natalie, and quickly took his feet off the desk, grabbed the remote, and shut off the TV. His face turned red. "Oh, Natalie. Sorry, I didn't see you there."

"That's okay, Eric. I don't think we should outlaw cars or guns."

"Hey, look," Eric started hesitantly. "Ah . . . last month when we first met, I told that stupid joke. I thought you were offended by the Cajun part. Charlie told me about what happened to your brother. I'm really sorry. I wanted to apologize sooner, but Charlie said to leave it alone. But I just couldn't let go of it. I really am sorry."

"It's okay, Eric. You didn't know. Hey, I got a good one for you," she said. "Thibodeaux is driving down the Interstate and Boudreaux is riding along. But Thibodeaux is only driving ten miles an hour. Traffic is passing them left and right, swerving all over the place to keep from hitting them. State Trooper Hebert sees this and proceeds to pull them over. Trooper Hebert ask Thibodeaux, *Why you goin' so slow?* Thibodeaux replies, *Mais, Ossifer, I always drives de speed limit, look ders a sign right der, an it says ten.* Trooper Hebert tells him, *Thibodeaux, you dummy, dats de highway sign. Dis is Interstate 10.* Hebert looks over on the passenger side, and notices Boudreaux shaking and sweating, and asks him what the problem is. Boudreaux says, *Boy, I sure wish you had stopped us ten minutes ago, when we was on highway 182!*"

"That's a good one, Hebert! So what you up to tonight?" Eric asked her.

"Let see, parking cars, directing traffic . . . oh, wait, I'm not working tonight," Natalie said, rubbing it in.

"Yeah, yeah, fine. Miss all the fun. See if I care."

* * *

Natalie picked John up at his cabin around dusk, and they headed over to Taylor Lumber. She found a suitable spot and spread out an old quilt. The night air was comfortably warm. Natalie propped herself up on her elbow, reclining halfway on the blanket, and made small talk with John. All around them, locals, summer residents, and tourists sat scattered about on blankets and lawn chairs. The air of expectancy created a sense of cozy camaraderie among the group gathered for the event, as strangers and neighbors alike chatted amicably.

Natalie nodded hello as she recognized familiar faces. Then she heard the laughter of children somewhere behind them. She turned and recognized some of the girls in her Girl Scout troop. They had some sparklers and were waving them around in the air. She called out to them and waved. They smiled and waved back, the hand-held sparklers making colorful arcs in the air.

When the evening sky grew dark enough, the fireworks began. The crowd oohed and aahed as sudden bursts of color lit up the night sky. Natalie and John sat side by side in comfortable silence.

All too soon, the fireworks were nearly over. The crowd heard numerous *thoof* sounds, as multiple fireworks were launched into the air. The multi-colored display suddenly bloomed in the sky above them, reminding Natalie of a huge bouquet of glittering flowers. The crowd cheered their approval, then flinched as a final barrage of eardrum-bursting cannon sounds fell upon their ears. The sky grew dark again, and the final wisps of smoke from the fireworks evanesced into the night air.

The spectators left slowly, seemingly reluctant for the magic of the evening to end. John felt the same way.

"Hey, I didn't eat much for dinner. Feel like grabbing a bite to eat?" John said.

Natalie smiled, pleasantly surprised that John had initiated the idea. "Sounds great! What are you hungry for?"

"A whitefish sandwich, actually."

"Sounds good to me. We could walk and get there faster with all this traffic," Natalie said as she looked around her.

They walked the mile to the restaurant, and the place was packed when they arrived. John and Natalie sat at the only empty table left. They ordered and were served soon after.

"You must have connections here to get served so quickly on a busy night like this."

"Just my good looks, I guess." Natalie smiled and waggled her eyebrows comically.

John took a bite of his sandwich.

"So, do you think Hollywood will ever make a movie out of *From Hell to Paradise?*" Natalie asked, then took a bite of her sandwich.

"God, I hope not."

"What do you mean?"

"I mean, they offered me close to a million dollars for the rights a couple of years ago."

"Wow, why didn't you go for it?" Natalie wiped her mouth with her napkin and took a larger bite.

"You said you love that story?"

Natalie nodded in agreement, unable to talk with her mouth full.

"Lot of people do. I love it. Most of all, Amy loved it. I told them the only way I'd sell it, was if I had creative control."

"What'd they say?"

"Nope. Even if they'd said yes, it'd still be a lie. They'd just do what they wanted, then settle out-of-court for the lies and for the promises that they'd break."

"Is it that bad?"

"Oh God, Natalie. You don't know the half of it. It's the strangest damned place you'll ever encounter in your whole life. I mean it. A bunch of crooks and gangsters. And the sad part is, most everyone in the system will acknowledge that the system is corrupt, but no one will take responsibility to fix it. In fact, they *feed* off its corruption. And then these people talk about how corrupt *Washington* is? What a bunch of hypocrites."

Natalie could tell she'd gotten him started on a subject he was passionate about.

He continued his diatribe. "And there's all these little off-shoots that talk about how screwed-up Hollywood is. But they're the first ones on stage to receive their awards, and get their pats on the back."

"Why don't you just make the movie yourself?"

"That's a big *why* when you're a radical moderate like myself. I had one fellow tell me he'd finance the film if I'd cut out the love scene. I had another lady with another agenda tell me she'd put up the money if I'd make the leading couple gay."

Natalie laughed so hard, she almost spit out the drink of coke she'd just taken. "Oh, that is rich," Natalie said catching her breath.

"Anyway, if it ever came together, it would make a wonderful movie. But I'd rather not see it done, if not done right."

"I respect that."

"Betsy didn't feel that way. She was furious when I turned down the deal."

"You haven't finished your sandwich," Natalie scolded him.

"Talking about Hollywood made me lose my appetite. I'll be right back." John stood up, picked up the check off the table, and started walking toward the cashier.

"Nice butt," Natalie said spontaneously as she watched John walk away. She'd no sooner said it when she thought, *Natalie! You and your big mouth.*

John hesitated for a split second, without looking back, then proceeded to the cashier.

I can't believe I said that, she said to herself.

John came back to the booth and sat down. Natalie felt very uncomfortable.

"Been a long time since anyone's said anything like that to me. Thanks."

Natalie felt relieved. "You're welcome."

* * *

Natalie and John arrived back at his cabin and sat in her VW, talking. Finally, he realized the time.

"I'd better let you go home. You have to work tomorrow," he said.

"Do you want me to come in?"

"I appreciate you babysitting me, but you don't have to worry. I'm not gonna check-out. Not tonight, anyway."

"I'm not babysitting you," Natalie insisted.

"This is the second time you've pulled me out of my cabin."

"Well, this is not a public service. I've enjoyed myself very much, both times."

"Thanks, for everything."

"You're welcome. I'll stop in and check on you."

"Public service?"

"Friend service."

John smiled, and got out of the car. When he got to his door, he turned and shouted, "You, too."

Natalie yelled back. *"Me too*, what?"

"Nice you-know-what."

Natalie smiled, and drove away.

SATURDAY, AUGUST 9TH

HESSEL, MICHIGAN was host to one of the finest antique boat shows in the world, every year on the second Saturday of August. John looked at the empty slot where he'd always kept his Chris-Craft Runabout. Ever since the accident, his boat had been stored in Ted's boathouse.

John sat on the end of the dock, looking at the placid, blue-green waters. He thought about all the times he and Amy had sat there on the dock doing nothing, just being together. His heart constricted within him. He felt the weight on his chest again. It threatened to crush and suffocate him. He gasped, and tried to pull some oxygen into his lungs. It hurt so much to think of her. But he *wanted* to think of her. To remember. Remember all the sweetness and joy she had brought into his life. Remember the many adventures they'd had together, exploring the wilderness that surrounded them.

For the first time since her death, he wanted to go back to those special places. And he wanted Natalie to go there with him. John took a deep breath and then squared his shoulders.

*   *   *

Natalie and Ted sat inside Ted's cabin, drinking coffee and looking at his newest photographs. They heard a knock at the door. They looked up and saw John looking in through the screen door.

"I just put the boat in the water, thought you two might like to go to the boat show for a couple of hours."

Natalie and Ted exchanged furtive glances. This was the first time since the accident that John had come so far out of his shell. Natalie smiled brightly at John. "That would be fun! How about it, Ted? You up for it?"

Ted knew John's invitation was sincere, but sensed that three would be a crowd. He graciously declined. "Sorry, kids. I've got a lot of developing to do."

"Can't it wait, Ted?" Natalie cajoled. "It's a gorgeous day, and there's a whitefish sandwich over at the food booth with your name on it."

Ted smiled at them. "No, you two go on without me. Have a good time."

Natalie smiled and shrugged her shoulders at John. "Okay, have lots of fun in your *dark-room*!" she said facetiously.

Natalie exited the cabin, and she and John walked down to Ted's boathouse. John climbed into the boat, then gave Natalie his hand and helped her into the passenger's seat on the left side of the boat.

"Are you back on night shift now?" John asked her.

"No, I got the day off for the boat show. I figured *someone* would ask me to go," she said with a grin.

John started the engine and gingerly backed the runabout out of the boathouse. Then he turned the boat around, and throttled slowly to avoid creating a wake. Once they cleared the shallows, John accelerated to a comfortable cruising speed.

"Before we head to the boat show, I'd like to show you something," John said.

He cruised the path made by the channel markers, weaving gently around the lush, green islands and sheltered bays. The gleaming, wooden boat skimmed along the smooth surface of the water, leaving a soft, rolling wake behind them. The noise of the engine startled a Great Blue Heron that had been stalking his dinner in some shallows off to their right. It uttered a loud squawk and took flight. John cut back on the throttle. The boat bobbed gently on the water as they watched, transfixed. They heard a whooshing sound as the great bird flapped its large wings, its legs trailing behind. As it climbed into the air, it tucked its head back onto its shoulders in a S-shaped curve. They watched as it flew out of sight.

John turned the boat in toward the shallows, cut the engine, and dropped anchor. "We spent a lot of time right over there in those shallows, catching fish," John said pointing. "Amy and I."

Ted had joked to Natalie once that John wasn't much of a fisherman.

"More like *talking* about fish than *catching* them, from what I've heard," Natalie teased, trying to keep things light.

"You want to hear a *fish* story? *I'll* tell you a *fish* story. This one you won't believe, I guarantee you. When Amy was about four years old, we had a cookout up on Johnson Creek, right by the little dam. Amy was sitting on the dam with my friend, Rick. She had a little fishing pole, and was drowning worms."

John choked up and fell silent for a moment, not trusting his voice. Then he continued.

"Rick had a rod and reel that he'd borrowed from a friend. A very *expensive* reel. The friend didn't want to lend it to him, but Rick finally talked him into it.

"My friend Joe and I were sitting on the shore, having hotdogs and brews, when we hear a gunshot upstream. About half-an-hour later we see five baby ducks swimming downstream with no mama. It wasn't hard to figure out what had happened, so we decide to rescue the ducklings, and take them to the DNR.

"Joe and I are in the water, up to our necks, with a fishnet, trying to sneak up on the ducks. Finally, we get one of the ducklings in the net, but the weave on the net is so big, that the duckling is falling out of the net. So we walk over to the dam where Rick is fishing, and we're yelling at him to get the cooler, so we can put the duck in there.

"Now, Rick had been fishing for hours, and hadn't caught a thing. He set the pole down on the dam, poured the ice out of the cooler, and then reached out to try and get the duckling. At that exact moment, a fish grabs his line, and starts to pull the expensive, borrowed pole toward the water. Amy sees the pole being pulled toward the water, tries to grab it as it's pulled off the edge of the dam, and falls headlong into the water.

"Anyway, Rick got the duck put in the cooler, we fished Amy out of the water, got the rest of the ducklings, and then went to work trying to find the borrowed fishing pole. Believe it or not, we found it. It was underwater, on a ledge about six feet down, right in front of the dam. The good news – the fish was still attached. The bad news – it was pregnant, and we had to throw it back. True story, I swear to God."

John and Natalie laughed together.

"You're really witty," Natalie said. "I see your personality in your writing. Some of the stuff in *From Hell to Paradise* cracked me up. Especially the title, when I found out that *Hell* and *Paradise* were towns in Michigan."

"I haven't felt so humorous lately."

"You're getting better. I can see it. I can feel it."

He sighed. "I don't know."

"Hang in there, John," Natalie said softly.

"You know, I really appreciate what you're doing for me. Getting me out of the house. Getting me to talk. I just realized that I've been so wrapped up in myself, I hardly know anything about *you*."

"What do you want to know?"

"How about your life story?" John replied.

Natalie looked at John. "This could take a while."

"You've got a captive audience," John said, motioning to the water that surrounded them.

"I grew up in a little town called Milton, just outside Lafayette, in southwest Louisiana. We lived on a country road, alongside a bayou. Behind our house were dense woods with a small creek running through them. I was a real tomboy. I used to hang out in those woods with my cousins that lived about a mile down the road from me."

Natalie smiled fondly as she relived the memories. "We used to go adventuring through the woods with BB guns and machetes, cutting off the heads of water moccasins, and shooting the big black and yellow banana spiders that made their webs in the branches."

"Man, you *were* a tomboy," John remarked.

"My mom stayed at home while my dad worked. He was gone a lot, sometimes a month at a time on the oil rigs in the Gulf. He made pretty good money, but we hardly ever got to see him. But he made up for it when he was home. He'd come home with a twinkle in his eyes, and a carload of presents for my mom, my brother, and me. *Laissez les Bontemps roule! Let the good times roll!* was his battle cry."

"You said you had a really tough childhood," John remembered.

Natalie hesitated. "When Joey was three years old, my dad had a really bad accident. He was replacing some shingles on the roof, when he slipped and fell off. He broke his back in three places. The doctors told him he could never go back to work. We lost our house and had to move into an apartment. Dad started drinking. It got really bad."

John could tell she really didn't want to talk about it. "I'm sorry. I didn't mean to bring up bad memories."

"It's okay. I moved on, and made something of my life in spite of it. I graduated from high school with straight A's and got a scholarship to go to U.S.L. – University of Southwestern Louisiana. Then I enrolled in the police academy. After graduating, I ended up on the New Orleans police force. I was there until Joey died."

"What made you decide to become a police officer?"

"I wanted to help people. When I was a kid, I used to go to the movies a lot. I mean a *whole* lot. I was a movie junkie." Natalie laughed at herself. "I used to love seeing the bad guys get caught. I thought about being a doctor, or a lawyer. But, for the most part, they only helped people *after* the damage was done. I thought that if I was a cop, I'd be able to *prevent* people from getting hurt. Or at the least, keep the criminals from hurting people *again*."

"So, how did you end up here, in the U.P.?" John asked.

"I tried to go back to work, but I couldn't handle living in that city anymore. The carnival atmosphere there seemed like a macabre nightmare. Everywhere I looked, people walked down the street, go-cups full of alcohol in their hands. Don't get me wrong. I have a drink now and then. But I saw what alcohol did to my dad, to my brother. When it gets out of control, people get hurt."

John understood completely.

Natalie continued. "Anyway, my college roommate invited me to stay with her for the summer. She had moved from New Orleans to Mackinac Island a few years before. I'd just finished your book the day before she called. The timing was uncanny. I took an extended leave of absence and came up to stay with her at her cottage. I fell in love with the area and decided that it was a good place to make a fresh start."

"How did you get back into police work?"

"During my stay on the island, I took a little road trip to explore the surrounding area and do some camping, and came up here to the Snows. There's an herbs and art shop outside Cedarville. A guy there offered kayak classes. I'd never kayaked before. Man, I did it one time, and I was hooked. Totally! We paddled out on the bay, and through the channels. Saw the Great Blue Herons in the marshes. It was the most amazing experience I'd ever had in my life. I loved the peace and quiet up here. Mackinac was nice, but a little too hectic for my taste.

"The day I was supposed to go back to Mackinac, I ran into a marine officer, and we started chatting. He told me about a position that was open on the Clark Township Sheriff's Department. One of the deputies had recently retired. I thought about it for a few days. It seemed so nice and peaceful up here, so different from the craziness I'd left behind in New Orleans. So, I applied for the job and was hired."

"So, tomboy, how do you like working around a bunch of men?" John smiled at her and waited for her reaction.

Natalie smiled and rolled her eyes at him. "They can get under my skin occasionally, but I really do love working with them. Beats working with a bunch of women. Don't get me wrong. One on one, I get along fine with women. But for the most part, as soon as you add more into the mix, it starts to get ugly. The gossiping and cattiness gets so bad that I always have to bail."

"Have you ever been married?"

"No." Natalie stopped talking. There was a moment of awkward silence. John tried to fix his blunder.

"I'm sorry, that's probably none of my business."

"No, that's okay. It's just that I've never talked to anyone about it before." Natalie hesitated for a moment, and then continued. "We were engaged to be married. We'd planned the wedding, sent the invitations and everything. Then Joey died. I was devastated. I felt like it was my fault he died. I was the one that had invited Joey to spend the summer with me in New Orleans. If it wasn't for me, Joey would still be alive." Natalie's voice broke. She swallowed hard. She was determined not to cry. Between the two of them, there had already been enough tears for a lifetime.

"I turned to my fiancé for the comfort and support I needed so badly. He couldn't handle it. Just when I needed him most, he shut down emotionally. I still don't understand it. He came to me a few weeks after the funeral, and gave me a song and dance number about being promoted at his job, and having to transfer to Houston. Two weeks later, he was gone."

John kept silent and let her finish.

"I never let myself get involved with anyone after that. I didn't want to risk that kind of hurt again." Natalie sat up straight in her chair. She didn't want to talk about it anymore. She looked at John and made herself smile. "Well, enough about me." She looked down at her watch. "Whoa! We'd better hurry if we want to make the boat show."

John grinned. "No problem." He climbed back and pulled up the anchor, then returned to his seat. "I'll show you what this baby can do. Hold on!"

He throttled the engine, and they were off. He glanced at Natalie. She turned to him suddenly and her smile widened to a grin.

"I get it!" she blurted out.

"Get what?" John yelled back.

"The name of your boat. *Almost Paradise!*"

John grinned back at her.

The wind rushed over them, whipping at their clothes and hair as they sped along. The flag on the back of the boat jerked and snapped noisily, adding to the din. Natalie looked over and saw John's hand on the arm rest. She placed her hand on his, and they cruised along the smooth blue waterway.

* * *

As they neared Hessel Bay, John slowed the boat to a crawl. The marina was chock full of antique wooden boats of every description – a sea of waxed, shiny wood surfaces that winked and flashed in the August sunshine. They dropped anchor on the east side of the harbor, and went ashore. Natalie wanted to stroll around and see everything, but first she needed some fuel.

"I'm starving, how 'bout you?"

Without waiting for John to answer, she headed for the food tents. John shook his head in amusement and followed in her wake. They waited in the long line at the booth until it was their turn. John purchased four whitefish sandwiches, and refused Natalie's offer to pay.

"It's my treat, he said."

"Thanks, John. That's nice of you." Natalie said. They sat on a couple of large boulders on the shore, and wolfed down their lunch. The Sault Swing Band started playing in the gazebo behind them. They heard the lively strains of Glenn Miller's *In the Mood*, and Natalie started patting her foot in time to the music.

"I love these guys," she said enthusiastically. "This boat show always reminds me of a Louisiana Fais Do Do."

"What's a Fais Do Do?"

"It's a Cajun festival that has lots of good music, good fun, and of course, good food," she laughed as she waved her sandwich in the air.

"Do you miss Louisiana?" John asked her.

"Not much. The winters here can get pretty long, so along about February, I miss the warm weather. I miss the crawfish, going crabbing with the cousins, and doin' the two-step," she reflected. "But I don't miss the craziness. It's a culture of extremes. Puritans or perverts. Abstinence or excess." She paused for a moment, then added with a smile. "God, I *do* miss the food, though."

John laughed heartily.

"Hey, but how can I complain," she said as she started on her second whitefish sandwich.

They sat for awhile, soaking up the sunshine and enjoying the music. Natalie noticed that John kept looking over at the large tented area behind them. At the edge of the tent were eight-foot tables butted together to form one long, continuous table. Sitting there with stacks of books all around them, were authors from all over the state of Michigan. Festival goers chatted with the authors, bought books, and had them signed.

"You miss that, don't you?" she asked.

"Miss what?"

"The book stuff." She pointed to the group of authors signing at the tent.

"Amy used to come with me when I did booksignings. I miss it. I miss *her.*" A shadow passed over his face.

"I understand, John. I do."

John didn't respond to her comment. She decided to change the subject.

"How did you come up with Mark Emerson for a pen name?" Natalie asked.

"Mark Twain. Ralph Waldo Emerson."

"Two of my favorites. Have you ever read Emerson's essay, The American Scholar?" Natalie asked him.

"Absolutely," John replied.

"So many writers just use words for ornamentation, but Emerson uses words to convey ideas. The beauty of his writing is in the ideas conveyed, and the simplicity with which he conveys them," Natalie commented.

"My sentiments, exactly. That piece got me thinking about so many things."

"Like what?" Natalie asked him.

"I'm more fascinated by *why* people believe what they believe, than *what* they believe. Learning is such an exciting adventure, and the whole process of learning is so fascinating to me. When we're young, we have so many questions; we're like a sponge. We start with a premise, and move forward to a conclusion. Maybe our conclusions weren't always right, but at least the *process* was honest. But as we get older, we get so dishonest. We start with conclusions, preconceptions, and then work backwards to try to prove what we've already concluded. It's so dishonest. And most of our beliefs are just a smorgasbord of *other* people's beliefs. We don't even have convictions that are our own. I don't agree with everything Emerson wrote, but his writing helped me to get honest, and look at the process, and helped me to become more selective in determining my core convictions," he said.

"You're so articulate. And you have something to say. I hope you keep writing."

John thought about what she'd said. He used to love writing. The only thing he'd loved *more* than writing was spending time with Amy. He had never even entertained the idea of writing again after Amy had died. Until this moment.

"John, you need to express yourself. Not just because others need to hear what you have to say, but because, well, because you need to write. For you."

John didn't respond. He just looked off across the water. But her words set his mind in motion.

"Would you like to go look at the art booths?" Natalie asked.

"Sure. Let's do it."

They walked up by the food booths, swung around the public ramp and headed toward Mertaugh's. They strolled along, stopping here and there, to examine the beautiful works of art; especially the booths brimming with pottery, quilts, and Natalie's favorite – hand-blown glass.

Natalie stood at the booth, agonizing over which piece to buy. "I like the emerald green perfume bottle," she said, "but I really love that cobalt blue vase." After a few minutes of debating, she decided to get both.

Natalie paid for her purchases. The artist running the booth – a bearded man with sagacious, smiling eyes – carefully wrapped them up, and bagged them for her. Natalie thanked him, and she and John headed back to his boat.

"We'll have to go to one of his glass blowing demonstrations sometime. They are amazing," Natalie said.

"Sounds fun. I'd like to."

* * *

The sun hung low in the western sky as they finally headed for home. Overhead, the sky was brilliant blue, abruptly changing to a light orange, then deepening into brilliant tangerine near the horizon. The water was deep purple, the land on either side of them, silhouette black.

As they neared John's cabin, Natalie mentally prepared herself for what she had to do next. They pulled up and docked. John jumped out first. Natalie threw him the mooring lines to tie off the boat. He extended his hand and helped her out of the boat. As she stepped onto the dock, she was so close to him, that for a brief moment, she thought he was going to pull her to him and embrace her. Natalie wanted him to. She was sure John *wanted* to. But the moment passed. They walked down the dock and stood near Natalie's car.

"John, I need to tell you something."

Something in her tone made John's facial muscles twitch.

"Greg Reynolds changed his plea to guilty. There's not going to be a trial, only a sentencing hearing." Natalie stopped and peered at John in the waning light to see how he was taking the news. "You'll get a chance to speak about your loss in the courtroom. Many times, what the families say during that time, can affect sentencing."

John's face was grim, his voice, forceful. "I'll be there."

FRIDAY, AUGUST 29TH

MACKINAC COUNTY COURTHOUSE was a beige, art deco, stone building that had been built in 1936. It was a veritable skyscraper in the tiny town of St. Ignace, standing four stories high. The interior of the building reflected the rich heritage of a time when buildings were fashioned from fine woods and solid rock wrestled from the earth. The first floor had a high, ornate tin ceiling painted soft cream. Tall, elegant art deco light fixtures hung on long chains from the ceiling, emitting a soft yellow light that bounced off the dark, polished wood-paneled walls and the gleaming, rose granite floors. On either side of the main entrance, wide sweeping staircases made of the same dark wood as the paneled walls, led to the floors above that held the district and circuit courts.

John and Natalie sat alone on a wooden bench just outside the circuit courtroom. At the last minute, John had refused to go inside. He just couldn't deal with it. He sat there without speaking, wringing his hands and looking off down the hallway. Natalie sat beside him in silence, her hand resting on his upper back. On the wall opposite them hung a large, black clock with a white face. Its loud, ominous tick echoed in the empty hallway. The disconcerting image of a time bomb flashed through Natalie's mind. She glanced surreptitiously at John. She saw the strain in his face. His jaw was clenched, his face taut with emotion. Abruptly, John's head snapped around and he was face to face with her. Natalie flinched. The sudden movement had startled her.

"How much longer is this going to take?" he blurted out.

"These things usually go pretty quick."

The words had no more than come out of her mouth, when the large wood doors to the courtroom swung open, and the hallway started to fill with people. Sam Brown, the prosecuting attorney, walked up to John and Natalie.

"John, we did everything we could. Judge Warren, he's kinda, well . . . " Sam paused.

"What do you mean?" John asked.

Greg Reynolds came walking through the courtroom doors with his cousin, Mike, and his attorney, Doug Krieger. They stopped in the hallway, their backs to John and Natalie. Greg smiled and shook Doug's hand, then slapped his cousin on the back.

John was dumbfounded. He looked at Sam questioningly.

"What's going on?" Natalie demanded.

Sam looked down at the granite floor. He couldn't stand to look John in the face as he delivered the crushing news.

"He got time served and five years' probation. A slap on the wrist."

John exploded, leaping to his feet. "He *what?!*"

Heads turned as John's voice grew louder.

"He killed my little girl and he gets five years' probation?!" John was crying now, his fists clenched, his face beet-red.

"John, you've got to calm down," Natalie pleaded.

"Calm down?! Calm down?!" he shouted.

Now everyone was staring at him.

"That son of a bitch killed my little girl! That son of a bitch killed my Amy and you want me to calm down?!"

Natalie and Sam grabbed John's arms trying to restrain him.

"I'll kill you, you bastard! I'll kill you!" John struggled to free himself.

A nearby officer ran over to assist Sam and Natalie. He stood in front of John and blocked him with his body. John continued to rant at Greg as tears poured down his cheeks. He clawed the air with his hands trying to get at Greg who was a good twenty feet away.

"You're a dead man, do you hear me?" he screamed. "You're a dead man!"

* * *

It was eight o'clock in the evening. The sun wouldn't start its final descent for about a half-hour. When they'd arrived at John's cabin, Natalie left the back door of the cabin open. The screen door kept the mosquitos at bay, and allowed the clean, cool air and the sounds of frogs and crickets to filter in. She left the cabin lights off, with the exception of a table lamp near the sofa, and a small, halogen light over the sink in the kitchen.

John sat on the couch, red-eyed, and distraught. Natalie rummaged through his kitchen cabinets until she found an unopened bottle of scotch. She poured the scotch into a tall glass filled with ice. She knew John needed its numbing, sedative effects. If she couldn't calm him down, she worried about what he might do next. She handed him the drink as she sat down next to him, then watched as he took several large sips.

"I understand how you feel, John, but you gotta let it go."

"Five years' probation? What kind of crap is that?" he said bitterly.

"I know what you're going through. The s.o.b. who killed my little brother lost his drivers license, and spent three months in jail."

"You knew it was gonna go like this didn't you?" he accused.

"I thought he'd get two years in jail and probation. I didn't think he'd just get probation. This judge is a . . . "

"You told me he'd pay." John was still pretty agitated.

"He will, John. We . . . you have a civil case against him for wrongful death."

"It won't bring back Amy. You told me he'd pay."

"John, all the hate in the world isn't gonna bring back Amy. Two months after the s.o.b. that killed my brother got out of jail, he got juiced up, ran a red light, and got hit broadside by a semi-truck. I was so glad that bastard was dead, but it still didn't bring Joey back."

John sighed and took a few more swallows of his drink. His shoulders slumped forward and he seemed to calm a little. Natalie fell silent for a while. She heard a scratching sound at the screen door and looked up to see Felix waiting to be let in. She got up and cracked the screen door slightly. Felix slipped through the narrow opening, ran straight to his food bowl and started wolfing down his dinner. Natalie closed the screen door and sat back down on the couch next to John.

"John, I don't know what to say. All I know is that you are a wonderful man. You have to go on. You have to remember the wonderful times you had with Amy, and keep living. For Amy's sake. For my sake, John."

Natalie paused. She took a deep breath and exhaled slowly. She was afraid to continue, but she decided to risk it. "I care for you, John. I haven't been able to let anyone into my life since Joey died."

John sat silently, staring at the floor. She willed him to look up at her, but he kept his head down, refusing to meet her gaze.

"Reaching out to you has helped me to see just how much Joey meant to me, and how he'd feel if he knew I was just existing, instead of really living . . . " She summoned all her courage. "John, I can't go on just existing. I need you, John. I need you," she pleaded.

John didn't react.

"I'm gonna go now," Natalie said abruptly, feeling embarrassed and rejected. She walked toward the back door.

"Natalie," John said softly. He got up and walked over to her. He took her hands in his and looked into her eyes. "Maybe we could go somewhere tomorrow night. Somewhere nice."

Natalie smiled. "You asking me out, John?" she said gently.

"We've been out before," he corrected her.

"No, John, we've been out, but we've never been *out*."

"Then I guess I'm asking you out."

"Then I guess I'm saying yes." John let go of her hands and Natalie reached for the screen door handle.

"Tomorrow," he said. "I'll pick you up around seven. I was thinking we could have dinner on Drummond Island."

"That sounds nice." Natalie leaned toward him and kissed him on the cheek. She opened the screen door and walked out. He stood there watching her as she crossed the deck and slipped around the corner, disappearing from sight.

SATURDAY, AUGUST 30TH

DRUMMOND ISLAND was only about a twenty-five minute drive from Cedarville to the ferry docks in DeTour, then another ten-minute ferry ride to the island. John looked at his watch again. They'd have to get going if they were going to make the 7:40 ferry.

He stood in the living room of Natalie's cabin, waiting for her to finish getting dressed. He would have sat on the couch, but Abby and Salty had commandeered it already. They lay there with their heads down in their usual sulking, *why-are-you-leaving-me-again* pose, their eyes following John as he started pacing back and forth. John looked over at their melancholy expressions and felt sorry for them. He walked over to the sofa and crouched down next to Abby and stroked her head.

"Don't worry, girl, I'll have her back home soon."

Abby licked his hand and then tried to lick his face. He pulled away just in time.

"Whoa, girl, don't get me all mussed up!" He petted Abby's head one last time and stood up.

"I'm ready." Natalie had walked into the living room without John noticing.

He turned around and his eyes widened. Natalie blushed. She fidgeted with embarrassment as John stared at her.

She wore a gossamer, pale blue cotton dress, luminous against her bronzed skin. It had spaghetti straps, and a tight fitting bodice that was laced up, yet still open, exposing a modest amount of cleavage. The material flowed out from an empire waistline, leaving her narrow waist and curvaceous hips to the imagination. The dress was moderately short, exposing shapely, tanned legs that tapered into delicate ankles. Her manicured feet were encased in strappy, low-heeled sandals made of buttery-soft, chamois colored leather that laced part way up her calf.

It was only recently that John had noticed Natalie's natural beauty. And up until last night, he'd only seen her as a friend in time of need. But tonight, he saw her in a different light altogether.

Her eyes, normally hazel, changed color depending on what she wore. Tonight they were a mesmerizing, silver-blue. She wore makeup that accented those exotic, almond-shaped eyes and long dark lashes. Her high cheekbones were dusted with a soft pearly mauve that matched the glossy shine on her full, sensuous lips. And her hair. John had never seen Natalie with her hair down. It was either swept up off her neck and pinned up, or in a ponytail. Tonight it was down. The soft lights of the cabin bounced off her long, dark hair as it cascaded down her back in soft ringlets. Some of the tendrils swept to the front and gently framed her oval face. She was gorgeous.

"I'm ready to go," she said again, feeling very awkward.

John just stood there staring, not saying a word.

"What?" Natalie said to John, unsure of his reaction.

"You look . . . " He stopped.

"What?!" she asked more urgently.

"You look incredible," he said softly. He felt as if the temperature in the room had suddenly increased. Now it was *his* turn to fidget.

"Well, uh, I guess we'd better get going if we're going to be on time for the ferry," he said, flustered.

He walked over to the door and opened it for Natalie.

"See ya, guys," she said to Abby and Salty as they exited. John closed the door behind them.

"Do you mind if I drive?" John asked her.

Natalie was surprised. This was the first time he'd driven in all the time they'd spent together.

"Not at all. Can we take my car?" she asked.

"Sure." John was puzzled as to why she wanted to take the VW. "You don't want to put the top down, do you?"

"Are you kidding? I worked on my hair for an hour," she laughed. "Just thought you might enjoy driving my car."

"Sure, why not," he said agreeably.

"You *do* know how to drive a stick, don't you?"

"I used to have one of these babies when I was in college. Not in such good shape, but it ran."

John walked around and opened the door for her. Natalie climbed in the car, and from his view, John couldn't help but appreciate her beauty – every inch of it. From head to toe, and everywhere between, he was captivated by her grace and charm.

John walked around to the other side of the car and started to get in. *Oh, dear God*, he thought. He was thoroughly aroused. He wasn't prepared for this. At all. He hadn't felt this way in a long, long time. He didn't know how to handle it. He climbed into the car and immediately started babbling. Anything to get his mind off of how he was feeling. Anything to keep Natalie from seeing how awkward he felt.

"My first year in college, U of M, I lent my bug to a friend for the whole school year. I lived on campus, and didn't really need it. She lived in Detroit, and she didn't have a car, and she needed a way to get back and forth to Ann Arbor from Detroit every day. Anyway, I lent her my car. When the school year was over, I got the car back, and it seemed to be in good shape. About a month or two later, I had to replace the transmission. These things happen. I didn't blame her. But man, it cost me a bundle, and I was trying to put myself through school and . . . "

John took a deep breath and continued. "Anyway, several years later, my last year in school, I'm sitting in a coffee shop with Betsy and some of her friends, and the conversation got on the subject of VW's. This guy next to Betsy starts telling us a story about a girl who borrowed a VW from a friend during her freshman year at U of M, and how she drove it back and forth from Detroit to Ann Arbor at 70 miles-an-hour in third gear for almost the whole school year before she found out that it had a fourth gear! So I asked what the name of the girl was, and . . . "

"John?"

"Yeah?"

"We're gonna miss the ferry."

"Oh, yeah." His face reddened. He started to reach for the ignition.

"John?" Natalie said softly.

"Yeah?" He turned his head her direction.

Natalie leaned toward him, reached her hand around the back of his head, and planted a slow, gentle kiss on his lips.

"Let's go."

John sighed deeply, letting go of the tension in his shoulders. "Yeah. We'd better."

*   *   *

They drove along in comfortable silence, John watching the road, and Natalie watching the scenery. It was breathtaking. She had passed this way many times, but never tired of the view. In the background, the azure sky and indigo waters provided a permanent canvas for an ever-changing landscape as they drove along. They passed rocky points and little bays, sandy beaches, and spreading marshes. Clumps of bright green birches contrasted with the dark cedars, and giant, exposed white pines, seventy to eighty feet tall, stood at the water's edge, their branches bent away from the direction of the prevailing winds and flattened on the windward side, giving them a wild, rugged look. Here and there, patches of goldenrod and purple asters added splashes of late summer color. The waning sun provided a Midas touch, washing everything with a golden glow.

They arrived in DeTour just in time. John pulled onto the ferry and parked. An attendant showed up a few minutes later and John handed him a twenty for the fare. The attendant made change, and with a polite thank you, walked away.

While they waited to depart, Natalie noticed a huge ship that had entered the DeTour Passage.

"Look! It's a saltie!" Natalie pointed toward the huge, thousand-foot freighter as it slowly made its way through the passage.

"What's a saltie?" John asked.

"It's an ocean-going freighter. You can tell from the rust stains and the three angled masts. You don't see very many of them anymore. Since the break up of the Soviet Union, there's been less of a demand for North American grain, consequently, fewer salties."

John was impressed. "Wow. Smart *and* gorgeous."

Natalie grinned. "Actually, that's the only ship I know. I just got lucky on that one."

A few minutes later, they pulled up to the Drummond Island dock. The ferry hummed with the sound of the hydraulic lift as the ramp slowly lowered to the dock. It began to disgorge its cargo of tourists and islanders. John started the car and drove off the ferry. He headed up M134 about eight miles and then turned left onto Townline Road.

"Have you ever been to Bayside before?" he asked.

"No, I've been to the Wayfarer's Mart on the south side of the island, but this is the first time for Bayside. I've heard the food is incredible. A friend of mine told me that she'd eaten in fine restaurants from Minneapolis, to New Orleans, and everywhere in between, and her meal at Bayside was the best food she ever tasted in her life."

"Wow! That's pretty high praise," John smiled. "I hope it lives up to your expectations."

Natalie smiled back at John. "I'd be happy just eating a fish sandwich at Albany Bar, just as long as you were there."

John reached over and squeezed her hand. Conflicting emotions welled up inside him. For the first time in a very long time he felt cherished and cared for by a woman. He had learned to live so long without it, he hadn't realized how badly he needed the companionship; how thirsty he'd become for someone who genuinely liked and listened to him. On the other hand, he felt guilty for being happy. Survivor's guilt, they called it. He felt he had no right to be alive and happy when Amy's life had been cut short so tragically.

He glanced over at Natalie and his heart immediately went out to her. She had been through it, too. She had confided to him the heartbreaking details surrounding Joey's death. He realized at that moment that she needed him for her own healing process, just as he needed her.

He took a left on Tourist Road and within five minutes they were pulling into the parking lot of the restaurant. They exited the car and walked into the restaurant. Housed in a low, wooden building, the restaurant incorporated alternating cozy and wide-open spaces after the style of Frank Lloyd Wright. Large, plate-glass windows brought the beauty of the outdoors to the diners. Its rustic decor was offset by fine, white linen table cloths and elegant table settings.

A tall, willowy young woman with a Spanish accent, approached them. She was dressed in a white silk blouse with French cuffs, and a long black skirt.

"Good evening," she said, "do you have a reservation?"

"Yes," John replied, "Harrison."

She walked to the hostess stand and examined her seating chart. "Would you like to sit inside or out on the terrace?"

John looked at Natalie.

"Outside sounds nice," she said.

The hostess nodded. "Come with me, please."

They followed her to a small table toward the edge of the terrace.

The hostess waited as John pulled out Natalie's chair and seated her, then himself. She smiled broadly at them as she handed them their menus.

"Your waiter this evening is Friedrich. Please, enjoy your dinner."

Their waiter appeared shortly. He was blond and blue-eyed. He smiled and greeted them as he lit the candle on their table.

"May I get you something to drink?" he asked.

John looked at Natalie. "What would you like to drink?" he asked her.

"I'd love a glass of white wine."

"We'll have a bottle of Pinot Grigio, Santa Margherita," John said after scanning the wine list for a few moments.

"Very good." Friedrich disappeared from the table.

Natalie looked around. There were about ten tables scattered across the terrace, all covered in the same white table linens and table settings as their counterparts inside. Only three other couples were dining on the terrace, their murmured conversations and low laughter creating a pleasant atmosphere. The ambiance was further enhanced by the view. A path lit by footlights, wound through a copse of trees and ended at the water's edge. Waves lapped peacefully at the shore, and a soft breeze stirred in the treetops. Sounds of a piano playing in the main dining room drifted out onto the terrace. Natalie relaxed and sat back in her chair. She studied her menu for a few minutes. Making a decision was hard for her. Everything looked so good.

Presently, Friedrich returned with their bottle of wine and a wine bucket and presented the bottle to John. John nodded his approval and after he'd gone through the ritual of tasting the wine, motioned for Friedrich to fill their glasses.

"Are you ready to order?" he asked them.

"Well, I'm having a hard time," Natalie responded. "What do you suggest? I love salmon."

Friedrich smiled and pointed to a salmon dish toward the bottom of the menu. "This is my favorite. Grilled salmon topped with ginger medallions and a honey-teriyaki glaze."

"Sounds great! That's what I'll have," she said.

"Do you have any specials not listed on the menu?" John asked.

"Yes, tonight we have Chicken Genovese. Medallions of chicken breast, sauteed in a Chardonnay, lemon-butter sauce, topped with artichoke hearts, roasted red peppers and sprinkled with capers. It is served with a side of Fettuccine Alfredo."

"Sounds like a winner." John replied.

"Very good," Friedrich said. "Would you care for an appetizer? The crab-stuffed mushrooms are excellent."

Natalie nodded and looked at John. "I'd love some, but only if you promise to help me eat them."

Friedrich nodded and left.

Natalie took a sip of her wine and looked thoughtfully at John. She wanted to know everything about him and his life before she met him.

"You said you and Betsy met in college? In an art class, right?"

"Oh, this should make for wonderful dinner conversation," John said, mildly sarcastic.

"I just want to know more about your life."

"Are you uncomfortable being with a married man?" he asked.

"I already told you I understand your situation. You said she wants a divorce. I've seen the way she treats you, John."

"That's the funny thing. She kicks me out of the house. She takes all her stuff from the cabin. She says she wants the divorce, but she hasn't made any effort to get it. No letters from her attorney, nothing."

"That's strange." Natalie responded.

"Not for Betsy. She's played stranger games."

"I'm sorry. Maybe I *did* bring up the wrong subject."

"It's okay. I've put you in an awkward position."

"I want to be here, John."

"Me too."

*　*　*

After dinner, John and Natalie sat in silence, enjoying each other's company. The piano caught his attention when it started playing a song that he recognized, and he broke the silence.

"When I was in college, I lived in a house with some classmates. The house belonged to this elderly man that had just lost his wife. He was so lonely, and welcomed having us around."

Natalie smiled gently.

"Anyway, he gave us the run of the house. In the living room was this old Steinway Piano, a baby grand. I didn't know how to play piano, but I could play a nice big fat C major chord, with double octaves in the bass. I'd put the top up on the piano, depress the sustain pedal, and hit the chord with all I had."

"Like at the end of *A Day in the Life*, by the Beatles."

"Exactly. It was so beautiful. I could have crawled up inside that chord and stayed there forever."

Natalie nodded in agreement.

He continued. "You're gonna think this is sort of weird, but at that moment, I realized that life was supposed to be harmony and beauty, like that chord. I looked around me and saw all the evil and the pain in the world, and I realized that, somehow, humanity had lost that chord."

"You and I are a lot alike. Guess we're both in search of the lost chord." She smiled ruefully.

"Moody Blues, 1968."

"Yeah. I just got the re-mastered CD."

"You must believe in the supernatural?" he said, more as a statement than a question.

"I don't believe that everything that happens is supernatural, but I *do* believe that supernatural things happen," she observed.

"I hear ya. It drives me crazy when I hear someone say that everything happens for a reason. You know, they stub their toe and they say, God made me stub my toe, or they drop their fork, and they say, it must have been fate that I dropped my fork."

Natalie realized what John was implying. "When Joey died, everyone tried to tell me something that they thought would help ease the pain. They all had their own little convoluted philosophies to explain pain and death. I grew up having people tell me that the bad times came from God, to help me better appreciate the good times. All those bad times did, were to make me afraid to enjoy anything good in my life. I think everything happens with a cause, but not for a reason."

"Do you believe there's evil?"

"You forget, I was a New Orleans police officer. You bet your butt I believe there's evil. I've seen horrific things in my work. That's why I love animals. They love so unconditionally. Only humans use their freedom of will for cruelty."

"Only people have the stupidity to be destructive, and the intelligence to be cruel," John said.

Natalie looked at John strangely.

"Betsy always says that," John explained.

"Russell said that exact thing to me, once."

"Here we are talking about the mysteries of the universe . . . I should be exploring the mysteries behind those beautiful eyes. They are so beautiful, and filled with compassion."

John reached over and put his hand on hers. She looked into his eyes trying to probe their depths. Her pulse quickened. She suddenly turned bashful. She wasn't used to having a man look at her that way. Natalie looked away and noticed an older couple at the other end of the terrace, staring at them. She'd noticed them looking their way earlier, but hadn't thought anything of it before. Now it made her uncomfortable.

"What's with those people, John? They keep staring at us."

John looked over at them. "Hmm. I met them once at a real estate convention at Grand Hotel. I think they're clients of Betsy's."

"Can we go now?" Natalie blurted out.

"Sounds good to me." John slipped a couple of large bills inside the leather check holder on the table and rose from his chair. He pulled Natalie's chair out for her and they left the restaurant.

When they arrived back at Natalie's, they sat in her car talking.

"I'm sorry about this evening," John apologized.

"Sorry? Sorry about what?"

"I guess I didn't know how to act. What to talk about. It's been a long time since I've felt this way."

"I had a really good time. Anything we talk about is fine with me. I feel very comfortable with you."

"I suppose I'd better go. You've got to work tomorrow."

"No, actually, I have to work the bridge walk on Monday, so I have the day off tomorrow. John, I had a really good time tonight," she paused. "And I don't want it to end."

John searched her face, trying to read it.

"Please stay."

* * *

John and Natalie lay in her four-poster bed, arms and legs entwined. *See You There* from the *Whisper from the Mirror* CD played, as candlelight flickered and danced on the ceiling. She gazed at him, drinking in his tousled golden hair and half-closed eyes. He reached over and caressed her face with his hand, tracing a line from her mouth up to her nose. He tweaked it gently and smiled.

Natalie smiled back. "When I first met you, my heart hurt so much for you. I just wanted so badly to help you. After we watched the fireworks together, I came home and put Joey's pictures out. And I realized that by trying to help you to go on with your life, I was helping myself to do the same."

She stopped for a moment and looked away, trying to find the right words. She looked back at him again, and what she saw in his eyes gave her the courage to continue. "After the boat show, I knew I loved you."

He was silent for a moment, then spoke. "You know what you said last night, about how Joey would feel if he knew you were just existing?"

"Yeah, I remember."

"I thought about it all night. All I'd been able to think about before that, was that it was my fault Amy was dead; that if I hadn't taken her along that day, she'd still be alive. But last night, I thought about how Amy would have felt without her daddy, or how she'd feel now if she knew . . . if she knew how many times I've thought of ending my life. And I was ashamed of myself."

"Life is hard for the living, John. We're the ones that have to go on."

"Yeah, I know. It just hurts so much to think that she will never get to grow up, to fall in love, to have children. All those things." He choked up and could say no more.

Natalie looked at him tenderly. "God, I know, John. Joey was so full of life. He was so smart. Had so much ability. I can't imagine what . . . " She paused. "But what if it had been me or you, instead of Joey, or Amy. They would have had to go on. We wouldn't have wanted them to grieve forever."

"I know."

"I think grieving is important. But there's a point where it becomes destructive. You've got to move past it. I really believe that we'll see them again someday. That's what carries me day by day and gives me strength and comfort. I can't even *imagine* how unbearable the sorrow must be for those that don't have that hope."

They lay there silently for a few moments.

"I love you, John. Every moment I spend with you, I love you more."

John looked away and didn't respond for a while. Finally, he spoke, his head still averted. "Those are really hard words for me to say. I never thought I'd ever say them again."

"Did you love Betsy?"

"Madly. She was so different, Natalie. You wouldn't have believed it. She was so passionate about life, about her art, about my success. She was a real giver."

"Do you still love her?"

"I don't know if this will make any sense to you. But the woman I loved died after we moved to Hollywood. My dad had just died the year before. I felt like I'd lost the two people that meant the most to me in the whole world in the space of a year. And I felt like life was over. But the next year, Amy was born. I took one look at her, and my whole life changed. I knew that I'd fallen in love forever, and I knew I could go on."

Natalie held his gaze.

"Do you understand what I'm trying to say to you, Natalie?"

"I'm not sure."

"I'm saying that I know now that I can go on."

Natalie's heart swelled within her. She smiled radiantly at John, her eyes starting to tear.

"I hear ya, John."

John pressed his lips against hers. They kissed passionately, then held each other close. Natalie snuggled near to him, her head resting on his chest. The comforting sound of his heartbeat lulled her to sleep.

SUNDAY, AUGUST 31ST

STARLIGHT filled the Northern Michigan sky overhead, and in the distance, the glimmering, shifting shapes of the Aurora Borealis could be seen. Greg Reynolds lay back on the bed of his pickup truck, his legs dangling over the tailgate. He looked up at the profusion of stars scattered across the sky.

He took another swig of the bottle of Jack Daniel's, now almost empty, and climbed back into his self-pity. He'd gotten five years' probation from that whole Harrison kid fiasco. The straightjacket the cops had on him was insufferable. He had to watch every step he took, or he'd be back behind bars for a long time. If that wasn't bad enough, he'd lost his job when the local authorities had left him rotting in jail before his sentencing hearing. And, Tyler, that son of a bitch, was suing him for the money he owed him. The nerve! If he ever managed to get that little twerp alone again, he'd rid himself of one debt, that's for sure. Debts! That burned him the most. Since he'd lost his job, he hadn't been able to keep up with his bills. That led to the ultimate blow. His most cherished possession, his brand new, black Dodge Ram truck, would soon be repossessed. He took a final swallow of Jack Daniels. "Fuck you, God! It's not fair!" he shouted at the night sky. The more he thought about it, the angrier he became. "Why wait? I'll go take care of that little shit right now!" Greg sat up. He looked at the now empty bottle in his hand and threw it at the nearest tree. It exploded into several large shards and he hooted with laughter.

Despite the generous amount of liquor that sloshed around inside him, Greg was still coherent enough to find his keys he'd dropped earlier near the driver's side of his truck. The metal keys glinted in the dim moonlight, as he bent down and closed his hand over the key ring. He started to straighten and felt the earth shift beneath his feet. He wobbled a bit, noticing that the heavens above him seemed to spin. He blinked a couple of times and rubbed his eyes with his left hand as if that would remedy his condition. Leaning heavily on the truck door, he rested for a few moments. The world seemed to stop spinning around him, so he opened the door and climbed into his truck. Starting the engine and shifting into gear, he looked for signs of the two-track he'd come in on. It took a moment for the thought to form in his alcohol-dulled brain.

"Oh. Lights. Lights would be good here." Greg flipped on the headlights and aimed his truck in the general direction of the dirt road in front of him. He managed to make it to the highway without incident. He turned right and headed up M129 toward Pickford. He looked at the large digital clock on his dash. 1:00 a.m. He wondered if Tyler would be home by now. If not, he'd just park his truck somewhere close, and throw Tyler a little surprise party when he came home. Greg grinned and howled at the crescent moon that hung low in the night sky. He veered back and forth, attempting to keep his truck between the ditches. Five minutes later, he slowed his truck to a crawl as he passed Tyler's house. The house looked dark and deserted, punctuated by the empty driveway. There was only one other place Tyler could be at this hour. He stomped on the accelerator, and the truck flew down the highway.

Just before Pickford, Greg turned right on a gravel road and headed east for a half mile. Finally, he reached his destination. He pulled into the driveway, narrowly missing the deep culvert on his right.

The house was a homely affair. Grey asbestos tiles covered the sides of the small, two-story farmhouse. A set of cement steps led up to the narrow front porch. The whole building, porch and all, seemed to lean a little to the right. In spite of its shabbiness, it had a tended, cared-for look. Two tractor tires graced the front yard, brimming with marigolds and petunias. Their cheerful daytime colors were gone, painted over with somber grey shadows and silver moonlight.

Greg cut the engine and turned off his lights. He noted only one car in the driveway in front of him. Jenny's. *Even better,* he thought.

He walked up the steps and banged on the front door.

"Jenny, you little slut. I know you're in there. Open this door, or I'll kick it down." Adrenaline flooded his body and combined with the alcohol, his anger detonating the deadly mixture. He pounded on the door again, then rammed the door with his shoulder.

Jenny screamed in fear and cowered behind the locked door. "Greg, get out of here, or I'll call the police!" she cried.

Using his body as a battering ram, Greg aimed his shoulder at the weaker, hinged side of the door. He propelled himself forward and crashed through the door. Jenny screamed and tried to run. He grabbed her and slapped her down on the couch, and fell on top of her, pinning her down with his weight. He clawed at her shorts, trying to rip them off and kissed her roughly, bruising her mouth. Jenny let out a muffled scream and struggled beneath him. She bit his lip, drawing blood.

Greg was enraged. He pulled back a moment. "Why you little slut! You'll pay for that!" He pulled his arm back, his fist clenched, intending to deliver a brutal blow.

Suddenly, a hand from behind, grabbed his arm and twisted it behind him, wrenching him off Jenny. It was Tyler.

Jenny fled to a corner of the living room, frightened and crying.

"You son of a bitch." Tyler slugged Greg. Greg was too drunk to put up a good defense. He fell to the floor, howling in pain, his nose pouring with blood. Tyler reached down and pulled Greg toward him by his shirt collar and punched him in the jaw, knocking him to the floor again. Greg crawled away backwards, trying to make it to the front door before Tyler laid into him again. He got up, dizzy from the exertion and loss of blood. Tyler grabbed him again and threw him out the front door. Greg crashed headfirst into a porch post with a sickening thud. Reeling from the pain, he stumbled down the steps and fell face first onto the ground.

Tyler screamed at him. His neck muscles were distended, his face distorted with fury. "If you ever come back here again, if you touch her, if you so much as *look* at her, I swear to God, Greg, I'll fuckin' kill you!"

Greg got up from the ground, wiping his bloody face with his shirt sleeve. He gave Tyler a scathing look.

"I mean it, Greg!"

Greg walked over and opened the door of his pickup.

He yelled back at Tyler. "You can have the whore. She's a lousy fuck anyway!"

Greg jumped into his truck, intending to make a quick getaway. "Shit!" He was blocked in by Tyler's truck.

Tyler ran to his truck and grabbed his gun off the rack behind the seat. Greg made a sharp left and drove through the yard, rolled over one of Jenny's flower beds, and headed toward the highway. Tyler leveled the rifle at the driver's side and looked into the sights.

Jenny screamed, "Tyler, don't! Let him go!"

Tyler frustrated, raised the gun into the air, pointed toward the sky, and fired.

* * *

John bolted upright in bed. A cold sweat broke out all over his body, causing him to shiver. His breath came quick and shallow. Natalie felt the bed jar and she was instantly awake. She looked at her alarm clock on the night stand. It was 2:00 a.m.

It was the same hideous dream. The nightmare that had plagued his sleep since the accident. The dream was always exactly the same. His hands shook as he covered his face with them. Then he pushed his hair back out of his eyes.

"John, What's wrong?" Natalie took his hands in hers to steady them. "I'm right here, John. It's okay."

John exhaled slowly and looked at her bleakly. "It's always the same. I can't make it go away. I keep having the same nightmare. It'll go away for a few days, and I think I'm rid of it. Then for no reason at all, it starts all over again."

"It was just a bad dream, that's all." Natalie tried to comfort and reassure him.

John was still really shook up. "You don't understand. I can't take it much longer."

"John, it's okay. It was a nightmare. It wasn't real."

"No, it's not, Natalie. It really happened. My little girl was really killed. I can't take this anymore, Natalie."

"John, you're going to be all right. It's just gonna take some time," she said soothingly. She pulled him close to her and held him tightly. After a few moments, she felt him relax a little.

He pulled away from her and looked at her despairingly. "I keep having this dream. About the accident, but it's a little different every time. Sometimes Amy isn't with me. Sometimes she is. Sometimes it's Betsy, or even you sitting next to me. But there's always a man, a hunter, in camouflage, standing by the side of the road. He's pointing a gun toward the car, and then I hear a shot, and then I wake up."

Natalie looked thoughtful. "John, you told me earlier tonight, that you felt guilty about taking Amy with you."

"Yeah."

"I don't understand. Was she not supposed to be with you?"

"Amy never came with me, neither did Betsy. I always went to the cabin on the Friday night before Memorial Day, to open it up. Betsy and Amy always came up on Saturday morning."

"So Amy wasn't supposed to be with you."

"No."

She thought on that for a while. Then she looked directly into his eyes. "John, is there any reason anyone would want you dead?"

He was taken aback. "Geez, Natalie. What in the hell are you talking about?"

"There's just so many things that don't fit in all of this."

John got up and started putting his clothes on.

"Natalie, I've got enough to deal with, without having to deal with this crap."

"I'm sorry, I just . . . "

"I've gotta go."

"John, don't go. You're upset."

"I'm gonna go for a drive, clear my head."

John headed for the door. Natalie followed him.

"I didn't mean to upset you." She grabbed a silk robe off a peg hook near the bedroom door, and tied it around her as she followed John out into the living room.

John was rattled. "It's not you, Natalie. I've just gotta go. I'll call you tomorrow." He kissed her on the forehead and walked out the front door.

Salty had heard the distress in his master's voice. He jumped up from the sofa and came over to Natalie. He sat near her feet and whined softly. Abby still lay on the couch, but her head was up, assessing the situation. Natalie stroked Salty's head absentmindedly, watching as John drove away in his car.

3:00 A.M.

MOONLIGHT shone through the large picture window in Greg's trailer. Except for the glow put out by the television set, the room was engulfed in darkness. Greg had dragged himself home an hour ago, and had made a half-hearted attempt to cleanse himself of the dried blood on his face. His nose had finally stopped bleeding. It was swollen but not broken. Good thing, since a visit to the emergency room might have aroused too much attention from the local deputies. He hadn't bothered changing his bloody shirt. It was too much effort for one night.

He sat there in his favorite armchair, a worn-out brown and gold plaid recliner. He nursed a beer with one hand and the large knot on his forehead with the other, holding an ice pack to his head for a while until it was numb. He stared unseeing at the flickering light of the television as he plotted his next move.

In the wooded lot behind Greg's trailer, a figure crouched silently. Dressed in black, the shadow crept forward. The intruder made it to the edge of the woods, lifted a rifle shoulder high, then looked through the gun's scope, zeroing in on Greg's chest. Greg took a sip of his beer, then rested it on the arm of his chair.

A single shot reverberated in the night air, followed by a light plink, as the bullet pierced the picture window and hit its intended target. The can of beer fell to the floor, spilling as it rolled to the edge of the TV cart and came to a stop. The beer continued to drain from the can, soaking the green shag carpet. CNN droned on about violence in the Middle East as Greg slumped over in his chair, dead.

8:00 A.M.

SUNLIGHT bathed the cloudy, morning sky a deep crimson. Russell Townsend looked up at the lowery sky and knew some bad weather was on its way. He knocked loudly on the side door of the Harrison cabin. A car pulled up behind him and he turned around. Natalie got out of her cruiser. She strode up to him, her eyes blazing with anger.

"What are you doing here, Russell?"

"Greg Reynolds was murdered early this morning."

"I heard. Charlie called me a little while ago. What's that got to do with John?"

"You heard him say it, Nat, in front of God and everybody."

Natalie was incensed. "Charlie just told me that Greg tried to rape Jenny Breckner last night. Did you ever think that Tyler Kendricks might have something to do with this?"

"I hadn't heard, but I'll get to Tyler. Right now, Mr. Harrison is our prime suspect."

"Just because a grieving father has an emotional outburst? You have no probable cause, Russell."

"Yeah, well, I got a *probable* search warrant, Nat."

"How in the hell did you get a warrant, Russell? Judge Warren?"

Russell's failure to answer was all the affirmation she needed.

"That son of a . . . "

Russell cut Natalie off. "Tread lightly, Nat."

"That makes about as much sense as the five years' probation he gave Greg."

"Kind of a moot point now, Natalie." He turned away from her and pounded hard on the door, causing the window panes in the door to rattle.

John had just managed to drop off to sleep when the loud pounding sound startled him awake. He sat up in bed and groggily reached for his jeans lying on the floor nearby.

"Just a minute!" he called, wondering who was pounding on his door at this hour on a Sunday morning. He walked over to the door and pulled it open. He was surprised to see Russell Townsend standing there in full uniform. Natalie stood beside him, dressed in a t-shirt and jeans. He was wide awake, now. *This can't be good news,* he thought as he looked at their unsmiling faces.

"Natalie? Officer Townsend? What's up?"

Charlie and Eric pulled up in separate cruisers.

"Mr. Harrison, we have a warrant to search the premises," Russell said. He pushed past John and walked into the cabin. Natalie followed close behind.

"Search the premises? Natalie, what's going on?"

Natalie looked at John. "Someone killed Greg Reynolds."

Russell started to look around the cabin.

"You think I did it?" John said, as Charlie and Eric entered the house.

Before Natalie had a chance to say anything, Russell turned toward John, and spoke from across the room. "You certainly had motive, sir."

"But I didn't . . ." John tried to answer.

Natalie cut John off. "Yeah, well he didn't have opportunity. He was with me, all night. He just left my house a couple of hours ago."

John turned quickly and looked at Natalie.

Charlie broke in. "Is that true, Mr. Harrison?"

Natalie locked eyes with John for a moment, then turned to Charlie. "Of course it's true. We were together all evening, went to dinner on Drummond Island, then came back to my cabin. John spent the night. Left a little after six a.m."

"I asked Mr. Harrison," Charlie said, giving her a stern look.

"John, don't answer any questions," Natalie said.

"Natalie, if you're trying to interfere with this investigation, you're doing a pretty good job of it," Charlie said sharply.

Eric walked up to them. "Do you own any firearms, sir?" he said to John.

John pointed to a cabinet in the corner of the living room. "In the gun cabinet, over there."

John walked over to the gun cabinet that Russell was standing in front of. Everyone followed. The doors to the cabinet were open and the wood around the lock was splintered. Russell opened the door. Two guns stood upright in the rack. A third slot was empty.

John was perturbed. "My 30.06 is missing."

Natalie blurted out, "Oh, come on. This is so obvious. Lots of people in that hallway heard him say, *I'm gonna kill you.* Tyler was there. What a perfect opportunity."

Charlie gave Natalie a warning look. She stared back at him defiantly.

"Natalie, can I speak with you outside?" His voice was low and simmering.

"But . . ."

"Natalie. Outside," Charlie commanded. He walked outside expecting her to follow.

Natalie looked at John helplessly and followed in Charlie's wake.

Russell resumed his interrogation. "Do you have any more firearms, sir?"

John pointed across the room at his desk. "In the desk. Top drawer."

Eric walked over to the desk and opened the drawer. He looked at John quizzically. "There's nothing here, sir. Just a box of shells."

John looked dumbfounded. "What? What are you talking about?" He crossed the room in three strides and looked down into the empty drawer.

*   *   *

Outside, Natalie and Charlie were standing by Charlie's cruiser, having a heated discussion.

"The man has an iron clad alibi, Charlie."

"He could have left your place at six, and done the job, and come straight over here."

"When was Greg killed?"

He looked at Natalie. "I never said."

Natalie didn't respond. Charlie opened his car door and started to get in.

"Dispatch took a shots-fired call at 3:05 this morning. Russell found his body around 3:10."

Natalie twisted a stray lock of hair with her finger and tried not to look relieved. "Well, see. Told you."

"You know, you do this little thing with your hair when you're covering for somebody."

"He didn't do it, Charlie."

Charlie sighed, and raised his eyebrows. "Yeah, well. Tell him not to leave town."

"Yeah, sure."

"And Natalie, I don't want you within a mile of this investigation. You're too close to John to be objective." He shut his door, started the car, and then leaned out the window. "Oh, and Natalie. You're working the bridge walk with Russell tomorrow."

Natalie smiled lamely. "Oh, great."

Charlie backed out of the driveway and drove off.

Eric came out of the house with John's shotguns in his arms and put them in his car. Russell came out next. John appeared at the open screen door.

Russell stopped and turned back to face John. "Want you to know sir, that our investigation is ongoing, and that we request that you not leave town until otherwise notified."

"Yeah, yeah. He's not going anywhere," Natalie said, as she walked toward the cabin.

"I had eleven years as a detective in Detroit. I think I can handle this," he said as he walked by her. He got into his car, slammed the car door, and drove off, flinging gravel and dust as he went.

Natalie looked back toward the door to say something to John, but he wasn't there. She sighed heavily and walked back inside. He was standing at the kitchen counter, staring out the window. He was understandably upset. She walked over to him, and he turned around to face her. She put her arms around him and they embraced.

"I didn't do it, Natalie."

"I know, John. I know."

REVELATIONS

1:00 P.M.

THE BULLET HOLE stared back at Eric, echoing the violence that had taken place in the early hours of that morning. Eric bent and looked through the picture window of Greg Reynold's trailer. He watched the red dot as it danced around on Greg's easy chair. Finally, it came to rest in the center of the masking tape X.

"Got it!" Eric yelled.

In the woods about a hundred yards away, Natalie steadied the surveyor's laser on the tripod. She tightened the adjustment screws. "Right . . . here," she said to herself, then yelled across the field to Eric, "Got it."

Eric started running toward her. Natalie, preoccupied, didn't notice. She was looking down, scanning the ground about her. Eric arrived a minute later, winded from the short dash across the field.

"Charlie is gonna have our badges if he finds out we're doing this," he wheezed.

"Yeah, probably so," Natalie said, continuing to look around on the ground. Then she stopped and looked right at Eric. "Why in the hell didn't Russell do a trajectory test this morning? And why didn't you guys tape this area off?"

Eric finally caught his breath. "Hey, I'm not the man in charge, dear. I just do what I'm told."

Natalie shook her head in annoyance at the lack of procedure.

"Hey, Natalie, I got a good one for you. Boudreaux decides that he wants to take up ice fishing. So he goes to the library, reads some books on the subject, and decides that he's ready. He goes to the nearest frozen lake he can find, sets up all his equipment, and proceeds to cut a hole in the ice. Suddenly, he hears a loud voice from above, *There are no fish under the ice!*"

"So if our shooter was right there . . . " Natalie interrupted, talking to herself while pointing to the tripod.

Eric continued. "So, anyway, he picks up all of his stuff, moves some distance away, and proceeds to cut another hole in the ice. Again, the voice from above says, *There are no fish under the ice!* So Boudreaux moves all the way to the other end, and starts to cut another hole. Again, the voice from above says, *There are no fish under the ice!* Boudreaux finally gives up, looks up, and asks, *Is that you, God?* The voice answers, *No, Boudreaux, this is the ice rink manager!*"

Natalie was too focused to laugh.

"Find any footprints?" Eric asked.

"That's what I'm looking for. I think I'm looking in the ice rink, though. With all these pine needles, I doubt our shooter made any."

Imitating the voice of the ice rink manager, Eric said, "Look underneath the needles!" He bent down, and started whisking away the layer of needles on the ground. In the soft dirt underneath, a faint outline of a shoe print could be seen.

"Wow. Nice goin'," Natalie congratulated.

"No patterns, but we can at least get an approximate shoe size," Eric said.

Natalie measured the print in all directions, and wrote down the measurements in her notepad. At that moment, she heard the swishing sound of someone walking through the tall weeds behind them, and then a familiar, rumbling voice.

"Thanks for inviting me to the party."

Natalie turned, relieved to see Ted.

"Hey, Ted. Thanks for coming. Did you bring your gear?"

"Got it all." Ted held up the large bag that was in his huge, bear-paw hand.

"Good. Let's start with pictures of this print, right here. Get some of the area, some from this point of view toward the window of the trailer," Natalie directed.

Ted pulled out his camera, found the particular lens he needed and attached it. Soon he was clicking away.

"Have you questioned Tyler yet?" Eric asked Natalie.

"That's my next stop. As soon as we're done here."

"If he did it, and he was trying to frame Mr. Harrison, why didn't he take the rifle and put it back in Mr. Harrison's cabinet?" Eric asked her.

"I don't know, but I do know John didn't do it. Therefore, I have to assume that whoever did it, was trying to make it look like John did it. But they couldn't just take the gun, commit the crime, and return it. That would be too obvious. John wouldn't be that stupid. So our shooter had to make it look like John had tried to set it up to look like someone had tried to set *him* up," Natalie answered.

"Whoa, wait a second! Who's on first? You want to say that again?" Eric was confused.

Ted stepped up to the plate. "What she's saying Eric, is that our killer is either really stupid, or really smart."

Now, Natalie was confused. "What do you mean, Ted?"

"Well, if he's really stupid, he'd just steal the gun, kill Greg, and return the gun."

Eric said, "And if he's really smart?"

"Then he's got to put himself in John's shoes. John opened the door to this when he threatened Greg at the courthouse, and I think it's safe to assume our killer was present when John made those comments. If our killer wants to do this convincingly, he has to put himself in John's shoes, act like John would act," Ted answered.

Natalie broke in. "Yes, but our killer *hasn't* acted like John would act. John's not a cold-blooded killer. He wouldn't have premeditated this. John is a grieving father.

He would have acted on impulse, and he wouldn't have cared who knew that he killed Greg."

Eric said, "Maybe he just got back to his house, came to his senses, and broke open the gun case to make it look like someone else did it."

Natalie answered. "Self preservation isn't in John's nature, at this point. He's borderline suicidal."

"Well then, someone really dumb did this. That's all there is to it. And Tyler sure fits that bill," Eric stated.

"Don't underestimate Tyler," she came back.

Ted interjected, "It's the breaking open of the gun case that really throws me."

"Me too," Natalie replied.

"Why?" asked Eric.

"Because it's really stupid," she said.

"Yes, or, it indicates another alternative," Ted asserted.

"Another alternative?" Natalie waited.

Ted answered. "Maybe someone was trying to make it look like someone really stupid did it."

By now, Eric was totally bewildered. "Oh, man! Leave me out of this conversation. You onion peelers lost me at hello." He walked off a few paces, bending low to the ground, scanning the area for more evidence.

"Who else had motive but Tyler and John?" Natalie asked herself aloud.

"Find that out, and you've probably found your killer," Ted finished.

Eric straightened up and waved his arm in the air to get their attention. "I don't know about our killer, but I just found our murder weapon." Eric held the rifle up with his handkerchief, trying not to taint the evidence.

Natalie walked over to where Eric was standing. "What in the hell kind of investigation did you and Russell do out here this morning?"

"Hey, don't get on me. Like I said, I just work here. He told me he'd scanned the area, and that he didn't find anything," Eric answered defensively.

Ted spoke up. "Well, it's John's gun, no doubt."

Eric pulled back the bolt and stuck his nose up to the chamber. Then he brought the chamber to eye level, and looked through the barrel. "Smells like it's been recently fired, and *looks* like it's been recently fired."

"Yeah, yeah. And we'll only find one set of prints on there, too. Yada, yada, yada," Natalie replied.

"We've got to take it in, Natalie," Eric said.

"Of course we do, Eric. Just give it a day or two."

"Natalie! Withholding evidence? I don't think so. We *will* lose our badges. Maybe more."

"Look Eric, Russell was obviously sound asleep when he was out here this morning. No one knows about this, but us. Just wait a day or two, come out here, and say you found it. Please, Eric. If Charlie finds out . . . I just need a couple of days."

"What would *Boudreaux* do?" Eric said, rolling his eyes in acceptance.

Natalie couldn't help but laugh.

*　*　*

Natalie pulled up to the dilapidated farmhouse and parked her cruiser in the driveway. She started toward the front door of the house, but noticed it was inaccessible. Someone had done a makeshift job of putting the wrecked door back in place, by nailing several boards over it. Natalie decided to walk around to the back of the house and look for another door to knock on. As she rounded the corner of the house, she saw a thirty-something woman with long, permed, blonde hair tied back behind her neck, wearing a faded blue sun dress with a daisy print. The woman was bent over some tomato plants in her garden, picking the last of the summer harvest.

"Jenny?" Natalie approached as the woman straightened up. "I'm Officer Hebert."

Jenny had a detached expression on her face. "I've already answered Officer Townsend's questions," she said.

"Would you mind if I asked you a few?"

"I suppose not."

Natalie looked at the bruise on Jenny's face. "Does that hurt?"

Jenny shrugged her shoulders noncomittally. "Not really. I'm used to it. I mean, from Greg. Guess I won't have to deal with that anymore," she said.

"Greg hit you before?"

"Greg and I used to go out. He hit me every time he felt like it. I finally had enough. I started goin' out with Tyler. He was good to me. Greg didn't like it. I don't think he cared about me, he just couldn't handle me goin' out with Tyler."

"Jenny, what time did Greg come to the house last night?"

"He showed up a little after one o'clock. I was watching Saturday Night Live. It had just ended."

"What happened then?"

"He was yellin' at me to let him in. I wouldn't, and so he broke down the door. He pushed me down on the couch, and was all over me. It all happened so fast."

"Where was Tyler?"

"He went to the store. He came in and pulled Greg off me, and they started fightin'. Greg was really drunk. Tyler threw him out the door, and then went for his gun. He was gonna shoot Greg, but I begged him not to. But he did fire a shot off in the air, just to scare him."

"Then what happened?"

"Greg drove off. I was gonna call you guys, but Tyler wouldn't let me. He said he'd take care of Greg."

"Did he?"

"You mean, did he kill Greg? No. He sat up and watched TV for a few hours. I sat with him, just to calm him down. He finally went to bed around 6:30 or 7:00, and that's when I called you guys."

"Why did you call the police when Tyler told you not to?"

"I was afraid he might kill Greg or something. I couldn't stand it if anything happened to Tyler. He's the only man that's ever treated me right."

"Was Tyler mad at you for calling the police?"

"A little. But he got over it," she said with a shy smile.

"And he was with you, here, all night?"

"Yes. Yes, he was," she said, as if trying to make up her mind.

"Is Tyler around?"

"No, he left right after Officer Townsend left."

"What time was that?"

"That was about 10:30."

"Okay. Thanks, Jenny."

Jenny nodded silently, then turned and bent back over her tomato plants. Natalie turned and walked back to her cruiser and got in. She sat for a moment, thinking about her next move. Then she started her car, pulled out onto the road and drove off. She hadn't gone more than fifty yards, when she saw an elderly woman standing in front of a neat, white Victorian with gingerbread trim, watering a bed of roses that climbed up a trellis to the right of the front porch. Natalie pulled over and stopped. The elderly woman turned toward her questioningly, the forgotten hose in her hand now watering the already-green lawn. Natalie got out of her car and walked up to the diminutive woman. At five-foot-six, Natalie literally towered over her.

"Ma'am, I'm Officer Hebert. Do you mind if I ask you a few questions?"

The woman shaded her eyes from the sunlight and squinted up at her. Natalie thought immediately of her own grandmother. The woman wore a pink housecoat with matching slippers. Her silver hair was pulled back into a neat bun, and her thick-lensed, gold-rimmed glasses magnified the sweet, blue eyes that looked up at her inquisitively. When she opened her mouth, however, the grandmotherly image was replaced by one of a bantam rooster – small, but feisty.

"You don't look like a policeman. Where's your uniform?"

"I, I got called in early this morning, and didn't have a chance to put it on," Natalie stuttered slightly, caught off guard by the woman's directness.

"Must of been 'cause of the ruckus they were making over there last night."

The woman suddenly remembered the hose in her hand. She turned abruptly and tottered across the yard to turn it off.

Natalie tried to look patient while waiting for the woman to finish. Instead of returning to where Natalie stood waiting, the woman wobbled over to her porch, slowly climbed the steps, and sat down in a white, wooden rocking chair. Natalie wondered if the woman forgot she was there, or had decided that the conversation was over. While she wondered what to do next, the woman waved her over.

"Well? Are you going to come sit down and talk, or what?"

Natalie almost rolled her eyes in exasperation, but checked herself. Bantam rooster or no, she had been trained from her youth to respect the elderly. She walked across the yard and up the steps of the porch, and sat down in a matching rocking chair, next to the woman.

"Now, what were we talking about again? Oh, yes, the ruckus last night." The woman rocked slowly back and forth without saying anything for a few minutes. The chair creaked as it went back and forth, back and forth.

"Could you tell me about that?" Natalie finally blurted out.

The woman gave her a disapproving look. "I'm getting to it. Would you like a glass of tea? It's awful warm outside." Again, the chair creaked as it went back and forth, back and forth.

Natalie could swear she saw a twinkle in those blue eyes. The woman was having a little fun at her expense.

"No, thanks anyway." Natalie got the message and settled back in her rocking chair and set it in motion. She made herself relax and pretended she had nothing better to do all day. She glanced secretively at the woman and thought she saw the corners of her mouth turn up slightly in a smile. After what seemed like forever, the woman finally spoke again.

"It was awful. I heard this fella yelling outside the house. That's what woke me up. I'd seen him there before, but not for a long time. He's yelling, then he kicks down the door. Then I see the other fella pull up. This fella I see over there all the time. He runs inside. I hear yelling, then the first fella comes flying out of the house. There's some more yelling, and then the second fella goes to his truck and gets a gun out of it."

"A hand gun, or a rifle?"

"A rifle, of course. They're still yelling at each other. The first fella drives off, and then the second fella fires his gun up in the air."

"About what time was that?"

"I looked at my clock when I woke up. It was 1:10."

"Thanks for your help." Natalie suddenly stopped rocking and practically bolted from her chair and started down the steps of the porch.

"It was about 1:15 when I called the police. But no one came out until around ten this morning."

Natalie stopped and whirled back around toward her with a puzzled look on her face.

"You called the police?"

"I call *every* time there's a ruckus over there. Someone usually comes out right away. But not last night."

"Thank you. Thank you very much."

"You're welcome." The elderly woman shut her eyes. A contented smile spread slowly across her face, and the chair resumed its creaking as she rocked back and forth, back and forth.

Natalie smiled and shook her head. She turned and walked across the yard, and got in her cruiser. She picked up her police radio handset, and started to depress the call button, then stopped. She put it down, picked up her cell phone instead, and scrolled down until she found the number.

"Yeah, Dispatch. This is Officer Hebert. I need to find out if you had a domestic disturbance call for us last night, at around 1:15am." She paused for a moment. "Can you tell me who took the call?" She paused again, listening to the reply. "Thanks." Natalie breathed in deeply, started her car, and drove away.

MONDAY, SEPTEMBER 1ST

THE MACKINAC BRIDGE was the location for a special annual event on Labor Day. Every year, the two southbound lanes of the bridge would be used to handle the vehicle traffic for both directions. The two northbound lanes would be blocked off, so that people from all across the state, country, even the globe, could make the five-mile walk across it.

The event presented a unique challenge for local law enforcement, who would be called upon to oversee the bridge walk. It was necessary for them to arrive at four a.m. just to organize the crowds that began to gather almost as early.

Before sunrise, throngs of people would already be gathered in a fenced area on the northeast side of the bridge, waiting for hours in anticipation, trying to be among the first to head south across it. As the mass of humanity grew, the chatter of excited voices would become almost deafening.

The walk would begin at seven a.m., with the governor in the lead. Soon afterward, the festive, packed crowd would start to funnel out of the fenced waiting area, like a herd of cattle going through narrow pen gates. Inevitably, someone in the crowd would start making a mooing sound. People would laugh at the joke, then the mooing would be picked up and echoed by others to the amusement of all.

Busloads of people would continue to arrive, even after the initial start of the bridge walk. The buses would continue to make trips back and forth, disgorging their passengers, until the last group of walkers headed across, around eleven.

Natalie rode to the event that morning with Russell in his cruiser. Most of the ride had been in silence. Once they arrived, she tried to stay as far from him as possible. She'd stopped in on John the night before, just to check on him, and had found out that Russell had been there several more times that day, hassling him, investigating Greg's murder.

Natalie struggled with her thoughts. She didn't know *for sure* where John had gone after he'd left her place at two a.m., but she believed him when he said he'd gone for a drive to clear his head. She was troubled, because she knew in her heart that even if John *had* killed Greg, she still would have covered for him.

The threat of rain hovered over the event all morning. When the last of the bridge-walkers started across, Natalie and Russell put up the barriers. About an hour later, when the last group had just cleared the bridge, the rain finally hit.

The rain hammered down, forcing them to seek refuge in the only available shelter – Russell's cruiser. Even though the windows were up, Russell insisted on having a cigarette.

"You should stop smoking. It's a nasty habit," she said with disgust.

"I will, someday," Russell snapped.

"You should stop bugging John, too."

"*That* I won't do." His face was rigid with anger.

"Won't you even entertain the idea that someone else might have killed Greg?" Natalie fumed.

"I have. But Greg's cousin Mike isn't gonna kill his only friend and meal ticket, and Tyler Kendricks has an alibi."

"So does John."

"I know he wasn't at your house Sunday morning, Nat."

Natalie grew defensive. "Are you spying on me, Russell?"

"I was just doing my rounds," he retorted.

Natalie fell silent.

"Look, I don't blame you for covering for the guy. I know you care for him. I don't even blame him for blowing Greg away. I mean, after what the guy did to his little girl . . . " Russell choked up and looked away.

"He didn't do it," she insisted.

Russell didn't answer her right away. He watched as the rain sheeted down his window. Then he said, "Well, if he didn't, then maybe Tyler's alibi is bogus. Or maybe cousin Mike had a dumb-ass attack."

"Have you questioned him?"

"I'll get to it. Just let me do my job, Natalie."

"No comment," Natalie said sarcastically.

"Look, let's call a truce, okay?" Russell turned and looked at her.

She was surprised at the look of pain on his face. She suddenly felt sorry for him and decided to change the subject. "You've been up here almost nine months, and I hardly know anything about you," she said.

"Not much to know."

"Bet you never thought you'd get this much action when you came up here."

"Yeah. Still not as crazy as Detroit, though."

"Why'd you leave Detroit?"

"Oh, lots of reasons." Russell laughed. "No, actually, only one reason." His face grew somber.

"*What?*" Natalie asked.

"I went through a bad divorce."

"I didn't even know you were married."

"Yeah, me neither," he laughed bitterly. "She couldn't handle being married to a homicide detective."

"I'm really sorry. How long ago?"

"Couple of years."

"How old are you?"

"Thirty-six. You?"

"Hey, I'm a woman. You can't ask that."

"Sorry."

"But, as long as I'm still getting carded, I don't mind saying. Thirty-three," she grinned.

"Thirty-three!" he said. "Have *you* ever been married?"

"No. I was engaged once, but it didn't work out."

"What happened?"

Natalie looked out at the rain. The way the rain beaded and slid down the window reminded her of tears. She thought about Joey.

"I'd rather not talk about it. It was an awful time in my life. It's painful to even think about it."

Russell nodded in understanding. "I've seen a lot of pain in my thirty-six years." He was quiet for a moment. "But hey, my parents told me that pain and suffering make you a better person." Natalie sensed resentment in his voice.

"If you're talking about suffering injustice because you choose to do the right thing, or suffering to help someone else, that's one thing. But if you're talking about suffering because you're too stupid to come in out of the rain . . . "

"Not much difference, really."

"Stupidity isn't much of a cause, Russell. If you believe it is, then I hope you enjoy pain and suffering, because a lot of it's gonna be coming your way."

"It's part of the universal order, Nat," Russell philosophized.

"More like universal disorder, Russell. Pain and suffering are an indication that something is out of order. Like, Oh! Maybe that bullet doesn't belong in my arm!"

"Pain can be ignored."

"So can the oil light on your dashboard. Hey, you can even break the warning light out if you don't like what it's trying to tell you. But it won't make the problem go away. If you don't attend to the problem, your engine's gonna seize up."

"Yeah, well maybe I'll get around to checking under the hood someday," he said with a chuckle. "Hey, let's go over to Mac City. I'll buy you a fish sandwich at Scalawags."

He started the cruiser and pulled out onto the bridge.

Natalie added, "Yeah, sound's good. Then how about we stop at Darrow's, and I'll buy you a piece of cherry pie ala mode?"

"Where in the hell do you put all that food, Miss Skinny?"

"It's called having two dogs that have to be walked, make that *run*, twice a day," she laughed.

"Maybe I should get some dogs," he said, pinching the small roll around his waist.

Natalie couldn't let this opportunity go by. "Maybe you should get a girlfriend," she said, then waited to see his reaction.

"Too complicated."

"No one in your life?"

Russell looked gloomy. "Nah, no one."

TUESDAY, SEPTEMBER 2ND

THE DONUT HOLE in Natalie's hand was dripping icing onto her lap as she pulled into the station parking lot. She held her foot on the brake and licked her fingers clean before putting the car in park. After cutting the engine, she leaned over and fished a wet nap out of the pocket of her jacket. Once she was satisfied with her clean-up job on her hands and the spot on her pants leg, she got out of her patrol car and walked up to Charlie and Eric who were standing outside.

Eric grinned at her. "Hey, Natalie. I got a good one for you," he said.

"I'm not in the mood, Eric."

Eric's eyebrows went up questioningly and he raised his hands in protest. Charlie motioned to her as he walked to his cruiser.

"Let's take a ride, dear," Charlie said. Natalie followed without a word. They drove through town, and as they passed the bakery, he chuckled.

"Hey Nat, have you made friends with the new owners yet? I sure miss being able to show up at three a.m. to drink coffee and munch on donut scraps."

Natalie smiled. "No, I've met them, but I haven't gotten around to hinting about how we do things around here. Until we get in good with the boss, we'll have to resign ourselves to going there when they're open, like everybody else."

Charlie sighed. "I hate it when my routine gets changed. I'm *still* getting used to living without my Jersey Muds. Remember those?"

Natalie shook her head.

"No, I guess you wouldn't. The Bon Air closed down a few years before you moved here. I used to *love* going there once a week to have a sundae they called the Jersey Mud. It was served in a tall fountain glass so you could see all the layers. They'd start with chocolate syrup, then put a layer of chocolate ice cream, then chocolate syrup, then vanilla ice cream, then *more* chocolate syrup, then marshmallow creme, then a layer of powdered malt and then top it off with a cherry. That was the *best* sundae in the world."

They pulled up at the Hessel marina and Charlie turned the car off. He sat back and looked over at her.

"Charlie, you didn't bring me along to talk about donuts and sundaes," Natalie remarked.

"You got that right," he said. "Let's get some air."

They got out and walked around to the front of the car. Charlie sat on the hood of the car, while Natalie leaned against the front fender. She fidgeted nervously, wondering what he was going to say. Charlie sat there quietly for a while, his face cupped in his hands, looking out over the waters of the bay. It was a warm, sunny day. The bay was unruffled, flat as a pancake. A gull lighted on the railing near the public ramp and eyed them closely, waiting to see if they had any food to offer.

Charlie kept his eyes on the water. "Natalie," he said, "what are you trying to do?"

The tone of his voice made Natalie tense up all over. "What do you mean?"

"I mean, do you like your job?"

Natalie looked over at him, trying to read his face. "Of course, I like my job. What are you getting at?"

"Do you know what kind of shit you can get in for withholding evidence in a criminal investigation?" Charlie turned to look at her. His face was solemn, his forehead wrinkled with worry.

Natalie shook her head and said softly, "Eric. That little . . . "

"Eric *likes* his job. Now, do you want to tell me what's going on?"

Natalie's temper flared. "What's going on is, Russell's doing a lousy job, that's what's going on. He's so convinced John did it, he's not even looking anywhere else. I went out to the crime scene. He hadn't even taped off the area. He did no tests. Any idiot could have found that weapon. He thinks he's some kind of one man show."

Charlie sighed, then looked off again across the water.

"What's with him, anyway? I just don't get him," she complained.

"Russell's a tough one to get. He doesn't let anyone in," Charlie said.

"He told me why he moved up here and everything. I feel for the guy, but it's no excuse for shoddy work."

"Why *did* he say he moved up here?"

"Because of his divorce. His wife left him 'cause she couldn't handle the police-wife thing."

Charlie laughed. "Is *that* what he told you? I know his ex. She was raised up here. Her daddy was a police officer. Sally's a good girl. She hung in there as long as she could."

"What happened?"

"Russell's mommy and daddy have a lot of money. A *lot* of money. He never really cut the strings with them. Sally got tired of them making all their decisions. She gave Russell the ultimatum."

"Guess he made the wrong choice, huh?"

"He's here because he couldn't hack it in Detroit. He wasn't a team player. Other officers felt he was gonna get someone killed. He got on the force to begin with because of mommy and daddy's influence. When he couldn't hack it there, mommy and daddy got him his job here."

"Geez, the guy's older than me," she said.

"Well, that's why Russell doesn't like himself very much. I think he really wants to break away from his parents. But you let someone else run your life long enough, you just give up."

Natalie sat silently for awhile, deep in thought. Then she said, "How in the hell did he get that search warrant?"

"Judge Warren is a good friend of mommy and daddy's."

Natalie looked over at Charlie. She hesitated, then spoke softly. "Charlie, there's something I need to tell you." Charlie turned to look at her. "I was over on Mackinac Island at the end of June, up at Grand Hotel. I saw a picture there that had been taken that weekend. It was a picture of Betsy Harrison . . . and Russell."

She saw Charlie's face register surprise and shock.

"Russell?! That doesn't make any sense."

"It doesn't make any sense to me, either. I mean, maybe the picture was innocent. John told me that Betsy sold Russell's parents their cottage. The picture was taken at a real estate convention. Maybe Russell's parents were there. Russell was there. You know? Friendly."

Charlie looked dubious. "Yeah, maybe."

"But Russell's been so dogged on John. I mean, you accused *me* of not being very objective."

Charlie thought for a moment. "Normally, in a murder, I'd follow the money – find out who stood to gain with Greg Reynolds being dead. But I don't know about this one." Charlie paused. Natalie could see he was disturbed about what she had told him. "See what you can find out."

Charlie walked back to his side of the car to get in. Natalie followed his lead. She opened her door and looked over at him. "I thought you told me to stay away from this investigation."

Charlie paused, his car door wide open as he looked over the top of the car at Natalie.

"Yeah. Well, just stay out of Russell's way, okay?"

Natalie nodded in agreement, and got in the car.

*   *   *

Natalie turned onto Portman Road, then pulled into Greg Reynold's driveway. She saw his cousin Mike walk out of the front door and load a stereo into Greg's truck. Natalie shook her head, incredulously. He was looting the place. Natalie got out of her cruiser. Mike looked up at her.

"What in the hell are you doing, Mike?"

"I'm getting my stuff."

Natalie walked over and peered into the back of Greg's truck. It was piled high with various and sundry items: a large color TV, a stereo, a red toolbox, a set of weights and a weight bench, and several grocery bags stuffed with an assortment of food, music cd's, and several bottles of alcohol.

Natalie looked askance at Mike, her eyebrows raised. "Taking Greg's truck, too?"

"It's my truck now. The bank was gonna repo it, and I'm just taking over the payments on it."

"You're not taking anything anywhere, Mike. This is a crime scene."

"Ah, shit. You guys couldn't solve a crime if you saw it happening. Everyone knows Tyler killed Greg."

Natalie crossed her arms and looked at Mike. "Why's that, Mike?"

"First of all, 'cause Tyler wanted Greg's girl."

"Greg's girl?" Natalie said in disbelief.

"Jenny."

Natalie shook her head in amazement at Mike's stupidity.

Mike saw she wasn't buying it, so he tried another tack. "Greg owed Tyler five thousand dollars, which he knew he'd never get."

"Well if Greg's dead, Mike, Tyler's never gonna get his money back, duh?"

"Tyler's a dumb shit, ain't he? Besides, he woulda come over here and got Greg's stuff if I didn't. I just beat him to it."

"Seems to me like you're the dumb shit, loading up Greg's truck. Maybe *you* killed Greg."

Mike guffawed loudly, his disgust evident on his face. "I didn't kill my cousin."

Natalie spoke through gritted teeth. "Get in *your* truck, Mike, and get out of here, *now.* And if I find you back here, or if so much as a pencil is missing from this place, I swear to God, I'll lock your butt up."

Mike laughed. "Yeah, right. Around here, you can shoot little girls and not go to jail."

Natalie's face flushed red and she stepped up to him. His amusement turned to surprise as she kicked his feet out from under him, wrestled him onto his stomach, and cuffed his hands behind him.

Her chest heaved and she panted from the effort. She wiped the sweat from her face. "Yeah, we'll see about that," she said grimly. "Burglary. And I just saw your eye wink. That's resisting arrest. Ouch. I think I just felt you hit me. That's assaulting an officer."

Natalie pulled him to his feet, and pushed him forcefully toward the cruiser.

"Now I know why Russell enjoyed kicking Greg's butt so much," she said.

"Russell was just paying him back for all the times Greg kicked his ass when we were kids."

Natalie stopped short, stunned by Mike's remark. She recovered quickly, grabbed his elbow, and shoved him into the back seat of the cruiser. "Get in, you son of a bitch."

* * *

Natalie lay on her four-poster bed, dressed in an over-sized white t-shirt that read 1994 New Orleans Jazz Fest. It had a picture of a dancing alligator on it, holding a pink umbrella in one hand and a saxophone in the other. She lay on her back with her knees bent, her right ankle resting on her left knee. Abby and Salty lay curled up on either side of her. She looked up at the ceiling as she cradled the phone next to her ear. A soft breeze blew the curtains back and forth as the crickets outside her window started another end-of-summer concert. She heard the phone on the other end ring several times before he answered. He finally picked up and she heard his voice.

"John?" she said softly. "It's me."

His voice was low and tender. "Hey, how's it going?" he said.

Natalie sighed. "Oh, man. Tough day. I'm sorry I wasn't able to stop by today. Just so much going on. Working on this investigation."

"Yeah, your friend Russell stopped in again today. He keeps hounding me."

"He's not my friend, John."

"The guy just won't let up. He thinks I killed Greg Reynolds."

"I'm sorry, John. Russell has a big chip on his shoulder."

John was silent for a few moments. "Natalie . . . " he paused. Suddenly his voice sounded tired and worn out. "I'm not sure how much more of this I can take."

Natalie became alarmed at the despair in his voice. "John, don't you give up on me now. I love you. I *need* you."

"Yeah, I love you too."

"Just hang in there," she coaxed. "I know you didn't do it. Look, I'm going to be tied up for a few days.

I've got some things I've got to check out. *Please,* go hang out with Ted for a few days, okay? Just so you're not alone."

"Yeah. I'll try," he sighed. "I'd better let you get some sleep. You've got to work tomorrow."

"Don't forget I love you, okay?"

"I won't," he said softly.

"Goodnight," she whispered.

WEDNESDAY, SEPTEMBER 3RD

THE DOOR was still pretty battered looking, but Tyler had patched it up with scrap lumber, figuring it would do its intended job until they could afford to buy a new one. Tyler knelt down to screw the bottom hinge to the frame.

Natalie pulled up in her cruiser and walked up to the front porch. She waited patiently while Tyler finished his task. Once he was done, he stood up and looked at Natalie.

"Tyler, I need to ask you a few questions."

"Shoot."

Natalie raised her eyebrows.

Tyler looked back at her and smiled wryly. "Just an expression. Look, I didn't kill Greg. It couldn't have happened to a nicer guy, but I didn't do it."

"Greg owed you a lot of money."

"How would I get it back if I killed him?"

"Greg hurt Jenny."

"Like I said, couldn't have happened to a nicer guy, but I didn't do it."

"Who *did* do it, Tyler?"

"I don't know. Maybe Mike. If I were Mr. Harrison, I'd of done it in a heartbeat, but I don't think he did."

She probed Tyler's face with her eyes and saw something genuine there. "Why'd you keep hanging out with those jerks?"

Tyler sighed. "Hell, I don't know. We were friends all our lives. I don't know. I guess I wouldn't have met Jenny if it wasn't for Greg."

Natalie gave Tyler an understanding look. "Yeah, you would have."

"When I met Jenny, I wanted to make something of my life. Still do."

"That's good, Tyler," she said, then changed the subject. "What about Officer Townsend? Russell? Mike told me Greg knew him when you guys were kids."

"Yeah. We used to hang out together. Russell's parents had a place on Marquette Island. I thought they owned the whole island. Probably do."

Natalie smiled and shook her head in agreement.

"They used to come up in the summer from Detroit. Russell started hanging out with us. His parents never woulda let him if they'd known. Anyway, Greg ran the show. We were all kind of scared of him. He had that look in his eye, like he'd kill you if you didn't do what he said. Even as a kid. He'd beat Russell up whenever he didn't do what Greg wanted him to. But Russell kept hanging out with us. Until we all got arrested."

Natalie was surprised. "Russell was arrested?"

"Yeah. Breaking into some cabins. But his parents made the whole thing go away . . . for *all* of us. Anyway, Russell's parents never let him hang with us after that."

Natalie thought for a moment. "The night we arrested you guys, the night when Amy Harrison was killed, Russell said he'd had to deal with you guys getting drunk and firing your guns before."

"Every Friday night. Like clockwork."

"Like clockwork?"

"We'd get off work. Go out to Greg's, get drunk, and target practice. Sometimes Russell would come out and shoot a few rounds with us. Sometimes he'd just sit there with his hand on his gun, trying to intimidate Greg."

Natalie was dumbfounded. "Tyler, tell me about what happened the night Amy Harrison was killed."

"I made a beer run. When I got back, Greg and Mike were already shooting it up. Greg made me put a whiskey bottle on my head, and stand out by the sand bags."

"Yeah I saw those. You always do your shooting into those?"

"I *always* did. Most the time Greg and Mike did too, but sometimes they'd just shoot anywhere they felt like shooting."

"Do you remember what time Russell showed up at Greg's?"

"Nah. We were out back. He came out of the back door of Greg's trailer with one of Greg's 30.06's in his hands. We thought he was just there to do a little target practice. Then we started hearing all these sirens. Russell just sits there. About a half hour later, he gets up and goes ballistic. He cuffs me and Mike, and starts taking us around front. Greg follows us the whole way screaming at him, saying he's gonna kill him. We got out front, and Russell was all over Greg. That's when you drove up."

"Jesus!" Her head was spinning. "I gotta go." She started walking to her cruiser, and looked over her shoulder at Tyler.

"Tyler, don't talk to *anyone* about what you told me, until I tell you, okay? Please?"

Tyler nodded his assent. Natalie jumped in her cruiser and took off.

* * *

John sat on the green corduroy couch in his living room. He held Amy's stuffed moose in his hands as he looked out over the water. A pair of white mute swans flew in and skidded to a stop on the water right in front of his dock, but John didn't even notice them. One moment, he'd be thinking about Natalie and the joy and healing she had brought to his life. The next moment, memories of Amy would flash into his mind. He'd start to feel the pain of his loss again, and the weight of survivor's guilt would lay heavy on his heart. The journey through those peaks and valleys of emotions was exhausting and draining. He felt so tired of it all, and wondered what was the use of anything.

Then finally, he remembered Natalie's encouragement to live his life the way Amy would have wanted him to.

He felt a wave of peace wash over him, and he relaxed his grip on the stuffed moose he held in his hands. He was thankful to have met such a tender, compassionate woman, who genuinely cared about him. It had been a long time since he felt loved and cared for in that way. He heard a knock at his side door and his face lit up with a smile.

"Natalie!" he said to himself.

He jogged over to the door and stopped short when he saw who was at the door. It was Betsy. At least, he *thought* it was Betsy. She had the same emerald green eyes and auburn hair. But instead of the usual super-short power suit and spiked heels, she was demurely dressed in a long, pale lilac sundress. Instead of the perfectly-styled hair she'd sported for the last several years, her long, flowing tresses stirred gently as the light breeze caught them and lifted them off her shoulders. For a moment, John was speechless.

"Betsy," he finally managed to say. "I didn't hear you drive up."

"I parked over by the lake. I went for a walk, and then I ended up here."

"What do you want?"

"John, can I come in?"

"Betsy, we have nothing to say to each other."

"John, please, I need to talk to you."

John opened the screen door for her and she walked inside. He motioned for her to go before him, and as she passed by, he caught a whiff of perfume that he remembered her wearing years ago. Lily of the valley. They walked into the living room. John didn't know what to make of her. She turned and looked at him hopefully.

"Maybe a cup of coffee?"

"Sure." John went over and started a fresh pot of coffee. Betsy stood there hugging herself with her arms and then walked over to a bookshelf. John came back into the living room and Betsy was standing by the bookshelf, sobbing. He saw a framed picture of Amy in her hands.

"She was so beautiful," she cried.

"Oh, God, Betsy. Please don't do this."

Betsy overflowed with remorse. "And I was such a lousy mother."

John didn't respond, but his eyes grew moist. She turned to face him. Her face was stained from tears and mascara. "And such a lousy wife."

"We went through a lot, Betsy," he said gently.

"Nothing can justify how I was. I was so neglectful of Amy, and so horrible to you. John, I came here to tell you that I'm sorry. I'm so sorry." She put her head down on her arms and started sobbing again.

John grabbed several tissues from the box on the coffee table and walked over to her. He put his arm around her and pried her away from the bookshelf. He wiped her eyes dry, and handed her a fresh tissue to blow her nose.

"Betsy. Don't do this to yourself."

She looked up at him, the tears continuing to flow. She buried her head on his chest for a moment, then sighed and looked back up at him.

"Can you forgive me, John? Do you think you could forgive me, and that we could try to put our lives back together? We could do it, John," she begged. "Please say yes. I want . . . we could . . . we could make another Amy together," she looked at him beseechingly.

John burst into tears and began to sob uncontrollably. He held Betsy tightly in his arms, wishing that he could just turn back the clock and do his life over. He pulled Betsy even closer to him.

"Oh, God, Betsy."

"I miss her so much," she wailed.

They stood there holding on to each other through their tears, crying until there were no more tears left in them.

Betsy looked up at John again and held him in her gaze. "I want to try again, John. I want to try and get back what we had. I want to be the woman I used to be. I want to be the couple we used to be."

"What are you saying, Betsy?"

"I want to try to put our marriage back together again, John. I'll quit real estate. Go back to art. You used to love it when I would paint, remember? You would sit and write, while I would paint. It could be like that again. And we could have a child, another little girl, just like Amy."

"We can't get Amy back, Betsy."

"I know that, John, but we can have a little girl, that we both love. And I won't miss her growing up this time. I'll be there, to help raise her. We can both love her."

John was in turmoil. "Betsy, this is just guilt talking. I'm not criticizing you. I understand how you feel. It's the same way I felt. If only I hadn't taken Amy to the cabin with me, she'd still be alive."

"No, John, this isn't about guilt. This is about me changing, and it's about us. I love you John, and I want my life to change. I've already wasted too much of my life. I don't want to waste anymore. I want to be with you."

"Amy . . . I mean, Betsy. She looked so much like you," he explained.

Betsy smiled gently. "I know."

"Betsy, this is pretty sudden. And there's someone else in my life, now. I need some time to think about all this. Some time to sort things out."

"I understand, John. I do. Take all the time you need."

Betsy paused, then took a deep breath. "John, before you decide, I need you to know something." She hesitated and looked at him. "Oh, God, this is so hard." She took another deep breath. "I've been having an affair with someone. While we were together. While Amy was still alive."

"Betsy, I don't want to hear any more."

"I just don't want us to start over on false pretenses. I want everything to be out in the open. I broke it off with him, and it's over between us. And I want you to know that I love you. That I've always loved you."

Betsy put her fingers on the locket hanging around her neck and held it up to John. It was the locket John had given Betsy when Amy was a year old. It contained a baby picture of Amy.

"Amy helped me find my way home."

John looked at the locket, then into Betsy's eyes.

He thought of all the good times they'd had before everything had fallen apart, and his heart melted. He wiped the tears from her cheeks and looked at her tenderly.

"God, I'd forgotten how beautiful you are."

Betsy rose up on her toes and kissed John on the lips. At that moment, the side door creaked open, and someone walked inside.

"John, I . . . " Natalie stood in the hallway and stared at the two of them. John pulled away from Betsy, upset and flustered.

"Oh, God. I . . . " Natalie trailed off in mid-sentence, too shocked to even know what to say. She turned and darted out the door.

"Natalie!" John ran after her. Natalie didn't turn around. She just kept her head down as she headed for her car. John caught up to her and grabbed her elbow and swung her around. She was in tears.

"Natalie. It's not what you think."

Natalie didn't respond. She kept her head down, refusing to meet John's eyes. Betsy came out of the house, and walked up to them. She smiled gently at Natalie.

"I'm so sorry. I'll leave you two alone to talk."

Betsy started walking toward the road.

"Do you need a ride to your car?" John asked Betsy.

"No, I'll be fine," she assured him.

Natalie wiped her tears away and looked at John, her face full of hurt.

"What's going on, John?"

"It's not what you think."

"You said that already. I don't know what to think. Tell me what to think, John."

He looked into her eyes and saw the pain and confusion. "I think she's changed."

"I'd say so. She didn't even look like the same woman. She was actually nice to me."

"She wants to get back together. Give up her business. Have a baby together."

Natalie thought she couldn't hurt any more than she did now. She was wrong. John's remark cut her to the core. "I was kind of hoping *we* could do that together." She looked up at him dismayed. "Oh, John. John! You need to slow down. You're really emotional right now. She's emotional. You can't run on your emotions here."

She paused, looked down at the ground, and then stamped her foot, trying to regain control of her *own* emotions.

She collected herself and said, "Okay, John. My emotions aside. Maybe she has changed. Maybe this is what you want for your life. But just take some time," she pleaded. "Give the dust a chance to settle. Don't make an emotional decision. This is a decision you'll have to live with the rest of your life."

"No kidding, Natalie."

"Please don't get defensive, John. I love you. I want the best for your life." She faltered for a moment and her eyes started to tear again. "If this is the best for your life, I want it for you." Her voice shook and she stopped talking until she could trust it again. "But *I* just might be the best for your life. If I am, I want *that* for your life. Do you understand?"

"Yes, Natalie, I do."

"I'm sorry. I'm not pressuring you. You need some time to sort things out. And I've got so much going on in my head right now, I can't deal with this. I've got to do my job."

"I understand."

Natalie felt her heart breaking when she looked into those blue eyes of his. Her voice trembled again as she said, "Um . . . I think . . . I think it would be best if we didn't see each other for a while," she managed to get the words out without breaking down. "Until you figure out what you want to do with your life," she added. "In the mean time, I'm going to try to figure out who killed Greg Reynolds, and get you cleared."

"I appreciate all you're doing, Natalie. I . . . I'm just really confused right now," he said gently.

"Me too, John. Me too."

She walked to her cruiser. "I'll see you around, okay?" Her voice sounded strangled and unnatural in her ears.

"Yeah."

SATURDAY, SEPTEMBER 20TH

THE AIR had changed today. Something about it was different. It smelled different. Felt different. Natalie observed it happen every year since she'd moved here. It happened on a different day every year, but it always happened. And everyone who lived in Northern Michigan could tell when that day had arrived. They knew summer was over.

Everything was happening in Natalie's life all at once. She'd tried to handle the pressure, and to keep working too. But it was all too much for her. Being back on night shift for the last two weeks hadn't help much either. So yesterday she told Charlie she needed a month's leave-of-absence, effective immediately. Try to clear her head, and put things together. Hang out with Abby and Salty. Spend some time on the water.

Natalie sliced through the cool, blue waters of the bay with her paddle. Ted had told her that *the greatest cargos of life come in over quiet seas*, and this was the one thing, the one place, that always seemed to induce that serenity. So many times, when life had tied her in knots, she would come here, and soon, the rhythmic stroke of her paddle, and the tranquil surroundings, would wield their healing powers.

For a while, she glided along silently without paddling. She looked down into the clear, placid waters, delighted by the play of water and light off the limestone boulders on the lake bottom, and the quick darting shadows of the perch as they ran for cover to the lake weeds undulating below her. She looked at the tree-studded islands nearby, then up at the vibrant turquoise skies. She soaked in the warm September sunshine.

She began to sift through the thoughts in her mind, gently turning each one over, examining them with calm objectivity. A sudden splash caught her attention. She looked over toward the marshy shoreline and saw a lone turtle sunning himself on a half-submerged log, his sunbathing companion having just deserted him. Natalie chuckled. She figured the other turtle had seen what appeared to be a giant log heading toward him, and had lost his nerve, choosing the safety of the lake, rather than to remain exposed on the log above.

Finally, her morning trek was over. She paddled parallel to the shore. Abby and Salty came running full-throttle from the direction of her cabin, barking excitedly in celebration of her return. As she paddled toward the shore, she prayed a simple prayer.

"God, I know you love me and want the best for my life. Please let me know if I'm fishing in the ice rink!"

WEDNESDAY, OCTOBER 15TH

THE LEAVES had turned burnt orange and cadmium yellow, eye-popping bright against the dark tree trunks. The ones already fallen from the trees blanketed the ground in a crazy-quilt pattern, stitched together with the still-green grass that lay underneath. Natalie drove along M134 with her window open slightly, gulping down the cool, October air. She detected the rich, pungent scent of decaying leaves, laced with the sugary maples and the lung-cleansing cedars and pines. The sky above her was a brilliant blue, void of clouds except for a few white, puffy ones that rimmed the horizon.

She pulled up to the Harrison cabin and saw Betsy's Mercedes in the driveway. John's car was gone. She knocked politely on the side door and waited. Betsy opened the door a few moments later.

"Officer Hebert. Natalie?" she said smiling.

Natalie nodded.

"John isn't in right now. But he should be back soon." Her tone was kind and gentle.

"Actually, it's *you* I'd like to talk to," Natalie replied.

"Me?"

"Can I come in?"

Betsy nodded and opened the screen door for her.

"Please. Would you like some coffee?"

"No, no thanks. Look . . . "

"Would you like to sit down?"

"Thanks," Natalie said gratefully. She walked over and sat on a side chair. Betsy sat on the couch across from her and waited for Natalie to speak.

"I've been doing a lot of thinking. I want you to know that I'm not trying to steal your husband. I just want what's best for him."

"Natalie. I'm not angry. I'm not even jealous. Well maybe a little, but I have no right to be. I was out of the picture. I told John I wanted a divorce. You helped him so much. I don't know if he'd have made it without your support."

"I love John, and I want him to be happy," Natalie said. "If that's with you, then okay. If it's with me, okay. I just care about him."

"You don't think I do?"

"No, I didn't say that. I'm just concerned about his motives. He's so vulnerable right now."

"Losing a child isn't something you get past overnight," Betsy said gently.

"I agree."

"Are you questioning *my* motives?" she spoke candidly, but without any malice in her voice.

"No. I mean, I don't think so. I know you've both been through a lot." Natalie paused, and shifted gears mentally.

"Look, I need to talk to you about something. Some-*one*."

Betsy looked puzzled for a moment, then she finally caught on. "You mean Russell Townsend. John told you about my affair?"

"No, John didn't tell me. John knows about you and *Russell*?"

"He knows I had an affair, but he doesn't know that it was with Russell. John wouldn't let me tell him who it was."

"Just so you know, I haven't seen or talked to John since that day," Natalie said.

"That's very considerate of you. Look, I'm not trying to get between you and John either, if that's what will make him happy."

"I'm sorry if I misjudged you."

"Same here," Betsy replied. "So how *did* you find out about Russell?" Betsy asked.

"I just sort of put two and two together."

"I hope John hasn't put it together. I don't know how he could. I broke it off before I came to see John that day."

"How did Russell feel about that?"

"He's . . . I think he's obsessed with me. He just can't let go. He keeps calling me. I need to talk to him soon, to spell it out for him. But I'm afraid to tell him about John and me . . . I mean, if John and I get back together."

"You shouldn't try to deal with this yourself. When a man can't hear the word *no*, he can be very dangerous."

"I know. I wanted to tell John, but he has so much to deal with right now."

"Let *me* talk to Russell." Natalie stood up.

"I'm glad you came here today," Betsy said.

"I just want the best for John. Take care, okay?"

"I will." Betsy walked Natalie to the door.

Natalie paused and looked at Betsy. "I'd appreciate it if you didn't tell John I was here today."

Betsy nodded. "It's between us."

"Thanks," Natalie said, and walked out the door.

Betsy watched as Natalie got in her car and drove away. She stood there for a long time without moving, then slowly closed the door.

TUESDAY, OCTOBER 28TH

THE WINDOWS of the boathouse shook in the autumn wind, as Ted struggled to bolt them down. He was just finishing his ritual of readying the boathouse for winter, when Natalie cut through the yard and walked up to him.

Ted looked surprised and pleased to see her. "Well hey there, stranger."

"Hey Ted. What are you up to?"

"Getting this thing closed up for the season."

"John take his boat?" She looked back over toward John's cabin. There were no cars there.

"Couple of weekends ago. What's up with you two?"

"Didn't John tell you?"

"Nope. And I didn't ask."

"Betsy wants to get back together with him."

"I saw her car over there a couple of times. Haven't seen you for a while. I didn't know why. Now I do."

"Yeah, well, I took some time off. I just needed to get away from everything. He needs some space to figure things out. I need some space." She looked back over toward John's cabin again.

Ted smiled. "Maybe he's wondering where you've been, too."

"I was thinking about stopping over and talking to him. Maybe in a few days. I've got Friday off."

"Natalie, you and John are *right* for each other."

"*I* think so, but *he's* gotta figure that out."

"So, what have *you* been up to?"

"I went back to work last week. Night shift again. Yuck! I haven't been around mentally, that's for sure. I've got some stuff on my mind that just won't let go."

"You need to talk about it?"

"Actually, I need to ask a favor."

"Shoot."

"Oh, God, don't put it that way."

"Natalie. What's going on?"

"Ted, I need you to make copies of some photographs for me. Only I don't want you to see them, and I don't want to see them, either."

"Well, how in the hell am I going to do *that*?"

Natalie looked down at the ground. She started to tremble, then stamped her foot to get control of herself.

"I hate this job."

"Natalie, just spit it out."

"They're photos that were taken of Amy, after she was shot."

"Oh, God, Natalie. What's going on?"

"I have to find out something, Ted. I don't think Amy's death was an accident. I mean, I think someone was trying to kill *John*. Amy wasn't supposed to be with him that day. I think it was a fluke that somehow, *she* ended up getting killed. I don't know how or why, but everything I'm finding out is pointing that direction."

Ted blew his breath out. "I need a strong cup of coffee." He started walking toward his cabin with Natalie trailing behind.

They walked into the cabin. Ted went straight for the pot sitting on the warming plate and started fixing their coffee.

"Ted, I need to see those photos of the cougar."

"They're right there on the table."

Natalie fumbled around through piles of photos unsuccessfully. Ted brought Natalie her coffee, and then set his down on the table. He reached out and picked up the correct pile, and handed her the photos.

"I'll never know how you do that," Natalie said.

"I've got them all filed in my head. What's the cougar got to do with this?"

Natalie went to the second picture in the stack. She handed him the photo. "This."

"What about it?"

"These photos were taken the day of the accident. That's Russell's cruiser in the background. Right over on Blanchard."

"Yeah?"

"I've never seen you botch an exposure in all the time I've known you. I wasn't going to say anything."

"That's not a botched exposure."

"I know that, but I thought it was a botch job the day I saw it. I thought the light on Russell's car window was an overexposure."

"Natalie, you know me better than that. I'd toss it, and do it again. That's sunlight."

"I know. I figured that out. What time did you take these pictures?"

"Probably around five. I'd only taken half the roll when I heard the sirens. Natalie, what are you saying?"

"I've been putting together some pieces of a puzzle in my head. And they're all starting to fit. And it's horrible, Ted. It's horrible."

"You think Russell had something to do with this?"

"Why is his car sitting there *before* the accident? Why did he show up at Greg's house so quickly after the accident, but before the emergency vehicles arrived at the scene? If he was in the area, why didn't he answer the 9-1-1 call when Amy was shot? *Why?*"

"I don't know. Why would he want to kill John? He doesn't even know the man, does he?"

"I think I know why he wanted to kill John. He may *still* want to kill John. Betsy might be in danger too, and I need those copies of Amy's autopsy photos to prove it."

"Why don't you go to Charlie? Tell him what you know."

"The only person around *here* who has the forensic expertise I need is Russell. But I have a friend who works in the lab in New Orleans. That's why I need those photos."

"Okay, well, you're right. I *don't* want to see those photos. And I know *you* don't want those images in your head, either. So, I'll figure out a way to do it. When do you need them?"

"I've got the case file in my car. I need to get it back before anyone finds out it's missing."

"Better get it back before *Russell* finds out it's missing." Ted shook his head. "You be careful, girl."

"I will."

*   *   *

Natalie walked into the darkened station with the case file in her hand. A lone street light shone through the partially opened window blinds. As Natalie walked past the window, broken rectangles of light flickered over her face and torso. She walked over to the file cabinet and slipped the file back in place. The drawer clicked shut, and Natalie breathed a sigh of relief.

Behind her, in the far corner of the room, the neon end of a cigarette glowed in the darkness.

"Doing a little late night work, Nat?"

Natalie's heart lurched in her chest. Her legs felt like they would collapse beneath her. She whirled around to face him. "Damn, Russell! You scared me!"

Russell didn't respond.

She laughed nervously. "I told you, you should stop smoking."

"I told you, I will someday," he said flatly.

There was a long silence. Natalie wondered what to do next.

"So you think I killed Greg Reynolds," Russell said.

"What makes you think that?"

"You seem to have your own investigation going, And I'm the only one that apparently isn't supposed to know it."

"So how did you meet her, Russell? How long have you been having your fling with Betsy Harrison?"

"Whoa! Seems like you *have* been doing some investigating. A year and a half is hardly a fling. I may be guilty of having an affair with a married woman, but I'm not guilty of murder. I met her at a real estate convention in Detroit."

"I don't get you. She doesn't love you."

"That's where you're wrong. You're not a very good investigator, Nat. You've got to pick up every stitch. Two rabbits running in the ditch."

Natalie detected a noticeable slur in his voice.

"Yeah, yeah, must be the season of the witch. I know the song," she said.

Her eyes adjusted to the light. Russell tipped up a bottle of whiskey, and took a swig.

"You're drunk, Russell," she said in disgust.

"I'm not drunk. I know exactly what I'm saying."

"Then you're crazy."

"Being crazy isn't so bad. It's going there that drives you nuts."

"You can stop what's going on."

"Hey, I'm just playing the hand I was dealt. Just like Judas, don't you think?"

"Judas had a choice, Russell. Just like you."

"I'm just a little puppet on a string," he laughed bitterly.

"Not if you don't want to be."

"Maybe, it's too late for me."

Natalie walked to the door, and opened it. She stood in the door and looked back at Russell. "It's your turn to decide, Russell. You'd better decide while you still can. *If* you still can."

Natalie walked out, leaving Russell alone in the darkness.

*   *   *

Natalie arrived home and trudged up the stairs to her cabin. She was bone-tired. Abby and Salty waited eagerly as she unlocked the door and stepped inside. They must have sensed her fatigue, for instead of jumping on her as they normally did, they sat there whining softly. She tossed her keys into a basket on the side table and squatted down in front of them. Putting her arms around both of them, she hugged them close to her. Abby licked her face in understanding.

She sighed wearily, stood up and took her jacket off, then her shoes. After putting on her nightgown, she cracked her window slightly, and the cold, crisp air filtered in. She looked out the window for a moment. In the sky above, Orion shimmered against black velvet. She yawned, then turned and walked over to her bed. She climbed under the covers and pulled her lavender down comforter up to her chin. Abby and Salty jumped up on the bed and curled up on either side of her. Within minutes, she was sound asleep.

*　*　*

Natalie sat up in bed, confused. She was wide awake, her heart thumping in her chest, every muscle in her body tense. She switched on the lamp on her night stand. The dogs. They weren't on the bed anymore. They were at the front door, growling and barking ferociously. She quickly opened the night stand drawer and pulled out her spare gun. She switched off the lamp and flung the covers off, slipped out of bed and snuck over to the bedroom door. She leaned forward a bit and peered out into the darkened living room.

"Abby! Salty!" she hissed. They recognized her tone of voice and fell silent. Natalie strained to hear any sounds the intruder might make. All she could hear was the blood pounding in her ears. A porch board creaked softly. She shivered from the cold. Her hands were frozen and bloodless, and she fumbled as she tried to take the gun's safety off. The screen door creaked open, and she heard a knock at the door. Natalie held her breath.

"Natalie?"

She recognized John's voice. Natalie blew out her breath in relief.

"Just a minute," she yelled.

She put the safety back on the gun, and returned it to the night stand drawer, then hurried over to the door with Abby and Salty on her heels. She turned on the porch light, unbolted the door and opened it a crack. John stood there on the porch, his hair rumpled, his face rough with beard stubble. His shoulders were slumped and his hands were in his pockets.

"I couldn't sleep. I missed you so much," he said simply.

Natalie flung the door open wide and leaped at him, wrapping her arms around his neck. She kissed him hard on the mouth and he responded, his lips meshing with hers. As they kissed, he put his arms around her and carried her still entwined around him into the house, kicking the door shut behind him. Finally, she pulled her lips away from his. He put her down and looked into her eyes.

"God, I missed you," he whispered.

She smiled back at him. "I missed you too." Then without hesitation she said, "Now that you've woken me up and scared the hell out of me, you can make me breakfast."

"Breakfast? It's only three a.m."

Natalie ignored his comment. "I want eggs Benedict with hash browns on the side. Be sure you cook the ham slices nice and crisp. I'll start the coffee."

"You're a real pain in the butt, you know that?" John smiled at the feisty, loveable woman standing in front of him. He tousled her hair and tweaked her nose.

Natalie stepped backwards out of his reach and put her hands on her hips and lifted her chin defiantly. "Yeah. I know. You are too. Maybe we're God's gift to each other," she challenged, then broke into laughter.

A draft blew in from the bedroom and Natalie shivered. She turned and ran back into her room to close the window, then put on a fuzzy blue robe and her Tweety Bird slippers before walking back into the kitchen. John was bent over, rummaging around in the fridge, looking for the ingredients he needed. She slapped his butt playfully, startling him. He hit his head on the inside of the fridge, nearly dropping the carton of eggs on the floor.

"Ow! That *hurt*, woman!" He straightened up while rubbing his head. He looked at her from head to toe, then raised his eyebrows at her choice of attire. "Wow, don't you look sexy," he said grinning.

Natalie smiled impishly back at him. "Yes, I do."

As they sat eating breakfast, John took a sip of his coffee and smiled at her, feeling like a goofy adolescent, smitten with puppy love. For the last fifty-five days, he'd tried not to think of those beautiful hazel eyes that sparkled back at him; that sweet mouth that curved into a kind, loving smile; the fragrant scent of tangerine and orange blossoms that radiated from her skin and hair.

John was reluctant to break the mood. He sighed and took another sip of his coffee. "I'm meeting Betsy in Petoskey on Friday morning. I'm going to tell her then." He paused. "I love you, Natalie, with all my heart. The only reason I even went through any conflict at all, is because Betsy reached into my heart and pulled on the Amy strings."

"I understand, John." Natalie cupped her hand over John's and stroked it lovingly. "Are you worried about how she'll react?" she said.

"Yeah, I am, kinda. I think she'll be okay, though. Betsy is a strong woman. I think she'll understand and move on with her life."

He stood up and took his last swallow of coffee. "I'd better let you get some rest."

Natalie set her fork down and swallowed her last bite of eggs Benedict. She rose from the table and walked over to him, put her arms around him and leaned her head on his chest. He pulled her close and kissed the top of her head.

"John, I have to tell you something, and please don't ask me any questions. I think I know who killed Greg Reynolds. I just need a couple of days. Please be patient," she said softly. "This will all be over soon."

FRIDAY, OCTOBER 31ST

THE LIGHT of the sun peeked above the horizon. The pale blue sky deepened in color, and soft pink rays shot through the wispy, pearl gray clouds that drifted just above the horizon. Finally, the sun crested, and blazed across the surface of the lake. Natalie rested her paddle, and looked at her waterproof diving watch. It was 7:17 a.m. She paddled toward shore, then pulled her kayak up on the beach where Abby and Salty were waiting.

She started toward the cabin, the dogs following behind, until Abby spotted a squirrel and gave chase. Salty ignored the squirrel, choosing Natalie's company instead.

Natalie sat at her kitchen table eating a huge stack of pancakes slathered in butter and maple syrup when she finally heard Abby whining at the front door. She got up and let her in. Abby was panting heavily. Natalie swore she saw a smile on her dog's face. She knew Abby never meant any harm to the squirrels. It was just her way of having fun.

"Come on, girl," she said. "Time for breakfast." She filled their bowls and sat back down to finish her meal.

Normally, she ate only fruit before noon. But lately, she'd been ravenous, and on this morning, the sirens' call of pancakes and coffee had been too strong to resist.

Natalie puttered around the house all morning, doing chores, waiting for the phone to ring. She looked at the kitchen clock. It was eleven. She'd overnighted the photos to Randy on Wednesday. *He had to have examined them by now*, she thought. *Why doesn't he call?*

She knew Randy would call her eventually, so she kept moving to keep herself busy. The next time she looked at the clock, she was in her bedroom putting away the laundry. The alarm clock on her night stand read 12:02. Time for lunch.

There was some leftover fried chicken in the fridge. Natalie fixed herself a salad, fished the two last pieces of chicken out of the fridge, and sat down at the table. Abby and Salty suddenly appeared at her feet and sat there patiently, looking at her with their tongues hanging out, their eyes full of longing.

"Okay, okay," she said. She tore a couple of meaty chunks off the breast she was eating and tossed them toward Abby and Salty, who snapped them up before they hit the ground. They looked back up at her to see if she would maybe toss them another morsel.

"Nope. That's it, kids. You know you're not supposed to eat table scraps, anyway."

Once she finished eating, Natalie got up and cleared the table, then did the dishes. As she dried the last dish, she looked up at the kitchen clock again. *Geez, Randy. Why haven't you called yet?* She dialed his number and got his answering service. She left a message for him to call as soon as possible, then hung up the phone. She decided to head over to the station and talk to Charlie. She hoped Randy would call soon.

* * *

Natalie pulled into the station parking lot around one o'clock. She got out of her VW and walked inside. Eric was sitting at his desk, filling out paperwork.

"Hey Nat, you look nice today," he said.

Natalie gave him a curious look. She was wearing her favorite pair of faded button-fly Levis, a tight-fitting black, turtle neck sweater, and her black, Converse, high-top tennis shoes. She wasn't dressed up by any means, but Eric was used to seeing her mostly in uniform. She walked over to her desk and laid her cell phone down. Charlie came out of the men's room.

"Charlie, can I talk to you?"

"Sure."

She tilted her head in Eric's direction and raised her eyebrows at Charlie. "Privately?"

"Sure, let's go outside."

Charlie opened the door for her and followed her out. They stood in the parking lot in front of Natalie's car. She folded her arms and looked at him.

"I think I've got this whole thing put together."

"What whole thing?"

"Who killed Greg Reynolds."

"I'm all ears," he said.

"You told me that normally, in a murder, you'd follow the money. Find out who stood to gain with Greg Reynolds being dead. Remember?"

"Yep."

"I think someone stood to gain, but it wasn't money. I'm waiting on a phone call that I think will put this whole thing together."

"Like I told you, stay out of Russell's way."

"What if Russell did it?"

"Like I told you, stay out of his way."

Charlie headed back into the office. Natalie followed.

Eric looked up from his desk. "Hey, Natalie, some guy from New Orleans called on your cell phone. I hope you don't mind me answering it."

"Did he leave a message?"

"Mais ya, he did, cher'." Eric held up a piece of paper and started reading. "Let's see, his name was Boudreaux Thibodeaux Gaston Leroy at . . . "

Natalie grabbed the paper out of his hands. "Okay, knock it off."

She picked up her cell phone from the desk and walked outside. She got in her car and held the piece of paper up to read it, then dialed the number.

"Randy?"

"Sorry I didn't get back to you sooner. I just got the photos this morning," he said.

"What did you find out?"

Randy was blunt. "You've got some real incompetents doing your lab work there. This wasn't a three-hundred-yard shot. More like . . . maybe thirty yards. Fifty tops."

"You sure, Randy?"

"Absolutely. The damage this bullet did? This bullet was pretty close range."

"Okay, Randy. I owe you one."

"When you coming down to visit?"

"I'm not sure. Say hi to the guys for me, okay?"

"Sure. See ya, Nat."

*   *   *

It was 1:45 p.m. when she arrived at John's cabin. No one was there. She went over to Ted's and knocked on the door. He opened the door and peered out at her.

"Ted?" she said through the screen door.

"Hey, Natalie."

"Have you seen John?"

"This morning, but he left early."

"Oh, that's right. I forgot all about it. He's in Petoskey. I need to talk to him. To both of them."

She started to leave.

"Natalie?"

She turned back around and stopped. He walked out of the cabin and joined her.

"I was thinking about something that you said on Tuesday," he said.

"Yeah?"

"I went over to Reynold's field with my high-power lens. There's too many trees. There's no straight shot from where those guys were shooting, to the road where Amy was killed."

"I know that, Ted. This will all be over soon," she called over her shoulder as she ran to her car.

Natalie glanced down at her wrist watch. She headed down the highway on her way to Petoskey. It was two p.m. exactly. Off to her left, Lake Huron was the color of lapis lazuli. The wind picked up, and started whipping across the lake, creating large, frothy whitecaps. As she passed by Nunn's Creek, she glanced over and saw a single bald eagle sitting on a spit of land. Something must have disturbed it, for it suddenly took flight and soared right over the top of her car. The sight barely registered in her mind, she was so intent on her thoughts.

Natalie turned and headed south down I-75. She thought about the timing of that day that had changed so many lives. She realized that the day John and Amy had headed toward their cabin, she must have passed them on I-75 on her way to pick up the prisoner in St. Ignace. Her heart ached. If only she could turn back the clock, she would gladly give up her future with John, for Amy to still be alive. If only.

Natalie pulled up into the Harrison driveway. She got out of the car and stood there, remembering the first day she came here. She half-expected Betsy to come storming out of the house again, eyes blazing, her mouth set in a grim line. Natalie walked up the driveway. Betsy's car was there. Natalie knocked, but there was no answer. She walked around to the back of the house, thinking maybe Betsy was in the back yard and hadn't heard her knock. The back door was ajar. She knocked on the door, but again, no answer.

Natalie stepped inside the kitchen and called out to see if anyone was there. She glanced around, then started to walk out. But just before she exited, she saw a phone bill laying open on the kitchen counter. She picked it up and looked at it. Her face turned white. She dropped the bill on the floor.

*   *   *

Natalie drove down the highway with her left hand on the wheel. She held her cell phone with her right hand and dialed with her thumb. Then she held the phone to her ear. *Damn! All circuits busy!* Every few minutes she would retry, only to get the same busy signal. Finally she put the phone down and focused on the road.

The traffic was horrible. She wove in and out of it, trying to get ahead of the congestion. She hit her steering wheel in frustration, as an elderly man in a white Dodge ahead of her drove ten miles under the speed limit. The traffic was too heavy in the other lane to even think of passing him. "Damn it! Get out of the way!" she cried.

*   *   *

John backed out of his parking spot at Cedarville Foods. The clock on his dash said 5:33 p.m. He nodded politely, allowing a young boy and his mother to pass in front of his car. The boy was dressed in a Harry Potter costume. The gusting wind tugged at his cloak and caused it to billow out and flap behind him. John had seen a few ghosts and goblins earlier when he'd driven through a nearby neighborhood. It was Halloween Night, and clusters of children darted like bats from house to house, swooping in to claim their sugary treats.

About ten minutes later, John arrived at his cabin and went inside. He put the groceries away methodically, can goods in the bottom cabinet, the loaf of bread on top of the fridge, the dairy products inside. Closing the refrigerator door, he turned to go into the bedroom, when he heard his cell phone ringing. He picked up the phone and hit the receiver button.

"Hello?" His brows furrowed in concern. "Betsy, slow down. What's going on? Where are you?"

Betsy was crying. "I'm at Russell's cottage. John, he's obsessed with me. I think he's going to kill me." She was nearly hysterical now.

"Betsy, where's Russell now?" John was frustrated, trying to make sense of her frantic babbling.

Betsy looked out of the cottage window. "He's outside by the lake. He's come unglued, John. I'm really afraid. You've got to help me!" She looked out the window again and saw Russell walking slowly toward the house.

"Oh, my God. He's coming back!" she wailed. "John, help me, please!" The phone went dead.

John shouted into the phone. "Betsy? Betsy?!" He ran to his desk drawer and yanked it open.

The drawer was empty. He'd forgotten that his 9mm pistol was missing, along with his 30.06, when they'd searched his house that morning. He had no shotguns either, since they'd been confiscated that same morning. John ran out the door, and leaped into his car.

As his car hurtled down the country road, he prayed that he would reach Betsy in time. His cell phone rang again.

"Betsy!" he shouted.

"John, it's me." It was Natalie. "Listen, I have to tell you . . . "

He cut her off. "Natalie, Betsy's in trouble."

"Where are you?" she asked.

"I'm on my way to Russell's cottage. I just got a call from Betsy. She said she thinks Russell is going to kill her!"

"John, don't go there," she said, her voice urgent, and sharp with fear.

"I *have* to go, Natalie."

"John," she pleaded. "Don't go. There's more . . ."

The line went dead. John had already hung up.

* * *

The sun had set by the time John pulled up outside Russell's cottage. John could see the dim light of oil lamps, and the flicker of firelight from the fireplace, coming from inside the cottage. He had barely exited his car when he heard a gunshot. He ran toward the front door. "Dear God," he cried as he flew up the steps and burst through the door.

Betsy was standing in the kitchen, crying and shaking, holding John's 9mm pistol in her hands. Russell was lying on the floor. A red stain had formed on his shirt, spreading outward from his chest. Betsy dropped the gun on the floor, and bent over as if in pain, hugging herself as she wailed piteously.

John was in shock. He stood there motionless, his mind reeling in confusion. Finally, he went over and knelt by Russell's body, trying to make sense of what had just happened. Russell's opened jacket revealed an empty shoulder holster.

Behind John, Betsy straightened up and pulled something out from the waistband in the back of her jeans. She had a strange look in her eyes. The flickering firelight had turned her face a sickly orange. She smiled as she pointed Russell's .38 Smith and Wesson revolver at John's back.

John turned and looked up, back over his shoulder, at her. The confusion on his face morphed into astonishment.

"Betsy, what are you doing?"

"I'm going to kill you, John," she said calmly. She grinned at him and followed his movements with the gun as he rose to his feet and turned to face her. She repositioned the gun, making sure it was aimed at his heart.

"What are you doing?" he said again, incredulously.

"No one will ever know. My husband came here in a jealous rage, and he and my lover shot each other. Who will ever know?"

"Betsy, you're out of your mind!"

"No John, I know *exactly* what I'm doing. I gave up everything I ever wanted so you could write your stupid crap. I sacrificed everything for you!" she screamed at him. Betsy faltered for a moment. This time, real tears started to trickle down her cheeks. "You were going to take everything away from me."

"Betsy, you *know* I wouldn't do that to you."

She threw back her head and stared at him. "No. Nice try," she said coolly. "I want it all, and I'm going to get it. You'll be gone, and I'll have everything." She smirked at him, confidently. "The property, the rights to your silly works, and . . . "

"You did this for *money*? You killed Russell, and now you're going to kill me for *money*?!"

"For money. And for revenge."

"Revenge?"

"Yes, revenge. At you for ruining my life. At Russell, for killing my little girl."

"What are you talking about?"

"Don't you get it, John? It was a collaboration. At least Russell thought it was. He would have done anything I wanted him to. He was going to kill you, and make people think Greg Reynolds accidentally shot you. Then he thought we'd live happily ever after together. He didn't know I was going to tell the police that he'd killed you because he was obsessed with me. You'd be dead, he'd go to prison, and that would have been that. But *you* had to take Amy with you."

"You killed our daughter, Betsy?" John's face turned pale and he felt as if he would throw up.

Betsy erupted in anger. "No!" she screamed at him "It's *your* fault! It's *all* your fault. Amy wasn't supposed to be with you. You were the one who was supposed to die, damn you!" Her eyes narrowed to slits and she looked at him accusingly. "Do you know how sickening it was to fuck this bastard, knowing he'd killed my little girl? But I had to set this up. I had to get rid of him, and I had to get rid of you."

"Oh, God, Betsy. This can't be true. *You* caused all this," he choked on his words, barely able to speak. "You killed our little girl," he whispered.

"She wasn't *our* little girl, John. She wasn't *your* child."

"Do you really think it would make any difference to me if she *wasn't*? I loved Amy, with all my soul."

The gun shook in her hands. Conflict raged within her. The devastating reality of the events that she had set in motion was finally beginning to dawn on her. It seemed, as if for a moment, that the walls that she had built around her heart might crumble – that genuine remorse might win out over the bitterness she harbored. Then her face hardened.

"*You* caused all this. It's your fault! It's your fault!" She looked at the ground and repeated herself, trying to persuade her own mind, and somehow cleanse herself of guilt. "It's your fault. It's your fault."

John's face was wet with tears. They ran down his cheeks and splashed onto his shirt.

"Betsy, you need help," he said.

A strange miasma shrouded her eyes.

"*I* need help, John?"

Her movements became robotic. She planted her feet shoulder-width apart. She steadied the gun with both hands, as the corners of her mouth twitched spasmodically.

"Goodbye, John."

The ticking of the tall grandfather clock in the corner was amplified in the otherwise silent room. John stood frozen in place, unable to believe what was happening.

Suddenly, a loud noise shattered the silence. Betsy fell backwards, a look of stunned disbelief on her face. The gun fell from her hands and clattered to the floor. She crumpled to the floor and a pool of blood started to form on the linoleum beneath her. She lay there without moving. John rushed to her side and leaned over her. He checked her pulse. She was gone.

He looked back and saw Russell had pulled himself up on one elbow. He was clutching the gun from his leg holster in his hand. Russell's strength gave way, and he collapsed back to the floor and closed his eyes. John knelt down next to him. Russell opened his eyes. There were tears in them. He looked at John beseechingly.

"I'm sorry," Russell whispered hoarsely. "I'm so . . . " He breathed in one last time. His eyes stared up at John, blank and unseeing.

John looked down at his own hands. They were covered in blood. The horrific images of Amy's death came flooding back to him. He wailed in agony. He crawled on his hands and knees to Betsy and hovered over her body. The complete destruction of his world was too much for him. He couldn't handle it anymore. He had to stop the pain. He saw the .38 lying on the floor and picked it up. He pressed the cold metal barrel against his temple. His hand shook as he cocked the hammer. *I can end this right now. I don't have to hurt ever again. It will all be over soon.*

He looked down and closed his eyes, then quickly opened them again. Something gold and shiny had caught his attention. He looked down and saw Betsy's locket on the floor next to her body. The one with Amy's picture in it. He hesitated. He heard footsteps running up the outside stairs and coming into the cottage through the open door.

Natalie stopped short, horrified by the carnage before her. She looked and saw John on his knees with a gun to his head.

"John!" she cried. "Don't! Please don't do it!"

"How could they do this?" he cried.

"Please don't add another death to this."

"What's the use, Natalie? They think I killed Greg Reynolds. They'll think I killed Betsy and Russell, too. What's the use?"

"Listen to me, John. We know that Russell killed Greg Reynolds. We know he tried to kill you, too. They'll believe you, John. I believe you."

"So what if they believe me. What's the use?"

"Is this what Amy would want, John? *Is it?!*" she shouted.

"There's no hope, Natalie."

"There's always hope, John. There's always hope. If you die, who will remember Amy? There is no remembrance in the grave, John. You have something to live for. To remember Amy. Someone to live for. You have me. You have *us*! John, please live for *us*!"

John dropped the gun to the floor. Natalie ran to him and held him as he collapsed in her arms. She didn't know how long she'd have him, but she had him now, for this moment. She would take each moment as it came.

THE STARK NAKED
21-DAY METABOLIC RESET

THE STARK NAKED 21-DAY METABOLIC RESET

EFFORTLESS WEIGHT LOSS, REJUVENATING SLEEP, LIMITLESS ENERGY, MORE MOJO

BRAD DAVIDSON

WITH LAURA MORTON

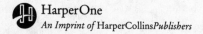

HarperOne

An Imprint of HarperCollinsPublishers

THE STARK NAKED 21-DAY METABOLIC RESET. Copyright © 2015 Stark Books, LLC.
All rights reserved. Printed in the United States of America. No part of this book may
be used or reproduced in any manner whatsoever without written permission except
in the case of brief quotations embodied in critical articles and reviews. For information
address HarperCollins Publishers, 195 Broadway, New York, NY 10007.

HarperCollins books may be purchased for educational, business, or sales
promotional use. For information please e-mail the Special Markets Department
at SPsales@harpercollins.com.

HarperCollins website: http://www.harpercollins.com

FIRST HARPERCOLLINS PAPERBACK EDITION PUBLISHED IN 2017

Designed by Terry McGrath

Library of Congress Cataloging-in-Publication Data is available upon request.

ISBN 978–0–06–236922–2

17 18 19 20 21 RRD(H) 10 9 8 7 6 5 4 3 2 1

This book is dedicated to my
beautiful wife, Maria, and my
amazing children, Joseph, Isabel, and
baby Gavin, for their support, sacrifice,
and belief in my crazy pursuits.

To my parents, Mike and Rose Davidson,
for grinding every day of my younger years
and giving me the opportunity and security
to take risks and pursue my dreams!

Contents

Preface

A T THIRTY-TWO YEARS OLD, I looked in the mirror and saw the body I had always wanted and strived for. However, despite looking outwardly amazing, I was keeping a dark secret that was eating away at every fiber of my being. This burden weighed heavily on me day and night.

You see, I was living a totally fake life. On the outside I was the picture of health, and yet I was the furthest thing from being healthy.

Yeah, I looked great, but I felt *horrible*.

Sure, I had those amazing six-pack abs, but I couldn't get going in the morning or function throughout the day without a steady supply of caffeine pumping through my veins. I was severely lethargic and irritable. My thinking was sluggish and foggy. And though I was physically exhausted during the day, I was totally wired at bedtime, so at night I couldn't sleep. Not a wink. To top it off, my sex drive was completely gone.

I could no longer handle my lack of integrity, my daily pursuit of hiding behind my physical image, and my continuously feeling awful on the inside while promoting healthy living as a personal trainer. Overnight, I realized that everything I had learned, believed, and stood behind for so many years as "the truth" in the world of health and fitness had misled me to my harsh reality.

As a fitness professional, I was petrified I would lose my clients, my business, and my reputation as one of the leading trainers in Southern California if anyone found out how weak and tired I felt. I hid my dirty little secret from my colleagues and clients as best I could. I couldn't hide it from my wife, though. When I wasn't working, she bore the brunt of my mood swings.

Of course, my doctor's solution was prescribing the use of hormone replacement therapy and medical drugs like Lipitor to reduce my symptoms and the risk of early death.

Early death! What was wrong?

My doctor diagnosed me with andropause (male menopause). I felt so ashamed and disappointed in myself the day he told me that, at thirty-two, I had the testosterone levels of an eighty-year-old man. For a guy who made a living as a fitness professional, this was a real punch in the gut. From where I stood, it was as if I had hit rock bottom. To be sure, my belief system about health and fitness—that looking fit equaled health—was *completely* shattered.

I meet people daily who are stuck living my old life. They struggle with low energy, are inexplicably overly emotional, are unable to sleep or have interrupted sleep patterns, lack a desire for sex (even if they don't talk about it), and battle to keep their bodies looking great despite hitting the gym 5 days a week.

I imagine many of you might be familiar with this feeling, you know, hiding your true self from the world. Pretending to be bulletproof, invincible. Saying everything is great when it isn't. I hear it from my clients all the time.

Can *you* relate to any of these frustrations?

If you're anything like me, you're probably strong enough to keep yourself from eating too many calories.

You're certainly strong enough to force yourself to exercise harder or more often, even when you don't feel like it.

You're definitely strong enough to avoid carbs at all costs.

And, by God, you're strong enough to suffer through the latest juice-cleanse craze . . . just to prove you can or because all your friends are doing it.

But I have a really important question for you: *Are you strong enough to follow in my footsteps and do what it takes to get your health and your life back?*

To truly get my health and life back it took *vulnerability*. Yup. Vulnerability to admit that maybe I didn't know it all—and maybe, just maybe there is a better way of life. Vulnerability to humbly ask for help, and then to be open to exploring different ideas I thought were foolish at first, but ones I was willing to try if it meant healing myself for the greater good and for the rest of my life.

Yeah, I was more than willing to put myself out there for that.

Over the past eight years, being strong enough to be vulnerable has dramatically improved the quality of my life. But more important to me, it has led to the creation of this program, the Stark Naked 21-Day Metabolic Reset.

Why did I decide to name this program "Stark Naked"?

Simple. In German, the word *stark* means "strong." (That's why I named my first company Stark!) And there is no greater form of vulnerability than being naked, is there?

Once I overcame my early andropause and healed my metabolism, the root cause of my symptoms, through the natural methods I share in this book, I made a vow to live my life in the most authentic way. No more lies.

So I am not going to pretend to be an unassailable guru with all the answers. I can only share my journey of what got me healthy and how I've helped thousands of people do the same.

Here's something else you need to know up front.

I am not a medical practitioner or a research genius. I am a top-tier performance coach who works with people on an individual basis and gets excellent results. I won't have the answer for everyone, but it is highly likely that I can help you improve the quality of your life . . . in a very big way.

There is no doubt this book will challenge your current strategies and beliefs, but if you're struggling as I was years ago, that challenge is exactly what you need. It will challenge the rules that have been hammered into your head over the years about what it takes to not only look good, but to feel good too. There are going to be things I ask you to do that go against everything you've ever been told. Be vulnerable and try them. I did, and they changed my life. I just need 21 days to make you a believer.

Before we start you need to ask yourself this important question: *Are you strong enough to be vulnerable enough to step out of your comfort zone and try something new . . . perhaps something that goes against everything you think you know for the next 21 days?*

If the answer to this question is *yes,* you're going to rock this plan.

If you're not sure, put yourself in my hands for the next couple of hours as you delve into my story and the "why" of my program. If I can't convince you of the merit and reasons you should give your body a reset based on what you read, well, maybe you're not ready yet. I hope you'll get there someday. When you're ready, or when you just realize you feel lousy and want to feel better, I'll be here for you.

Here's one more thing to consider. If you are the kind of person who likes to cut to the chase—and you know who you are—you can jump right to Chapter 11 and dive in to the Stark Naked 21-Day Metabolic Reset. Think of Chapter 11 as the "how" and the rest of this book as the "why." The plan has been designed to be easy to follow and ready to do as a self-contained chapter.

Although I'd like to believe that most of you will want to understand why my program works the way it does—especially because it breaks from traditional thinking in so many ways—if you really just want to get started, go for it. No harm, no foul.

If you feel the need to slowly dip your toes in the pool before actually diving in—and believe me, that's going to be most of you—the rest of the book is for you.

Introduction

MY LOVE AFFAIR WITH EXERCISE began when I was in eighth grade. It started the day my father brought home my first set of free weights and taught me the proper way to work out in the confines of my bedroom. Even though the space was extremely limited, I thought, "If *I* can get into shape in this tiny space, *anyone* can!"

My first military presses made me feel as though I was on a teeter-totter, trying to balance my arms and keep the weights steady in my hands. I was terribly wobbly and unsure of myself, but I was immediately hooked on the idea of getting fit! From that moment on, I dedicated my life to looking good and wanting to help others feel better about themselves too. I wanted everyone to feel what I felt.

You see, I was that kid in the eighth grade who started to work on his body right around the time his body was changing, so when I bulked up, got into fantastic physical shape, and was ripped from my arms to my abs, everyone took notice—especially the girls. Man, I liked how that felt!

When I was old enough and able to afford it, I moved to California to pursue the world of physical fitness as a personal trainer. What guy dedicated to his body didn't dream of someday working out on Venice Beach with Arnold Schwarzenegger and Franco

Columbo? I must have watched *Pumping Iron* a hundred times!

Although I loved being a trainer, my true passion for health and wellness was ignited when I was thirty-two years old. As for most of us, it took an awakening—the kind no one really wants to have, but sometimes needs—to understand something's got to give or there will be a significant price to pay in the future.

Okay, I'll come clean. Like so many people in my field, I'd grown a bit overconfident. I was that guy who thought he was invincible— living large, moving at a fast pace, eating what I genuinely believed were all the right foods, and hitting the gym hard. From the outside, I was doing everything right, and yet I felt awful. I had terrible insomnia, and my energy level and sex drive had hit rock bottom. My body was starting to change too. Despite being a top-tier trainer, fat was creeping in around my washboard middle, and I felt weak.

As if that wasn't bad enough, one morning I awoke to discover I was missing patches of hair from my beard. At first, I thought my wife was playing a joke on me by shaving little strips off in my sleep, but she swore she hadn't.

Suddenly worried, I went to see my doctor to check things out. After a battery of tests, he informed me that I was suffering from low testosterone caused by . . . wait for it . . . *stress*!

Stress?

In my early thirties, I was told by my doctor that I was in early andropause (male menopause), brought on from high levels of stress. *WTF!*

My total testosterone level was akin to that of a typical eighty-year-old man. *Huh?*

I knew I was tired, *way too tired* for a guy my age. I could tell my metabolism had slowed down a bit, because I was lethargic and had begun carrying around my waist a new and unwanted thick layer of belly fat—something I couldn't seem to get rid of, no matter how hard I tried (not what you'd expect to hear from a trainer). But I couldn't believe my health had deteriorated that much over the last few years.

I was secretly hoping my clients wouldn't notice my ever-expanding waistline. To hide it, I wore baggy clothes over my love handles, thinking I was being superclever. After all, who wants to work out or take fitness advice from a fat trainer?

There I was, selling health and vitality, and my life was so far from that ideal image. I was such a fraud. When I finally stopped lying about what was going on, I had no choice but to accept my situation for what it was and not what I wanted it to be. My condition couldn't be fixed over a weekend or by just catching up on some much-needed sleep.

Don't get me wrong. That would have been great, but it wouldn't have solved my real issues or been effective for me long-term, because my body was crying out for help. The biggest problem I was having wasn't my testosterone levels. It was that I wasn't tuned in or listening to my body and hadn't been for a long time.

My body was like a computer that had frozen. No matter what I did, all I got was the sad Mac face. What do you do when your computer or phone won't respond?

You reset it!

The harsh reality was that I needed an overhaul—a reset. And since I was aware enough to understand that metabolism is the key to health, I knew I needed an entire *metabolic reset*. (Cue the dramatic music here!)

"Hi. My name is Brad. I was a personal trainer living a complete lie!"

Whew! I feel so much better having this out in the open! Now that I have confessed this about myself, want to know a dirty little secret? Many personal trainers live with this same story. They overwork, overexercise, and don't get enough sleep, because they're trying to keep up with the needs of their busy high-achieving clients. They become experts at maintaining an external image of being fit, when in fact they are just like I was back then—anything but!

The reality is, this affliction isn't exclusive to personal trainers—

lots of people live this way (maybe even you) and don't even know it. And if they do, they're more than likely afraid to do anything about it, because it will upset their "perfect" and "comfortable" routine.

Sound like anyone you know?

When my doctor told me I was sick, I knew the time had come to make some serious changes, but I also knew my usual approach wasn't going to work. My high-achieving, stress-filled, aggressive lifestyle was actually the root cause of my low testosterone and my extreme lethargy, among other side effects, including my low mojo, or sex drive, and weight gain.

But how?

Clearly, exercising hard and eating what I thought was healthy were totally backfiring. *I could not "out-exercise" this new low or "eat" my way to health.*

I had to discover a smarter way to approach my health and reset my metabolism, one that worked for me at a time when I didn't feel like doing *anything*! I needed a solution that could stand up to the stressful demands of my hectic life and work schedule while healing me. Once that happened, my new lifestyle had to prevent another breakdown in my health.

It wasn't easy. There were a lot of starts and stops and lots of trial and error along the way.

I was a human guinea pig, experimenting on myself for months at a time. I experimented with nutritional strategies like eating an extreme Paleo diet, intermittent fasting, and multiple variations of cleanses. I manipulated my exercise protocols, trying high-intensity short-duration exercise, long-drawn-out cardio, corrective exercise, and modified-strongman training. I did extensive lab work testing supplement strategies. I studied functional medicine, obtained advanced certifications in Functional Diagnostic Nutrition, and hired numerous experts in these fields looking for clues to the answers my body needed.

Finally, I found the approach to nutrition, exercise, recovery, and sleep that healed my metabolism, and my andropause reversed itself. My energy was through the roof, my mood was optimistic, my sex drive was back, and, best of all, my body began to look like the body of a qualified trainer again.

And then I had an epiphany. If this plan worked for me, I was certain I could help others with it.

Why?

I had finally found the answers that helped set me on the right path to where I not only looked good, but felt great too. This was what every client of mine truly wanted, but never articulated. As a result of these strategies learned and perfected, I now use this exact system on all of my private clients at Stark, which allows them to experience the same reset and benefits I experienced.

And now, with *The Stark Naked 21-Day Metabolic Reset* these exact same benefits are *yours* for the taking too.

A Lifestyle Plan Designed for You

Finally, there is a lifestyle plan that meets your needs and will help you to live your healthiest life ever, from the inside out. Stark Naked is the only lifestyle plan designed for all of you who believe life is meant to be lived, not just endured, who want to live life on *your* terms!

If you describe yourself as busy, stressed, overcommitted, and tired, you are a person I call a *high achiever*. Don't get freaked out by that term. You don't have to be a titan of business or a guru of greatness to be considered a high achiever.

If you constantly push yourself beyond the limits, have a strong desire to be the best at whatever it is you do, have a drive to be successful, but have become ambivalent about the impact of stress on health, dismissing it as the "price you pay," *you* are a high achiever. If, no matter how much you accomplish, you can't shake the ever present feeling that there are still items on your infinite "to do" list, *you* too are a high achiever.

High achievers can go from being in fifth gear to crashing, and they need 2 or 3 days before they can flip their "on" switch to "off" during a vacation—though they can never really unplug. In general, high achievers are incredibly driven individuals who are in a constant state of stress, focused on a desired outcome, and willing to do whatever it takes to accomplish that outcome. High achievers have an ability to dig in and keep going, pushing through barriers even when everything seems to be against them. Failure is not an option!

Does any of this strike a chord?

It should, because this massive population keeps multiplying and includes young professionals, Gen Xs, Gen Ys, baby boomers, stay-at-home moms, working moms, busy executives, business leaders, law-enforcement professionals, professional athletes, and any others who claim they are constantly on the go.

Could this be *you*?

Three years ago at the age of sixty-three, iconic head football coach Bruce Rollinson, from Mater Dei High School in Orange County, California, stepped into my office to talk about a strategy to revamp his health, energy, and fitness. Why?

He wanted to earn the respect of his players as he demanded that they get more serious about their health. The prior year, his team had their first losing season since he took over as head coach in 1989. It was time for the mighty Monarchs to make a comeback. The coach was tired of seeing pizza boxes in the locker rooms and observing his players not being in top physical condition. He hired a new strength coach to help get the kids into shape. I have so much respect for a coach who leads by example.

When he started working with me, Coach Rollinson weighed 227 pounds. His cardiovascular risk markers were elevated, he wasn't sleeping well, and he really struggled with afternoon energy crashes that were negatively affecting his mood and focus during practices.

To make matters more challenging, he had suffered numerous injuries to one knee that initially limited what we could do in the area of exercise.

In my eyes, Coach Rollinson is the ultimate example of a high achiever—even in his sixties. He's a fierce competitor who was nowhere near ready to walk away and retire from coaching. He still had a lot more games left to win, and he knew it. He just needed some support to reset his metabolism, so his body and energy could keep up with his drive and hunger to keep coaching football.

Within six months, we transformed his body, which dropped 40 pounds. Not only did he reset his metabolism and have the energy to be a better leader; his team totally transformed too! His team ended the next season with an 11–3 record, making it all the way to the CIF Championship game. I will never forget their game at Anaheim Stadium that year against their rival school, Servite High. Coach Rollinson let me bring my ten-year-old son into the locker room before the game, and he got to run out onto the field with the team. Three years later, Coach Rollinson is still going strong. He has kept his metabolism optimized, has maintained his weight, and is keeping his health and energy in check. It's going to take more than age and stress to get Coach Rollinson to retire.

No matter where you are in life, it's not too late to take control of your health and well-being. All it takes is 21 days and a commitment to stay the course.

It's Time to Make a Lasting Change

Get ready for a dynamic shift in the way you think and live.

The Stark Naked 21-Day Metabolic Reset is designed to teach you why you feel the way you do, show you how to reset your metabolism (fix what's broken), and then help you to apply these healthy-living principles to your individual lifestyle. In just 21 days, you will feel great, look fantastically healthy, and perform at an amazingly peak level with more energy than you've ever had or thought possible. When you get right down to it, energy is our greatest asset in this game of life; if your energy isn't up to par, everything suffers.

Today, my schedule is the busiest it's ever been. Not only do I train clients and advise them on nutrition, while traveling the world teaching groups of other high achievers how to reset their metabolism and develop resiliency in their stressful and demanding lives; I also balance those tasks with my responsibilities as a husband and dad. As a result of my time spent perfecting this plan, I can show you how to have that same kind of balance in your life too.

The majority of mainstream diet and fitness advice promises a quick fix, but I have discovered that quick fixes require you to either deprive or abuse the body, in short, to stress out the body. Your body does *not* need more stress. Even when I was diagnosed with andropause and feeling my lowest, I didn't want to believe I was sick. I knew I felt bad, but I still wanted to believe I could work this problem out with discipline and effort. In reality, like you, I was simply exhausted, not sick. My body needed the exact thing I generally considered to be a sign of laziness and weakness. What it needed was the four-letter word *r-e-s-t*!

Say what?

Yes, *rest.*

I grew up with a father who instilled a fierce work ethic in me. He told me that hard work was the essential foundation of success. Quitting was never an option in our house. Neither was being lazy. One of my dad's yearly goals at his job was to win the perfect attendance award. He took so much pride in winning it several years in a row.

In a recent private consultation with a very successful man, our conversation happened to turn to the virtues of rest. He looked at me and said, "Brad, I will be honest with you. I have not taken a full week off of work since I started my business in 1983." Although I am sure this is his secret to becoming hugely successful, imagine the sacrifices he has made physically, emotionally, and otherwise to make that statement.

Now, I realize most of us don't understand the word because we are people on the go, but rest is the magic pill when it comes to health and fitness. High-performance athletes tout the virtues of their off days and the impact that has on their performance. And that's why I made rest and sleep a huge part of this plan. In fact, it's so important to the success of your reset, I dedicate a whole chapter to the benefits of sleep. *Do not skip it!*

Cutting back on exercise when you're physically shot is also important to your recovery, and that's another key element in your reset plan. Believe me, too much exercise combined with one crazy fad diet after another can be a very dangerous thing. In my case, I was actually breaking down my body by trying to combine traditional theories of nutrition (like eating a no-complex-carbohydrate, primarily high-protein clean diet), overexercising, and believing (based on my highly motivated work ethic) that I had to outwork everyone else if I was going to succeed. I wanted to accomplish great things and look incredible at the same time. I got away with that mentality for a while, but slowly that way of thinking and living caught up with me and then *wham*!

I know a lot of you reading this book live life *very* committed to the fire in your belly and accomplishing as much as possible in your life. You likely grew up hearing such sayings as, "You can sleep when you're dead" or "The harder you work, the luckier you get," and perhaps took them literally. That's why you likely work as hard as you do, as a result find yourself in a state of complete fatigue, and think it's actually *normal* to feel that way.

I've got news for you. It's *not* normal to feel this way.

In fact, if you can give me 21 days, I can open your mind, body, and spirit to a totally new "normal." But you've got to be willing to give up your old ways of thinking and try some new things that may rock your world at first.

Hey, I get it. Getting stuck in a rut happens to the best of us. Believe me, I hear it every day. Clients come into the gym and say things like:

"My energy is horrible without caffeine."

"I can't sleep."

"I need to take a sleeping pill to get any sleep."

"I have zero sex drive."

"I force myself to exercise every day, but my body does not reflect my efforts."

"I am looking for answers, and all I can find are the common extreme ones that say I need to sacrifice more and try harder. I need to cut more calories, eat less carbs. I'm not exercising enough or hard enough. I'm supposed to suck it up and try harder!"

"I am at my breaking point!"

"No pain, no gain, right?"

Wrong!

This book will turn everything you think you know about nutrition and fitness on its head and show you what "great" and ultimately "normal" should really feel like. The Stark Naked 21-Day Metabolic Reset is not about healing you from a disease or turning you into a fitness model. If that's what you're looking for, move on to the next fad diet book. I'm not your guy. I'm good at what I do, but I am neither a medical doctor nor a magician.

Besides, looking good but feeling horrible doesn't cut it in my world. Those aren't the results we are after here. This book is a long-term lifestyle plan for those in need of a metabolic reset to elevate their readiness and resiliency, so they can conquer the game of life.

Think of it as a comeback.

Take Control of Your Health and Fitness for the Very Last Time

If you're tired of being tired, sick of being sick, over being under-sexed, starving for better health, and dying to finally live your best life ever—then you are finally ready to take control of your health and fitness for the very last time. Why?

The Stark Naked 21-Day Metabolic Reset is the ultimate tool to build resiliency into your high-achieving lifestyle and allow you to wake up every morning with the "juice"—that necessary motivation—to conquer life one day at a time. Allowing yourself this chance to reset will refuel that inner hunger and drive for being great and getting the most from every day of your life. It will make life fun again!

The reset plan in this book is the exact strategy I use with the professional athletes I train who want to resurrect or extend their careers, the powerful overachieving CEOs who are running on low energy and experiencing unwanted brain fog, and the overextended parents trying to be all things for their kids and suffering from constant fatigue and moodiness.

This book holds the keys to the kingdom. They're yours for the taking. All you have to do is grab them and unlock the door.

You are about to make a paradigm shift. Don't let fear stop you! I have found that most people will go to greater lengths to avoid what they fear than to obtain what they desire.

Here's the thing. Fear kills everything—especially your greatest potential. So often, people come to me afraid of what the future holds—and some, for very good reasons. They've been warned by their doctor that if they don't get a handle on their health, the worst doom-and-gloom outcome is imminent. Frozen by fear, they throw their hands in the air and give up without ever trying. They worry that if they don't get back into shape, their spouse will leave them, they'll get sick(er), they'll miss more days at work, and so on. If . . . if . . . if . . .

Playing a game of "What If" Roulette is a horrible way to live!

I'm here to tell you that *fear is a reminder of what is possible.* Use it to motivate you! This is *your* life. It's not your parents', your kids', or your spouse's. It isn't measured by your job title, your bank account, the car you drive, the watch on your wrist, or even the size of your waistline. It's about being in the moment—the here and now. The master of mindfulness Jon Kabat-Zinn says, "You can't change the tide, but you can learn to surf." That philosophy speaks to me, a California boy, on every level, and that's exactly what I chose to do when I took control of my health and wellness.

Welcome to your new journey, your great comeback! It's not too late to have the life and health you've always wanted.

What You're About to Read

It's important to understand right out of the gate that the Stark Naked 21-Day Metabolic Reset isn't a diet. It isn't a fad. It isn't a quick fix, and it isn't some gimmick that will backfire the minute you screw it up.

Face it: you can't will yourself to feel better. There is no magic bullet. The only true answer is to change your lifestyle by getting healthy and living your best life. In order to do that, you must first fix what's broken. This is the playbook that will show you how to do that.

The first three sections of this book show *why* my program works, including the research and data to support my plan. Part One is all about what has happened to you—what got you to this broken state and why you feel the way you do. It explains the metabolic breakdown process, what caused it, and the symptoms you're likely feeling from it, such as low energy, lack of sleep, zero sex drive, and your body's lack of response to your dieting and exercise attempts.

Part Two explains the massive impact of stress on your body and what you can do to alleviate it. Whether you realize it or not, stress is at the root of your metabolic breakdown. This section of the book is designed to explain the three major culprits that elicit the stress response, causing the Metabolic Breakdown Cycle, *high-achieving lifestyle, toxicity, and food-driven inflammation;* these eventually lead to altered hormones and the ultimate consequence, *total metabolic lethargy*. If these three areas are left out of control, they will eventually destroy your metabolism by first altering your hormones and eventually completely wiping out your metabolism, destroying your energy, body, and desire for life. You can't beat a stress issue by adding more stress. You have to reduce or eliminate it from your routine, and this section will illustrate the reasons why.

Part Three will teach you about the Stark Naked lifestyle and how to get the most out of your 21-day reset. In this section, I will explain why you are going to focus on getting more sleep and why cutting back on your exercise program will help you recharge your broken metabolism and lay the groundwork for your new life as an optimized high performer. I will also give you cutting-edge mindset solutions to help you thrive throughout the Reset. I'm not going to sugarcoat things. The first week can be tough, but this section will show you how to win before you start by helping you buffer daily stress and learning to lead a resilient, optimized life after completing the Reset. Remember it's your current lifestyle choices that have beaten you down. You cannot expect to reset your metabolism and then successfully go back to your old way of living. You have got to fix what's broken and then live a new healthier way of life that supports your reset metabolism—not destroys it.

Parts Four and Five detail how my program works. Part Four is the Stark Naked 21-Day Metabolic Reset. Everything you need for success is in Part Four. If you are eager to start right away, go ahead and jump ahead to Part Four and start rocking. But trust me, as your body and energy begin to transform, eventually you are going to want to know the reasons why my program works, because it defies everything you thought you knew. When that happens, simply go back and read Parts One through Three to learn the "why." You'll be glad you did!

Part Five shows you how to live the Stark Naked life *optimized* after you complete the Reset. Once you feel great again, you won't ever want to return to your previous way of living. The way to an optimized life, in which you have built resiliency into your high-achieving lifestyle, can be found here.

I want you to know that I will be with you every step of the way. You are not alone on this journey, and you don't have to be afraid of the road that lies ahead. I assure you, I've been where you are right now. I know exactly how you're feeling. Together, we will walk this path to better health and wellness and discover what it truly means to not only look, but also feel great.

Are you ready to get started?

Me too!

Let's go!

▶ PART ONE

YOU'RE HAVING A BREAKDOWN

1

You're Having a Breakdown—
a Metabolic Breakdown

"CARBOHYDRATES ARE THE DEVIL!"

"Eating fat makes you fat!"

"Do a cleanse!"

"Learn to control your caloric intake."

"Eat more protein!"

"No, wait. Protein kills!"

"Eat vegetarian."

"Go raw."

"Go vegan."

"Go gluten-free."

"Don't eat sugar."

"Don't eat wheat."

"Don't eat dairy."

"Don't eat at all. Just juice!"

Is anyone else confused by all the nutrition and diet information being thrown at us today?

What makes navigating this maze of information even harder is that these "theories," "diets," "plans," and "programs" are each highly researched and, for the most part, backed up by bona fide scientific research by doctors who all tout the health benefits their program allegedly provides.

Worse yet, each program promises to become the next miraculous solution to improve *anyone* and *everyone*.

So who is right? Welcome to my worst nightmare!

If you are bewildered when it comes to eating right and choosing the best foods for you, you are not alone. A 2012 food and health study presented by the International Food Information Council Foundation showed that 52 percent of Americans surveyed thought it was easier to figure out their taxes than healthy eating.

There are so many nutrition plans, diets, and options available, it's no wonder people don't know which way to turn. The biggest problem is that most of the information out there is conflicting! Worse, it's often driven by a larger-than-life personality who has a need to be right. Even if the information being offered has merit, it isn't always geared toward your individual needs. That makes it truly hard to know who to trust or which program is best for you.

And that's a big problem, because what you eat has a huge impact on your health. Everything you're doing to eat "right" is probably wrong.

Fad Diets Aren't the Answer

These days I don't really think of myself as a personal trainer as much as a health and performance coach to many of today's highest achievers and some of the fittest people on earth. In fact, one of my clients, who is the most sought-after real estate coach in the country, refers to me as *his* performance and energy coach! I take that role and title very seriously, because he is a guy who is on the road 230 days a year, speaking to capacity crowds day in and day out, someone who absolutely needs his energy and performance to be at peak levels all the time.

Over the years, almost all of my clients have come to count on me to know about the latest information in all areas of health, nutrition, and fitness, which means I need to be on top of the latest and not so greatest next fad diet that overpromises and underdelivers. They ask me, because most of them want to try it, have tried it, or know someone who has tried it, and so on.

I have sifted through just about every theory, program, and promise *and* the science that backs those diet plans. After going through each from every point of view, I have discovered one very important thing. *Most are not sustainable for long-term success, especially for people like you—the high achievers of the world.*

Although they may initially create some positive results, eventually each one of those trendy fad diets will stop working. Some are actually so dangerous that over time you may actually start damaging your overall health. That's because most nutritional strategies today are designed for the overwhelming number of people who are looking for shortcuts to weight loss, expecting a magic pill to cure their bad habits.

I recently had a client tell me he was considering going on a 15-day juice and coconut-water cleanse.

"Are you moving to Gilligan's Island?" I asked.

He looked at me as though *I* was the crazy person in the room. He was stunned by my straight-faced reaction. I really think he believed juice and coconut water were healthy choices for 15 days. Sure, he might have lost some weight, but the second he went off that diet, he would have put it right back on and wouldn't have earned any benefit for his effort.

"The only reason I can think of to sustain yourself on fruit juice and coconut water for two weeks is if you're stranded on a deserted island," I said.

Seriously, if you are going to put yourself through a program of any sort, doesn't it make more sense to learn how to sustain yourself on a food-based program that you can live by and maintain for the long term? More so, one that has multiple health benefits beyond weight loss?

It's like asking a dermatologist for a remedy for your wrinkles, when your real issue is dry, flaky skin, red blotches, and brown spots. People just can't see past the wrinkles!

People have been led to believe that weight loss is the sole solution to all our health and fitness needs and that because a program makes you lose weight quickly, it's a good program. People who choose a juice cleanse are typically unmotivated to do the necessary work to sustain long-term results. They're looking for a shortcut to weight loss, a magic cure, a quick fix. They're into fad diets, not *health* and *wellness*. They may see weight-loss benefits from the next hot diet plan, but they aren't necessarily getting healthy or creating a lifestyle that will sustain habits to maintain their weight loss. They are merely creating a temporary mindset that achieves their immediate desired result, but no long-term payoff.

For example, if you go on a low-fat diet, you may lose a little weight in the beginning, but in the long run you end up having issues with low energy, lack of sex drive, a sluggish brain, depression, and increased body fat due to a lethargic metabolism. Your brain and your hormones need fat to function optimally. You get the quick initial weight-loss result, but you are trading optimal health for a number on the scale. It's not ideal.

Likewise, removing carbohydrates from your diet creates some weight loss and improved energy on the front end, but if deprived of carbs long enough, the thyroid is guaranteed to struggle and slow down, which will lead to low energy and eventually unwanted fat gain. *Translation: If you're not eating carbs, but gaining weight—now you know why!*

Fad diets are not the answer for people looking for a lifestyle that will sustain both feeling great and looking great. They are not long-term solutions, but simply stressful ways to manipulate your body to quickly force weight off. Here's the bottom line: to obtain long-term weight loss, *you must fix the problem that is causing fat storage* and not damage the body more just to drop numbers on your scale.

Eating "healthy" and working out longer and harder aren't the answers either. I meet so many people who think they're doing everything right and making good food and exercise choices, but realizing zero results! It's so darn frustrating! As a matter of fact, most people start noticing they're feeling even worse as time goes on.

"If I Am Doing Everything Right, Why Do I Still Feel So Bad?"

My client Misty is a thirty-eight-year-old mother of four living in Oregon who was highly committed to eating healthy and routinely exercising, but she was at her wits end because she wasn't getting the kind of results she wanted. Misty is a stay-at-home mom who also works as an onsite apartment manager in the complex where her family lives, so she juggles a lot of responsibility. She paid attention to her diet and believed she was making good, healthy choices about what she was putting in her body. Misty was extremely disciplined, avoided fast food and processed foods, watched her caloric intake, and focused on eating a clean, whole-foods diet most of the time. I totally believe she only put the foods she told me about in her system. Her efforts had rewarded her with excess weight gain instead of a slimmer body. Emotionally she felt so bad, she started taking antidepressants, which only brought on severe fatigue.

During Misty's quest for answers she constantly concluded that she must be eating too much or not exercising enough, because no one could give her another rational explanation for her weight gain. She tried every diet she could find—low-fat, low-carb, and low-calorie—you name it, she tried it. She was willing to try anything just to lose a little weight and feel better.

Her frustrations with exercise were no different. Her only answer was to spend more time in the gym or suck it up and exercise with more intensity. This wasn't an easy task for someone who had to summon up all her natural energy just to get from her bed to the coffee pot in the morning and pray for a kick-start. Caffeine became her lifeline to survive the day ahead of her.

During our first meeting, Misty was shocked when I told her there was no exercise program that would give her the results she was looking for and she should dramatically reduce her exercise commitment every week to start with. I am always amazed at the reaction I get when I first tell new clients that.

"Are you crazy? I will blow up like a balloon if I exercise less."

That's the usual response I hear from people when I tell them this. Misty had fallen hard for the old-school approach of doing more and trying harder to the point of exhaustion. Her body was overstressed.

I did some testing on Misty to see what was really breaking down in her body. Her diagnostic results showed that her liver was overwhelmed from all the coffee she consumed throughout the day and from excessive amounts of exercise. The second thing her results showed was that Misty was experiencing extreme food-driven inflammation. The foods she was choosing to eat were certainly considered healthy foods, but for Misty they were contributing to her problems.

These two conditions were placing extreme stress on Misty's metabolism and causing what I call the Metabolic Breakdown Cycle. Her metabolism had gone into self-protection mode. What Misty needed was to stop the deprivation and exercise abuse and reset her broken metabolism.

It's as simple as this. If I want my car to go faster but I have four flat tires, what will help more? Fixing the tires or pushing the gas pedal as hard as possible to the floor?

You first have to fix what's broken!

Understanding Your Metabolism

After many years of rejuvenating worn-down high achievers, I have discovered the Metabolic Breakdown Cycle. This is the breakdown process that slowly destroys your metabolism and prevents you from experiencing great energy, amazing clarity, a rockin' body, and a youthful sex drive.

Metabolism is one of the most misunderstood of the body's systems. A lot of people talk about "metabolism" and yet few really understand what it is or how it affects health and vitality. This is especially clear whenever I ask my clients what they think metabolism is. Most people say metabolism is the amount of energy a person's body burns or that it has something to do with the thyroid. When I push a little farther for clarity, some say that when the thyroid gets sluggish, they have a slow or sluggish metabolism and that's why they get fat. Although that is all true, over the years I have come to understand that our metabolism is really so much more than that.

Even medical professionals have varying definitions. The classic thought on metabolism is that it is the sum total of all chemical reactions in the body.

However, my favorite definition of metabolism comes from *The Schwarzbein Principle,* by Dr. Diana Schwarzbein and Nancy Deville: "Metabolism is the combined effects of all the varied biochemical processes that continually occur in your body on a cellular level. These processes enable every individual component of your body to function, making it possible for you to think, digest food, move, and perform all the functions of a living, breathing being."

These metabolic processes include such things as hormone production, tissue regeneration, digestion, elimination, and immune responses. In fact, *everything* going on in your body impacts the sum total of your metabolism. If any one of these processes gets a little out of balance, your metabolism pays the price.

Okay, what does that really mean? And more so, what does that mean to you?

For example, if your liver is congested and working on overdrive, it will have a huge negative impact on your metabolism by slowing down your thyroid hormones. Your liver is largely responsible for converting the mostly inactive form of the thyroid hormone, T4, into the active form, T3. It really doesn't matter how little you eat or how hard you exercise; those things won't help your congested liver, heal your damaged metabolism, or prevent the result: unwanted fat storage.

Recent studies have shown that metabolism isn't just a set of automatic physical processes—it's also affected by the emotional connection between the mind and body. What we think and feel impacts our body chemistry. That means everything from stress to pleasure has a profound impact on metabolism.

Think about that for a moment. *Everything that happens in your daily life affects your metabolism!*

When stress hormones get out of whack or stress levels stay chronically elevated over time, they cause a cascade of problems, from wrecking your digestion to causing hormone imbalance and chronic fatigue. I see living proof of this every day in my clients who suffer the effects of stress in their daily lives before doing the Stark Naked 21-Day Metabolic Reset, and there's lots of research proving my point, including studies that show high stress loads can block the production of sex hormones for men and women. As soon as those hormones are out of balance, your metabolism starts falling apart and you will eventually hit the wall from total adrenal burnout. When that happens, you're shot.

Stress is the trigger that breaks homeostasis, the body's ability to maintain internal stability, and affects metabolism. What this means is that you can be eating what some expert deems a "perfect" diet, but if one of your metabolic processes is dysfunctional, your metabolism is going to start to show problems until that dysfunction is fixed. For example, you can eat a low-carb diet, exercise fifteen times a week, and do a thousand crunches a day, but instead of the hard body you're pushing so hard to get, all you're going to end up with is a miserable, frustrating existence.

One of the biggest challenges I face with clients is getting them to believe they aren't being cheated by a faulty metabolism. They are cheating themselves by living the way they do. Oftentimes, clients come to me saying things like, "I can't lose weight because my metabolism is slow," "I don't have the energy," or "Only skinny people have a high metabolism."

I hear the most absurd excuses from people, when in fact it's really a basic metabolic breakdown in their body machinery. Most everyone is born with a healthy metabolism, but, sadly, instead of preserving it, most people will spend their lifetime running it into the ground.

The Metabolic Breakdown Cycle

In the Metabolic Breakdown Cycle, stress, caused by your high-achieving lifestyle, a congested liver, and food-induced inflammation, eventually disrupts hormonal levels, leading to a lethargic metabolism.

METABOLIC BREAKDOWN CYCLE

STRESS (High Achieving Lifestyle, Toxicity, Food-Induced Inflammation) ⇨

Altered Hormones ⇨ Lethargic Metabolism

Physical signs that you are experiencing the Metabolic Breakdown Cycle include low sex drive, intense food cravings, difficulty waking in the morning, low energy throughout the day, gaining fat even though you are eating less and exercising more, sleep issues (exhausted in the morning, can't sleep at night), foggy thinking, increased joint pain, and lack of enjoyment in life.

Your Achilles' heel is the stress hormone known as *cortisol*. Cortisol is a steroid hormone released by the adrenals in response to stress and a low level of blood glucose. Its functions are to increase blood glucose through gluconeogenesis, to suppress the immune system, and to aid the metabolism of fat, protein, and carbohydrates.

Unfortunately, this hormone has gotten a bad rap over the years, but I believe it's misunderstood. Depending on your situation, cortisol can either be your best friend or your worst enemy. We've all heard remarkable stories of superhuman strength in a crisis, such as a woman being able to lift a car off her child with one arm or a man breaking down a door during a fire—that's cortisol working at its finest.

If you ever find yourself being pursued by a lion someday, you better hope your "fight or flight" response is able to fire on all cylinders and release optimal amounts of cortisol to save your life. But too much of this mighty powerful hormone, and it can easily become your worst enemy. Too much cortisol in your system for too long will leave you exhausted, fat, brain-dead, sex deprived, and depressed. As a high achiever, you're probably feeling like this right now. It is the insatiable desire to push physical and mental limits, to create more success in life, and to constantly be better that drives you into a chronic high-stress state. Your body doesn't know the difference between running from a lion or being stuck in traffic—meaning, to your body, stress is stress.

When your body is picking up signs of trouble, it essentially has one way to respond—and that's "fight or flight." Of course, unless you're living in the wilds of East Africa, it is unlikely that you will come across a real lion in your day-to-day activities. As a matter of fact, most likely you will rarely experience the kind of life-or-death situation that our early ancestors relied on the "fight or flight" response to protect them from.

A natural response that developed to help us survive acute bouts of stress is now misfiring within our bodies. As a result of this unnecessary stress response, we are unintentionally being robbed of our health and happiness. Worst of all, it's our own fault. We've created a world of false lions chasing us from the moment we wake to the moment we finally fall asleep—if we fall asleep.

You see, everything you do that causes stress in your life is a lion. The alarm clock startling you out of bed in the morning is a lion. The caffeine in your Starbucks coffee is a lion. Eating a poor breakfast or, worse, skipping breakfast altogether is a lion. Battling traffic is a lion. Dealing with fires at work, managing e-mails, deadlines, negative coworkers, jerk bosses—*all lions.*

Having an argument with your significant other or feeling guilty about missing your child's big game or recital? All these are situations that trigger the same response as a lion chasing you.

Eating what you think is a healthy lunch, not realizing that the almonds and corn you put on your salad may actually be creating large amounts of inflammation (and therefore stress) inside your body—yup, more little lions.

After work you force yourself to hit the gym for your high-intensity workout, because you've read it's the best way to lose your ever-increasing belly fat. What you don't realize is that you've been running from lions all day! By the time you get to the treadmill, you're already completely exhausted, but your body has to dig deeper to find the energy to help you survive yet another bout of stress. You drag your now completely wiped-out self home, grabbing another small cup of coffee-flavored lion on the way.

You force down a bland no-carb dinner, because you've heard that carbs at dinner make you fat. Then you pour yourself a large glass of red lion—oops, I mean wine—to help you unwind and quickly fall asleep on the couch. Your significant other startles you awake and then tells you to come to bed—causing your subconscious to search for the immediate danger. More lions.

As soon as you lie down, he or she starts to get a little frisky, but guess what? Nothing happens on your end, because even if you wanted to, you can't get turned on. You've got no mojo! Great—another lion!

Here's the good news. *It's not your fault your mojo is lacking.*

Your body is inherently wired for survival. When the body thinks it is at high risk, nothing else matters. It wants to keep you alive. There is no way it's going to allow you to get distracted by a possible roll in the hay and end up dead! So you're left lying in bed for the rest of the night, upset and embarrassed, and your now-racing mind is creating more non-life-threatening emotional and mental high-stress situations—releasing more lions. More lions means more cortisol, leading to hormonal disruption, and eventually a lethargic metabolism. It's a vicious and never-ending cycle!

And that is the metabolic breakdown. You will never beat a stress problem by applying more stress.

Eating healthy and exercising are supposed to be fun, simple, and enjoyable. They should be your secret weapons to solve your basic health problems, to help you look great and feel your best. But for too many of my clients—and probably you too—they are two of the most ferocious lions.

When (Seemingly) Good Food Makes You Feel Bad

As a health and wellness expert, I constantly find myself in the unexpected position of having to steer my clients away from eating certain foods that most of us would deem healthy and nutritious, such as blueberries, salmon, broccoli, whole grains, and most nuts. Often, the suspicious culprits are causing digestive intolerances and other disorders that my clients would never have considered were tied to the "healthy" diet they thought they were eating.

Eating healthy and *eating right for your body* are two separate issues. Even if you are eating *healthy* foods, your body may not be metabolizing those foods in a *healthy way*. Inflammation results, causing more stress, bloating, joint pain, water retention, and foggy thinking. Basically, you feel like crap and may not even know it. People learn to live feeling bad. Worse, they accept it as *normal*. It's not normal.

My client Misty was eating all the right foods that were traditionally considered healthy—but for her they were internally raising hell. I remember an e-mail I received from Misty questioning the value of gluten and dairy. Was all of the information she was reading and hearing in the media on the "dangers" of both just hype, or did she really need to be careful? Believe it or not, I commonly get questions from my clients about these, since most nutritionists deem wheat and dairy quite necessary staples in the diet for good health.

Let me regain my composure from that last statement and get the sour taste out of my mouth from having to say it.

Okay. I'm back.

Bull! Neither is necessary!

While following the exact 21-Day Reset outlined in this book, Misty removed all the most common food triggers from her diet, including gluten and dairy, reduced unneeded stressors on the liver, focused on gentle daily liver support, and reduced her exercise. Within 21 days Misty lost 10 pounds and 3 inches off her waist. She no longer needed or craved coffee for energy.

When the time came, I allowed Misty to reintroduce gluten and dairy in the form of pizza after she had had been on the program for 60 days (pizza, mind you, a food that was given to an NFL athlete client of mine during training camp by the team's nutritionist and told it was an amazing source of protein and good carbs!).

Guess what happened?

The retaliation by her body was downright violent. She was extremely fatigued and miserable the following day. She also took multiple unwanted trips to the bathroom. Ouch! Not fun!

Misty had never noticed a reaction to pizza like that before, but definitely recognized the lethargy and depressed feelings from her prior life. She got such great results on the Reset, because she found the source of her Metabolic Breakdown Cycle and fixed it! She was simply eating the wrong foods for her body! Instead of fueling her with great energy, the foods she was eating were really robbing her of her best life and causing serious harm to her metabolism.

I know exactly how Misty felt, because I grew up unaware that an ailment I was suffering from was the result of a reaction to food. I vividly remember being a kid who sucked on four inhalers a day and struggled for every gasp of air; I watched my mom cry because she didn't know what to do to alleviate my struggles to breathe. I spent my early childhood on a dairy farm. I grew up thinking cow's milk was a must and good for strong bones. I consumed an awful lot of dairy, sometimes drinking more than a gallon of milk a week on my own. But milk, as it turned out, was the direct cause of my asthma. Too bad I didn't figure that out until I was thirty-two years old. But once I did, it was amazing how much easier it was to exercise, sleep, and relax, because I was no longer struggling with asthma or being loaded up on the medicine in inhalers.

Just because food is considered healthy and nutritious by someone else's standard, it doesn't mean your body can break it down, assimilate it, or tolerate it in a way that makes it healthy for you.

If you have a digestive disorder or severe food allergy, you already know this. However, if you are unaware of the foods and poor eating habits that might be placing unnecessary stress on your digestive process or causing inflammation, irritation, or other adverse reactions—you could go on feeling bad yet thinking you are eating healthy for years!

Here's what I mean. Are you someone who eats lots of raw veggies thinking they are good for you? Believe it or not, raw vegetables can cause severe bloating and acid reflux. The fructose found in fruits such as mangos, pears, apples, watermelon, grapes, cherries, dried fruits, and fruit juices can cause abdominal pain, bloating, and diarrhea. In some cases, it can even trigger symptoms in patients who suffer from irritable bowel syndrome (IBS) who don't normally have trouble digesting fructose.

Or maybe you're familiar with these habits. Almost all of my clients are people who are constantly on the go—meaning they are up and out of bed early and often out of the house before the sun rises. By the time most people are rolling out of bed and turning on the morning news, they've been to the gym, showered, and are already at their office or well into their day. For many, breakfast is something they might eat on weekends. This is a huge mistake. We all grew up hearing the line, "Breakfast is the most important meal of the day." And for good reason—it is. You wouldn't head out on a long road trip on an empty tank of gas. Why would you start your day on an empty stomach?

Believe it or not, coffee—even a venti triple latte—*is not a meal!*

But what if you do eat breakfast?

A bowl of Kashi cereal with fat-free milk and a banana may be deemed a healthy breakfast by many, but in reality it's the worst way to start your day! You are far better off eating pure protein such as chicken or bison in the morning than carbs. Why?

Your body is designed to be at its peak energy level between 7:00 and 10:00 A.M. If you don't feed it the right foods to wake your brain up and stabilize energy, you'll be dragging all morning, grumpy, and struggling with hunger. By lunch, you'll be so hungry, you'll more than likely blow it, eating all the wrong foods and sending all of the wrong messages through your system.

On the Stark Naked 21-Day Metabolic Reset, you will learn to eat three perfectly balanced, healthy meals throughout the day for *your* metabolism that will leave you feeling satisfied while stabilizing your blood-sugar levels, which will help level and maintain your mood and energy.

A lot of people supplement their diet by consuming energy drinks instead of eating food. They actually believe these sugar- and caffeine-laden drinks are good for them. Although these drinks might be popular, believe me, they're the devil in disguise. There is nothing in these drinks of any redeeming value. In fact, for many people, the stimulants in these drinks can actually cause problems, such as elevated blood pressure, palpitations, and muscle tremors.

These are all examples of "healthy" foods that may actually be damaging your body and making you feel really bad. So many people never make this connection!

Later in this book you will learn the most common food-sensitivity stressors that are crushing people's metabolisms. We have isolated these over the last two years by looking at labs from hundreds of high achievers just like you. To give you an idea of what I'm talking about, here are some of the other common foods that were causing me problems: salmon, beef, apples, corn, soy, and gluten. These are considered some of the healthiest foods we eat, but consuming these foods was only causing me harm, because my body couldn't break them down and they were, therefore, holding me back from all the promises of eating that healthy diet. It was a real catch-22 until I finally figured it out.

Anyone want to take bets that you're in the same boat?

When you remove the wrong foods for your body from your diet—even if they're thought to be healthy or good for you, these foods are actually acting as toxins in your body—there will be a short-term impact. I've noticed that clients who give up sugar, dairy, wheat, or processed foods go through a period of major discomfort as they purge the toxins from their system. I've even had clients reduce their carbohydrate intake and describe their symptoms a few days later as "flu-like," including a headache, fatigue, achy muscles, and brain fog. What's happening there is the body is making a metabolic switch from burning glucose from carbohydrates for energy to burning fat and protein instead, and that causes those horrible feelings.

So here's the only bad news about doing the Stark Naked 21-Day Metabolic Reset. Depending on your individual state of health and current nutritional strategies, you might have to suffer for a few days before you begin to feel the benefits of the program.

The good news? This transitional period will pass. And once it does, you will start to feel so good you won't believe you ever allowed yourself to feel that bad.

There's actually a name for this process—the Herxheimer reaction—which is feeling worse before you feel better. Dr. Herxheimer noticed that the symptoms of many patients suffering from syphilis would actually intensify before improving. Interestingly, those patients whose discomfort was the worst during treatment were the strongest and healed the fastest.

Although Dr. Herxheimer's discoveries took place more than a century ago, there is a tremendous amount of relevance to what I see with my clients every day. Anytime you make a radical change in lifestyle, especially when it comes to your diet and health habits, your body will have a strong reaction. From my point of view, the more severe the response, the better the result will be.

Three months into her new lifestyle, Misty sent me an e-mail saying she was down 17 pounds from the start of the program and was superexcited, because she had just returned from purchasing new skinny clothes for summer. She also shared she had been off her antidepressants since we changed her lifestyle and has an amazingly happy outlook on life. The best part of all is that she is experiencing extreme enjoyment being an energetic, present, and naturally happy mom to her children. As for me, receiving these types of e-mails on a regular basis is the best part of my job!

The Downside of Overexercising

Believe it or not, too much of a good thing can actually be destructive and harmful to your health. I see so many of my clients experiencing the downside of overexercising. If you want the greatest benefit of your time in the gym, your recovery has to offset your training volume. If it doesn't, then all of that excessive exercise is only damaging you, not enhancing you. There is a reason the greatest athletes on the planet sleep 10 to 12 hours per night. They learned early on that their bodies need that much time to rest to enhance recovery from their high volume of physical exercise. Doing this allows them to excel in their field and outperform their competition.

Once you are eating the right foods for your body and your metabolism isn't in a stressed state, it only takes a minimal amount of exercise to get great results.

Don't believe me? Check this out. Most of my professional athlete clients train only 4 days a week for no more than 45 minutes at a time, and they get *insane* results. If you're training more than that and not seeing the kind of results you'd like, I assure you the Metabolic Breakdown Cycle has begun and you need to take steps to fix whatever's broken in your system before you will be happy with your health and fitness results.

Breaking the Cycle

Logically, the solution to solving a stress-driven cycle is not to add more stress to the equation, like a calorie-deprivation plan or more exercise. You can't deprive a high achiever like yourself of carbohydrates, fats, proteins, or calories and expect to perform at an optimal level. You also can't remove yourself from your high-stress, goal-driven world. This will only result in feelings of loss or displacement and depression.

So what is the answer? The ultimate fix for a broken metabolism is to slow down and give your body a break. You must *reset* and *optimize* your metabolism, creating a resiliency that helps you withstand your enemy, *stress*.

Recovery, better known as *rest*, is the one thing you probably don't think you need or make time for, yet it's the one thing science has been showing us makes a major difference in staying healthy and having the stamina to conquer your dreams. Recovery is how your body recharges itself. It's how it replenishes all your hormones, and it's how your body recovers from the stress you deal with each day. Research has shown that what separates the highest performers in the world from average performers is an increased ability to recover.

In a 2009 study by Eric G. Potterat, in which elite military performers (Navy SEALs) were compared to nonelite military performers, it was discovered that the elite participants demonstrated more substantial heart-rate dipping (the amount of change in heart rate from waking to sleeping) during daily living than the nonelite participants. When these elite performers slept and the parasympathetic nervous system took over to induce recovery, their heart rate dipped by 29 percent versus a 21 percent dip for the nonelite. The greater dip meant they were getting more restorative sleep even when sleep periods were dramatically reduced. We're not all going to be Navy SEALs, but we can all stop focusing on trying to outwork everyone and start focusing more on recovery.

So guess what? From eliminating food-induced inflammation to emphasizing sleep, recovery is the critical component of the Stark Naked 21-Day Metabolic Reset.

Yes, sleep. I figured out that if I can get you to sleep better, you will get better results. Sleep is literally your secret to feeling amazing, looking great, and having the stamina to reach all of your goals in life. It's your greatest ally and the ultimate fountain of youth. Best of all? It's a lot cheaper than Botox and filler!

Still don't believe me? Research from 2007 links greater heart-rate dipping with lower risk of all-cause mortality, and elevated heart rate in general is associated with an increased risk of cardiovascular and noncardiovascular death. That's a scary thought when one of the most common things I see with new clients is an elevated morning resting heart rate.

And if that hasn't convinced you, maybe this will. Cheating your sleep is making you fat!

"Tired" and "fat" seem to go together like peas and carrots, peanut butter and jelly, and pizza and beer. There is no doubt that lack of sleep is related to an increase in hunger and weight gain. Research done by Columbia University looked at eighteen thousand men and women between the ages of thirty-two and fifty-nine and discovered some shocking realities about cheating sleep. Those who slept 4 or less hours a night were 73 percent more likely to be obese than those who slept 7 to 9 hours, and those who slept 5 hours a night were 50 percent more likely to be obese.

If you're not getting enough sleep, your metabolism cannot be supercharged, thereby keeping you lean and healthy.

You're going to hear this a lot throughout this book, but the real secret to great performance in any arena is the ultimate competitive advantage provided by *recovery*. All great performers know this. Have you ever noticed how great performers always share how hard they work, flaunt their crazy exercise regimes, and announce their drive to be the best? What they never share, though, is their game-changing recovery strategies.

Great performers focus on recovery, but they never let their competition know that's their secret. They want them to believe they work insanely hard and never have time to rest. And that's the reason they win, and others don't.

It's Time to Relax and Conquer

When it comes to feeling great, it isn't about working out harder and longer. Feeling great through this method is an empty promise. That old-school approach of using misery, deprivation, and discipline to do whatever it takes to lose weight and look good is over.

Done. As in diddy, diddy, done, done.

It's not about the latest fad diet or calorie count. It's not about overexercising.

Got it?

If you want to really stand out in this world, in your arena, regardless of what it is, then stop stressing your body and overworking and start focusing on the ultimate competitive advantage by learning to *relax and conquer.*

Let's face it. True high achievers won't really slow down or actually take a break until they feel it's critical. And that's exactly why you need this metabolic reset!

You won't slow down or take a break because . . .

You feel "guilty" if you aren't "busy."

You feel "lazy" if you aren't "working."

You feel "useless" if you aren't "doing" something—anything.

Have I hit a nerve yet?

Look, I get it. I work with high achievers every day, and here's what I know for sure. Until you teach high achievers the benefits and the rewards of saving their energy, looking better, getting more done, sleeping better, wanting and having more and better sex, they won't stop—won't take a break and definitely will never see the benefits of resting their body. Trust me, even if you don't know it or aren't willing to admit it yet, these are the things high achievers care about—and rightfully so.

Logically, high achievers need to be supported differently than lazy people who would prefer to never get off of the couch. High achievers need fats, proteins, vegetables, and carbohydrates every day, because they have to manage their stress and replenish that energy they are wiping out day in and day out from their high-stress lifestyle.

The strategies of the Stark Naked 21-Day Metabolic Reset and lifestyle plan are designed to heal the damage caused by the Metabolic Breakdown Cycle and protect your reset metabolism so you don't repeat the cycle over and over again.

Now that you know something's broken, you can choose to fix it.

You can accept feeling awful or choose to feel awesome and full of energy, living your *best* life in good health.

▶ PART TWO

STOP FOOLING YOURSELF AND FIX WHAT'S BROKEN

2

What Do You Mean Stress Is My Problem?

The Impact of High Cortisol Levels

WHAT DO YOU MEAN *stress* is my problem? I don't feel stressed!"

I wish I had a dollar for every time I heard that statement from one of my clients. Even if they are the most stressed-out people on the planet, most of them don't know it!

The majority of us live our complete adult lives dealing with and pushing through symptoms of stress such as anxiety, foggy thinking, bloating, weight and fat gain, lack of sex drive, and sleep issues, just to name a few. According to the Centers for Disease Control (CDC), *up to 90 percent of all illness and disease is stress-related.*

Stop and think about that for a second. How is it possible that my clients aren't aware of their stress?

Because stress isn't always recognizable. In fact, the most dangerous thing about stress, especially for high achievers, is how easily it can creep up on you or, worse, how fast you can learn to accept it as normal.

Ignorance is bliss—except when it comes to stress! When stress is allowed to linger in the body for too long, there's nothing blissful about it. When you don't know how much stress is really affecting you, you can't possibly understand the toll it's taking. Although the impact of stress is different for everyone, one thing that's for sure is that overwhelming stress can and usually does lead to serious health problems, from weakening the immune system, to high blood pressure, weight gain, sleep loss, lower sex drive, memory loss, skin conditions, and heart disease. Stress is one of the major causes of breakdown in the body.

Look, our everyday lives are full of common hassles such as traffic, deadlines, relationship conflicts, money concerns, child-care issues, and everyday experiences that can trigger a stress response in the body. Stress becomes so frequent that you may not recognize the impact it's having on you. I know it's easy to believe that a little symptom like being a slow starter in the morning is simply something that comes with the territory for those with drive and a work ethic, but the truth is, it's an early sign that stress is negatively impacting your health.

For the majority of my clients, stress is a part of their daily functioning, so much so that they may actually believe they're thriving because of it.

I have a news flash! They're not. No one really does.

Sure, in small doses, stress can act as a great motivator, but when it comes in large waves for long periods of time, eventually you will crash and burn, because your mind and body cannot take the emotional and physical toll.

Stress is a normal physical response to events that make you feel threatened or upset your balance in some way. When you sense danger, whether it's real or not, your body's defenses kick into the "fight or flight" reaction, or what experts often refer to as the stress response. This response is the body's way of protecting you from danger. If everything is status quo, this response helps you stay focused, energetic, and alert. However, if you're constantly overwhelmed with what the body perceives as a threat or problem, you will eventually be stopped cold in your tracks. Prolonged stress can cause major dam-

Physical Reactions to Stress

Stress impacts everyone differently. Some of the most common symptoms are characteristics of other ailments, so it's easy for most people to brush them off as something else. These "side effects" often include:

- Insomnia
- Clenched or tight jaw
- Teeth grinding at night
- Digestive issues
- Difficulty swallowing
- Tight throat or the feeling of a lump in the throat
- Antsy behavior
- Increased heart rate
- Restlessness
- Achy muscles or muscle tension
- Tight chest or chest pain
- Dizziness or light-headedness
- Hyperventilation
- Sweaty palms
- Nervousness
- Stammering
- High blood pressure
- Low energy
- Fatigue
- Mental slowness
- Negative thoughts
- Constant irritation
- Forgetfulness
- Lack of concentration
- Being easily overwhelmed
- Frustration
- Apathy
- Helplessness
- Low sex drive
- Retreating from friends, family and work (avoidance)

age to your health, mood, body, relationships, and overall quality of life—no matter how great your diet is or how much you exercise.

This chapter is going to take a deeper look at how stress is like an energy vampire that feeds on the body and explore the significant impact it has on us. When you're in a chronic state of stress, it literally robs you of your best self and, therefore, your best health. What if you made some changes and instead of it taking three cups of coffee and a shower to really wake you, you were able to pop right out of bed without an alarm clock and actually enjoy your cup of coffee instead of requiring it for survival? Imagine how much more you could accomplish in your day by waking recharged and ready to conquer the world every morning.

I know most of you believe you handle your stress well, but the likelihood is you probably don't. *Don't wait until things have gotten so bad you need medical intervention to keep you going!*

Over the years, I've met hundreds if not thousands of CEOs and successful businesspeople who have had some type of optimism training. They have been taught to view everything as perfect! Those are the clients that tend to scare me the most.

Why?

Just because you believe your life is stress free, it doesn't mean stress isn't causing damage to your body. For example, stress causes your sex hormones to drop, which means you won't have any sex drive. Your insulin is blunted, causing your blood sugar to skyrocket and your brain to shrink. Your thyroid slows, which means the metabolic pathway for creating energy is disrupted, and the result is total lethargy and unwanted fat gain. These are hardly the traits of a high performer.

A lot of specialists and doctors refer to this condition as "accelerated aging," which is what I was suffering from when I was diagnosed with andropause. Although the idea of accelerated aging may be medically accurate, no one under the age of sixty-five wants to hear that, let alone accept it. I know I didn't!

The accelerated aging process robs you of your quality of life years before you hit rock bottom (more on that in Chapter 6). However, instead of proactively dealing with it, so many people I see in the gym or at one of my seminars choose to ignore it or, worse, glamorize it as one of the traits it takes to truly become successful. I don't want you to be one of those people who hits rock bottom. Once you understand how the stress response works and how it affects your body, you'll be eager to use the 21-Day Reset and get back to your best self.

To understand this better, let's start by exploring what triggers our stress response.

Stress: Your Ultimate Bodyguard

The stress response is triggered by three different categories of stress stimuli. The first category is *life-or-death stress,* which is caused by any situation that threatens your survival, such as almost getting in a car accident or waking at 4:00 A.M. and realizing an intruder is in your house. When life-or-death situations arise, you want to have the necessary energy to respond well. That's why it's important to reduce the drain on your energy reserves from non-life-threatening stress.

The second category is *mental/emotional stress,* which is generated in response to life's challenges and demanding situations. Mental/emotional stress can be caused by life-altering events, such as the death of a loved one, divorce, or the loss of a job, or ordinary events, such as speaking in front of an audience, dealing with a jerk boss, having your spouse yell at you, or simply sitting in traffic. Your mindset determines your response to these types of situations and dictates how your stress response will be activated. With non-life-altering stressors like being stuck in traffic, if you start focusing on negative things that *could* happen, such as being fired for arriving late to a meeting, you will ignite the stress response. Your mind spins with all sorts of terrible possibilities, creating a sense of alarm based on fantasy. In reality, everything is actually okay.

Much of the advice available on how to handle stress deals with this category. If you've read any of it, you know that to prevent your stress response from firing in these non-life-threatening situations, you need to learn how to develop a "bulletproof" mind by curbing your propensity for creating negative outcomes and calming your mind down with activities such as yoga or meditation. In his book *The Way of the SEAL* and online training program *The Unbeatable Mind,* Mark Divine has developed one of my favorite approaches for developing a bulletproof mind.

Even after you've worked hard to build a strong mental outlook, as I have, it's easy for this type of stress to rear its ugly head. A few weeks ago, I was overwhelmed and tired. My wife and I had recently had our third child, so sleep deprivation was causing my mind to play games with me. Tom Ferry, a world famous real-estate coach, walked into the gym at 5:30 A.M. to get a workout in and immediately asked me if I was okay. I don't hide my emotions well. I replied, "Yeah, but my world is out of control. I am feeling so overwhelmed right now."

With a little snicker, he looked around the gym and said, "That's interesting. Your world looks calm and stable to me. You sure it's out of control, or is your thinking making it out of control?"

That simple question brought me back to reality and helped me realize I was creating situations that weren't really happening. It is so easy to let your mind get the best of you and trigger your stress response.

Lifestyle stress is the third category. Reducing lifestyle stress is essential to the Stark Naked 21-Day Metabolic Reset and ultimately will become a part of your everyday lifestyle. Throughout this book you are going to zero in on your most common lifestyle stress triggers and remove them. Lifestyle stress is caused by how you are living your life, your personal behaviors and habits. Cheating sleep, not drinking enough water, eating the wrong foods at the wrong time, and drinking too much coffee are examples of behaviors that trigger the stress response. If you can control these stressors, your life will dramatically change for the better. Let's look at how stress is robbing you of your ultimate energy, focus, and body.

How the Body Responds to Stress

The stress response begins in the brain. When your brain receives signals from your body that something is wrong, it sends an "Oh sh-t" signal to the section of the brain called the hypothalamus. The hypothalamus is a major control center for hormone production, and its primary function is to keep the body in a calm, optimized state. When the hypothalamus receives a stress signal, it works through your nervous system and its crime-fighting partner, the pituitary gland, to heighten your body's ability to respond to danger. The hypothalamus and pituitary trigger your adrenal glands to immediately release the hormone adrenaline followed by the hormone cortisol.

Adrenaline triggers your heart to beat faster, pushing blood to the muscles, heart, and other vital organs. The increase in pulse rate and elevation in blood pressure cause you to start breathing more rapidly and the airways in the lungs to open wide, allowing you to take in extra oxygen that gets carried to the brain, increasing your alertness. Adrenaline also triggers the release of blood sugar (glucose) and fats from storage in the body to help give you the energy to fight or run away from danger. This adrenaline response is so fast, most people don't even realize it's happened; they just know they feel really weird. The adrenals then follow up by releasing the stress hormone cortisol. Cortisol is released to make sure the body stays in this heightened state for as long as it takes to deal with the threat. Once the threat has subsided, cortisol levels decrease, allowing the body to go into recovery mode and replenish itself for the next life-or-death situation.

Your Inner Hulk, or When Stress Becomes Your Evil Foe

The transformation of Bruce Banner into the Hulk in the movie *The Incredible Hulk* is an excellent example of the stress response in action—and how it can become your worst enemy. A quiet child, Bruce Banner grew up in a very stressful environment. He lived with an abusive father and was constantly picked on by school bullies. Extremely intelligent, he eventually became a nuclear engineer for the military. During a test of a bomb he created, Banner was exposed to high levels of gamma radiation, transforming him into the Hulk. Because Banner had such a stressful childhood, his stress response system was very sensitive, and as soon as his body released the stress hormone adrenaline, the brutish Hulk would emerge.

Like all of us, the Hulk does not respond well to stress. He has a childlike intelligence, makes poor decisions, and becomes a very destructive menace to society. Sound anything like how you respond when stressed? Every once in a while the Hulk would do something heroic, but just like our own typical responses under stress, those times are few and far apart. Banner eventually discovered strategies to manage his response to stress, so that the Hulk would only emerge under extreme situations, not at the drop of a hat.

We all have a Hulk inside of us. It can be used for the greater good in extreme situations, but most of us have yet to obtain control of our inner Hulk. Your inner Hulk emerges most frequently from mental/emotional triggers, like sitting in traffic. I love watching the Hulk appear in cars around me in Southern California traffic. The inner Hulk causes people to honk and scream, slam

---

Chef Amar Santana, owner of Broadway by Amar Santana
Laguna Beach, California
Age thirty-two

▶ *Chef Amar Santana is one of Orange County's rising stars in the culinary world with his wildly successful flagship restaurant Broadway by Amar Santana in Laguna Beach. A chef's lifestyle is a big ball of stress. Their days start early and end late! Good luck getting them to eat a healthy diet, let alone find time to exercise.*

Amar's life was no different when he came to me looking for help. He had put on 50 pounds over the prior year and developed horrible sleep habits. His diet consisted of eating one calorie-laden meal at night, and most of his sleep came during a 2-hour nap he snuck in at some point each day. He was only thirty-two years old, but he looked much older because he was exhausted. On top of that, Amar felt overwhelmed and was tired of being overweight.

Although Amar has had success in the past with exercise pro-

their steering wheels, and drop not just F bombs, but A–Z bombs.

You definitely want your inner Hulk to emerge in life-or-death situations, but having your inner Hulk appear during a traffic jam or from drinking too much coffee is far from beneficial for you. It is actually very damaging. When cortisol is chronically elevated, your body is stuck in the revved-up fight-or-flight response all the time—which may sound good, but the impact is actually horrible. That would be like trying to reach 90 miles per hour on the highway with your car in first gear! Worse, a lot of people are stuck in that mode trying to sleep at night. Good luck with that!

High achievers are prone to abusing the fight-or-flight response, because they get used to living in this heightened Hulk state and consider it a "normal" way of life. They are experts at ignoring stress signals and have absolutely no idea that their stress response has

---

grams and extreme diets, he had never committed to making a change in his lifestyle. As with most programs, if you don't make a lifestyle change, the weight comes right back, and the stress from the extreme dieting and exercise actually contribute to more fatigue once the program is stopped.

After completing the Stark Naked 21-Day Metabolic Reset, Amar lost 14 pounds, which was a fantastic jump-start to his weight loss program and the incentive he needed to help him stick with it. The best part? He was able to fall asleep at night without relying on alcohol, and his sleep was uninterrupted through the night. Also because he no longer needed the 2-hour nap each day, he had plenty of time to add exercise back into his lifestyle.

Today Amar's life is still crazy stressful, but once we reset his metabolism, we were able to build resiliency to stress into his routine. He sleeps, which is critical, he stabilizes his blood sugar by eating the right foods at the right times throughout the day, and he is no longer dehydrated.

kicked in. I hate to break it to you, but although you may believe you're superhuman, just as my kids do when they put on their superhero costumes, you are not. When you run around like the Hulk for too long, your stress-response system begins to falter from overwork, causing the Metabolic Breakdown Cycle to start, leaving you exhausted and feeling bad all the time.

There is a price to pay every time your stress response is turned on.

Stress and the Metabolic Breakdown Cycle

As we learned earlier, cortisol elevation in acute life-or-death bouts is awesome, but when it's left stuck in the "on" position 24/7, it creates problems. When you are stuck in a heightened state, you will actually feel invigorated and alive. It's called an adrenaline rush, and you feel as though you are conquering life, but as it stays on, you slowly become "tired but wired" and eventually become downright exhausted. That's The Metabolic Breakdown Cycle at work.

Let's look at this a little closer. Chronic cortisol release has a negative effect on all other hormones. Remember that the body is built first and foremost to survive at all costs. This means your body will do whatever it takes to survive right now! It doesn't care that the actions it takes will lead to a heart attack in five years. It only cares about surviving *now*. When you live in a constant state of stress, the body is continuously being forced to take action for your immediate survival. Unfortunately, this is at the expense of all other metabolic systems.

Chronic cortisol elevation affects your body in numerous ways, but for our purposes I am going to focus on what I feel are the "Big Four," meaning the effects that have the greatest impact on you: elevated blood sugar, suppressed sex hormones, an underactive thyroid, and extra belly fat. When your body is exposed to long-term elevated cortisol, these Big Four will leave you fat, sluggish, uninterested in sex, and far from your intellectual peak.

Cortisol and Blood Sugar

When cortisol is elevated, the body upregulates glucose and fats for instant energy, but blunts the effect of insulin, essentially rendering cells insulin-resistant. Not only are blood-glucose levels high, but insulin is unable to perform its regular function of maintaining normal glucose levels. This puts extra stress on the pancreas, as it continues to produce increasing amounts of insulin in response to high glucose levels.

If cortisol is elevated 24/7, your blood sugar will also stay elevated. Long-term elevated blood sugar has been shown to negatively affect our brains, actually taking away from our intelligence. Research has linked elevated blood sugar to a reduction in the size of the hippocampus, the part of the brain responsible for memory. In his book *Why Isn't My Brain Working?*, Dr. Datis Kharrazian shows that millions of Americans are affected by brain damage caused by blood-sugar imbalances.

Elevated blood-sugar levels also increase fat levels, because muscle cells are not allowed to accept the glucose into the cell due to the dampened insulin response. Eventually the liver has to do something with the excess buildup of glucose in the bloodstream, so it recycles it as fatty acids and shuttles it off to be stored as fat.

So many people believe that you have to overconsume carbohydrates to create blood-sugar issues, but to validate my point that blood sugar can become an issue due to stress alone, I have even seen the impact of high cortisol levels on blood sugar in high-level athletes, especially top-level CrossFit athletes, who avoid carbs like the plague. They haven't had a carb in five years, yet they are prediabetic. Controlling cortisol is critical for long-term blood-sugar management.

Cortisol and Sex Hormones

Did you know stress can suppress your sex hormones? Yes, you read that right. Stress and sex don't mix. In men, elevated cortisol levels reduce the production of testosterone, an essential component for a healthy sex drive. In women, it causes a cascade of hormonal imbalances resulting in low libido. Low sex-hormone levels can rob you of your sex drive, take away your overall zest for life, and even lead to an early death.

Prolonged cortisol elevations also decrease the liver's ability to clear excess estrogens from the blood, leading to estrogen dominance and accumulation of fat on the hips, thighs, back of the arms, and chest. This estrogen buildup also has a negative effect on the thyroid, which I'll explain next. You have to get your cortisol under control if you want your sex hormones optimized. In Chapter 5, we'll explore in more detail how stress robs your mojo (yes, a whole chapter on mojo!), but for now the crucial point is this: when cortisol levels are elevated, sex-hormone production is slowed.

Cortisol and the Thyroid

Chronic stress and elevated cortisol levels wreak havoc on your thyroid in a number of ways. A proper amount of cortisol is very important for normal thyroid function. Cortisol works in a synergistic fashion with the thyroid hormone at the cellular level, making the thyroid hormone work more efficiently. When cortisol levels are too high, the brain will reduce the body's ability to make more thyroid hormone, which over time results in sluggishness, extreme fatigue, and other symptoms of hypothyroidism. Basically, your body is too busy focusing all its energy on keeping your inner Hulk amped up to maintain proper thyroid function, leading you to the extreme consequence of the Metabolic Breakdown Cycle.

Last, as mentioned in the previous section, when cortisol levels are elevated, so are estrogen levels. High levels of estrogen interrupt thyroid function by increasing levels of the thyroid-binding protein thyroxine-binding globulin (TBG). Thyroid hormones are bound to this protein and inactive while they travel through your body in the blood. Once they reach your cells, they become unbound and active to do their work. If there is too much TBG, thyroid hormones remain bound, unable to get into cells and therefore unable to do their work. Hypothyroid symptoms are the result.

Cortisol and Belly Fat

Cortisol has the ability to trigger fat loss and fat storage. For example, cortisol triggers fat release during controlled periods of exercise, as long as you don't eat carbohydrates prior to the exercise. But when cortisol is chronically elevated, it promotes the storage of fat and relocates excess circulating fat to your abdomen. If left unchecked, this results in weight gain and a resistance to weight loss. It gets even worse when insulin joins the party.

Insulin activity shuts down the fat-releasing activity of other hormones like cortisol, and when these two are partying together, they trigger the release of the major fat-storage enzyme lipoprotein lipase. Hello, belly fat. Welcome to the cortisol and insulin fiesta. Olé!

In addition, consistently high blood-glucose levels and blunted signaling of insulin leads to cells that are starved of glucose. But those cells are crying out for energy. This causes your appetite to fire, leading to overeating, as your body compels you to replenish for the next time your life is at risk. This is when we usually start devouring all our comfort foods, like ice cream, that combine fat and sugar. And, of course, unused glucose is eventually converted to fatty acids by the liver and stored as body fat, primarily around the belly.

Adding Insult to Injury

Wow! We are on a cortisol roll. We have covered the Big Four negative impacts on your body caused by elevated cortisol levels, so let's just add a little insult to injury.

Not only does stress destroy how we feel, look, and perform; it's also a key player in increasing our risk of disease and early death. Hypertension (high blood pressure), hyperlipidemia (elevated lipids), and hyperglycemia (elevated glucose) have all been linked to elevated cortisol levels. Individuals with a high waist-to-hip ratio (which identifies visceral obesity, excessive fat accumulation around the organs within the abdominal cavity) are at a greater risk for developing cardiovascular disease, type 2 diabetes mellitus, and cerebrovascular disease.

As you can see, stress destroys your ability to live optimally. Do you understand now how vital it is for you to wrap a lasso around your cortisol and get it under control?

Mike, SWAT team member
California
Age forty

▶ *When I first met Mike as a potential client, I immediately knew our biggest struggle was going to be working around his insane sleep schedule. The first day we met, he had been so busy with SWAT calls, he had only averaged around 3 hours of sleep a night over the prior 72 hours. Combine that with the constant stress of raiding houses of dangerous criminals, uncertain of what's waiting for him on the other side of the door each time, and he had the perfect storm for an extremely stressful lifestyle.*

Mike had been a collegiate fullback. When we met, one of his primary goals was to get his college body back before turning the big four-oh. He had three months to make it happen. His starting weight was 225 pounds, which was promising, but his body fat of 18.2 percent was far from ideal. Mike wanted to keep his weight above 210, but get his body fat back to 10 percent. He also wanted more energy to train harder, which Mike knew was

How the Stark Naked 21-Day Metabolic Reset and Lifestyle Control Your Inner Hulk

All three categories of stress can trigger your inner Hulk when not managed appropriately, but the main culprits are the category-three lifestyle stressors. You're probably not even aware of them. Imagine if Bruce Banner knew that cow's milk triggered the Hulk to emerge. Would he drink it every day? No way, but we do silly things like this each day. Now I am not saying that cow's milk is a trigger for everyone, but you would be amazed at the number of people it does affect.

Reducing poor lifestyle choices that trigger category-three stressors is the foundation of the Stark Naked 21-Day Metabolic Reset

lacking because he was forcing himself to go to the gym every morning instead of being excited about working out.

Oh, how I love a good challenge!

Since I knew Mike's work schedule wasn't going to change, I immediately put him on the Stark Naked 21-Day Metabolic Reset, so I could quickly fix what was broken inside Mike's body and establish a healthy foundation to create a resiliency to the stress of Mike's work and lifestyle. I wanted Mike to reach his goal instead of continuing his frustrating cycle of constantly fighting himself and getting nowhere despite trying.

After the initial 21-day phase, Mike's weight dropped to 221 pounds and his body fat to 14 percent. He lost 10 pounds of fat and added 6 pounds of lean muscle mass just by resetting his metabolism and allowing his body to recover from his extreme stress. Today at forty years old Mike weighs 215 pounds with a body fat of 10 percent and holding! His energy is through the roof, his training in the gym has gone to a whole new level, and, as he puts it, "I haven't felt this good since I was in my early twenties." I call that a win for both of us!

and lifestyle. Throughout this book you are going to zero in on the three most common triggers—a stressful lifestyle, toxicity, and food sensitivities—remove them, and learn to calm your inner Hulk. I've taken all of the guesswork out of it for you. This program corrects the poor lifestyle decisions triggering your stress response. Just follow the program exactly as laid out, and you can rest assured that the multiple Hulk triggers robbing you of your best self are being removed. If you skip any of the strategies to reset your metabolism in Chapter 11, you are allowing a Hulk trigger to run free and prevent your metabolism from a full reset. It's only 21 days!

Give your inner Hulk a break! Your health, energy, waistline, sex drive, and those around you will thank you.

Make a commitment to take control of your lifestyle and apply the given strategies in this book to support your liver, remove food-driven inflammation, enhance your sleep, balance your daily or weekly exercise and recovery, and feed your high-performing lifestyle in a new way, so your inner Hulk only appears when you really need it!

Reducing the lifestyle stressors that trigger your inner Hulk is the key to resetting your metabolism.

The eleven fundamentals of the Stark Naked 21-Day Metabolic Reset in Chapter 11 (see page 204) remove the multiple Hulk triggers robbing you of your best self. The first four are specifically designed to reduce your stress load and help you get better control of your cortisol.

1. Hydrate.
2. Sleep 7 to 9 hours a night every night.
3. Drastically reduce your intense exercise.
4. Commit to daily acts of relaxation.

Your Liver Needs Some Love

The Impact of Toxicity on the Body

WHETHER YOU REALIZE IT OR NOT, we live in a really toxic world. When I speak of toxins, I don't mean just pesticides or hazardous waste. What I am referring to is anything, whether a chemical or poison, that is known to have a harmful effect on the body. There are currently over eighty thousand known chemicals in our daily environment. Fifteen thousand of these are used in high volumes in the United States. Today, the United States produces over 300 billion pounds of chemicals a year. The average American is directly exposed to over 1,500 pounds of these chemicals annually, many of which are known carcinogens, substances directly involved in causing cancer.

That's a lot of dangerous chemicals to be swimming in! When asked, most people are unable to name one single toxic chemical that is a known health risk, and yet they live among thousands of them every day. As a society, we tend to have an awful lot of faith that big industry has our ultimate safety in mind over their own profits when it comes to creating and marketing the products they sell us.

What's even more frightening to me is the number of toxins our children are exposed to—even before they are born. This concerns me so much, because I have three beautiful children whose blood-brain barrier won't be fully developed until around the age of twenty, leaving their brains unprotected from these chemicals. It's scary to think that my little boy Gavin, born in October 2014, was exposed to hundreds of different toxins before he was even born.

Research presented by the Environmental Working Group shows there could have been as many as 287 different chemicals passing through the umbilical cord directly into the placenta. Of these, 217 are known neurotoxins, poisons that affect the brain and nervous system, and 180 are ones that we know cause cancer in humans and animals. The reported chemicals are coming from herbicides, house-hold products, consumer products, stain and oil repellant used in fast-food packaging, flame retardants, and pesticides.

Even though my wife took great care of herself throughout her pregnancy, it would be virtually impossible for her to avoid these tox-ins. They're everywhere and enter the body through the food you eat, the air you breathe, the water you drink (especially from that pretty and convenient plastic bottle), the clothes you wear, the products you use to clean your home, the cell phone you're talking on, and the lotions and balms you lather all over your skin every day thinking you're caring for your body, when you are actually wreaking havoc on it by adding to the toxicity.

What's the result of all of this exposure? Unfortunately, our bodies have become a toxic dumping ground, and we are paying a massive price for it.

Once our bodies have been exposed to these harmful toxins, they are processed through the liver and kidneys. Whenever possible, our body eliminates them in the form of sweat, breath, urine, and feces. Toxins not eliminated are retained. Because toxins are so dam-aging, the Stark Naked 21-Day Metabolic Reset is designed to help you cleanse the toxins from your system and relieve the stress you've unknowingly been placing on your body over the years, or as I like to call it, "love your liver," every day.

If you're the grumpy morning person everyone avoids talking to before 10:00 A.M., the person who needs to hit the snooze button on your alarm multiple times, stealing every last possible minute of sleep before getting out of bed, someone who needs a couple of cups of coffee to calm the beast and wake up before you can function in the world, then you are *definitely* someone who will benefit from loving on your liver. (Naturally, your kidneys are part of the detoxification process as well and will be supported in this process, but in an effort to keep things supersimple I've chosen to focus on the big driver of detoxification, your liver.)

How do you accomplish this?

First, eliminate the toxins you are eating and drinking. Without realizing it, most people eat and drink so many toxic substances, thinking they aren't causing any additional stress on the body, contributing to the onset or flare-up of a disease, or creating complications for themselves—but they are.

For example, caffeine is a favorite vice among my clients. But it's also one of the most taxing stressors on your liver and adrenal glands. One report I read from the Department of Molecular and Cell Biology at the University of California, Berkeley, stated there are up to one thousand chemicals in a single cup of coffee.

Alcohol is another major culprit. Aside from the hangovers, headaches, and other occasional unpleasant side effects, drinking alcohol depletes nutrients, especially B vitamins that are needed for metabolism and . . . what was that darn word I was looking for?

Oh yes, *memory*!

That's what causes the occasional forgetfulness about what went on the night before! Worse, breaking down alcohol exhausts your liver, making it harder to eliminate the unwanted poisons from your body. Not to mention that too much alcohol can damage or destroy liver cells. That's not to say you should never drink alcohol—you can.

Like everything, moderation and drinking some green tea before a night out on the town will help your liver function a little more effectively. Staying superhydrated is always a good idea too!

And finally, there's sugar. Kicking the sugar habit is hard, but it's so worth it. If I can get clients off sugar for 21 days, they rarely go back. It's akin to any drug detox program out there, because sugar is as addictive as most drugs. Think about it. Eating anything with refined sugar only makes you want to eat more. The brain depends on blood glucose for its energy. Eating sucrose can cause a plethora of problems, especially when it comes to blood-glucose levels.

Remember that famous trial where the attorney used the Twinkie defense, claiming his client's irrational behavior was impacted by his high-sugar junk-food diet? Although I am not sure I believe Twinkies will cause you to do crazy things, I do know this: There's no real nutritional value in eating one!

If you want to get off the sugar train once and for all, you have to start by cutting down or eliminating all refined sugars from your diet.

Guess what?

Refined sugar is hiding in the most unexpected places, such as those "healthy" juice drinks you think are good for you, your favorite marinara sauce, and every meal replacement bar! Read the labels on some of your favorite so-called healthy foods sometime and I'll bet you'll be shocked by the amount of sugar you'll discover among those ingredients. Eliminating sugar isn't easy, but once you kick the habit, food will start to taste better, and you will start to feel better too.

Now, I want to be up front and tell you the Stark Naked 21-Day Metabolic Reset is not an extreme detoxification program. If it were, you'd probably quit before seeing the kind of results you're looking for.

How do I know?

Like so many of my clients, I have punished myself over the years by trying many different extreme detox protocols. In fact, I was obsessed with wanting to understand them, because clients would come to me asking about them or after doing one. Most often, their results were consistently negative. Curious and perplexed, I didn't know the reason why, but I wanted to find out so I could help right the wrong.

Sure, they lost weight, but their body fat didn't change or, worse, it actually got higher. That meant they just stripped off muscle instead of fat, which is never desirable. In my mind, a detox should only be done if it will improve one's health, not worsen it. Although a detox cleanse may indeed help you shed a few pounds, it's likely that the lost weight is primarily water, which will come right back on as soon as you veer off the plan—even the slightest bit. This only leads to frustration and setbacks.

So how can you see effective results from a detox?

I have seen great success with my clients by simply removing any unnecessary sources of daily liver burden, so the liver can focus on the backed-up toxic junk that has been stored in your fat. Doing this enhances the liver's ability to work more efficiently with less effort. The body is designed to constantly filter toxins we ingest. If we can aid in that process, we will feel and look better.

What does this mean for you? Sorry to say—okay, not *that* sorry to say—that it means you will have to go without coffee, alcohol, and sugar for 21 days. But guess what? It's only for 21 days!

Give yourself 21 days, and you will experience the ultimate benefit: enhanced fat burning.

Yep, you read that right!

When the liver can catch up on the work it has fallen behind on, better fat metabolism is the outcome. After the 21-day Reset, if you still feel you want to include these toxins in your diet, I will teach you how to strategically reintroduce each of them without undoing all of the progress you've made.

A Healthy Liver

Your liver is the second-largest organ in your body (your skin is the largest). The liver is extremely valuable to the human body. It is responsible for over six hundred metabolic activities and actually has the ability to regenerate after being damaged.

Your liver is designed to survive at all costs. When your liver is overwhelmed, it goes into major survival mode. It will focus less on making sure your metabolism is firing on all cylinders and more on protection. It will start storing as fat the toxins it can't process and clear immediately.

How does this impact you? I don't care how much you control your calories and kill yourself on the treadmill, if your liver is overwhelmed, you are stuck in neutral—meaning that even if you're doing all the right things, you will never meaningfully move the needle on the scale.

If you want to get the most out of the Stark Naked 21-Day Metabolic Reset, it's important to understand the major role your liver plays in your everyday life. Most people know they have a liver, but few understand its function and purpose, so let's break it down to help you understand why a healthy liver is essential to your health and ultimately your success.

A healthy liver:

Cleans toxins and wastes from your blood. It polices your blood looking for toxins that are a dangerous threat to your body. When a toxin tries to sneak in, the liver ambushes the threat, cuffs it, and escorts it out of the body via pathways like sweat, breath, urine, and feces. This is a good thing, or like my daddy used to say, "Don't let the door hit you where the good Lord split you!"

Looks for the VIP citizens known as vitamins and minerals. It processes these highly valuable assets and prepares them, so your body can use them to work properly. Vitamins and minerals are used for things like enhancing your immune system, aiding in digestion, producing energy, protecting your cells from damage during stress and exposure to toxins, protecting your body from viruses and bacteria, and building strong bones and teeth.

Plays an important role in digestion. It is the central hub for metabolizing all calories and is responsible for processing proteins, fats, and carbohydrates. It is involved in protein synthesis, processing amino acids from broken-down protein so the body can use them. The liver makes a greenish-yellow gooey substance called bile, which is stored in the gallbladder. This substance is critical for the digestion and absorption of fats. The liver is also responsible for aiding in the management of blood sugar. The liver can store excess glucose in the blood as glycogen to be used in times of low blood sugar or other emergency energy needs. A healthy liver processes proteins, fats, and carbohydrates efficiently, allowing you to enjoy the benefits of better energy, low body fat, and a sharp mind.

Makes cholesterol. Relax! Cholesterol is a good thing. It's the backbone of your sex hormones. It also makes the base proteins needed for blood clotting.

Metabolizes steroidal hormones, such as the sex hormones and aldosterone (controls the balance of sodium, potassium, and water in your body), once they are done doing their job in the body. You will learn more about the liver and sex hormones later in this chapter and in Chapter 5, but they essentially control your sex drive. When the liver efficiently breaks down aldosterone, water retention is under control and you're able to keep your blood pressure in check. It can also slow down those pesky bathroom trips during the night.

An Unhealthy Liver

Now, that's what happens in a beautiful, optimally functioning liver—something few of us have. In reality, that is far from how most people's normal livers function these days. Many of my clients will try to defend themselves and their livers by showing me their "excellent" liver enzyme levels on recent blood work. However, I am usually the bearer of bad news when I have to explain they're not off the hook, because their liver is still suffering and causing them major problems.

How do I know? I run a simple urine lab test called the Urinary Bile Acid Sulfates (UBAS), which looks at liver function efficiency by testing its role as a filter of bile acids. Bile acids are a normal component of blood that your liver is responsible for clearing out. If you have a sluggish or overwhelmed liver, bile acids build up in your blood, forcing the kidneys to convert them to sulfates and excrete them through your urine. When sulfates are present at high levels in the urine, it's a clear sign your liver is working overtime and not keeping up with its workload.

Here's the scary part. Every person we ran this test on had elevated UBAS levels, yet the majority of those people had normal liver enzyme labs. What this tells us is a normal liver enzyme result doesn't necessarily mean you're safe.

If you have never had a UBAS test but have normal liver enzyme levels and are wondering if your liver is having an effect on your health, your cholesterol profile can give you a pretty good idea. The majority of your total cholesterol is produced in your liver. When your liver starts to get bogged down by stress, toxins, and too much sugar and fat consumption, cholesterol production can be thrown off balance. One of the liver's jobs is to use low-density lipoprotein (LDL) cholesterol to stimulate bile-salt production to help deal with fats in the blood. When fats in the blood begin to accumulate because of a sluggish liver, the need for LDL cholesterol and bile salt increases. An elevation in LDL cholesterol and triglycerides (a marker of how much fat is in the blood) is a sign that your liver is in overdrive. Your liver is not efficiently burning fat and is more than likely clogged up and tilted toward storing fat instead of metabolizing it.

Now that I have your attention, let's explore how your sluggish liver may be affecting your energy, weight, and mojo.

Sluggish Liver, Low Energy, Weight Gain, Low Mojo

A sluggish liver will have a dramatic effect on your energy. Toxins build up in the blood, reducing its capacity to carry oxygen and nutrients required for energy production. The result is constant fatigue. It can also have a negative effect on your energy by slowing down your thyroid.

The thyroid needs the liver to activate its hormone, so the body can actually use it. When activation is slowed, the thyroid struggles to do its job. When that happens, your metabolism is forced to slow down, and fatigue results.

As far as weight gain goes, a sluggish liver is forced to store fat instead of burn it, leaving you with a nice buildup of fat, especially around your belly. It's tough enough to exercise when your liver is storing fat and your circulation is poor, but combine that with a slow metabolism that prevents your thyroid from optimally burning energy during exercise, and it's next to impossible to lose weight. This is what causes most people to just give up on their weight-loss goals.

Finally, a sluggish liver is causing your sex hormones to go haywire. The liver is responsible for the elimination of excess estrogens. When the liver is backed up, this process is slowed and estrogens begin to build in the body, causing an imbalance. Women, this creates all kinds of havoc in your world. The buildup of estrogen can cause symptoms such as insomnia, fat accumulation around the hips and thighs, mood swings, foggy thinking, enhanced PMS symptoms, water retention, hair loss, and headaches.

Men, this buildup of estrogen can interfere with your fertility (impotence), sexual function (low sex drive and erectile dysfunction), and put you at risk for circulatory problems, heart attack, and stroke. Not to mention fat accumulation around your chest (yup, moobs, or man boobs) and thighs, thinning of your body hair, and depression. No fun if you're a guy who wants to maintain his manliness!

At Stark we track and monitor everything monthly to make sure people are making positive progress. If they aren't, we can make quick adjustments, so people aren't wasting time or effort. One month we noticed that my former business partner Todd's body fat had gone up out of the blue. Worse, his skin folds in the estrogen areas started creeping up too. He was laying down fat on his chest and especially his thighs. We refer to that as "feminizing" at Stark. He swore up and down he was following the protocols we designed and was blaming my team for feminizing him.

We dug real deep and discovered he had switched his body wash and lotion recently to products that were packed full of estrogen-mimicking parabens, and they were taking a toll on Todd's manhood. We had him go back to his old body wash and lotion and gave him some extra liver support for 30 days, and his body returned to his nonfeminized masculine body, or at least what he thinks is his masculine body.

Now do you believe me when I say it's worth your time and effort to support your liver?

The Impact of Chemical Toxins on Your Liver

In his book *Achieving Victory Over a Toxic World,* Dr. Mark Schauss writes that in retaliation against the toxic burden, the body will store toxins in fat and actually turn down the internal temperature to help

Signs and Symptoms of a Sluggish Liver

- Elevated LDL cholesterol
- Low HDL cholesterol
- Elevated triglycerides
- Expanding waistline
- Weight gain on the hips and thighs
- Abdominal bloating
- Inability to digest fatty foods
- Loss of appetite, especially in the morning
- Skin issues like psoriasis, eczema, acne, rashes, and itchy skin
- Low energy especially in the morning and after meals
- Unstable blood sugar
- Dizziness
- Sleep disturbances
- Moodiness
- Depression
- Hot flashes
- Irregular periods
- Intolerance to alcohol
- Intolerance to caffeine
- Swollen feet
- Swollen abdomen
- Bad breath
- Dark urine or stool
- Easy bruising
- Body odor
- Sensitivities to smells from perfumes, chemicals, paints, and cleaners

keep these toxins at bay. This slight drop in body temperature slows the resting metabolic rate enough to cause unwanted weight gain. If you've ever attempted an extreme approach to weight loss, you have probably experienced the wrath of all the toxins being released in the bloodstream too fast from the fat, eventually making you sick.

Eating a clean diet and limiting your caffeine, alcohol, and sugar intake will take some pressure off your liver, but there are so many more toxins that you're being exposed to on a daily basis that are causing health problems for you. Environmental pollutants burden you as well. But the toxins I've seen that cause the most trouble are found in the solvents used to make cleaning and personal-care products, the products you are choosing to put in your environment and even rub into your skin. Before you slather on your favorite body lotion, I want you to turn the bottle around and read the ingredients. Ask yourself this one simple question: *Do I know what all these chemicals are?* If your answer is no, why in the world are you putting it on your skin?

According to the Federal Food, Drug, and Cosmetic (FD&C) Act, cosmetics are defined by their intended use as "articles intended to be rubbed, poured, sprinkled or sprayed on, introduced into, or otherwise applied to the human body . . . for cleansing, beautifying, promoting attractiveness, or altering the appearance." Under the FD&C Act, cosmetics and their ingredients are not required to undergo approval before they are sold to the public. This includes skin moisturizers, perfumes, lipsticks, nail polish, mascara, facial makeup, shampoos, hair coloring, toothpastes, and deodorants.

I have even found scientifically proven dangerous chemicals in products for babies. Parabens, for example, have been shown to be an estrogen-mimicking chemical in rats and the methyl form has been found in the cells of breast-cancer tissue. I found methyl parabens in an old bottle of baby bedtime lotion. When my daughter was a baby, I had rubbed this on her after her baths, thinking I was being a loving father. I also remember my wife complaining about my holding my daughter when I had cologne on, because it made her smell like a man. Imagine my guilt when I researched the safety of colognes and found that my cologne at that time was rated as the most dangerous.

The average woman puts three to five hundred chemicals on her skin before leaving the house every morning. The typical perfume has over two hundred different chemicals alone! As a result of all of that primping, your liver is bombarded with toxins and angry at you before 8:00 A.M.! And the only person you can blame is yourself! Ouch!

Generally, the Food and Drug Administration (FDA) regulates these products after they have been released into the marketplace. There is no preapproval system in place except for color additives, such as those found in self-tanners. This means that manufacturers may use any ingredient or raw material in a product and sell it without a government review or approval. Parabens, for example, are used as a preservative and aren't just found in baby products. It is estimated that they are present in 75 to 90 percent of all beauty products. The parabens and chemicals in these products are being linked to issues like hormone disruption, infertility, cancer, headaches, skin irritants, allergies, and liver and kidney damage, to name a few.

Phthalates are another scary family of chemicals that are usually hidden on labels. These are typically hidden in the word "fragrance" on most products that have a smell and in nail polish. Phthalates have been shown to also be an estrogen mimicker and are linked to cancer and liver damage. The European Union has completely banned dibutyl phthalate (DBP) from cosmetics and baby products. That's scary. What do they know? What are we turning a blind eye to?

The list of "at risk" chemicals in solvents is constantly growing. It's time to wake up to the reality that solvents could be a major source of toxic overload for you and may be causing you some serious issues. It's my opinion that smelling great isn't worth losing my testosterone over. Wow. That brings back serious memories of a young man in my middle school who wore so much Polo cologne, he literally had a green cloud floating above him. Makes you cringe even more now, doesn't it?

Most of us apply somewhere in the neighborhood of 126 unique ingredients to our skin daily without giving any of them a second thought. But we should, because chemicals from all of our coveted beauty products don't pass through the digestive system, where they might be filtered. Instead, they head right into your bloodstream and therefore can be extremely toxic and quite dangerous to your health. According to the Environmental Working Group, one out of every 120 products on the market contains ingredients certified by government authorities as *known or probable human carcinogens*. One out of every 13 women and one out of every 23 men—12.2 million adults—are exposed to ingredients that are known or probable carcinogens every day through their use of personal-care products.

The regulatory requirements governing the sale of cosmetics are not as stringent as those that apply to other FDA-regulated products. In fact, cosmetics and toiletries are some of the least regulated and scrutinized products available. Although companies are not required to substantiate performance claims or conduct safety testing, if safety has not been substantiated, the product's label must read "WARNING: The safety of this product has not been determined."

Most people falsely believe that if a product is on the shelf, it can't be harmful. Of course, we all know that's not true. Cigarettes are a great example of that.

But hardly anyone thinks of perfume or body lotion in that same category. And really, why would you? Companies are required to list all the ingredients in order of use, but they are not required to test their products for safety, so no one understands the risk of using those products they believe are good for them. To be fair, that doesn't mean that all cosmetic companies don't have safety standards, but it does mean that many such claims as "natural," "botanical," and "organic" are useless. The FDA can take action against a product only if it has enough scientific proof that the product is actually dangerous.

Do yourself a favor and take some time to research all the products in your medicine cabinet or bathroom to see what toxins you are using on your skin or hair, brushing your teeth with, breathing in, or ingesting on a daily basis. If you can pronounce the ingredients or know what they are, it's a good bet the product is probably safe. Any ingredient that has too many syllables or is unrecognizable is most likely a chemical or toxin. Remove the dangerous products from your shelves. Your liver will thank you and, believe me, you will notice a significant difference in how you look and feel.

I have seen enough improvement in people who have removed questionable solvents that I now am down to using only two products: Dr. Bronner's Castile Liquid Soap and Jungleman all-natural deodorant. You don't need to give up makeup, nail polish, or moisturizers. There are products available that are nontoxic and better for your health. Once you know what you're looking for, you'll find a wide selection of aluminum-free deodorants, triclosan-free mouthwashes, fluoride-free toothpastes, and nontoxic sunscreens, moisturizers, shampoos, and other hair care products. The Resource Guide at the end of the book will help you find safe non- or less toxic replacements. I have even shared some of my favorite products.

Check out the Environmental Working Group's website (www.ewg.org) and their awesome new app called SkinDeep. These two sources will allow you to search through all your lotions, creams, soaps, cleaners, and so on, discover which ones are toxic, and find safe brands.

How the Stark Naked 21-Day Metabolic Reset and Lifestyle Support Your Liver

The Stark Naked 21-Day Metabolic Reset uses a number of naturally proven ways to support your liver. First, we will be removing our three high-achieving lifestyle addictions—coffee, alcohol, and sugar. It is critical to remove these for the initial 21-day period, because they are each a major burden on your liver. Additional ways that are non-supplement-driven include drinking warm lemon water first thing in the morning to stimulate your liver, removing protein- and fat-based breakfasts that are hard on a sluggish liver, and extending the detoxification period by replacing a solid breakfast with a green smoothie that supports the liver. (I get into this in greater detail in Chapter 11.) You will also be reducing your fat intake for the initial 21 days, so your liver can catch up on metabolizing the stored, clogged fat. You have to do everything you can to give your liver a break while you are using the natural liver-aid solutions in the Reset period. If you don't, the Reset won't be as effective, and you will have wasted your precious time and energy only removing the new toxins entering your body and not clearing the ones stored in your fat.

If you drink a lot of coffee, you will notice two things early in the Reset. First, you're going to have a nasty headache for the first few days. Second, you are going to be crazy hungry. The headache is obvious and expected because of the caffeine withdrawal, but why the major increase in appetite? Is this a starvation diet?

The answer is no! This is not a deprivation diet. In fact, I'd prefer it if you didn't think of it as a diet at all.

You will be hungry because coffee is a major appetite suppressant. Without it, you are going to find yourself constantly thinking about food for the first few days. During my most recent reset with my wife, I was so unbelievable hungry and grumpy during the first 5 days; no matter how much protein and how many vegetables I ate, I couldn't be satisfied. I was constantly focused on my watch, counting down the seconds until I could eat my next meal.

But by day 7 everything changed. I was easily satisfied in between meals. Once the initial rough period was over, it became much easier to stay the course for the remainder of the 21 days. Yes, even I had to tolerate those first few days, but it was worth it. The rougher it is in the beginning, the better the results you usually see in the end.

To make it worth your while to suffer through those first rough days, focus on the benefits of cleaning up your liver. You will have more energy, the most valuable benefit of this program. Well, maybe the second most valuable. I've yet to have anyone complain about an increased sex drive! When your energy is up, your drive and hunger for life are elevated; everyone actually enjoys being around you and is inspired by you. Increased energy also means energy to have more sex. Exercise is actually enjoyable when you have more energy. Trust me, raw energy created from a revved-up, healthy metabolism blows caffeine-driven energy out of the water every time. There is no comparison—not even close!

Other benefits related to improved liver function are healthier, younger looking skin, better bowel movements, breath that doesn't smell as bad, early morning energy, fewer hot flashes, less body fat around the hips and thighs, a more stable mood, better brain clarity and focus, and improved sleep. Did I mention improved sex drive? Of course I did! What do you expect? I'm a guy, and we think about sex every 7 seconds.

Look, the bottom line is that if you want to get the most out of the Reset, you will commit to aggressively supporting your liver for the next 21 days. You will commit to no coffee, alcohol, or sugar without grumbling about it. In fact, maybe you'll even welcome the break. Just follow the Reset. If you do, the sky is the limit for your results, especially once your liver is back on your side of the field.

Love your liver during the 21-Day Reset by removing the three major toxins causing it to become sluggish and following the other liver-supporting elements of the Reset fundamentals in Chapter 11 (see page 204).

5. No coffee.

6. No alcohol.

7. Remove sugar from your diet—all sources of sugar.

4

Healthy Foods Gone Rogue

The Impact of Food Sensitivities and Food-Induced Inflammation

AFTER A HIGH-STRESS LIFESTYLE and liver toxicity, the final catalyst that triggers the Metabolic Breakdown Cycle is something most of you have likely never heard about, but it's probably the biggest reason you are not seeing the results you want with your current nutrition plan—*inflammation brought on by food sensitivities.*

Even if you believe you've been eating a healthy diet, you might be eating the wrong foods *for you,* foods that are causing inflammation and discomfort in the gut and other symptoms you're not connecting to what you're eating. By now you realize stress is negatively impacting your health, and you've likely heard about or have even tried the latest and greatest detoxification programs that promise to bring balance and harmony back to your liver. But how many of you have removed foods that you are sensitive to from your eating plan? Even if you're eating fruits, vegetables, and minimally processed foods, you might still be eating all of the wrong foods *for you,* and that could be causing your body stress.

Eliminating food sensitivities is a key component of the success of the Stark Naked 21-Day Metabolic Reset. Understanding the importance and role food sensitivities play in our digestion and health has single-handedly changed more lives than any other strategy I use with my clients. It is so powerful that I am shocked it hasn't become a more mainstream medical protocol.

Chris Speicher, cofounder of Speicher Group,
   a real-estate firm
Maryland
Age forty-three

▶ *Chris was introduced to the Reset when my client real-estate coach Tom Ferry challenged a number of his clients to try it. At first, Chris was leery, because he had major stomach and bowel issues. He couldn't sleep through the night without having to use the bathroom. He was always nervous about eating out in restaurants, because he didn't know what the bathroom situation would be like. He even hated going to concerts and sporting events for the very same reason. He had lived this way for over twenty years.*

No matter what he ate, he always felt sick afterward. He described the feeling as similar to constantly being nervous. He also suffered from severe and chronic joint pain.

Chris had tried everything to combat his condition over the years, following different diets, only eating vegetables, not eating vegetables, and so on, but nothing provided relief. He was constantly taking antacids and had recently finished a six-month dose of antibiotics prescribed by a gastrointestinal doctor. Still no relief. No doctor could figure out the cause of his discomfort, and no medication could seem to fix it. Chris believed he was going to live the rest of his life like this. He certainly didn't believe the Reset would help, but he had nothing to lose by trying it.

His response to the Reset was immediate and life-changing.

To figure out an individual's exact food sensitivities, an expensive lab test called the Mediator Release Test (MRT) is usually administered. The MRT is a blood test that looks at how your body responds to 150 different foods and chemicals and accounts for all reactions by noting the presence of chemical mediators, such as histamines, cytokines, and prostaglandins, released by your immune cells. A blind

Within the first couple of days, Chris felt a natural cleansing taking place. One week into the program his stomach issues had almost completely subsided. His joint pain went away, and his energy level skyrocketed.

By the end of week two, Chris had experienced his first week of solid bowel movements in more than two decades. He was committed to changing his eating habits for the rest of his life.

Why did he see these results?

Eating the wrong foods, even foods deemed healthy, was causing major inflammation and destroying his digestive tract. By simply removing those foods through the Reset, his symptoms began to quickly subside.

Being able to enjoying dinners out with his wife and sporting events with his buddies and not living in fear of the nearest bathroom gave Chris back his life. He has stuck to the approved-foods list in Phase 2, and his life is dramatically different than it used to be. He has not had any major digestive issues since starting the Reset. He feels healthier and more confident than ever. His clothes fit better, and he now sleeps like a rock—something he had struggled with his entire adult life.

At forty-three, Chris has taken up power lifting, and his strength over the last year has dramatically improved. His improved digestion is allowing him to rebuild muscle tissue and recover from his intense training, causing amazing results. Chris truly feels unstoppable!

peer-reviewed scientific study showed the MRT to have the highest level of accuracy of any food-sensitivity blood test (94.5 percent sensitivity and 91.8 percent specificity).

Thankfully, my clients are in pursuit of the ultimate energy and performance edge, so the majority of them have taken the MRT. When I get their lab results, I know exactly which foods to remove from their diet based on their sensitivity level.

I know what you're thinking. "Sure, you can have your clients take an expensive blood test. But I can't do that. I don't have the money, and my insurance won't pay for that!"

Guess what? You don't need to take the MRT. I've done the work for you!

So how can I remove the foods you are sensitive to without making you take the expensive blood test? Over the years, I have collected enough data to know the most common food sensitivities. I personally went through every one of my clients' MRTs from the last several years and tallied every food sensitivity. Based on that information, we've removed the foods from the Reset diet plan and compiled a list of approved foods for the 21-Day Reset period. Although this approach may not create an individualized list of food sensitivities for you, I guarantee most offending foods will be pulled from your diet on the Reset.

How can I be so confident?

The results speak for themselves. The approximately fifteen hundred people who have done the Reset and eaten only from the approved-foods list have seen tremendous results, including losing weight—anywhere between 8 and 20 pounds—feeling great, having

The Stark Naked 21-Day Metabolic Reset does not focus on removing immunoglobulin E (IgE) food allergens from the approved-foods list. If you know you have a food allergy, leave that food out of your diet.

more energy, sleeping better, experiencing less bloating and gas, and having greater mojo.

Removing foods you are sensitive to while reducing stress and supporting your liver leads to amazing results!

The Impact of Food Sensitivities on Your Body

First, it's important to understand that food sensitivities are not food allergies. They both cause inflammation, but food allergies are serious reactions that create what's called an immunoglobulin E (IgE) response from your immune system. When you ingest something that you are allergic to, such as peanuts, eggs, milk, or shellfish, your immune system releases what's called IgE antibodies to attack the allergen. This can produce symptoms in multiple areas of the body including your eyes (tearing, redness, itchiness), nose (discharge, itchiness, congestion), throat (tightness), lungs (shortness of breath, cough), skin (hives, swelling), or GI tract (vomiting, nausea) and trigger anaphylaxis, a severe whole-body allergic reaction. If untreated, anaphylaxis can kill you.

Food sensitivities also trigger your immune system, but not in a way that uses IgE. When you consume a food you're sensitive to, your immune cells are stimulated to release several different chemicals called chemical mediators. Some of the most well-known chemical mediators are histamine, cytokine, and prostaglandin. These cause a negative response in your body and symptoms such as migraine headaches, acid reflux, bloating, foggy thinking, depression, irritable bowel syndrome (IBS), asthma, arthritis, attention deficit disorder (ADD), and weight gain.

Unlike IgE food allergies, food sensitivities do not cause an immediate negative reaction in the body. Food-sensitivity symptoms can show up anywhere from 45 minutes to 3 days after you eat! With that kind of span in between meals, how in the world are you supposed to figure out the true culprit causing your symptoms? Was it what you ate for breakfast yesterday or what you had for lunch today that is causing you discomfort this evening?

Whenever I talk to people about food sensitivities for the first time, the classic response is usually, "I am completely fine with all types of food! There are no foods that bother me." I usually snicker whenever I hear that, because over time I have learned that most of us have grown so accustomed to feeling lousy that we are oblivious to the foods that are causing issues in our bodies.

The body is built in a special way to deal with small stressors that are constant, but not life-threatening. That is basically what these food sensitivities are: small stressors that affect the body, but are not considered life-threatening.

I spent the early years of my life growing up on a dairy farm in McMinnville, Oregon, and it was always funny to watch people's initial response when they got out of the car to visit us. The smell of manure overwhelmed their senses. It was all they could focus on initially, but the longer they hung around, the less the smell bothered them. That is, until they left the farm and then came back. Watching that initial reaction never got old.

Like those visitors, you've become used to your offenders and their negative impact on your body. They're just a normal part of your life. Before I took my first MRT, I experienced this firsthand—on the day I proposed to my wife. It was a perfect California day—blue skies and sunshine. My wife awoke to roses and loose rose petals all over our bed and bedroom floor, with a trail of flowers leading her out of the bedroom to where I was surrounded by bouquets of roses and coffee from her favorite coffee shop. I got down on bended knee and some-how successfully persuaded her to say yes!

We decided to have a nice relaxed lunch midday, and I ordered my favorite meat, beef. As usual, my left eye began to water. This hap-pened often, which I was told was due to seasonal allergies. It was something I had become so used to that I didn't think much about it and made a mental note to pop an allergy pill when we got home.

I surprised my wife at lunch with our plans for the evening: dinner with our close friends at Club 33, a private restaurant in Disneyland. She was superexcited. We went home to get ready for our big night. My left eye was still watering like crazy when we arrived at Disneyland. I had forgotten to take an allergy pill! I was miserable!

When our friends arrived, they were 20 minutes late and cautiously asked us if everything was okay. I thought that was a weird question to ask a couple who just got engaged. During dinner they finally confessed that they were late because, as they were walking up to meet us, they noticed my left eye watering so badly they thought I was crying. They actually thought my wife had turned down my proposal! They literally walked around the park in circles for 20 minutes trying to decide what they should do!

After taking the MRT, I discovered beef was one of the foods I was sensitive to. By removing it from my diet and then reintroducing it, I've discovered that it is beef that makes my left eye water really badly—not seasonal allergies. For too long I thought I had watery eyes and my only recourse for relief was an allergy pill, when in fact my misery was actually being triggered by a food I was eating every day.

What are other symptoms that can be caused by food sensitivities?

Food sensitivities can affect you in multiple ways. They can create digestive complaints like bloating, diarrhea, constipation, IBS, GERD (acid reflux), and abdominal pain. They can cause fatigue and insomnia. They have been linked to depression, anxiety, irritability, and brain fog. They can cause food cravings and water retention, leading to weight gain, and metabolic syndrome, a cluster of symptoms that increase your risk of cardiovascular disease and type 2 diabetes. These symptoms include high blood pressure, high fasting glucose levels, excess fat gain around your belly, and elevated cholesterol levels. Food sensitivities have also been linked to problems with your skin, sinus and nasal issues, and joint pain. Reduced joint pain and enhanced brain function are two of the most common results people rave about after doing the Reset.

Now do you understand why addressing food sensitivities is such a necessary and essential component to your overall success?

How the Stark Naked Metabolic 21-Day Reset and Lifestyle Reduce Food-Induced Inflammation

The food we eat is used for a whole lot more than just energy. It forms the building blocks of your metabolism. It is used to rebuild tissue, make hormones, and replenish neurotransmitters in the brain. If your digestion is not working properly, you're going to have a hard time assimilating the foods you eat, and your metabolism will suffer the consequences.

A major disruptor of good digestion is food your body is sensitive to. These foods may be considered healthy food choices, but if your body sees them as a threat, it will trigger your immune system, cause systemic inflammation, and release the stress hormone cortisol.

Eating what you think of as healthy foods—fruits, vegetables, nuts, whole grains—may not be giving you the fuel you need to reach your peak performance. If you are sensitive to a "healthy" food, it's causing inflammation and damaging your body. When you see the approved-foods list for the Reset, you will most likely be surprised at the foods that do not appear on it. During the Reset you will avoid blueberries, shrimp, most nuts, broccoli, and salmon, for example. These are just some of the foods that routinely cause inflammation for my clients.

I'll wait while you go back and read that list again.

I have a friend who didn't want to take the MRT, because he was afraid the only two foods he actually eats salmon and almonds, would be on his list of sensitivities. "What will I eat?" he asked.

I need you to understand that I am not saying these foods are unhealthy. They're not, and that would be ridiculous. They're very healthy foods, packed with essential nutrients and vitamins, but for you they may be triggering inflammation and causing problems. By eliminating these foods for a period of time, you'll be able to tell if you are sensitive to them. You have got to get away from the foods you are sensitive to and give your body a break from these non-life-threatening stressors.

Here's the good news. The elimination period is only 21 days! In Phase 2 when I show you how to optimize your metabolism, I will teach you how to reintroduce foods you are jonesing to have back in your diet to see if they are safe or still a problem. You will know the answer right away. You see, when you remove a trigger food from your diet for a period of time and then reintroduce it, if it's still a problem, it will be like going back to the dairy farm. You will be amazed at how severe the symptoms are that you had originally become so numb to.

"How in the world did I end up with these sensitivities in the first place?" is a very common question people ask, once they experience the difference eliminating trigger foods can make in their life. There is still a lot left for us to learn about how these sensitivities develop, but three of the most common ways suggested by research are genetics, overexposure (eating the same thing over and over), and chronic stress. There is that word "stress" again!

By following the Reset, you will reduce unneeded chronic stress loads. This relieves the burden on your gut and creates an ideal environment for it to improve.

The role of genetics is an interesting one and something I have studied a lot. We use a few different genetic tests to help us construct high-performance plans for our clients after they have rebooted their health by resetting their metabolism. When it comes to genetics Dr. Mehmet Oz said it best: "Genes load the gun, lifestyle pulls the trigger." You are far from doomed by your genetics. It's your lifestyle that causes the majority of your problems. You choose how you live. Knowing there are some foods you will never be able to tolerate makes things a lot easier. Those foods will always be a trigger for you, regardless of how long you stay away from them.

Overexposure is a major contributor to food sensitivity. Why?

Most of us like routine. Do you have the same thing for breakfast every morning? Or, like the friend I mentioned earlier, only eat a few foods? In this case, there can be too much of a good thing. I believe this is the reason so many of my clients are sensitive to foods like blueberries, almonds, salmon, and broccoli. These are all known "power foods" for your health, so they went into overachiever mode and ate them—all the time. Instead of incorporating them into a balanced diet full of variety, they decided to eat these foods every single day to be superhealthy.

Brendan Steele, professional golfer
California
Age thirty-one

▶ *Brendan Steele, a PGA Tour golfer, came to me at the end of his 2012 season, because he wanted to put some weight on to help increase his strength for driving distance and improve his durability to reduce back pain. Brendan was a slender 6 foot 2 and 172 pounds, but during our initial meeting and evaluation his body fat came out high for his size, and I noticed his lower stomach was very distended. I asked Brendan how his digestion was, and he responded that he had struggled with it for some time, but he had learned to just deal with it. I explained to Brendan that if he truly wanted to put on good muscle mass that is usable in his sport he had to get incredibly healthy first, and having bad digestion would prevent any possibility of that. Most people don't understand the importance of good digestion.*

It's amazing how many people actually struggle to put weight on. The Stark Naked 21-Day Metabolic Reset is not just for weight loss. It can also help people just like Brendan who need to put on weight.

We ran the MRT on Brendan to determine his food sensitivities and discovered he was sensitive to most of what he was eating! We had to completely revamp Brendan's diet. We started by hav-

If you're a true creature of habit who eats the same food day in and day out, even healthy food, you may be doing more harm than good by eating the same foods over and over without giving your system a break. If this sounds like you, now you know why the perfect diet of superfoods may be making you feel so lousy. Your body was not built to function on the same foods every day. It was built for variety.

To receive these amazing benefits of removing foods you are sensitive to, you just have to simply follow the approved-foods list for 21

ing him eat only from the approved-foods list of the Reset. We had to give his body time to heal itself. Whether you need to lose weight or put weight on, you have to start by fixing what's broken! Brendan had to have faith in me, because I knew he would initially drop a lot of weight in the first 21 days, and that was far from his goal. But that was bad weight, and it was holding him back from making progress.

His body continued to heal itself in Phase 2, and during the initial few months his weight dropped all the way to 160 pounds. This was not the outcome Brendan was looking for, but he remained patient with me and his trust and patience have paid off incredibly. Eighteen months later he now weighs 190 pounds, and his body fat is very low. Brendan has lost 10 pounds of fat and added 30 pounds of muscle over two full PGA Tour seasons. His newfound muscle mass and strength has added 8 miles per hour to his club-head speed, and his average driving distance has improved by over 20 yards. That's incredible improvement for an athlete already playing at the highest level of a sport. He also has not missed one round of golf due to back pain in over two seasons. When we started working together two years ago he was ranked 205th, and for the first time in his ten-year professional career he broke into the top 100 world rankings. And he's still climbing. Not a bad jump!

days. Don't veer from it, don't ask to make any changes, just stick to it for 21 days. It's simple. If it's on the list, you can eat it. If it's not on the list, you can't eat it.

For example, beans and lentils are not on the list for the first 21 days, so please avoid them. I have found that beans are a major cause of inflammation in a lot of people. The main reason for this is that beans and lentils contain oligosaccharides. Oligosaccharides are a complex sugar that is very challenging for humans to digest. Many experts believe the reason is that we either don't make the enzyme alpha-galactosidase needed to break oligosaccharides down or only make very small amounts. When oligosaccharides are present in the gut and the enzyme needed to break them down is either absent or in short supply, you end up with bloating, cramping, and unwanted gas.

That experience may be fun for kids ("Beans, beans, the musical fruit, the more you eat, the more you toot"), but for most adults it usually leads to embarrassment. Another reason to avoid beans is because they contain phytic acid, which can strip our body of essential minerals. Truth be told, we don't need any extra help chasing away more minerals. My goal is to help you retain the good stuff! So, for the Reset, stay away from the beans.

Last, if there is a food you know you have issues with and it's on the list of approved foods, please don't force yourself to eat it. Go ahead and keep it out of your diet.

Even if you believe you've been eating a healthy diet, you might be eating the wrong foods for you, which are causing inflammation and discomfort in the gut and other symptoms. During the Reset, you'll avoid the foods shown to cause the most inflammation and use other lifestyle strategies to get the most from your food (see page 204).

8. Follow the list of approved foods.

5

Warning! Danger Ahead

Why You Have Low Mojo

O H, YEAH, I'M GOING THERE. I am treading into territory few are willing to explore, and yet so many of you are dealing with it. I'm talking about not having sex. As a personal trainer, I hear all sorts of intimate details about my clients' lives, but the topic that seems to creep up more often than expected is a question many deal with and so few admit: "What in the world has happened to my mojo?"

You may be wondering why I find this an important topic to talk about in a book about health and fitness. I mean, isn't lack of sexual desire just part of getting older? *No!*

If you remember back to the Metabolic Breakdown Cycle, chronic stress leads to altered hormones, eventually leading to a lethargic metabolism. If your sex drive has disappeared, that's a huge warning sign that you are in the midst of a metabolic breakdown and on your way to hitting rock bottom. You may not have had a total breakdown yet, but believe me, untreated, you are well on your way.

If your mojo is not what it used to be, you are going to need to commit to the Stark Naked 21-Day Metabolic Reset, and fast, or you will suffer the consequences of a total breakdown, making it much harder for you to reset later. The Reset alone won't be enough to recharge worn-out sex hormones. It's going to take a full lifestyle overhaul and lots of catching up on lost sleep, so make sure to pay attention to Chapter 8, the sleep chapter, because sleep will become your greatest ally. But believe me, if it means getting your groove back, it's worth it.

When it comes to lost or low mojo, I find that most men either overcompensate by excessively bragging about their sexuality to their friends or clam up and say nothing at all, because in their mind their lack of sex drive equals a loss in manhood.

On the other hand, I find women openly discuss their loss of interest in sex or lack of attraction to their mate, as if it is a rite of passage with age. Most women past thirty-five who are clients of mine will readily admit that they know something is wrong with their hormones. They inherently understand something is off kilter and their sex drive is different than it once was. It's amazing how many women I see in the gym who say they'd rather knit than have sex with their spouse.

Has it really gotten that bad that you would rather knit than engage in the horizontal tango? Trust me! Life is better when sex is at the center of it.

Here's something to think about. If you would rather sleep than have sex, consider yourself closer to death than life.

In the movie *40 Days and 40 Nights* a young twenty-something played by Josh Hartnett vows to go 40 days and 40 nights without having sex to make himself a better man, a decision that almost kills him. When I was younger, 40 days of no sex felt like an eternity, but when I was beat down to a lethargic pulp, 40 days was an easy conquest. Did it make me a better man? Far from it—just ask my wife!

I was miserable and unmotivated in every area of life. Sex was the last thing on my mind when my total testosterone levels came in at 102 nanograms per deciliter (ng/dL)—a third of the normal low (300 ng/dL). These days, at forty, can I go sexless 40 days without dying? Yes, but it's far from ideal or my idea of a good time!

My wife recently had our third child, and her pregnancy was a challenging one. When she first announced that she was pregnant, I was excited, because that usually means an increased sex drive, but that dream was short-lived. This pregnancy, she was sicker than sick nearly every day for the first twenty weeks. There wasn't much hanky-panky between us during that period—and, of course, I understood. Naturally, I found a way to survive. You can bet that when the few opportunities did appear, I definitely rose to the occasion! Though, looking back, I honestly think my wife was taking pity on me. Us men—we really are such babies!

My wife figured me out very early in our relationship. If she wanted me to move mountains, she was very strategic in how she motivated me. When it came to our sex life, she realized I couldn't get enough of her; nine years later I still can't! It's one of the great perks of marriage that comes with healthy hormones. My wife knows exactly how to use her charm to motivate me to do anything—even hang the Christmas lights. She doesn't have to nag me! Nope. All she needs to do is come home with some mistletoe, put it over my head, give me an intense kiss and her sexy, seductive look, and I am putty. Those bad boys are usually hung in an hour!

Now, if you're a married man like me, we all know our women have the ability to get us with their womanly ways, but the truth is, anyone in a relationship understands that bringing home flowers for no reason, planning a surprise weekend away from the kids, cooking a romantic dinner for two, cleaning the house, or just about any small unexpected gesture goes a really long way with our significant other. I know my wife loves it when I give her time away from the kids, a night out with her girlfriends, a massage in bed that *isn't* meant to be foreplay (okay, maybe it is), or a foot rub after a long run or hike we took together. Sure, I know these things usually lead to the horizontal mambo, but I also know they make my wife happy. And as the saying goes, "Happy wife, happy life!"

But what happens when the fire goes out? When, no matter how hard you stoke the flames, there is no fire? What the hell happened? Where has your desire for sex gone?

Most of us believe a shrinking sex drive comes with aging, but I don't buy that and I don't like when I hear clients use that as an excuse. I train a couple in their mid-seventies who have sex at least two or three times a week. During a workout, the wife once inquired whether I knew of any supplements to slow her husband down a bit. "He wants it all the time!" she said.

She went on to explain that if he simply sees a small flash of any of her bare skin, he's all over her and won't stop until she gives in and has sex with him. I can tell she loves that he still pursues her so passionately at seventy-five years of age and he doesn't need Viagra to make it happen.

Guess what? That's the potential we *all* have when we take proper care of ourselves!

I believe we are supposed to still be enjoying sex late in life. Now that I am in my forties, I am convinced that I am just reaching my sexual prime, despite research to the contrary that says men reach their sexual prime much younger. When I was thirty-three, I wouldn't have believed that was possible. I had just come off training with the U.S. bobsled team, so my body looked amazing. According to my wife, I had the physique of a Greek god. I was 5 foot 10, I weighed 205 pounds, and my body fat was under 10 percent. When I looked like that, one would have assumed I had a sex drive that was through the roof. But I didn't. In fact, my mojo was so low that I would rather have slept than had sex. My greatest desire in life was sleep. This was not healthy for a man my age or for my marriage.

We are always told not to judge a book by its cover, and I was a walking, talking example of that back then. Just because the outside looked good, it didn't mean the insides were functioning as they should. I have seen more perfectly chiseled high achievers with destroyed hormones than those with optimal hormones. Sadly, it is usually the best-looking men and women who I find have done the most damage to themselves. Remember, fitness can mask health.

We live in a world where we are constantly told that if we exercise (a lot), eat superclean, and get really lean, we are guaranteed to have optimal hormone levels. With the optimal hormone levels, we are guaranteed to desire more sex. Right?

Wrong!

In his groundbreaking book *Why Zebras Don't Get Ulcers,* Robert Sapolsky discusses in detail how stress negatively affects sex hormones in men and women. In fact, it's such an important topic, he writes an entire chapter on it. I am going to give you a basic understanding of how stress (have you noticed a pattern here yet?) is the main culprit that is likely shutting down your sex drive. If you don't deal with reducing your stress load—and I mean now—your hormones will never operate at an optimal level.

How Stress Robs Men of Their Desire for Sex

When it comes to men and sex, our hormones, just like our needs in life, are really very simple. Testosterone is a great predictor of biological aging in men. When testosterone dips, we suffer—a lot. This decrease can affect everything from our sexual desires to the ability to get it up, our general state of happiness, our drive in life, and our body fat, muscle mass, and mental concentration; it can dramatically increase the risk of an early death.

Basically the higher your testosterone level, the younger you are on the inside. Conversely, the lower it is, the older you are, independent of your actual age. The *Journal of Clinical Endocrinology and Metabolism* published a study following 794 men from the San Diego area over the age of fifty. It found that at an 11.8-year follow-up the men with the lowest testosterone levels (less than 241 ng/dL) were 40 percent more likely to die than those with higher levels. Similarly, in an August 2006 article in the *Archives of Internal Medicine,* a team of

U.S. doctors determined that men over the age of forty had an 88 percent increased risk of death associated with low levels of testosterone. An *ABC News* article highlighted research from the New England Research Institute stating that one in four men over the age of thirty suffers from low testosterone. (I was one of them.)

The reference range for normal total testosterone is usually 300–1000 ng/dL; anyone with levels under 300 ng/dL is considered to have low testosterone. This is a huge range in my opinion. I can personally testify that at 1000 ng/dL sex is all you can think about, but at 300 ng/dL Megan Fox hardly catches your attention. What's frightening in this research is the direction most men's testosterone levels are headed in general. By the year 2025, researchers are predicting a 38 percent increase in men between the ages of thirty and seventy-nine who are plagued with low testosterone. Something has to change, or it won't be long before a majority of men are suffering from low testosterone and being robbed of their best possible lives. The scariest part for most men is that one of the last things to go in their health decline is their sex drive and the ability to get it up. By the time they reach that point, they're pretty jacked up. I believe that's why there is an elevated risk of early death associated with low testosterone in older men.

Why is this happening?

Your brain is the control center for producing the majority of your hormones. In Chapter 2 we explored its role in triggering the stress hormones that unleash your inner Hulk and keep you alive in times of trouble. It is also responsible for producing more sex hormones. With a healthy metabolism, when your brain receives signals that your mojo is running low, it sends signals to your testes to produce more testosterone and refill your mojo. It is programmed to keep your sex hormones in a balanced state at all times, so you function at an optimal level and desire sex.

The major issue impacting your mojo in this day and age is likely chronic stress. So what happens when your body is under stress?

As soon as the brain perceives stress and signals the release of your stress hormones, the whole system for making sex hormones is shut down. Consequently there is an immediate reduction in mojo-making hormones. The production process for these sex hormones cannot be flipped back on until the stress-response system is calmed down. A 2011 study conducted by the University of California, Berkeley, supports the correlation between stress and the shutdown of the sex drive.

When you think about it, it makes perfect sense. The desire to reproduce is the second most important of the human drives.

Do you recall the first?

To survive at all costs!

A beautiful woman can make men do all sorts of crazy things, and our bodies know it, so to keep the focus on survival in the face of danger, the reproductive drives are shut down.

So, let's say it's the year 2040, and you're facing a zombie apocalypse. Out of self-preservation, you've suddenly found yourself in a fight-or-flight mode because you are running from a zombie. Your body will automatically shut down the desire for sex to protect you. I don't care if Elle MacPherson or Brooklyn Decker crosses your path—when you are running for your life, you are not going to stop and ask the zombie for a time-out to try and score. Believe it or not, you won't even want to.

It has also been discovered that it's not just life-or-death stressors that cause this reduction-in-testosterone response. It's all kinds of daily stressors, including pain, illness, poor eating habits, psychological stress, emotional stress, lack of sleep, excessive alcohol, and even overexercising, that can easily slow down your testosterone production. Yes, you read that right—too much exercise bashes and beats your mojo into submission.

Take it from a guy who knows firsthand. That's what happened to me in my early thirties. I had overtrained and, without realizing it, overstressed myself into a state where I had severely low testosterone levels. Now let me follow up by saying that I know exercise in the right proportion is a great thing. But like everything in life, too much of a good thing—even exercise—can be damaging. Research is very clear that moderate exercise is great for our bodies, but extreme intense exercise can cause more harm than good. Experts have shown that when you combine a poor diet, lack of rest, and too much exercise, you drive that pesky stress hormone cortisol through the roof.

What is suppressed when cortisol is elevated? You guessed it! Your mojo.

For years I have said, "The more insane your exercise program, the more insane your nutrition and recovery strategies better be, or you're going to find yourself on the road to metabolic disaster." I don't want to see you headed on that path. I will give you great strategies for tracking and managing safe exercise and recovery in Chapter 9.

And if I haven't already made it clear, I am about to put the final nail in the coffin for you on how stress impacts your sex life. When you have low mojo, not only don't you feel like having sex, even if you do, your stress-signaling system is likely having a negative impact on your erections. In 2012 the drugs targeting erectile dysfunction were valued at $4.3 billion for the year. That's a lot of ED drugs driving erections.

So how is stress affecting your ability to get it up?

We know it takes an increase of blood flow to rise to your calling. A reduction in cardiovascular health is the major contributor to our limp-noodle epidemic, but stress can also prevent you from responding to your sexual calling. You have to be in a calm state to obtain and sustain an erection. If stress is elevated, it is difficult to get it up, and if by some chance you are able to, that stress response will most likely cause premature ejaculation. Every man has experienced premature ejaculation. Yeah, we joke about it, but most of us are hiding the truth that we have experienced the inability to either get it up prior to sex or keep it up, often because of nervousness during sex. That reality often deeply scars us with embarrassment and hang-ups that get into our heads, making it tougher to stay calm the next time a sexual encounter occurs.

Now that I've delivered the reasons for your low mojo, allow me to give you some good news. The Stark Naked 21-Day Metabolic Reset will dramatically improve your erections by drastically increasing your cardiovascular health and overall blood flow! (You can thank all of the green vegetables and water you'll be consuming for that!) It will also drastically reduce your overall stress load, making it much easier for you to relax before and during sex.

I bet when you bought this book, you weren't expecting this added bonus!

How Stress Robs Women of Sexual Desire

Buckle your seat belts, ladies. You're not immune either. We are going on the ultimate roller-coaster ride. Yes, we are going to talk about women's hormones, which are far more complicated than men's. They drastically change each month according to a woman's cycle. To make it even more confusing, birth control and menopause have dramatic effects on your hormones—and they're different for every woman. I could write an entire book on this subject, but for our purposes I am going to focus solely on estrogen, progesterone, and testosterone and the impact these three hormones have on a woman's body when they are out of balance. It can result in unnecessary fat gain, inexplicable depression, and even low sexual desire.

Understanding Estrogen and Progesterone

Ladies, stay with me here. This is a little more intense, but unlike us thick-headed, zero-attention-span men, I know you have the ability to absorb information at a deeper level, so I am going to dive in here with the hope that you want the information I am providing. I have met so many confused women over the years who feel miserable. They know their hormones are to blame, but are clueless about what's actually going on to create the way they feel.

In 2012 I had the opportunity to record a podcast with Robb Wolf, the author of *The Paleo Solution,* about how I help women balance their sex hormones to assist with fat loss. During my preparation for that interview, I came across an article by Dr. Jade Teta entitled "Female Phase Training: Training with the Female Cycle." The article discussed how to use different types of exercise in the different phases of a woman's cycle each month to create consistent fat loss. Dr. Teta's knowledge of women's sex hormones runs deep. As a result of reading that article, I reached out to him and have since developed a great personal friendship. Through my numerous conversations with Dr. Teta, I came to a better understanding of what women struggle with when dealing with unbalanced sex hormones and developed this Reset plan to help meet their needs.

Let's take a look at how your sex hormones are supposed to work and where the bulk of the chaos is coming from for most women.

Like a man's, your brain is also at the root of controlling and balancing your mojo hormones. However, in women the brain triggers different hormones at different times of the month. During the first half of your cycle the brain triggers the ovaries to produce estrogen; then it switches to triggering progesterone in the second half of your cycle. Your brain is also responsible for stimulating the ovaries to release eggs. Estrogen and progesterone perform a specific dance each month during your cycle, and they need to be in balance to work at their best.

During the follicular phase (days 1–14) of the cycle, estrogen is steadily rising while progesterone stays low. Estrogen peaks during ovulation, releasing a mature egg. Then during the luteal phase (days 15–28) the body increases production of progesterone, preparing the uterine wall for implantation of a fertilized egg. If fertilization of the egg does not happen, then both estrogen and progesterone dip at menses, and the process starts all over. When the cycle runs smoothly and the two hormones stay in balance, you breeze through your cycle sometimes surprised when your period shows up. You feel sexy and happy, you enjoy sex, PMS symptoms are almost nonexistent, and your waistline stays nice and trim. You and your significant other get the most out of life enjoying your sexy hourglass figure.

Estrogen Dominance

How many of you truly experience a regular monthly cycle?

Here's a fun idea. Ask your significant other what it's honestly like dealing with you during "that time of the month." Does your significant other strategically plan business trips around those few days every month? That could be a good sign your hormones are a bit off.

Estrogen dominance is usually the main factor disrupting a healthy monthly cycle. Estrogen dominance occurs when progesterone is deficient compared to estrogen. Some experts believe it's likely that as much as 50 percent of all menstruating women deal with estrogen dominance. That means one out of every two of you is dealing with hormones that are internally wreaking havoc, which can lead to symptoms like these from estrogen dominance:

- Anxiety
- Breast tenderness
- Bloating
- Depressed sex drive
- Fat gain around hips and thighs
- Fatigue
- Poor memory and foggy thinking
- Headaches
- Heavy bleeding during menstruation
- Irritability
- Insomnia

- Mood swings
- Enhanced PMS symptoms

If you experience some or all of these symptoms every month, there is a good chance you're dealing with estrogen dominance. If that's the case, it's time to take action.

When your hormonal balance is off so that estrogen is elevated and progesterone is too low, you will typically store excess fat on the hips and thighs and have a smaller waistline. This is due to estrogen's ability to prevent cortisol from storing weight gain around the waist, but experiencing estrogen dominance long enough will eventually lead to an expanding waistline as well. Most women notice this transitioning into menopause, as estrogen begins to decrease, leading to lower levels of both estrogen and progesterone and the resulting inability to offset cortisol and block fat accumulation around your midsection.

The first step to solving this problem is realizing that, just like for men, stress is at the root of the problem and the worst thing you can do is add more stress to the mix by attempting to eat less and exercise more. Your body has the ability to convert progesterone to cortisol to keep you alive, because survival is vital. Stress eventually causes progesterone to decrease, leading to estrogen dominance. Choosing to deprive yourself of food and punish your body with exercise as your weight-loss game plan creates too much of a stress response in your body, driving progesterone even farther downward and creating more estrogen dominance.

Over the years, I have met with many women whose hips and thighs have actually gotten bigger while their waistline has shrunk when they were eating less and exercising more, leaving them frustrated and angry. If that's how you are currently trying to overcome this problem, please do your body and sex drive a favor and stop!

You can't force the change! You have to fix the problem. You must first discover the cause of the imbalance.

There are three main culprits leading to estrogen dominance. Men, make sure you pay attention to this list, because it affects you too; estrogen dominance is becoming very common in men as well. Pay especially close attention to numbers 2 and 3 below. Estrogen buildup in men can lead to moobs (there it is again, that word for man boobs), fat gain around the hips and thighs, hair loss, loss of sex drive, impotence, hot flashes, and mood issues like irritability. There's a joke among my colleagues: it's not young, high-testosterone men who start wars; it's the crotchety, older estrogen-dominant men who trigger the wars and then send in their young testosterone-driven armies to finish what they started.

Source 1: The "Progesterone Steal" from Stress

Progesterone is considered by many to be the "mother of all hormones," because every other hormone in your body is made from it. When stress is elevated, the body can turn on what is known as "progesterone steal." When the adrenals are no longer able to keep up with the demand for cortisol production, the body has a backup plan to keep you going. That plan is to steal progesterone to keep your cortisol production moving.

Dr. Tina Marcantel explains this well in her article "Hormones and How They Interact": "Mother Progesterone feeds the loudest baby (cortisol), and the other children (DHEA [dehydroepiandrosterone, a natural steroid hormone], testosterone, and estradiol [an estrogen]) decrease in size because all the attention is being given to cortisol." Basically if your body is under stress and your brain is triggering the need for cortisol, your other hormones are going to suffer until the stress trigger is dampened. This is especially prevalent during states of adrenal burnout.

It's very common to find estrogen dominance issues in women who are exhausted from chronic stress exposure. This is also commonly seen during menopause and is one of the reasons a woman's waistline expands during menopause, even though her diet hasn't changed. Cortisol is stealing all the precursor building blocks of the sex hormones to keep it alive, and the other hormones (estrogen, progesterone, and testosterone) necessary to keep you skinny have been deprived so long, they barely exist anymore. Cortisol can be such a killjoy!

I have seen multiple women in their early forties showing signs of early menopause, and the one thing in common among all of them is their trashed adrenals from an overly stressed lifestyle.

Source 2: A Sluggish Liver

Another major player causing estrogen dominance is a sluggish liver. The liver is responsible for preventing estrogen from building up in your body. Estrogens are processed through the liver and shuttled out like all of the other toxins described in Chapter 3. When the liver is overwhelmed, the process of removing estrogens is slowed down, which causes estrogen to become stuck in the body. The result is that the estrogen side of the estrogen-to-progesterone ratio is elevated, leading to estrogen dominance, which causes you to experience the symptoms like fat storage on your hips and thighs, increased irritability, insomnia, fatigue, headaches, and foggy thinking.

To make matters even worse, when you combine low progesterone from stress with estrogen buildup due to a sluggish liver, you get that pesky Dr. Jekyll–Mr. Hyde monthly cycle. This is very common.

Now get this. The first line of defense for this hormonal imbalance recommended by our medical community is to add synthetic hormones to the mix in the form of a birth control pill, which is actually classified as a known carcinogen right along with tobacco and asbestos by the World Health Organization. Currently over eleven million U.S. women between the ages of fifteen and forty-four take oral birth control pills. Fifty-eight percent of users rely on the pill for other purposes besides pregnancy prevention. Some of the major reasons for use according to a 2011 Guttmacher Institute study: 31 percent use it for cramps or menstrual pain, 28 percent for menstrual regulation,

14 percent for acne. These are all symptoms of estrogen dominance.

I recently met with a young female athlete who was complaining of symptoms of estrogen dominance; specifically, she had a dramatic increase in body fat, and her PMS symptoms were noticeably rougher every month. After digging deeper into her medical history, I discovered she had symptoms of an extremely burdened liver. Four months prior to our first meeting she had stopped taking her birth control pills, because she felt they were making her too aggressive.

Unlike most women who are taking estrogen-based birth control pills, she was using the new form of birth control called Drospirenone (DRSP), which only contains progesterone. Remember, progesterone has the ability to convert into other hormones like cortisol. However, it can also convert to anabolic hormones like DHEA and testosterone. Although her birth control was doing a good job keeping her estrogen-progesterone balance in check, it was also allowing the excess progesterone to convert to anabolic hormones, making her significantly more aggressive. When she removed the birth control from her daily routine, her progesterone collapsed. Her elevated estrogen and a sluggish liver caused an extremely estrogen-dominant state. As a result, her body fat quickly elevated, especially around her hips and thighs. Her muscle mass and strength also diminished, and she went from being superaggressive to experiencing bouts of extreme anxiety, insomnia, and fatigue.

The Stark Naked 21-Day Metabolic Reset did wonders for her overwhelmed liver, allowing my client to drop 15 pounds in the first 21 days. For the first time in months, she was able to sleep again and no longer had mood swings or severe anxiety. She was able to fit back into her skinny clothes and had no severe PMS symptoms every month.

Source 3: Xenoestrogens (Environmental Estrogens)

In Chapter 3 we covered the chemicals you are exposed to from rubbing various beauty products onto your skin every day and the impact this has on your liver and sex hormones. One classification I want you to be aware of is xenoestrogens, synthetic chemicals that, once inside the body, can mimic estrogen. *Xeno*, from the Greek, means "foreign." We discussed parabens as an estrogen mimicker in Chapter 3, but there are additional environmental estrogens you are likely being exposed to. Other known xenoestrogens include:

Phthalates, commonly used in flooring and plastics and also found in perfumes, lotions, cosmetics, varnishes, nail polish.

Bisphenol A, found in the linings of most food and beverage cans and currently one of the highest-volume chemicals produced world-wide. The FDA has recently banned its use in baby bottles and infant formula.

Atrazine, an herbicide to control weeds, the second largest selling pesticide in the United States, banned in Europe in 2005. It is used on crops like corn and sugarcane and on golf courses and lawns.

Zeranol, currently used extensively as a growth stimulator in the beef and pork industries in the United States and Canada, banned in Europe in 1985.

Xenoestrogens are scary, and they are everywhere! Unless you want to remove yourself from society and go live deep in the wilderness of the Rockies, you are not going to escape xenoestrogens. The bottom line is this: you have to take the best measures to offset the damage these can cause. The Stark Naked 21-Day Metabolic Reset provides you with a good foundation of daily support to fight these substances, but you may wish to take your defense to another level and remove as many xenoestrogens from your lifestyle as possible.

Women and Testosterone

The last hormone I want to explore with you is testosterone, that scary manly hormone. Most women view testosterone as the hormone that creates gross-looking bulging muscles and hair in all the wrong places. Most of you want nothing to do with that bulky look. Trust me, I am not a fan either. More recently the role of elevated testosterone in polycystic ovary syndrome (PCOS) is another reason you want nothing to do with testosterone. Yes, testosterone is the primary hormone for men, and yes, high testosterone is associated with PCOS, but when testosterone drops in women it wreaks havoc within your body. It plays a major role in sexuality, helping with sexual desire and preparing you for sex with natural responses such as vaginal lubrication. When testosterone is too low, you no longer want sex, and if you have it, it's not especially enjoyable.

Low testosterone in women has been associated with the following symptoms:

- Anxiety
- Loss of libido
- Lethargy and lack of motivation
- Loss of muscle and strength
- Inability to climax
- Depression and mood swings
- Increased fat around your belly
- Elevated risk of osteoporosis
- Hair loss on the head and body

What causes low testosterone in women? The majority of testosterone for women is created by the adrenals. And though I realize I am starting to sound like a broken record, it cannot be overstated that the biggest culprit causing low testosterone in women is stress. When your adrenals have been mobilized to defend against stress, they are not allowed to replenish testosterone until the stress goes away.

Another very common trigger for low or reduced testosterone is the birth control pill. The pill works so well, it not only prevents you from getting pregnant; it actually reduces your desire to have sex in the first place by blunting testosterone. Last but not least, menopause is also another common cause of low testosterone. When a woman hits menopause, all hormones come crashing down, especially testosterone.

It's absurd how your current lifestyle is destroying your hormones, isn't it?

I hope testosterone just got a little less scary for you. If you're experiencing some of the symptoms talked about in this chapter, please follow the Stark Naked 21-Day Metabolic Reset exactly as it is laid out. It will be the start your body needs to revitalize your testosterone, rebalance your estrogen and progesterone levels, and give you back your swagger. If you choose to ignore these warning signs or, worse, if you have pushed yourself too hard for so long that not only are you dealing with a lot of these symptoms, but you are also exhausted all the time, you have entered the final stage of the Metabolic Breakdown Cycle, known as adrenal burnout.

> If your sex drive has disappeared, that's a huge warning sign that you are in the midst of a metabolic breakdown and on your way to hitting rock bottom. The Reset will help you get your mojo back.

6

The Consequences of Your Metabolic Breakdown

The Dangers of Adrenal Burnout and Hitting Rock Bottom

D O YOU WAKE UP FEELING TIRED? I mean inexplicably tired—as though you haven't slept enough, or at all, and you fear you can't make it through your day, even when you had 8 hours of sleep the night before? Or at the end of the day, are you so exhausted you can't make it through to the end of a movie without falling asleep?

Are you so tired that you are lacking your once virile sex drive? Do you suddenly experience random sugar or salt cravings you've never had before, feel depressed, or get sick all of the time? Do you find yourself uncontrollably irritable, unable to focus or remember things and basically lacking the joy and drive you once had in life?

If you answered yes to most (if not all) of these, you're in the final stage of the Metabolic Breakdown Cycle. You've definitely pushed too hard, too long, and your body has officially given up.

Welcome to the wonderful world of what is commonly referred to as adrenal burnout—meaning your adrenal glands are overworked and are functioning in a fatigued state. When the adrenals can no longer keep up, your body has basically given up its fight to keep you alive and has begun to shut down. Adrenal burnout has been a major buzzword in the world of high-performance athletes, but in the last few years it has become more mainstream among high achievers like you.

Most commonly associated with intense or prolonged stress, adrenal burnout occurs when the adrenal glands function below the necessary level. Your adrenal glands mobilize your body's responses to every kind of stress (whether it's physical, emotional, or psychological) through hormones that regulate energy production and storage, immune function, heart rate, muscle tone, and other processes. When your adrenals get fatigued, you have basically pushed yourself so hard for so long that the control system of the adrenals begins to wear out and shut down. Once they can't keep up with demands placed on them, you begin to suffer big-time.

Just about everything you do can and does impact your adrenals. If not managed properly and given enough rest, your adrenals will be overworked and forced to give up.

How do you know if you have hit the wall and are experiencing adrenal burnout?

Simple! Do you have any of these symptoms?

Getting light-headed when going from a lying to a standing position

Feeling overwhelmed

Hypoglycemia (low blood sugar)

Constant tiredness

Irritability and depression

Low blood pressure

Anxiety

Trouble staying asleep

Trouble getting out of bed in the morning

Lack of joy in life, everything is a struggle

Preference for sleep over sex

Severe brain fog and lack mental focus

No desire to exercise

If you are regularly experiencing three or more of these symptoms, then your adrenals are more than likely working in a state of adrenal burnout and your metabolism is seriously broken. Not only is the Stark Naked 21-Day Metabolic Reset an absolute must for you; your energy bank account is so far overdrawn, the bank is about to close your account unless you start replenishing the energy and fast!

I know this is going to be a tough adjustment for many of you, but the only exercise I recommend you do during the Stark Naked 21-Day Metabolic Reset is passive, such as taking walks in nature for 20 to 30 minutes a day. This is a secret recovery strategy I've learned the Russians use with their athletes. It's so secret they wouldn't even allow Ivan Drago to be shown doing it in *Rocky IV*. Okay, just kidding. It's not *that* secret, but you would be amazed who uses this strategy of walking in nature to enhance recovery and keep the metabolism running on all cylinders. Professional athletes, top CrossFit athletes, CEOs of very successful companies, U.S. Military Special Forces members, and yours truly take advantage of this strategy regularly. I will teach you how to use it to your advantage in Chapter 9, where I'll talk in greater detail about exercise during your reset.

In early January 2014, I received a phone call from the incredible world-class CrossFit athlete Becca Voigt. At age thirty-four, she has qualified for the brutally intense CrossFit Games seven years in a row and is recognized as one of the fittest women in the world. The CrossFit Games pride themselves on being the world's premier test of fitness. In 2014 over 140,000 people signed up for the CrossFit Open, hoping to earn a spot in the CrossFit Games. The 140,000 are eventually whittled down to the top 100 men and women in the world, who compete in multiple events challenging fitness and athleticism over a long weekend at the Home Depot Center in Los Angeles for the title "Fittest on Earth."

During our first conversation Becca told me she was suffering from adrenal burnout. She literally could not get out of bed in the mornings from excessive fatigue. She was emotionally worn out, lacking her usual drive for training and in life. Her necessary competition workouts were stalled, and her cardiovascular conditioning seemed to be slowly disappearing. Becca's body fat was suddenly elevated, and her old nutritional strategies of eating low-carb and superclean were no longer helping her usual six-pack or energy production. This was not a good sign. She asked me for my help to reset her system, so she could compete in the 2014 CrossFit Open that started in six weeks.

Things had to change for Becca, and they had to change fast! I quickly agreed with Becca's assessment that the biggest hurdle holding her back were her adrenals. They were definitely overworked and functioning in a burnout state. As with most overachieving athletes, I also found her liver very sluggish too. This combination can have a terrible impact on a high-performing athlete like Becca.

Our initial focus was to support her liver with strategies from the Reset while slowly increasing her carbohydrate intake to support her intense training volume, improving her body's ability to recover. How effective were these strategies?

Within two months, Becca went from struggling to get out of bed in the mornings to finishing second at the 2014 CrossFit Southern California Regionals and reaching her seventh straight CrossFit Games. If these strategies can rejuvenate someone like her, at the highest level of fitness competition, they can help any individuals reset their metabolism and get their adrenals back online—including *you*!

First, let's explore how you got here in the first place.

The Causes of Adrenal Burnout

Imagine for a moment that you are a race-car driver in the Indy 500. You're in total control of the car. You decide when to turn the steering wheel, apply the gas and brake, signal your pit crew that the car needs attention, and make pit stops for them to refuel and perform mechanical repairs. When your car is well cared for and finely tuned, the signal and demand system works smoothly, keeping your car operating at its peak performance and giving you your best chance of winning the big race.

Are you with me so far? In this analogy the driver is the brain, specifically the hypothalamus-pituitary complex (HP complex), the major control center for the glands that make hormones in your body. The hypothalamus connects your nervous system to your endocrine system through the pituitary gland and acts like a thermostat for your hormones. The hypothalamus receives input from your nervous system and triggers the pituitary to send specific signals to the different glands for hormone production and adjustments to keep them in balance, just like your thermostat regulates the temperature of your house.

A simple example of this is when the brain receives the input that you're moving from a lying to a standing position. The brain signals the adrenals to release epinephrine (adrenaline) to raise your blood pressure a little as you become erect. This happens in order to fight gravity and make sure blood stays in your brain, so you don't pass out. If your adrenals are exhausted and not working at optimum levels, you will feel light-headed and dizzy doing something as simple as going from lying to standing.

Think about that. Has this ever happened to you? If so, it might have been your body telling you your adrenals are running low on fuel just like a race car.

When your body, like the race car, is well cared for and finely tuned, it works at an optimum level, constantly maintaining a perfect balance to meet the performance demands. As the driver, you are constantly monitoring feedback from your car, correcting the positioning with your steering, applying the gas and the brakes at the right times to keep your car in the race around turns, and listening to your pit crew through radio communications. You're constantly getting feedback to keep you at your best.

But what happens when you decide to start ignoring feedback from the experts, thinking you know best? Trouble is waiting for you.

Let's say your tires signal you that it's time to make a pit stop and have them changed. Eager to stay in the race, you decide to override the signal. You decide that a pit stop isn't worth the time, so you fly right by the pit. Now things begin to get tough. The car is harder to control in the turns, but you know you can dig deep and overcome this with your superb driving skills. Next, you notice a warning light on your dash. It's the fuel gauge indicating that you'll need gas soon. Now, the smart thing to do would be to make a quick pit stop to change the tires and refuel, but no, you again override these signals, yet continue to demand that your car keep performing at its peak. The car is being pushed past its ability to maintain high-performance balance and will eventually break down. Do you really think you have a chance at winning the race this way?

Heck no! The smart thing to do would be to make a simple pit stop!

You have no chance of winning a race with this strategy. Those signals are all there for a reason, and a great driver pays attention to those signals and responds to them as needed. A horrible driver ignores the signals, believing he can push the car and win the race. Eventually the driver pushes the car too far, and it either breaks down or runs out of gas. Now the car is "dead" and unable to respond to any of the driver's commands. No matter how hard the driver pushes on the gas pedal, if there's no gas in the tank, there will be no response from the car.

This is what happens to your body when it's put under unneces-

A Simple Adrenal Test You Can Do at Home

Here's a simple test you can do at home to see how your adrenals are doing called the Orthostatic Hypotension Test. It's a test I run on every client I work with to get some clues as to how well their adrenals are doing. To complete the test you need a blood pressure cuff and a place to lie down flat on your back. Place the blood pressure cuff on your arm and lie comfortably, flat on your back, for 5 minutes. Take your blood pressure and record the systolic number (top number). Next come to a standing position and retake your blood pressure. Again record the systolic number (top number). See the chart below for results.

ORTHOSTATIC HYPOTENSION TEST RESULTS	
Systolic Change	*Possible Adrenal Finding*
Increases 6–10 mm/Hg	Healthy adrenal function
Increases 1–6 mm/Hg or does not change	Adrenals are under stress
Decreases 1–10 mm/Hg	Adrenals are struggling
Decreases more than 10 mm/Hg	Adrenals are exhausted

If your systolic number does not go up by 6–10 mm/Hg, you know you are in the Metabolic Breakdown Cycle, but if it drops more than 10 mm/Hg, you need to follow the guidelines in this chapter. You might not officially be there (you would need a 16-hour saliva cortisol DHEA lab to confirm this for sure), but it's pretty clear your adrenals have been overworked and are really struggling. It's time to give them some serious support.

sary stress. So many of us totally ignore our body's signals that something is wrong. We are determined to push through everything! You can't win in this game of life by ignoring the signals.

Your body is trying everything to force you to sleep, yet you keep slamming coffee and Red Bulls to push through! Your headache is screaming for water, yet you give it an aspirin!

Gentlemen, your body needs green vegetables to rise to the occasion, but your answer is Viagra to improve blood flow. Ladies, the fat accumulating around your hips and thighs is begging you to hit the stress-reduction button, yet you continue to do the opposite and keep grinding through workouts. When you choose to ignore the stress signals crying out from your body, forcing it to keep going, the adrenal glands eventually become overworked and start shutting down.

The HP complex will elevate the signaling, trying to get the lethargic adrenal glands to respond, but it too will eventually give out. Now, the overworked adrenal glands and HP complex are just like the run-down race car and no longer able to signal and respond.

If you are experiencing symptoms of adrenal burnout, your adrenal glands and the HP complex in your brain have been pushed too hard, too long. They can no longer keep up with the demands. The only answer is to make a pit stop and reset your metabolism.

How the Stark Naked 21-Day Reset and Lifestyle Repair Adrenal Burnout

Is it as simple as just following the 21-Day Reset to fix adrenal burnout?

I wish! You didn't reach this state overnight, and therefore you won't fix it overnight. You have been ignoring your body's signals for years; the fact is, adrenal burnout is a pretty extreme chronic state.

To resolve your adrenal burnout, follow the Phase 1 Reset and Phase 2 Optimized Nutrition Plan *and* change how you think about stress. The Reset and Optimized Nutrition Plan will help reduce the lifestyle stressors contributing to your burnout. To heal, you'll also need to address your mental or emotional stress. And that means *reducing* it in your life.

I know, it's a lot easier said than done. Rome wasn't built in a day.

It will take time, but like everything we've talked about so far, it will be worth it.

In Chapter 2 we discussed the Hulk response and used the example of people allowing their inner Hulk to be activated simply because they are stuck in traffic. There was no life-threatening situation, but how they perceived the situation and the thoughts that followed caused them to respond internally as if it were.

This type of response to stress only leads down the path to destruction—especially where your health is concerned. Remember, this is your time to *relax and conquer*!

How can you accomplish this?

If you really want to recover from adrenal burnout, you will need to take some time and make a list of mental and emotional triggers that bring out your inner Hulk. I know one of my inner-Hulk triggers is being late. I despise running late. I used to get very worked up when I was late for an appointment, especially if someone else was the cause of my tardiness. I still get worked up about this, but I've learned not to let my inner Hulk come out over it, because I now understand that I pay the price for that response.

Even so, there are times that test me. As a guy who grew up in the rains of Oregon, I hate how life in Southern California comes to a screeching halt with the slightest drizzle. The roads become gridlocked, and everyone is afraid to drive. If I have to drop my kids off at school in the morning, which is usually a major treat for me, and then get to a meeting with a client, it becomes a real challenge in the rain. I will feel my inner Hulk emerging, but I try my hardest to fight it, as I inch my way through the drop-off lane, watching the clock, knowing it's going to be close whether I'll make my meeting on time or not.

Once you've made your list of triggers, you will want to avoid those situations until you've learned to control them. If you find yourself experiencing the trigger, you will need to remind yourself that it's not a life-or-death scenario. No matter what, everything will be okay. You may have to practice deep breathing until you feel calm and in control. A mentor of mine George Ryan puts it nicely: "Take a walk on the beach in your mind for a few minutes," meaning find a calm place in your mind until you're at peace. Do whatever it takes to either avoid those stress triggers or keep yourself calm whenever you're experiencing them.

You will also want to take up some type of meditation to calm your inner Hulk. Meditation is one of the greatest tools available to high performers. There is a reason people like Oprah, Richard Branson, and Tony Robbins are constantly recommending meditation. It's a major competitive advantage for greatness. But if you are anything like me, when I close my eyes and try to think about nothing, I literally think about everything. It's far from relaxing, because I just end up getting frustrated. A couple of smartphone apps that I really like to use to help me reach a meditative state are *Calm* and *Headspace.* Find what works for you and use it regularly.

Last, you need to focus on two things we have yet to talk about—your recovery and sleep. Sleep is such a critical component in your

Keep Calm!

My favorite app for keeping my inner Hulk under control is *Calm.* It progressively relaxes your body until you hit a deeply calm and relaxed state. I use this app two or three times a day, because it keeps my stress under control and helps me feel my best.

Another app I really like is *Headspace.* I love to use this app before I speak, as it centers me and calms my mind, making me a much better speaker.

I also recommend any type of mindset training that helps you cope with stressful situations. I have included a few of my favorites in the Resource Guide.

When you combine a bulletproof mindset with a reset, high-performing metabolism, you can accomplish things beyond your greatest dreams!

reset, especially if you have hit the wall. Later, in Chapter 8, I am going to explain why it's so important and give you my best strategies for improving it. You will learn in greater detail why I believe sleep is the fountain of youth, the wellspring of your sex hormones, and the source of your energy and creativity.

Sleep is your secret weapon and greatest asset to recovering from adrenal burnout. Just following the Stark Naked 21-Day Metabolic Reset alone without committing to great sleep at this stage of the breakdown cycle will leave you with subpar results. Remember, you have to start making deposits back into your overdrawn energy account. This means you'll have to commit to 7 to 9 hours of quality sleep. If your schedule doesn't allow for that kind of time, you need to do some negotiating elsewhere. Real rejuvenation happens in sleep, and depriving yourself of sleep is one of the reasons you have ended up feeling this way. Everyone experiencing adrenal-burnout symptoms has cheated sleep at some point in their life.

Guess what? You can't win this game of life if you are cheating sleep. Period!

Plain and simple, either make some room for it or get ready to spend the remainder of your life being unproductive and feeling miserable. It's your call. I have yet to meet someone who complains about the quality of work, level of production, and general improvement in life as a result of sleeping more.

I have a confession to make. I have been known to be a little hardheaded from time to time. Sometimes it takes reliving pain a few times before I truly learn my lesson. I have lived the adrenal burnout nightmare twice in my life. The Stark Naked 21-Day Metabolic Reset pulled me out of my last adrenal-burnout state, and the Phase 2 Optimized Nutrition Plan has kept me living a beautiful life that is busier than ever.

Life is so much better when you live it with boundless energy. I want you to experience that more than anything! This plan is truly made for resurrecting those who find themselves in this ugly world known as adrenal burnout, and it's there to change trajectory for those of you who haven't hit rock bottom yet, but are on a collision course toward it. It will take some commitment and effort on your part to resuscitate yourself, but trust me you will learn to love giving back to yourself. It's okay to love yourself every day! In my opinion, it's your duty!

When you choose to ignore the stress signals crying out from your body, forcing it to keep going, the adrenal glands eventually become overworked and start shutting down. To resolve your adrenal burnout, follow the Phase 1 Reset and Phase 2 Optimized Nutrition Plan, reduce your mental/emotional stress, and prioritize sleep.

Jeff, ex-Navy SEAL, currently with Search and Rescue California
Age forty-eight

▶ *Jeff was referred to me because he was experiencing extreme lethargy. Just getting out of bed was a chore! As an ex-Navy SEAL, he found that lack of energy tough to take. He was tired of feeling and looking worn out and wanted answers. Jeff was once the physical and mental specimen every man dreams of being, but now he found himself far from the picture of the man he once was. He just couldn't understand why he was always so tired. No amount of sleep seemed to help him feel better. More didn't seem to solve his problem, and less just made it worse.*

His daily exercise regime with his current tactical team had no positive effect on how he looked or felt either. Usually, exercise gave him some kind of boost. But now it only made him drag more. Jeff really began to notice the effects of extreme fatigue when he was sent out on calls searching for lost hikers. Mountainous terrain that was once easy for him was now extremely challenging and taxing.

Despite eating the same as he always had, Jeff was slowly

gaining weight, getting fatter in areas that had never been an issue. As the days went on it, it took everything in him to just survive his workouts.

After running the Orthostatic Hypotension Test on Jeff to determine if he was suffering from adrenal burnout, my hunch proved right. His systolic number dropped 30 points when he stood up. Jeff was clearly experiencing adrenal burnout and needed to be rejuvenated.

As a Navy SEAL, this man possessed more mental willpower than you or I could imagine, yet his extreme willpower and drive were of no avail. His intense drive to force change was only creating negative change, which left him feeling frustrated and angry.

I love working with guys like Jeff, because I get to be the brakes, not the gas pedal. Unmotivated people need a cheerleader to push their gas pedal and get them off the couch to exercise; high performers like Jeff need a brakeman—someone to help them pull the reigns back and allow the body to recover from all of the demands placed on it over the years. Most high achievers just need a great strategy to reset and renew their systems to experience incredible results.

During our first meeting Jeff weighed in at 186 pounds with 16 percent body fat. His first goal was to get his energy and ambition back in life. His second goal was to get his Navy SEAL body back. Following the initial Stark Naked 21-Day Metabolic Reset, Jeff focused on recovering from an extremely high-stress lifestyle. He was amazed by his rejuvenated energy and drive. Within the first couple of weeks, Jeff actually looked forward to getting out of bed and enjoyed challenging himself in the gym again. His weight dropped to 180 pounds and his body fat reduced to 12.5 percent. Four months later, his weight held steady at 175 pounds, and his body fat percentage got back to where it was during his SEAL days at 9 percent.

▶ PART THREE

THE STARK NAKED LIFESTYLE FOR SUCCESS

7

Breaking Bad

Clarifying Nutritional Confusion

I F COUNTING CALORIES was the gold-standard way to get the best weight-loss results, I would not have written this book. Frankly, I'd likely be out of a job. I never learned how to count calories. It's not that I can't count or add. I surely can—unless you're doing reps in my gym! In which case, ten is never really just ten. But that's another story. However, when it comes to counting calories, well, I've never subscribed to that theory.

My original journey in the fitness realm started just as a personal trainer and strength coach. I didn't start to focus on nutrition until the late 1990s. When I started working at a high-end gym in 1998 that had a nutritionist on staff, I did what all the smart trainers did. I sent my clients to the nutritionist to enhance their results. At least that was the promise I was sold by the owner of the gym, and like my clients I bought into the better-diet-equals-better-results pitch.

Every diet that my clients received early on was focused solely on calories. I watched as each of my clients started to feel miserable, losing strength and stamina in the process. Worse, their body fat rarely came down. In fact, for many it starting going up. At the time, my uneducated answer was to train harder, do more reps, and eat less.

Hey, it was all about calories, and if they were eating too many calories, I was going to make up for it by having them expend more calories. This approach only left my clients feeling exhausted and frustrated.

The nutritionists told me it was my clients' fault. Their lack of results was due to overeating and lying in their food journals. How annoying was that?

My clients and I were at our wits' end. Something had to give, so I changed the plan. I started experimenting.

The first thing I did was to meet with the top three nutrition experts in my area and have them design nutrition programs for me. At the time all three focused on calories. I knew that wasn't going to work. Been there, done that. Still, I gave all three the same diet and exercise outline I was following, and I got three totally different answers for my calorie needs. I chose the one I felt was the best fit for me and the results were staggering. I put on 5 percent body fat in the first six weeks! I was furious! My goal was to drop body fat, not add it!

At my follow-up meeting, the grave conclusion was that it was my fault, I was lying about what I said I ate, and I needed to be more honest about everything I was eating. I didn't take this criticism well, as I tend to go above and beyond with my efforts. I was always told by coaches growing up that I was incredibility coachable. In fact, my coaches had to choose wisely what they asked of me, because I applied it exactly as requested. I was obsessed with getting results.

So in this case I had followed the diet outline perfectly and to the letter. Needless to say, I quickly abandoned that low-calorie, fat-gaining trap and started my own journey, which has led me to acquire knowledge and strategies over the years that are responsible for the success of this program.

Do High Achievers Really Overeat?

I have reviewed thousands of high achievers' diets over the years, including those of pro athletes, tactical athletes, CEOs, homemakers, entrepreneurs, high-school athletes, CrossFit athletes, and busy executives, and the one commonality among all of them is that the majority undereat. Their metabolisms are paying the price for eating too little, which is what makes them feel and look miserable. It's amazing how many women are losing their hair and have zero sex drive from caloric deprivation. Yet if you ask them what strategies they are using to change their outcome, they will say, "I know I eat too much, so I am watching my calories."

I am not naive, nor am I saying calories are of zero importance. If you weigh 120 pounds and eat 8,000 calories a day you will gain weight. However, I hardly ever meet anyone who is actually, genuinely overeating. Most of us are too busy to overeat. The only issue with calories for most high achievers is that they need to consume more! Scary thought, but it's the truth.

I've learned one very important fact: *no matter how few calories you eat, you will never succeed by depriving your metabolism of what it needs.* Doing this is a recipe for metabolic disaster.

There are far too many nutritional "rules" that cause confusion and hold us back from living our healthiest lives.

One Size Does Not Fit All

In Chapter 1, I listed several variations of popular diets and nutritional plans that most of you have either heard of or likely tried at one time or another. From these you can get some idea of what has gotten you to this broken state. Since the 1960s, research has been dominated by two conflicting observations. First, we are under the misguided impression that the so-called experts know how to eat healthy and maintain a healthy weight. Some do, some don't. Second, the obesity rate has nearly tripled since the 1960s, which suggests that something about these dieting approaches isn't working.

There have been tens of thousands of diet books and articles on health and nutrition over the years offering all sorts of plans promising all sorts of ideas, hypothesis, research, knowledge, science, and data to show "their" ideas work. Most experts believe their program is the be-all and end-all answer for every individual alive.

Is there one perfect program that works for everyone? I haven't found one yet. Sure, some are better than others. And some, well, I am not a fan of at all. I believe my plan is better than most, because it's a manageable lifestyle that can be maintained, but I will concede it too isn't perfect for everyone.

When it comes to nutritional health and wellness, my philosophy is pretty simple. *Find the foods or dietary patterns that help you in your pursuit of a long and healthy life.*

I have learned many strategies from various medical experts that have been incorporated into the Stark Naked 21-Day Metabolic Reset to help make sure you discover the benefits of true healthy living and maintain this new lifestyle. I get it. You don't have the time to be sick and rundown. None of us do. That's why I've taken the guesswork out of it for you.

I've also incorporated some great strategies learned over the years from fat-loss experts, because I believe having a lower body fat is a competitive advantage in all areas of high performance, except perhaps in Sumo wrestling. The remainder of the strategies you'll experience throughout this program have come from trial and error—lots of trial and error. These are strategies that have worked for my clients and for me.

Remember, what got you here won't get you there.

Busting the Six Nutritional "Rules" Holding You Back

There are six main nutritional "rules" that cause my clients the greatest amount of confusion and hold them back from living their healthiest lives. For many, these rules are set in stone. Yet few people I train have ever taken the time to research the validity of these so-called rules or why they should abide by them in the first place. As a result, most people believe and therefore trust that if they want to stay fit and healthy, these are the key things they're supposed to do, and they therefore dutifully follow along.

I've got news for you. These so-called rules are really nothing more than urban myths.

For example, you may believe it is necessary to eat five or six small meals a day to get your metabolism charged and live in an optimal state. Or you may believe you can't eat carbs—at all. Or, if you do eat carbs, you may believe you can't eat them at night.

Guess what?

Not one of those is true!

Warning: Not only am I going to challenge these so-called rules of successful nutrition; I am going to ask you to break them!

I know what you're thinking. "Say, what? Break the rules? No way! I can't do that! If I do, my metabolism will slow down, and I will get fat."

Stop it! Stop right now. Let's be honest with ourselves. If you're reading this book, your metabolism is far from optimal. Something has got to change! Maybe it's one of your precious nutritional rules!

I am only challenging you to try the Reset for 21 days. Then decide for yourself.

Here are the six nutritional rules *you* are going to break *now* to ensure your success.

Nutritional Rule #1: You must eat five to six meals a day to keep your metabolism at its peak and prevent you from going into starvation mode.

How many of you believe this one?

Okay, I will admit that I followed this advice for the longest time. As a good trainer, I even passed this knowledge on to my clients. "You must eat every 2 to 3 hours, or you'll risk your metabolism slowing and your body going into starvation mode," I'd preach.

Here's the truth. If this rule were an undeniable fact, science would back it up as the best way to eat. Well, it doesn't.

Science continuously shows no benefit from this rule, which makes this a myth. It is true that digesting a meal raises metabolism slightly, a phenomenon known as the thermic effect of food. However, it is the total amount of food consumed that determines the amount of energy expended during digestion. Eating three meals of 800 calories will cause the same thermic effect as eating six meals of 400 calories. There is literally no difference.

There is no nutritional benefit to eating smaller meals more often. Numerous studies are now showing it to actually underperform in comparison with larger, less frequent meals. A study published in the *International Journal of Obesity and Metabolic Related Disorders* put this to the test. All subjects ate the same number of calories, but they were divided up into different meal frequencies: six meals a day, two large meals a day, or fasting for breakfast. Zero benefit was found for higher-frequency meal consumption. There was no significant effect on metabolic rate or total fat lost by eating more often, even though the nutritional world has told us the opposite.

In 2012, a study published by Maastricht University Medical Center compared high-frequency meals with low-frequency meals, and the results were the opposite of what was expected. Resting metabolic rate (RMR) was higher in the low-frequency meal group, meaning the subjects' metabolism was more elevated. The study also found appetite control was better in the low-frequency meal group.

How can that be? What about blood sugar? Aren't small meals more often supposed to be better for blood-sugar control? Aren't we supposed to eat meals every 2 to 3 hours to control our blood sugar and keep our appetite under control?

According to this study, the low-frequency eating *reduced* overall glucose levels during the day, indicating glycemic improvements. These are just two of the many studies that have found that increased meal frequency creates no benefit to your metabolism and often decreases your ability to lose weight.

Perhaps you're wondering, "Okay, but what about my muscle mass. If I don't eat every 2 to 3 hours I will go into starvation mode, and my muscles will start to feed off themselves, right? I can't risk losing muscle mass, Brad."

I totally agree that muscle mass is critical. I even believe maintaining muscle mass is a great predictor of longevity. But let's take a look at an interesting study that may change your mind.

The *British Journal of Nutrition* reported a study on how the body and metabolism respond to fasting for durations of 12, 36, and 72 hours. If 2 to 3 hours is all it takes to go into starvation mode, then after 12 hours people should be crushed. By 72 hours they should be absolutely destroyed, right?

Wrong! At the 12- and 36-hour marks, the researchers found enhanced metabolisms, not sluggish ones. The starvation mode switch does exist, but it didn't kick in with the people in this study until the 72-hour mark. Rule busted.

Nutritional Rule #2: Always eat carbohydrates in the morning.

We've all heard this: eat carbohydrates early in the day for good energy and so you will easily burn them off with regular daily activity.

As a high achiever, you likely rely on having a lot of energy and a sharp, focused brain. If you lack energy or your brain is not in the game, your performance will suffer greatly. If carbohydrates were the answer for enhanced energy and performance, you would eat carbs with every meal, right? Logic would say that by doing so, you'd always have great energy and great focus, but I hardly find that to be the case. Most people we test and work with experience the opposite effect when eating carbs. They complain of feeling lethargic and sleepy after eating carbs. If you don't believe me, join me for a corporate speaking engagement following a pasta lunch. Most people want to take a nap—and some do, heads bobbing and eyes rolling trying to stay awake. It isn't my topic! What they need is some protein.

I remember game days back in high school. Our coach always encouraged the team to eat huge carb-loading meals before football and basketball games. He said the carbs were supposed to give us an energy edge. The problem was that the majority of my teammates and I would fall asleep on the bus ride to the big game from all of those heavy carbs! The last thing we wanted to do when we arrived at our destination was to play a game—let alone win! We could have been much better athletes if our coach understood the impact of all those carbs on his team.

The hormonal response to carbohydrates causes a rise and fall of insulin, which makes you tired. The rise in insulin triggers the brain to release serotonin, a neurotransmitter that calms and relaxes the brain. It's why Thanksgiving is so great at inducing your food coma. It's not so much the tryptophan in the turkey (that does help a bit), but the carbs you eat with the turkey that cause the rise in insulin and release of serotonin.

The reality is, carb loading before the big game or important match isn't good for any athlete. It was a misunderstood myth everyone bought into back then. Now that I am a coach and trainer, I want my competitive athletes showing up for their competitions supercharged, on fire, wanting nothing more than to be engaged in their competition, not dreaming of a nap. You can bet I am not feeding them carbs before the big event we spend so much time training for!

If your goal is to have a lot of energy, to be more focused and highly driven, then you need to *avoid carbs early in the day*. The Stark Naked

21-Day Metabolic Reset is built to support this concept by providing you with foods early in the day that keep insulin at bay and the brain turned on—not shutting down.

The ideal foods for great energy and brain power are protein and fat. They don't create the major spike in insulin that carbohydrates do, therefore keeping the brain from shutting down. Eating protein and fats early in the day is the foundation of true high-performance nutrition. Interestingly, you will notice in Phase 1 that you are not asked to eat these foods for breakfast. Why?

Detoxing your liver is a major focus at the start of the plan. If your liver is sluggish and you eat protein and fats too early in the day, it can make you nauseous. The liver is required to help break down the proteins and fats, so you need it humming along and not behind on its duty to get the most out of the protein and fat intake.

Nutritional Rule #3: Eating carbohydrates at night will make you fat.

Okay, great. So now you understand the reason you shouldn't eat carbs in the morning. But I know what you're thinking. "There's no way I am eating carbs at night! It will make me fat!"

I get it. We all want to look great. I want to look great as well, but this whole idea that eating carbs at night will make us fat is far from verified in the world of science. Yes, during the first half of sleep there is a dip in energy usage, but during the second half of sleep, in the REM cycles, energy expenditure takes off again. Believing that energy expenditure is so low during sleep that carbs will make you fat is ludicrous. Science is beginning to back the notion that eating carbs at night will not only make you lose more weight than spreading carbs throughout the day, but it will also enhance the quality of your sleep. It's a two-for-one special!

In 2011, a group of Israeli scientists found that those who ate 80 percent or more of their carbohydrate intake starting at dinner over the course of six months not only lost more weight and body fat, but also had fewer issues with hunger during the day. Why wouldn't you want those kinds of benefits from your nutrition?

Research has also shown that eating a meal at night with carbs in it helps induce sleep. It enhances pathways in our body that make us sleepy, whereas protein blocks those pathways making you feel more awake. Now, understand that this isn't the green light to start eating a bunch of junk carbohydrates before bed. High-sugar carbs will make you crash quickly, but they will disrupt overall sleep.

The research is clear. A higher-protein diet during the day and whole-food carbs like sweet potatoes at night is the key to success. Just follow the exact outline of the 21-Day Reset, and you will benefit from all this great cutting-edge research without having to think about it.

This rule is by far the hardest of the six biggies to get my clients to break. Everyone I work with believes that eating carbs is bad, so getting my clients to eat carbs at night is one of my greatest challenges. But when they finally give in and trust in the process and the plan, the results speak for themselves. The weight loss and improved sleep are enough to turn any doubter into a believer.

Still don't buy into it? Try it for 21 days. If you're not completely convinced, go back to your old ways. You've got nothing to lose, and everything to gain. I'll stake my name and reputation on it!

Nutritional Rule #4: Removing foods like dairy and gluten (wheat) is dangerous and will lead to nutrient deficiencies.

This rule is one of my favorites to debunk.

Here's an interesting fact. Every single one of us is walking around with multiple nutrient deficiencies that are caused either by genetic issues, poor digestion, lack of nutrients in the soil our foods were grown in, or simple lack of consumption. You definitely are and, despite my knowledge and awareness, I am too.

The value of proper nutritional balance is not very important to most people, but our bodies were designed to function at the highest level by absorbing vitamins and minerals from the food we eat. A nutritional deficiency occurs when the body doesn't absorb the necessary amount of a nutrient. Calcium, vitamin D, iron, potassium, vitamin B_{12}, magnesium, and folate deficiencies make it tough for your body to run optimally and can be the source of symptoms like fatigue, hair loss, muscle cramps, skin issues, digestion issues, stunted or defective bone growth, and even dementia, just to name a few. On a cellular level, nutrient deficiencies can impact bodily functions including water balance, enzyme function, nerve signaling, and metabolism.

In the past I've experienced numbness in my hands at night while I sleep. For me this was caused by B_{12} deficiency with a known genetic basis. Vitamin B_{12} not only helps with healthy nerve cells; it is also involved in red-blood-cell production, aids in the production of DNA, and helps make neurotransmitters in the brain. Interestingly, although my vitamin deficiency is genetic, vitamin B_{12} deficiency is becoming much more common today, especially among vegans and people who've had weight-loss surgery. The symptoms of B_{12} deficiency include numbness in the legs, hands, or feet; problems with walking and balance; anemia; fatigue; weakness; depression; a swollen, inflamed tongue; memory loss; paranoia; and hallucinations. If you have any of these symptoms, you can get vitamin B_{12} from eating more fish, eggs, and poultry.

Okay, you're probably confused. So let me explain.

If these nutrients are so important, why would I remove foods that would put anyone at risk for increasing their deficiencies? Good question!

First, the only reason dairy and gluten are of concern is because the typical American diet is so poor and devoid of nutrients that dairy and gluten-containing grains, such as wheat, barley, and rye, are often the only sources of nutrients at all. The reality is that nutrients are hidden in our vegetables and fruits, and those are what most people tend to have the hardest time eating.

"Eat your fruits and vegetables." We've heard that all our lives,

OTHER COMMON NUTRIENT DEFICIENCIES		
Nutrient	Where It's Found (Stark Approved)	Deficiency Symptoms
Vitamin B$_2$	Lamb, oily fish (mackerel), eggs, spinach, asparagus, collard greens, mushrooms	Anemia, cataracts, poor thyroid function, fatigue, bloodshot eyes, chapped lips, sore tongue and lips
Folate	Spinach, asparagus, avocados, mango, oranges	Anemia, poor immune function, fatigue, insomnia, elevated homocysteine
Zinc	Poultry, seafood, lamb, wild game meat, spinach, pomegranates, blackberries	Hair loss, diarrhea, impotence, loss of appetite, loss of taste, weight loss, slow wound healing, mental lethargy
Magnesium	Dark leafy green vegetables (spinach), avocados, fish, blackberries, raspberries	Nausea, vomiting, muscle cramps or twitching, insomnia, anxiety, restlessness, irritability
Vitamin D	Sunlight, egg yolks, fish	Osteoporosis, low calcium absorption, depression, bone ache, head sweating

right? Most of you probably know they decrease your risk of diseases like cancer and yet so few focus on eating those foods that benefit you most. If you are really worried about nutrient deficiencies, then step up and eat your fruits and vegetables. If you follow my program, like it or not, you will!

By increasing your consumption of these foods, you will avoid any nutrient deficiencies that might occur because foods such as dairy and gluten are no longer in your diet. We want dairy, gluten, and all of the other foods that commonly trigger inflammation removed for all of the reasons we explored in Chapter 4. That inflammation response is not worth the pathetic batch of nutrients you are getting from dairy and gluten, nutrients that you could be getting in abundance from your fruits and vegetables without the adverse reaction. This is killing two birds with one stone. Remove the irritants and enhance your uptake of nutrients. It's so simple!

Nutritional Rule #5: You have to restrict calories for weight-loss success.

At the very beginning of this chapter I stated that I don't agree with the low-calorie approach, but I really want to drive this point home, because so many people obsess about this so-called rule. In my opinion, there are much deeper and more important reasons holding you back than eating too many calories. According to Gary Taubes, who wrote the book *Why We Get Fat: And What to Do About It*, in 1878 the German nutritionist Max Rubner crafted what he called the "isodynamic law." This law claimed that the basis of nutrition is simply the exchange of energy, spawning the belief that "a calorie is a calorie." This means that no matter what the source of a calorie (fat, protein, or carb), the energy extracted from it or the work necessary to burn it is the same.

For over a hundred years science has been drilling this idea into us. Consume fewer calories than you burn, and you will lose weight. Consume more, and the number on the scale will increase. If you are gaining weight, you are simply eating too many calories. Therefore, the only solution is to eat less or exercise more. Get serious about your weight and do both.

Here's how this theory works. A pound of fat is 3,500 calories. If you eat 500 calories less than you burn every day, then after a week ($7 \times 500 = 3,500$) you will have lost a pound of fat.

Wow! I wish it were that easy. If that were the case, we'd all be walking around skinny and happy, and I'd be unemployed.

I'm always amazed by the variations in the way people approach this simple calorie-restriction idea. I remember speaking with one woman a few years ago whose trainer had her exercising twice a day, 7 days a week. He was only allowing her to eat 800 calories a day, assuring her it didn't matter what foods made up those 800 calories, claiming it could be birthday cake or Ring Dings; as long as she stayed at 800 calories, she would see results. Theoretically, she was burning more calories than she was consuming, so she should have gotten skinny overnight, yet the exact opposite happened. In her case, calorie deprivation backfired. The number on the scale went up from unwanted fat accumulation around her hips and thighs. How in the world could that happen when she was in extreme calorie deprivation?

Because calorie restriction for weight loss is a myth and not supported by science. In 2004, a study in the *Journal of Nutrition and Metabolism* divided overweight individuals into two groups. One group was fed a high-protein diet, and the other was given a high-carbohydrate diet. The high-carbohydrate group was fed an average of 300 fewer calories a day. At first glance, the study appeared straightforward. According to the "a calorie is a calorie" model, the lower-calorie intake group should have lost more weight, but the exact opposite happened. The higher-calorie, high-protein group ended up losing more weight and more fat in the study.

What? How can that be? Why did the high-protein group lose more weight, even though they consumed more calories? There are a few reasons.

First, food affects hormones. In this study carbohydrates triggered the release of insulin telling the body to store energy, not burn it. Second, the amount of energy the body uses to break down, assimilate, and absorb protein is much greater than what the body uses to break down carbohydrates.

The third and final possible reason the high-protein group may have lost more weight is the fact that protein consumption creates more satiety. That may not have been the case in this study if everything eaten was carefully monitored, but in real life it is easier to overeat on a high-carbohydrate diet. This study shows it's more important to focus on what you eat rather than how much.

So if it's not all about the calories, what causes us to put on weight?

The human metabolism is so complex. There are so many variables that can cause weight gain. The Stark Naked 21-Day Metabolic Reset deals with the three major causes of fat gain for high achievers—*stress* from a high-achieving lifestyle, *toxicity,* and *food-driven inflammation.* You can reduce your calories as much as you want, but if your metabolism is broken, the calorie pursuit is pointless and just fuels fat gain.

A few years back I was working with an NFL lineman who quickly needed to lose 25 pounds. This man weighed 372 pounds. A team was interested in him, but would only sign him if he could get his weight down to 350 pounds. Strangely, he was only eating 2,400 calories a day, not a lot for a guy that size. My initial comment was "You are starving yourself! My eleven-year-old eats more than you do!"

He told me that two weeks prior to our conversation the food delivery company he was using increased his calories from 2,400 to 2,800 calories a day, and his weight increased from 360 to 372 pounds. He was forced to return to 2,400 calories, as that was all he could eat without gaining weight. My client was exercising hard to try to lose the weight, but wasn't getting any result. He felt horrible, had no energy, and was not gaining any strength in the gym. He definitely wasn't lying to me about what he was eating. It's amazing how honest people are when specific changes in their bodies equal a bigger bank account!

Don't believe me? Just watch an episode of *The Biggest Loser.*

You become very honest and are willing to do anything for success. Since cutting calories was not an option, I had to make a quick decision. I remembered my client mentioning he was having weird cravings for things like dairy and wheat bread. That's when it occurred to me that there was something else going on. I immediately called the food delivery company he used for all of his meals and asked them to remove all the common foods that people have sensitivities to, those that we remove in Phase 1 of the Reset.

The result? Within eight weeks he was down to 340 pounds!

"I don't understand this," he said. "I have more energy than I have had in years! My strength in the gym is unreal! I haven't weighed this little since high school, and I am eating more calories! I should feel miserable right now from the effort and sacrifice to reach this weight, but I feel great! I have always been made to feel it was my fault, like I wasn't trying hard enough or I was lying to them on my low-calorie programs. No one believed me except you."

The sincerity in his words was the best part of our success. I simply replied, "We found the root cause of your broken metabolism, food-driven inflammation, and repaired it."

Nutritional Rule #6: Caving in to cravings is just a lack of willpower. Suck it up!

When it comes to cravings, a lot of my clients are very shy when talking to me about their habits. They see their hankerings for midnight snacks and novel food combinations as strange and weak.

Allow me to be the bearer of some good news. Cravings are a real issue in today's society. There are all kinds of theories behind cravings.

Some claim they are merely a given and need to be controlled by willpower, while others say the food industry discovers our addiction mechanisms and preys on them. When a potato-chip manufacturer says, "You can't eat just one . . . ," believe it.

After my first food sensitivity test was done, I discovered that the foods on my sensitivity list were the same foods I often found myself craving—a lot. This piqued my curiosity, especially because I found it really hard to break my addiction to those foods I was sensitive to—specifically maple syrup and dairy products. I wasn't sure how I would prove it, but I was certain there was a connection.

Every Friday, my high-carb cheat meal (which you will learn more about in Phase 2, the Optimized Nutrition Plan) was pancakes or waffles with a *ton* of maple syrup and ice cream. I loved the flavor combination of that dessert. However, once I ate it on Friday, I found myself having nearly uncontrollable cravings for it during the following week. It took every ounce of willpower I had not to give in to my desire for that dessert until the following Friday.

However, one Friday I ate those same foods, and my throat started to close up. The severe reaction almost choked me to death. Now, you might have thought this experience would have been scary enough to keep me from ever eating that dessert again—but it wasn't. My cravings were so strong that I continued with my Friday-night habit despite knowing it could kill me.

Originally, I thought it must be the gluten in the pancakes, until one weekend I was visiting my parents with my daughter and my mom made us gluten-free pancakes. Thinking I was in the clear, I poured maple syrup over the top and began to eat. Again my throat closed up, but this time it was the worst experience I'd ever had. And this time, it took place in front of my daughter.

Okay, now I began to worry I might be sensitive to all carbs. That breakfast was the tipping point that pushed me to have my sensitivity test done. Lo and behold it wasn't the gluten. It was the maple syrup and cow's milk that was roughing me up. Ta-dah!

I immediately went to IHOP and devoured a huge plate of pancakes with blueberry syrup—not maple—followed by dairy-free ice cream. Guess what? No choking response.

As I ran more and more of these tests, it suddenly became very clear to me that people actually crave the foods they are most likely to be sensitive to. My hypothesis gets proven with every client MRT that comes back. The foods my clients crave the most usually appear in their red zone—meaning these are the foods they shouldn't eat, because they trigger an intense inflammation response and do the greatest harm.

It is not clear why we often crave foods to which we are sensitive, but several theories have been proposed. Some researchers suggest that our bodies can become addicted to the chemical messengers, such as histamine or cortisol, that are secreted by immune cells in response to allergens in the body. It is hypothesized that, although eating foods to which you are allergic can cause a rash or sneezing, the body also may experience a soothing response from the presence of the chemical messengers, increasing the desire to eat more of that food.

Another theory proposed by a well-known immunologist is based on the science of how antibodies (a protein used by the immune system to identify and neutralize foreign objects) and antigens (unique parts of the foreign object) connect (bind) to each other. Antibodies can bind to more than one site on an allergen in the food; therefore, when there are very few antigens but a large number of antibodies present, the antibodies will become cross-linked and make large complexes. It is theorized that these large complexes can cause an increase in symptoms.

In this theory symptoms are caused by the large number of antibodies in relation to the number of antigens rather than being caused by the number of antigens. In fact, it is suggested that if you eat more of the antigen, you can decrease the number of antibody complexes by allowing each antibody to bind to an antigen rather than forming the large complexes, thereby reducing the number of symptoms. Normal metabolism works to remove the food antigens, and as the ratio of antibodies to antigens begins to rise, symptoms will begin to increase. Craving and addiction to food may be the result of the body's attempt to increase the number of antigens present and prevent the formation of the large antibody complexes that are associated with an increased number of symptoms.

Succumbing to food cravings to help alleviate symptoms provides short-term relief. The cravings and symptoms will return. This yo-yo effect is believed by some allergy specialists to be the reason why people who stop eating the foods to which they are allergic first go through several days when they feel worse before they start feeling much better.

The important thing to remember is that *you don't know how bad you're feeling until you eliminate the cause of your stress.* You have learned to live and, worse, accept living with feeling bad. Once you cleanse your body of the toxins that are causing you to feel your worst, you will appreciate what it feels like to be back at your best.

Breaking the Rules Is Fun!

Breaking the "rules" of nutrition can be scary and tough. One of the best strategies I have seen work is to complete the Stark Naked 21-Day Metabolic Reset with a community of family and friends. If you are married, do whatever it takes to get your spouse to join you on the Reset. Support, especially during the first week, is critical and leads to incredible long-term success. There's great power in numbers.

Craig and Cherisse Smyser are a couple in their early forties from Texas who went on the Stark Naked 21-Day Reset with Tom Ferry's original inner-circle real-estate group. Their results have been nothing short of life-changing. Here is their story, told by Cherisse:

About five years ago, I was working out in a gym 1 to 2 hours a day, 6 days a week, and I was in great shape, the best shape of my life. Then we moved back to Texas, and I found work as a preschool teacher. I stopped working out, and over the course of four years I gained about 35 pounds. Finally, I was able to go back to a gym, and although the weight came off a little (at the most, 10 pounds), it always came back on, even when I thought I was eating "right." I think my metabolism just kept my body at this new weight no matter what I did. Recently, I even tried Plexus Slim on a recommendation from friends. Nope. Nothing happened after four months using their pink drink.

Then my husband mentioned your Reset challenge, and we decided to do it as a couple. Craig ended up losing 10 pounds, and I shed 15! In three weeks! I feel amazing, and I'm looking forward to getting rid of another 20 pounds to get back down to the low 160s (I'm 5 foot 11). We are following Phase 2 and having no problems staying on it. And, although we look forward to that 7th-day high-carb meal, we don't feel like we need it. In addition, I have lost a total of 9 inches: 2 off my waist, 2½ off my hips, 1½ off my bust, 1 inch off each thigh, and ½ inch off each upper arm. And that's just in three weeks! Thank you for coming up with this program! It is finally something that my body responds to, and I feel so healthy. I love sugar, but I hardly even think about it anymore. I just didn't think that was possible!

One year later I received a follow-up e-mail from Cherisse. She and her husband were each down 30 pounds and loving life. This program is not a short-term fad diet. It's a life-changing alteration in lifestyle.

Breaking the rules can be fun, and oftentimes it takes a willingness to break the rules to find a pathway to success. Following the so-called nutritional rules is holding so many of you back. For the next 21 days I am going to ask you to put on a brave face and go rogue. Take a leap of faith with me and break the rules. You know as well as I do something has to change! What are you waiting for?

It's good to follow all the rules when you're young,
so you have the strength to break them when you're old.

—MARK TWAIN

I've broken all of the erroneous nutritional rules for you during your 21-Day Reset. The eleven fundamentals of the Stark Naked 21-Day Metabolic Reset (see page 204) help you to avoid the pitfalls of these so-called rules that are really holding you back.

9. Maximize protein and vegetable intake.

10. Follow carbohydrate and fat servings exactly.

11. Stick to three meals a day.

8

Sleep

Your Ultimate Ally

ONE OF THE FONDEST MEMORIES I have with my daughter, Isabel, was the first time she experienced the clear night sky at my parents' home in Oregon. She was just three years old and was mesmerized by how the bright stars lit up the night sky. Living in Southern California, she had never experienced anything quite like it. I had so much fun showing her the different constellations I grew up exploring as a young boy, like Orion's Belt and the Big Dipper. As we shared this father-daughter moment together, something extraordinary happened. Isabel got to see her first shooting star—and I was there to share in her excitement.

I grew up taking for granted the clear night skies of my home state. I suppose most of us don't appreciate what we have when we are kids until we are much older and can see those simple things through our children's eyes. As I think back, I vividly remember one night sleeping under the stars at summer camp. Like my daughter, I was enamored by the countless shooting stars I saw. I am quite certain I saw more shooting stars on that single night in Oregon than most people see in a lifetime.

It's not that the stars aren't as bright as ever—it's just that most people live in places where they will never see them unless they drive hours away. The city lights in most metropolitan cities at night are now so bright, they literally wipe out our ability to see the vastness of stars above us. According to the Tucson-based International Dark-Sky Association (IDA), the sky glow of Los Angeles is visible from an airplane two hundred miles away.

Thomas Edison and his invention of the lightbulb dramatically improved many areas of our lives. It also came with a cost. One of the biggest is the impact light has had on sleep.

I attended my first live fitness seminar in 2007 with world-renowned strength coach Charles Poliquin in Chicago. Charles was someone I had fanatically studied throughout high school and college. I read every article he ever wrote. Every month I'd rip through my new edition of *Muscle Media 2000* magazine looking for his next great tip to help make me bigger and stronger. So when I was able to attend this seminar and see him up close and personal, I was so jazzed to finally have the chance to spend 5 days learning hands-on from the master. The experience was awesome!

When I returned to California, the exercise strategies I learned helped me crush it in the gym. I had learned great new supplementation strategies to enhance fat loss, but the information that shocked me the most was the discussion we had about the one common thing that holds people back from getting results and performing at their highest levels.

The surprising roadblock? Sleep!

When I was younger, I had always viewed sleep as a sign of weakness. I truly believed you had to cheat sleep to achieve success. When he shared the nugget of information about its importance, I was utterly blown away. The man I admired so much totally shattered my beliefs about what it takes to become successful.

Why does this matter?

Cheating sleep is accompanied by serious health risks and has a major dampening effect on your overall performance. Studies show that a lack of sleep can cause us to gain weight and increase the risks of cardiovascular disease, high blood pressure, diabetes, and even mental disorders. Just to add an extra point to show how damaging lack of sleep is, cancer has actually been shown to grow two to three times faster in lab animals experiencing sleep dysfunction.

Research shows that our brains work much better with more sleep, allowing us to perform better on the field, in the office, and at home with those you love the most. Think about it. How much better do you function when you've had a good night's sleep rather than not enough?

Even so, there are many people who believe the need for sleep is a sign of weakness and laziness and a waste of time that robs our wallets. George Burns said it best: "Don't stay in bed unless you can make money in bed."

Even worse, there are those who think you must deprive yourself of sleep if you truly want to be successful. A survey presented in William C. Dement's book *The Promise of Sleep* shows that 80 percent of Americans actually believe you cannot be a success at work and at the same time get enough sleep. (As you will read later in this chapter, you *can* and *should* have both!)

Who developed *that* theory?

Believe it or not, it was the great overachiever himself, Thomas Edison, who was at the forefront of convincing us that sleep was for the weak. He prided himself on only sleeping 4 to 5 hours a night. For many, functioning on a lack of sleep, putting in long hours, and getting lots done has been a badge of honor, something to brag about.

I will admit there was a time in my life when I too believed that a lack of sleep was an essential requirement for success. I truly subscribed to the theory that if I wanted to get ahead in life, I had to outwork everyone else. That meant cheating sleep, burning the candle at both ends, and doing whatever it took to get the most hours out of each day. I still hear the motivational mantra I fell for at a young age,

"You can sleep when you're dead," or as Benjamin Franklin once put it, "There will be sleeping enough in the grave."

I've got some good news for you. By the end of this chapter, you, like many of my clients who have successfully done the Stark Naked 21-Day Metabolic Reset, will discover that getting 7 to 9 hours of sleep a night is one of the most important and vital components in

---

Marisol, schoolteacher, mother of two
California
Age forty-three

▶ *Marisol is an incredibly passionate teacher and mother of two great children. She loves the challenge and creativity required to keep her students focused, so she can guide and develop them, but her severe insomnia eventually caught up with her.*

When we first met, she struggled with how impatient and grumpy she had become with the students in her class and her own children. She was no longer the happy, creative, compassionate woman she once saw herself as. Marisol was tired of the belly fat she had accumulated and, worst of all, was literally tired of being tired all the time.

Her pattern was to grind and push through in spite of her fatigued state at all cost. In her mind, she had no option. She had to keep working. Eventually, that approach catches up with someone. She ended up crashing. She was getting sick often or finding herself unable to get out of bed for an entire weekend. This would happen multiple times every year.

When Marisol first came to me, her initial request, like that of so many others, was "Brad, I need an exercise plan to get rid of my belly. My current program is not working."

I knew Marisol would be disappointed when I told her exercise wasn't the answer she was looking for. She reluctantly agreed to

try the Stark Naked 21-Day Metabolic Reset, thinking I was off my rocker. It went against everything she, as an educator, thought she knew about fitness. Still, I convinced her we needed to deal with her fatigue first by helping her sleep again, if she truly wanted her old body back.

Within 3 days of starting the Reset, Marisol slept a full 7 hours without waking once during the night. Then it happened again, followed by another night, and then another. Marisol's fatigue slowly started to subside as her sleep became consistent, and her mood quickly began to change. Her improved sleep was leading to a more optimistic outlook; she was beginning to feel like her old self again.

By the end of the 21-Day Reset Marisol had completely rejuvenated her energy and creativity and was once again happy! She was actually having fun in her classroom and at home. Even her principal noticed a difference, not only with Marisol but also with Marisol's students. They were excelling in the classroom, because Marisol's enthusiasm was rubbing off on them.

Oh, yeah, I almost forgot. Marisol also lost 6 pounds and 3½ inches off her waist in the 21 days. As an added bonus, the acne she had struggled with her whole life also cleared up. Although this isn't an anticipated side effect for everyone, it certainly was one for her.

Marisol's metabolism had been shutting down because her liver was totally overwhelmed. It was making her sluggish, keeping her up at night, causing the weight gain on her belly, ruining her mood, and having a negative impact on her skin. Simply following the plan and loving her liver for 21 days allowed her to sleep again and greatly helped to completely reset her metabolism. Six months later she has kept the weight and inches off, and her sleep has remained amazing. She has not had an episode of crashing or getting sick in over six months and plans to maintain her newfound lifestyle for years to come.

your long-term success at everything you do. Not only will you discover the benefits of the Reset by improving the quality of your sleep; you will also learn to embrace the value of sleep. Once you do, you'll make sleep a priority.

Great success is achieved by finding the things others are unwilling to do and then doing them! Believe me, sleep is a part of that formula.

I love supporting high achievers, like you and Marisol, in this world. The impact you have is so powerful; one simple change like Marisol's can send out a ripple effect, creating change so vast you will never understand the impact a simple 21-day choice can make on the future of this world. There are enough tired, grumpy, irritable people in this world bringing it down. We need more people like you to make the change Marisol made and exude happiness, kindness, and passion for life.

Americans' Ongoing Struggle with Sleep

The CDC, in the April 27, 2012, issue of the *Morbidity and Mortality Weekly Report,* reported that 30 percent of all Americans are sleep deprived and are only getting 6 or less hours of sleep each night. They also found those who work more than 40 hours a week were dramatically more likely to be sleep deprived than those who worked 40 hours or less per week. According to some estimates, 90 percent of people with insomnia—a sleep disorder characterized by trouble falling and staying asleep—also have another health condition.

More than sixty million Americans struggle with getting enough sleep. If you're sleep deprived, meaning that you sleep 6 hours a night or less, you literally function as if you're under the influence of alcohol. This means that three out of every ten people around you right now are functioning as though they've been drinking. Now, there's a sobering thought!

I always tell my clients that the quickest way to keep themselves from being mediocre is to find a way to get 7 to 9 hours of deep rejuvenating sleep every night. When I share this information with my clients, most of them think that I'm nuts. In their mind, that's a third of their day. They can't give that precious time up for something as "wasteful" as sleep. But if they did, they, like you, would quickly discover that sleep is the greatest source of insane success and happiness.

Say what? The truth is, most people are struggling with issues that are preventing them from sleeping: stress, insomnia, disrupted sleep, or too many distractions in the bedroom, such as phones and other electronic devices that are not shut down at night. Whether you're aware of it or not, the sound of those devices dinging all night long actually interrupts your sleep. Your best bet is to shut those iPads and smartphones down for a good night's sleep.

Although the Stark Naked 21-Day Metabolic Reset can help resolve some of those physical issues, to reap the most benefits in the long run, once you feel better, you must commit to maintaining your sleep, or you will end up right back where you started—feeling horrible and run down in no time.

If I could promise you greater happiness and success in your life simply by challenging you to get more sleep, would you take that challenge?

Check this out. Science is now showing that 10 hours of sleep is ideal for extreme athletes. People who push their bodies to the limit actually need to give it more time to rest. Think about that for a second.

Look, I have studied the benefits of sleep on people from all walks of life. I have seen the impact it can have on energy, body composition, health, brain function, and happiness. It is extremely clear to me that people who make sleep a priority in their life have a tremendous advantage in all of those categories over those who choose to cheat sleep. It's the sine qua non for feeling, looking, and performing at your very best.

The Stark Naked 21-Day Metabolic Reset has been built on proven foundational strategies that will no doubt improve your sleep. Stress is the number one reason we fall victim to sleep disturbances, and the Reset is designed to attack that stress. Poor sleep is also a trigger for stress; therefore, once we reduce your stress, you will need strategies to protect your sleep long-term, so you don't end up back in the Metabolic Breakdown Cycle. At the end of this chapter, I will give you strategies to enhance and protect your precious sleep that I want you to start practicing now, so by the time you have completed your Reset, your sleep strategies will be dialed in.

I am such a great believer in the need for quality sleep that I have

---

Kendra, stay-at-home mom
Saskatchewan, Canada
Age thirty-three

▶ *Kendra is a stay-at-home mom of three. Before starting the Stark Naked 21-Day Metabolic Reset, she struggled with her weight after the birth of her last child and was frustrated by her lack of energy from sleep struggles. This combination made it difficult for her to survive her long days, let alone thrive during them.*

In the mornings, everyone knew to give mommy her space until she had her morning cup of coffee and some time to "wake up." Though she tried multiple diets and even attempted Cross-Fit to lose weight, she always seemed to find herself without the success she was looking for. Kendra got leaner and stronger, but the scale never changed. What Kendra really wanted was to see some weight drop on the scale.

The diets she tried were too restrictive for her. Within weeks she gave up on them. She was looking for a lifestyle change that would allow her to lose some weight, but one that would also increase her energy and provide options that didn't make it feel so

researched and developed strategies to not only help you fall sleep easier, but also improve the duration of your sleep. No more lying in bed waiting to fall asleep, or worse—no more nights of waking up between 1:00 and 3:00 A.M. and finding yourself unable to fall back asleep.

My wife, Maria, recently went back to work following her maternity leave after giving birth to our third child. During her first week back, our older children were on a week's vacation from school, and I got to stay home and watch them. As the week approached, my wife worried if I would be able to handle the responsibility. At the time, I couldn't understand why.

restrictive. As a busy mom, Kendra also struggled with sleep. Not only did she have trouble falling asleep, she also awoke during the night with a racing mind, which kept her up for hours.

Deep down, I knew if she was going to have any long-term success with losing weight, Kendra needed to improve the quality of her sleep. Within a week of starting the Stark Naked 21-Day Metabolic Reset, Kendra began to experience such a deep sleep that she started sleeping through the night for the first time in years. As soon as that happened, it wasn't long before the weight began to fall off. She lost 14 pounds within the first 21 days, and it's still coming off.

Kendra's weight loss took a backseat to the lifestyle changes she experienced from completing the Reset. Instead of being lethargic and grumpy in the morning, she was now energetic and happy. Her energy throughout the day went through the roof, allowing her to more effectively remain patient with her kids and provide a more engaged playful environment. She is now resilient to stress and in control of her world and the world she provides her children.

Four hours into day one I was exhausted! The energy required to keep up with our kids while caring for our new baby's needs was unbelievable. I was shocked by how tired I was at the end of the day—not to mention how grumpy I was! By late afternoon, the baby was crying, the older kids were complaining they were bored, and all I could wish was "Calgon, take me away!"

I was so relieved to have survived that week without any catastrophes, but even more so to go back to work. That was one of the most stressful, demanding, exhausting weeks I've had in a long time. Knowing how demanding being a stay-at-home parent is helped me understand my client Kendra's needs when she reached out to me desperate for answers to help her survive and thrive in the high-stress, demanding environment at home with young children.

The Risks of Sleep Deprivation

Don't sleep—at your own risk. But what happens when your lack of sleep puts others at risk?

Sleep deprivation has caused some of the greatest historic tragedies of the century. Not sure of what I am talking about? Ever hear of the Exxon Valdez oil spill, the space shuttle *Challenger* explosion, Chernobyl, Three Mile Island? All of these involved human error due to sleep deprivation.

If that seems too big to grasp, then look at it like this. Studies show that sleep loss and poor-quality sleep also lead to accidents and injuries on the job. In one study, workers who complained about excessive daytime sleepiness had significantly more work accidents, particularly repeated work accidents. They also had more sick days per accident. That might not mean that much to the average employee, but to a business owner that adds up to a lot of dollars.

Lack of sleep can slow reaction time as much as drinking does, and both impair driving. Fatigue from lack of sleep is estimated to cause around 100,000 auto crashes and more than 1,550 crash-related deaths a year. In the "Sleep in America" poll, taken by the National Sleep Foundation, 37 percent of Americans (103 million people) admitted to falling asleep while driving in 2011.

I remember a near disaster that almost ruined my life in my mid-twenties. I was training clients starting at 5:00 A.M. usually until 6:00 P.M. From there I would head to my second job of bartending special events. I could be out as late as 2:00 A.M. on some nights. Although I was making great money, I was severely sleep deprived. Even so, I was very proud of my intense work ethic, which was, in my mind, helping me climb that "ladder of success."

I had finished an event one Saturday around 8:00 P.M. I had been bartending at the beach and was driving back to my company's head-quarters to return the bar equipment and remaining alcohol. I was exhausted from being out in the sun all day and having a ridiculously long week. I had the AC cranked up in the car and the windows rolled down. I was trying anything I could think of to keep myself awake at the wheel. Unfortunately, it wasn't working very well. My eyes were heavy and I could feel my head bobbing around as I began drifting in and out of consciousness. I came up to an intersection and didn't notice the couple in the crosswalk with their toddler and a baby in a stroller. Thankfully, they saw me and quickly realized I wasn't slowing down for the red light. They backpedaled toward the sidewalk as I blew through the light. I came to as I just missed crushing the baby stroller.

Looking into those parents' eyes as I whizzed by, seeing their fear and their anger, and then experiencing my own guilt for what I had almost done is something I will never forget. My heart was racing, and I was panic-stricken by what had nearly transpired. I had no problem staying awake for the remainder of my drive, but I quickly gave up my bartending job. I couldn't handle the long hours and lack of sleep. It was taking a toll on my body, and I almost paid a price that was too high to ignore.

To this day I am no longer willing to drive if I am even the slightest bit tired or fatigued.

Cheating Sleep Is Making You Fat

The reality is, when you don't sleep, you are totally disrupting your hormones. These fluctuations range from an elevated appetite to collapsing sex hormones. It only takes one night of not sleeping enough to trigger a negative response. For example, one night of sleeping only 4 hours will cause your hunger to spike and your blood-sugar and insulin levels to take on the characteristics of insulin resistance (the prediabetic stage). In this condition you can't process carbohydrates properly, yet you crave carbohydrate-rich foods the following day, like breads, pastries, and candy, which end up being stored as fat instead of muscle.

The University of Chicago reported research showing that morning testosterone levels can drop by as much as 60 percent for those sleeping 4 hours instead 8. Combining these responses with the elevation in cortisol we talked about earlier and you have the perfect recipe for fat storage. You've been bombarded with the message that you simply need to exercise more and eat less to rev up your metabolism, but in reality the first place you must start is with your sleep.

Recent research has focused on the link between sleep and the peptides that regulate appetite. Ghrelin stimulates hunger, and leptin signals satiety to the brain and suppresses appetite. Shortened sleep time is associated with decreases in leptin and elevations in ghrelin, leading many people to be hungrier than usual the following day. To make matters even worse, sleep debt has a negative effect on the brain as well, because it impairs the frontal lobe, which is responsible for judgment, and stimulates the part of the brain that controls motivation and desire.

When you impair judgment while stimulating desire and increasing hunger, you create the perfect storm for creating and satisfying your cravings for your favorite high-fat, high-carbohydrate foods, like ice cream. That's why those people in the earlier study who only slept 4 hours a night were 73 percent more likely to be obese than those who slept 7 to 9 hours a night.

Lack of Sleep and Its Impact on Mojo

"Not tonight, dear. I'm too tired."

Are those words that have become all too familiar in your bedroom?

Sleep specialists say that sleep-deprived men and women report lower libidos and less interest in sex.

Depleted energy, sleepiness, and increased tension may be largely to blame. We already know that increased cortisol can impact just about everything! However, a recent study funded by the National Heart, Lung, and Blood Institute found testosterone levels dropped significantly in men who don't get enough sleep—the levels were the equivalent of those for men 10 to 15 years older. That explains the lack of sex drive, but lower testosterone can bring about other negative side effects, especially for younger men, including reduced libido and poor reproduction. But they may even find themselves unable to build enough strength through muscle mass and bone density, leading to lower energy levels, poor concentration, and chronic fatigue. Low testosterone levels are also linked to metabolic syndrome—a cluster of metabolic risk factors that increase the chances of developing heart disease, stroke, and type 2 diabetes.

Long-term sleep deprivation leaves major, long-lasting effects on hormone levels. Scientists from the University of Chicago found men who get less than 5 hours of sleep a night for a week or longer suffer from dramatically lower levels of testosterone than those who get a good night's rest. Their study, published in the *Journal of the Ameri-*

can Medical Association, found that the levels of the hormone are reduced dramatically to levels more similar to those 15 years older.

Lack of Sleep and Depression

Over the years, I've noticed that a lot of the high achievers I've come into contact with deal with bouts of depression. For them, it seems to come out of the blue. They feel blindsided. Interestingly, many of those people are also severely sleep deprived. In fact, most would be clinically labeled as insomniacs.

Trouble sleeping can be one of the first symptoms of depression. Research has shown there is a lot of correlation between insomnia and depression. One large study of ten thousand people, published in the journal *Sleep,* found that people suffering from insomnia were *5 times* more likely to develop depression! One of the best ways to improve mood and maintain a positive, happy outlook on life is to get enough sleep. Look, I know it's a lot easier said than done for those who can't sleep. But understand, if you're not sleeping, something is wrong.

What Professional Athletes Know About Sleep That You Should Too

A number of great athletes today share one common focus—sleep! I've read that LeBron James sleeps 12 hours a night. Roger Federer sleeps 11 to 12 hours a night. Usain Bolt, 8 to 10 hours. Venus Williams, 8 to 10 hours. Michelle Wie, 10 to 12 hours.

Highly trained athletes tend to be way ahead of the curve when it comes to taking care of their bodies. The rest of us who actually care about ourselves follow suit a few years down the road. Core training and functional exercise were once thought of as exclusive training techniques for the elite athletes of the world, but now most every trainer I know uses these methods with their clients. Current trends such as heart-rate variability monitoring for readiness levels and something called fatigue science—also known as the study of the impact of sleep deprivation—are at the forefront of cutting-edge training today. Fatigue science has become so hot that the San Francisco Giants used a well-known sleep expert, Dr. Chris Winter, to help give them a competitive advantage in winning the 2014 World Series.

In November 2012, the *Wall Street Journal* article "Sleeping Your Way to the Top" shared strategies from three NFL teams focusing on sleep to help improve field performance. Two of the three teams featured, the San Francisco 49ers and the Baltimore Ravens, eventually met in the Super Bowl a couple of months later. Some might write that fact off as a coincidence, but I wouldn't dare. These teams put a massive emphasis on the body's need for sleep, following scientific research showing that sleep enhances athleticism and gives a huge competitive advantage.

The Stanford University Center for Sleep Sciences and Medicine has been extensively studying the effects of extended sleep on athletic performance. In one study the researchers asked athletes from a variety of sports to focus on extending their sleep to at least 10 hours a night. The results were staggering.

Swimmers experienced increases in speed, improved reaction time off the blocks, faster turns, and increased kick strokes. Tennis players improved sprinting speed and serving accuracy. Football players experienced an improvement in their 40-yard-dash time by an average of $\frac{1}{10}$ of a second. I know a lot of NFL hopefuls who have paid thousands of dollars to shave $\frac{1}{10}$ of a second off their 40-yard dash. That $\frac{1}{10}$ of a second can be worth millions of dollars. Basketball players experienced huge increases in shooting accuracy.

There is also extensive research showing that when athletes get more rest, there is a major reduction in the risk of injuries. Naturally, this is optimal for those who rely on their body to function in peak condition day in and day out.

One study of teenage athletes found that those who slept at least 8 hours a night had a 68 percent reduction in injury risk compared to those who slept less than 8 hours a night. Talk to most teenagers today. They get nowhere near 8 hours of sleep, with their demanding schedules that include practice time, schoolwork, and other activities. It's no wonder injuries have steadily been on the rise for our high-school athletes.

Here's the bottom line. If you're an athlete looking for a competitive advantage that also reduces your risk of injury, you must put a major focus on getting more sleep. Start targeting 10 hours of sleep every night. It will absolutely help take your game to the next level. I guarantee it! There is no diet or training program that will provide the same reward in performance as optimal sleep.

The Advantages of Sleep Outside of Sports

Athletes are not the only ones who can enjoy the advantage of improved performance from sleep. We can all benefit from getting a good night's sleep. That's why getting 7 to 9 hours of sleep each night is one of the key components in the Stark Naked 21-Day Metabolic Reset. To further validate this connection between enhanced performance and quantity of sleep, let's take a moment and analyze what prevents most people from getting enough sleep in the first place.

Dr. K. Anders Ericsson did a famous study that declared it takes 10,000 hours of deliberate practice to become great at something. Most people who know about this study use it to validate their depriving themselves of sleep in order to get more done trying to reach greatness in the first place. Interestingly, there was one additional factor in that same study regarding performance that few people talk about. The highest performers in Dr. Ericsson's study also slept an average of 8 hours and 36 minutes a night.

Yes, they got over 8 hours of sleep a night. When was the last time you got 8½ hours of quality sleep? Sleep is critical to whatever you're chasing in life.

When you get the optimum amount of sleep, not only will your body operate better physically; your mind will function better too. Your thoughts will be clearer and more cohesive. You will be more alert and aware of everything in your surroundings. Dr. William C. Dement, in *The Promise of Sleep,* explores how sleep affects overall performance by looking at things like the ability to receive information, the ability to act on information, and the individual attention span. To support his findings, he turned to research from fatigue expert David Dinges, at the University of Pennsylvania, who found that when people were forced to sleep 4 hours a night for two weeks, their performance in these categories was severely impaired, especially toward the end of the 14 days. Basically, sleep loss made people stupid.

I don't know about you, but I completely know how that feels. As a new dad, I know there are plenty of mornings I wonder if I should even be driving a car! As soon as I can catch a nap, my mind and thoughts realign.

The performance advantages from enhanced sleep seen on the sporting fields were due to more than just better physical recovery. Physical repair and muscular recovery are definitely enhanced by more sleep, but two other key benefits of greater sleep are vital for high achievers in any arena: better cognitive function and better stress control. Dr. Michael Breus, known as the "Sleep Doctor," also feels that cognitive benefits play a huge role in enhancing the athletes' performance. Everyone can benefit from a brain that makes quicker, more accurate decisions. It doesn't take much to slow things down— just one night of sleep deprivation can decrease response time.

It should also come as no surprise that not getting enough sleep triggers the stress response in our bodies. Research on nonathlete populations found that those who are sleep deprived have much higher levels of cortisol in their blood the following day, and it takes up to six times longer to return to normal than for those in the control groups. Now that you know how damaging cortisol can be when its level is chronically elevated, simply getting more z's can build resiliency against cortisol. Simply stated, those who get more sleep are basically calmer and happier people, two great characteristics for better performance in any environment!

Most people are proud to show off their sleep deprivation as a badge of honor around the water cooler, but what they don't realize is how badly their lack of sleep is robbing them of their energy and mental ability to work at their highest level. Sure, they might be at the office, working long hours day in and day out, but they are likely not functioning in the most productive manner. If they are actually mentally checked out, completing mediocre work and getting a fraction of the work done in twice the amount of time, what's the point of punching the clock? If you want to stand out at work, increase your sleep. Within a matter of days of sleeping more these are the benefits you can expect to experience:

Better decision making

Better attention span

Better memory

Increased energy and reduced afternoon energy slump

Improved mood and therefore better working relationships

Increased motivation

Less risk of on-the-job injury

Less anxiety

Better ability to handle stress

More creativity

Better problem-solving skills

The Foundation for Great Sleep

Now that you understand the importance of sleep, I want to help you set up the best environment for it. There are two strategies I have learned over the years that are the foundation for a great night's sleep. These strategies are going to take a little extra effort on your part, but they are worth it.

The Stark Naked 21-Day Metabolic Reset will improve your internal environment and provide you with better-quality sleep, but if your external environment isn't in sync with these new changes, it will prevent you from having an optimum experience. To allow for a great night's sleep you must first set your room up. Once you've done that, you'll warm up for sleep each night just as you should warm up before you exercise.

The Bat Cave

I first learned about the "bat-cave theory" in 2007 at a Biosignature Seminar with Charles Poliquin. The bat-cave theory is simply the idea of making your bedroom resemble a bat cave. Dark and cold is the ultimate answer for great sleep. The darker the room, the more melatonin you produce, which allows for a more regenerative sleep. The temperature of your room should generally be cool.

On any given day, your body temperature naturally rises and drops. In the evening, your temperature naturally drops as your body gets tired, and at night it actually reaches its lowest point around 5:00 A.M.

We've all experienced how hard it is to sleep in a hot room. For most people, it's a frustrating night of tossing and turning combined with very little sleep. For optimal sleep, the ideal temperature of your bedroom should be between 65 and 72 degrees. The colder, the better, as your body needs to cool down to induce sleep. If your bedroom is too hot, it can cause insomnia, because your body cannot naturally cool down. As an added bonus, there is some scientific support that shows sleeping in a cooler room can even help you burn fat while you're asleep.

It's also important to keep your head cool. Research shows that the brain prefers being cooler to enhance sleep. A hot pillow can cause sleep issues. In a study done by the University of Pittsburgh School of Medicine, insomniacs who wore a cooling cap had an easier time falling asleep and stayed asleep dramatically longer.

Strategies to Create Your Bat Cave

- Put up blackout shades to create complete darkness. I want your room so dark you can't even see your hand in front of your face. It's a little eerie at first, but the payoff in better sleep is so worthwhile. Prices for blackout shades range from $30 to $200-plus, depending on quality and the size and number of windows.
- Set your thermostat at 65–72 degrees. This is the ideal temperature for sleep.
- Sleep with minimal clothing on to help keep body temperature down.
- Remove anything that is plugged in from your room. The bat cave is literally for the two best things in life: sleep and sex.

Warm Up for Better Sleep

The bat cave is an incredible setting for deeper and better sleep, but if you don't apply specific strategies before getting into bed, you can still end up staring into the darkness unable to check out. You have got to unplug from your overly stimulating world. Your brain and nervous system need a chance to calm down and allow the process of sleep induction to kick in. To warm up for better sleep, apply the following strategies:

- One hour before bed, unplug from the world by turning off the TV, computer, iPad, smartphone, and so on. The blue light that is emitted from these devices tells the brain it's light outside and therefore it's time to wake up—not sleep. Unplug from these and spend some time reading by yourself, read with your kids, talk with your significant other, take a warm bath, or meditate—anything that will reconnect you with yourself and those you love the most.

- Create and keep a Gratitude Journal. One of the most powerful tools I have found to date is writing in a gratitude journal each night before bed. Simply writing down three to five things you're thankful for each night before turning out the light is huge for enhancing sleep—and your life.

Sometimes duty calls, and we have to get on the computer in the evening. Choose screens that don't interfere with your sleep if you can and keep use to a minimum. To prevent insomnia from blue-light exposure, I have Flux installed on my Mac. In the evening it emits a light that is more red than blue to help keep my brain calm, so I can still easily fall asleep. I use the computer sparingly during this time, as I like to separate from my work as much as possible each night, so my sleep is not hampered.

I know, we are so used to being connected to the rest of the world through our tech devices these days that unplugging may be difficult. But give it a try for the next 21 days and see how it impacts your sleep.

Strategies for Challenging Sleep Issues

If you've applied the above strategies and sleep is still an issue, here are some advanced strategies for improving sleep. I find that clients usually fall into one of two camps: either they struggle falling asleep or they crash easily but can't stay asleep.

Trouble Falling Asleep

If you have a hard time falling asleep and the foundation strategies of the bat cave and warming up for bed have not worked, you're dealing with a source of unwanted stress before bed that needs to be calmed down. Try the following solutions.

Drink tart cherry juice. Two separate research studies have shown that people who drank two small glasses of tart cherry juice a day significantly improved the quality of sleep and increased its duration. Tart cherry juice works because it naturally raises your melatonin levels, which have been shown to have an influence on quality of sleep by regulating your sleeping-waking cycle. These studies also showed that people who consumed the tart cherry juice in the morning and before bed actually took fewer naps during the day, meaning they had more energy.

Do a deep-breathing meditation. Simple breathing strategies can really help calm down unwanted stress. Try using a relaxed deep-breathing technique: sit or lie in a very comfortable position, keep your eyes closed, and breathe in through your nose for 4 seconds and out through your mouth for 4 seconds. Focus on deep abdominal breaths; with each breath, you should feel your belly rise as you breathe in and fall as you breathe out.

Trouble Staying Asleep

If you fall asleep on the couch or are out cold within 5 minutes of lying down, you are showing the classic signs of sleep deprivation, but many of you struggle with sleeping through the whole night. It's become obvious people usually wake in one of two windows of time. Most high performers either wake between 1:00 and 3:00 or between 3:00 and 5:00 A.M. Let's explore some solutions you can try to better improve your sleep during these periods.

Waking Between 1:00 and 3:00 A.M.

I would guess somewhere between 80 and 90 percent of all high achievers we work with struggle with waking between 1:00 and 3:00 A.M. when they first come in. Usually this is due to dips in blood sugar at night, forcing the adrenals to pump cortisol to stabilize blood sugar, which wakes you up. Eating a snack before bed to make sure blood sugar stays stable is built into the Stark Naked 21-Day Metabolic Reset and usually solves this problem. If you are skipping this snack because you still believe eating before bed will make you fat and you are waking between 1:00 and 3:00 A.M., do yourself a favor and have the snack—problem solved. If you're eating the snack, then here is another solution you can try.

Chinese medicine shows us that people who wake between 1:00 and 3:00 A.M. are having issues with their liver meridian. Have you ever noticed that when you drink a little too much alcohol, you fall asleep quickly but end up waking sometime between 1:00 and 3:00 A.M. and then struggle with sleeping the remainder of the night?

Dr. Dayne Grove, my personal doctor of naturopathy and Chinese medicine, chooses to put his clients on a "liver tonic" as his first option for treating those waking during this window. Their immediate improvement in sleep is incredible. To battle this naturally, I have purposely built green tea into the daily outline in the afternoon. Green tea has a lot of liver-support qualities and also has an amino acid called L-theanine, which helps calm stress. If you are waking between 1:00 and 3:00, it's really important to drink the afternoon green tea during your reset.

Waking Between 3:00 and 5:00 A.M.

Waking between 3:00 and 5:00 A.M. is linked to the lungs in Chinese medicine, and excessive oxidative stress tends to be the cause. The answer here is to add more antioxidants into your daily diet. A good first solution will be making sure you use dark-skinned fruit as your nighttime snack before going to bed during the Reset, which you will read more about in Chapter 11. Dark-skinned fruits have more antioxidants. These include fruits like plums, berries, and cherries. The tart cherry juice discussed earlier is great for solving this sleep issue as well.

Applying these strategies can only improve the quality and duration of your sleep, supplying you with more energy, better focus, an uplifted mood, more sex drive, and a better body to enjoy sex with. Remember, sleep is the most critical component to your long-term success.

> Getting 7 to 9 hours of sleep a night is essential to your long-term success in everything you do. The Reset will improve your quality of sleep, resulting in better body and brain function.

Chris, CEO, Pure Game, age forty-seven
Tony, founder, Pure Game, age forty-seven
California

▶ _Chris and Tony run a nonprofit organization called Pure Game, which focuses on developing character in at-risk children through experiential learning. They use the game of soccer to help children break free from their current situations and negative mindsets. Imagine the energy needed to run around on the soccer fields all day teaching and mentoring at-risk children._

When we first met, Chris and Tony both struggled with sleep, leaving them dragging most of the time. They needed coffee and caffeinated teas to help push them through their days. Their hearts were in the right place, but their bodies wanted to be home in bed—catching up on their lost sleep.

When the two men started the Stark Naked 21-Day Metabolic Reset, I purposely had them start on a Friday. I knew they would struggle for the first few days once I removed their false energy source—caffeine—and I didn't want that to affect the kids they worked with.

As expected, they were both miserable for the first 3 days. They slept a lot due to their true low-energy state. Tony's sleep quickly became regulated, though. He began sleeping through the night in no time. I am always amazed at how much better most people sleep once I remove the stimulant caffeine. In fact, he was hitting such deep levels of sleep that he would sleep right through the crying of one of his own children during the night. His wife would have to wake him to go get their child!

Chris took a little longer to regulate, but by day 10 of the Reset, his sleep had settled in nicely too. Up until then, Chris had been routinely getting sinus infections that would keep him up at night. Ever since starting this program, however, his sinus infections have been greatly controlled, allowing him to sleep better and longer.

Together, their energy on the field is incredible! Their ability to lead their organization has dramatically improved, and their impact is growing at an incredible rate. The power of sleep is truly amazing! Tony and Chris are changing the future of our society and now they have the energy and stamina to impact and change the trajectory of lives for even more vulnerable children.

9

Exercise

Why *Less* Is More!

WHEN YOU SEE THE WORD "exercise," what do you associate with it? The most common response I get from clients is "punishment." These responders are divided into two camps:

Camp 1: Exercise is a bad punishment, so I am going to completely avoid it.

Camp 2: Exercise is a good punishment. The more I can suffer through, the better it is going to be for me.

Which camp would you pitch your tent in?

But guess what? The people in both camps are robbing themselves of their best possible lives. Why?

Both versions of "exercise is punishment" lead to excessive amounts of unneeded stress on the body, stealing your energy and happiness, increasing your likelihood of getting sick, accelerating your aging process, blocking your creativity, and destroying your desire to roll in the hay.

Those of you who currently live in the "exercise is bad punish-ment" camp probably bought this book believing it would be another prescription touting the notion, "Exercise is a must for success." You'd be partially right. Keep reading, because I think you're going to like what I have to say about exercise. By the end of this chapter you will see that more is not necessarily better, and as a result you may just change your stance.

Exercise Is Bad Punishment and Must Be Avoided

Exercise is a gift, a reward that a healthy body craves. It's my belief that if your body doesn't want to move, then your metabolism is most likely broken and needs to be resuscitated—or, as I like to say, reset.

When I first met my client Brandon, he was overweight and felt miserable. Brandon, forty-two, is the owner of a commodities-trading company. He weighed 320 pounds and slept somewhere between 2 and 4 hours a night. He had dark circles under his eyes, looked perpetually exhausted, and walked around radiating how miserable he felt to the world. The guy was suffering and was eager to make some vast changes. He was desperate to lose the excess weight he had somehow accumulated over the past few years. I will never forget the first words he said to me when we met.

"Brad, I haven't exercised in fifteen years, and I hate it. I know you're going to tell me I need to exercise. If that's your resolution to getting me fit again, this meeting is over. I will not exercise!"

Yeah, I could see I had my work cut out for me, but I knew Bran-don wasn't a lost cause. In fact, he was my ideal client.

With a big smile on my face, I replied, "No problem, buddy. For the first 21 days as my client you're not allowed to exercise, so don't even ask."

The look on his face was classic. I think his jaw hit the table, because no trainer had ever said that to him before. Like most people, Brandon had been misled into believing that exercise was the ultimate answer to getting healthy, and unless he was willing to hop on that train, he would never get results.

By now of course, you know I had a different plan for Brandon. Within the first week of starting the Stark Naked 21-Day Metabolic Reset, Brandon was sleeping a solid and valuable 8 hours a night—every night. The weight started to peel off rather quickly and without a lot of effort or pain.

Around 15 days in, my phone rang. It was Brandon calling to tell me he had so much energy that he was actually ready to start working out. I reminded him that our agreement was no exercise for the first 21 days.

"Call me on day 22," I said.

I knew what I was doing. You see, with a guy like Brandon, exercise was something I needed him to want. I couldn't force it. Not now, not ever. The longer I made him wait for it, the more he would want it. Sure, I have clients who exercise moderately during the 21-Day Reset period because they thrive on exercise, but these are high achievers who are cutting back—not starting a regime for the very first time.

When day 22 came, you can bet the first call I got that morning was from Brandon. He was begging me to exercise. In three weeks, he had dropped 17 pounds and 3 inches off his waist. He was now sleeping throughout the night, and his energy was off the charts. He was rested, energetic, and in a much better mood. His wife wanted to know what I had done with her old husband. He was a completely different man after just 21 days. Best of all, the man who once viewed exercise as the ultimate punishment was now eager and excited about it! His punishment had become his ultimate reward. Six months after starting his reset, Brandon has lost 70 pounds and continues to follow the program. One thing is for sure, he is *never* going back to his old unhealthy, sedentary lifestyle.

Once you make a shift in your thinking and see the value in taking care of yourself as a reward and not a punishment, you will start to unleash the true power of great health and fitness that lives inside each and every one of us. You will no longer despise the effort. You will embrace the process.

How do you make that shift? Simply follow this program and allow your metabolism to be reset. You've got to relax and conquer!

If you're like Brandon and see exercise as a form of punishment or as the last thing you want to do for yourself, then don't exercise for the next 21 days (as long as you're on the Reset plan). I promise, by day 22, like Brandon, you're going to crave movement!

I have yet to see anyone who hated the punishment of exercise complete the 21-Day Reset and not be ready and willing to exercise. It's not going to be you, is it?

Exercise Is a Good Punishment and Must Be Endured

Not long ago, I received an e-mail from another well-known professional CrossFit athlete, the New Zealander Ruth Anderson-Horrell, who was pursuing the title of "Fittest on Earth." Like Becca Voigt, Ruth, age thirty, competed in the CrossFit Games multiple times. In her e-mail she wrote that her stomach was severely bloated from water retention, her body fat was creeping up even though she was exercising like crazy, she was moody, her strength was dwindling, and overall her gas tank felt as if it was on empty all the time. Additionally, she was experiencing dizziness and nausea after certain types of short, high-intensity bursts of exercise. After investigating her daily routine more thoroughly, I quickly discovered her recovery methods were not appropriately offsetting her training volume, and her body was starting to give up. The stress from exercise was literally killing her body and making Ruth and everyone around her miserable.

After talking it over with Ruth and her CrossFit coach, Dusty, we decided the answer was to shut down training for a period of time, so we could reset her metabolism. Ruth agreed to follow the Stark Naked 21-Day Metabolic Reset to the letter along with focusing on getting 10 hours of sleep a night to really allow her body to replenish her diminished energy reserves.

The only exercise she was allowed to do for the first 7 days was recovery exercise. Together, we chose walking in nature for her.

Walking in nature? Really?

Yes! Believe it or not, it's such a powerful form of exercise to reduce stress and aid in accelerating recovery. Research done by the University of Michigan has confirmed that walking in nature does wonders for improving mental health and reducing perceived stress. Spending time in nature is also great for lowering blood pressure, heart rate, and stress load on the central nervous system. According to Yoshifumi Miyazaki, Japan's leading scholar on forest therapy, walking in the woods relieves stress and helps the immune system recover more efficiently. Miyazaki's research on walking in nature not only validated the previous benefits; he also found it created a general relaxation of the body, decreased the stress hormone cortisol, decreased fatigue, and increased psychological vigor. These were all things Ruth could benefit from in her overstressed and tired state, so it was a logical choice.

In the second week we allowed Ruth to add in 2 days of short higher-intensity strength-training workouts to make sure she was able to maintain her strength and not lose too much ground during her recovery phase.

At the end of the initial 21-Day Reset, Ruth was scheduled to compete in a CrossFit event. Her results were amazing. By dramatically reducing her training volume and focusing only on recovery for the

21 days prior to the event, she crushed the initial 3-kilometer run straight uphill, then back down, without any energy issues and completed 2 more days of competing in multiple fitness events without feeling fatigued or running out of energy. Her strength did not falter, as so many people expected it would because she had reduced her training volume. She had done no special training for this event. She had only rested and reset prior to competing.

Ruth's situation is a classic example of "fatigue masking fitness." Thankfully Charles Poliquin had made me aware of this phenomenon years ago by teaching me that *exercise is worthless if you aren't successfully recovering from it.* Ruth was like so many of you who believe more exercise is good punishment and are therefore overstressing your bodies, which is ultimately leading to severe fatigue and metabolic breakdown.

I don't want you to suffer from that anymore. Your metabolism needs a reset! It's time to take a 21-day break from your intense exercise.

As hard as it may be for you to cut back at first, try to remember Ruth's amazing results. She felt better, performed better, and received numerous compliments about how great she looked at the end of the 21 days.

Now, I think it is only fair to share that I originally didn't believe Charles's thinking on recovery. I thought more had to be better. I never focused on recovery. I took great pride in my extreme commitment to excessive exercise and my refusal to rest in between workout days, and yes, although I ended up with a body that looked great, I felt horrible. The *best* I ever looked in life was the *worst* I ever felt.

I guess you can say I've always been a glutton for punishment and used to have a tendency learn things the hard way. A lot of these exercise ideas that are considered great at quickly changing our weight, body fat, and muscle levels are also great ways to ruin our energy, happiness, and sex drive. When I finally realized the value of recovery, everything changed. It was a real "aha" moment for me. And I want it to be one for you too.

The Stark Naked Exercise Theory

The clients I have worked with over the years have led me to some interesting perspectives on health, fitness, and performance, especially for high achievers. The reality is that most of us after the age of thirty have basically lost the desire to look like a Spartan warrior or a Victoria's Secret model.

I said most. There are still a few of you out there, and you know who you are.

For the most part, by the time you've reached this stage in life, you've likely realized you've got a lot more important things to focus on than spending your day living in the gym obsessing over your abs.

Do you still want to look good in a swimsuit on your vacation? Heck, yeah! But do you want to spend 2 hours a day in the gym slaving away for it, making yourself miserable and starving yourself to get there? No way! You have more important things to do with your time. You have bigger responsibilities that require a lot more energy to take care of.

It took me a while, but in my early thirties I finally figured out that it takes a whole lot more than a hard, chiseled body to attract a quality woman. Now that I am a husband and father, my number one priority is to have the energy for quality time with those I love after putting in a long day at work, great stamina to have a long successful career, and insane health to give myself the best chance of waking up every morning on this side of the dirt for many years to come.

And if you are like my clients, this is what many of you truly crave too. The disconnect for people is that, when it comes to exercise, most of the information on fitness and nutrition isn't focused on these goals. It's focused on appearance. That's why you are probably exhausted, wiped out by stress, and yet still forcing yourself out of bed every morning to get to that spin class or run 3 miles before the sun comes up, thinking you are doing something great for your body. Sadly, most of you have been brainwashed into believing you must exercise hard to be successful. Worse, many of you believe the more *fit* people are, the *healthier* they are.

Well, like many other mistaken notions, I'm about to shatter that myth too.

The Stark Naked strategies on exercise shared in this chapter are the same tactics I ultimately used to restore my life and fitness and the exact protocols I recommend when restoring those for all of my clients. These exercise strategies will teach you how to use exercise to accompany your Stark Naked 21-day Metabolic Reset and enhance your energy, motivation, happiness, health, and sex drive.

Personal experience has changed my perspective on what our exercise needs really are when our lives become complicated with responsibilities and pursuits. I have more compassion and understanding than most trainers, because my life closely resembles the lives of many of you. I am so much more than a trainer these days. You see, my old life as a trainer was simple. I didn't have much responsibility outside of training my clients and focusing on exercise to look good. In my current life I have a family, am a partner in a business, travel the world for more than a hundred speaking engagements a year, and run multiple full-immersion destination retreats. My perspective on exercise needs has dramatically changed. Looks are still important, but without great energy I am worthless when it comes to keeping up with all of my responsibilities and pursuits. Unfortunately, I have learned that the hard way too!

Before I had children, I could never understand why people with young children looked so tired and worn-out all the time. My inner thought was "How hard can it really be to take care of little ones?"

At the time, it seemed pretty obvious to me. I thought these people simply didn't care how they looked.

That all changed the day I became a dad. *Wow!* I was shocked at how fast I got fat after our first baby.

Some mornings it took every last drop of energy in me just to peel my face off the pillow and go to work. The idea of working out myself was just too much! Instead, I used that time to steal a quick nap. My sleeping times were not up to me anymore. I could no longer be lazy and just lay on the couch all day on Sunday. I had dad duty.

Oh, yeah. I sing a much different tune these days. Now I have so much compassion for new parents, because they have no idea what lies ahead. Before I had kids, I thought the answer was easy. You just need to suck it up and add more time in the gym to ward off the accumulating fat, but in reality that's the worst call.

Another eye-opening experience for me came over the last few years and has led me to become an effective coach for busy working professionals. I always assumed sitting at a desk all day was easy and could never understand why travel took such a toll on people's bodies. I figured it was simply an issue of laziness and all these people needed was more exercise and better direction in food choices. I remember when I received my first fitness tracker as a gift. It was the original Nike Fuelband. At the time, I thought the 10,000-steps-a-day rule was a joke. In my mind, I'd reached 10,000 steps by 10:00 A.M. every day as a trainer. It seemed to be setting the bar too low.

Fast-forward a few years. Today I spend around 6 to 8 hours a day seated in front of my computer screen working. By 7:00 P.M. most days I have only accumulated 3,000 steps for the day. Life can change pretty fast when you find yourself busy doing things other than being a personal trainer. Looks like I need to go for a walk before bed.

I value the feedback of my fitness tracker now, because I am shocked at how little I move in my new life. In fact, it serves as a nice reminder to get up and move. I am equally surprised at how tired and stiff my body gets just sitting all day. Some days, no, make that most days, the last thing I want to do after being glued to my computer screen for hours is exercise. It takes me a lot longer to warm up than it used to, so I can get a good workout in.

But I do it. Why? Because I know it's good for my mind, body, and spirit, which makes it good for my total health.

The secret to long-term change and enjoying a great high-performance lifestyle with a great body is to switch from the belief that looking a certain way or weighing a certain number is better than first feeling great! Once you start feeling great, you will quickly begin to look and perform great in *all* areas of your life. When you focus on how you feel, specifically your greatest asset, energy, you are bringing your metabolism back online and onto your side.

When you punish your body and focus only on how you look, you abuse your metabolism and are therefore forced to fight it. That is why you feel so bad!

The Stark Naked 21-Day Metabolic Reset Exercise System

Before I present the Stark Naked exercise system, let me be very clear: as a trainer I do not develop weak, slow, skinny people. The people I work with are not on a twelve-week transformation challenge just to look great in the mirror. Their lives, like yours, are very complex. Their training and performance requirements are complex and require year-round focus, which creates amazing stamina, enabling them to perform for years to come. The system I am about to share with you is highly tested and proven. It is currently being used by professional athletes, SWAT team members, CEOs, sports agents, CrossFit athletes, famous speakers, authors, Hollywood stuntmen, pastors, busy moms, high-performing businessmen and businesswomen, my wife after our third baby, and myself—just to name a few high achievers.

I don't build weak people. I build long-term, resilient high achievers. With this strategy you will get the most out of your body for the rest of your life.

Remember, intense exercise, which I love, like high-intensity interval training, lifting weights, spin class, and boot camps, are applying stress to your body. Extended overexposure to stress is at the core of your broken metabolism. I've said before and I'll say it again: *you cannot beat a stress-based problem by throwing more stress at it.*

You also cannot develop a resiliency to stress if you have not recovered from the damage of your past stress. Like any professional athlete, you need an off-season!

When you're trying to mend a broken metabolism, you have to remove as much unneeded stress as possible from the body, especially while you are resetting it. That's why we reduce intense exercise during the 21 days of your reset.

It's only three weeks! Your body will not fall apart! Remember, Ruth's body actually looked better and had better energy and strength in competition after she dramatically reduced her exercise volume for three weeks. Think of this as your personal off-season.

Here are a few of my favorite ways to focus on recovery:

Take a relaxing walk in nature. (Personally, I love the beach!)

Take a 10- to 30-minute catnap daily. (NASA uses this strategy with its astronauts, because it helps their brains work better.)

Get a massage, but avoid deep-tissue work, as pain creates stress. Get one of those relaxing Swedish rubdowns that makes you fall asleep and drool.

Do daily stretching and mobility work.

Practice meditation.

Get an acupuncture treatment.

Do cardiac output exercise, which is aerobic exercise that calms the body down. Try keeping your heart rate around 130 beats per minute (bpm; beats per minute can be tracked on a heart-rate monitor). Joel Jamieson taught me the value of this three years ago and it was life-changing for my fitness.

Here are my current daily, weekly, monthly recovery strategies:

Daily	Weekly	Monthly
Evening walks outside	Cardiac output exercise (twice a week)	Full-body massage (twice a month)
Calming app (2–3 times)		
10-minute afternoon nap	Stretching and mobility work (twice a week)	Acupuncture for stress (twice a month)

Phase 1: Recovery Exercise

The first step in creating a body that is resilient to stress and possesses the stamina for long-term high performance is to rebuild your aerobic system. This begins with *cardiac output exercise,* which is low-level exercise that causes the chambers of the heart to stretch, allowing more blood to be pumped with each beat, thereby providing more oxygen to meet the demands of exercise. Positive benefits from this type of training seen in our clientele include a reduction in resting heart rate and blood pressure, a reduction in fatigue buildup during high-intensity exercise, deeper sleep, enhanced resilience to stress, increased energy, increased happiness, better quality and quantity of sex, and a calmer mind.

The best time to introduce a higher volume of cardiac output exercise is during the 21-Day Reset, because this increase in movement and blood flow not only decreases stress, but also aids the lymph system in detoxification, enhancing the benefits of the Reset nutrition program. We are not using this type of training for fat loss; we are using it along with the Reset to remove all the roadblocks that are keeping long-term fat loss from happening.

RECOVERY EXERCISE GUIDELINES		
Frequency	**Duration**	**Exertion, Heart Rate (bpm)**
3–5 days per week	20–45 minutes	4/10, 120–140

SAMPLE EXERCISES FOR RECOVERY EXERCISE
Walking or jogging in nature
Walking or jogging on a treadmill
Using an elliptical machine
Doing sled pulls
Using an Airdyne bike
Swimming
Rowing

Note: You can choose one exercise for the duration or combine several for the total time. The goal is to remain at an exertion level of 4/10 or keep your heart rate in the 120–140 beats-per-minute zone for the entire time.

PERCEIVED EXERTION SCALE	
10	Maximal
9	Extremely Hard
8	Really Hard
7	Hard
6	Difficult
5	Challenging
4	Moderate
3	Easy
2	Really Easy
1	Resting

RECOVERY EXERCISE WORKOUTS *Example 1: Using One Exercise*		
Exercise	**Duration**	**Exertion, Heart Rate (bpm)**
Walking or jogging in nature	5-minute warm-up	2/10, 100–120
	30 minutes	4/10, 120–140
	5-minute cool-down	2/10, 100–120

Note: Walking or jogging in nature is my favorite choice of recovery exercise. There is something very powerful and calming about doing your recovery exercise workouts out in nature. I highly recommend you use nature to your advantage during your recovery workouts.

RECOVERY EXERCISE WORKOUTS *Example 2: Using Multiple Exercises*		
Exercise	**Duration**	**Exertion, HR (bpm)**
Elliptical (warm-up)	5 minutes	2/10, 100–120
Airdyne bike	10 minutes	4/10, 120–140
Rowing machine	10 minutes	4/10, 120–140
Sled pulls	10 minutes	4/10, 120–140
Elliptical (cool-down)	5 minutes	2/10, 100–120

If you are someone who struggles with the idea of only doing recovery exercise and not training hard for a couple of weeks, here are some guidelines for you. Remember, the people who get the best results are the ones who reduce their high-intensity exercise during the Stark Naked 21-Day Metabolic Reset.

HIGH-INTENSITY EXERCISE GUIDELINES		
Frequency	**Duration**	**Exertion, Heart Rate (bpm)**
0–2 days max	20–45 minutes	7/10 max, 130–170* max
* The HR will go up and down with effort and rest periods. The goal is to have your heart rate be in this range for the majority of the workout.		

SAMPLE EXERCISE PROGRAMS FOR HIGH-INTENSITY TRAINING
Lifting weights (avoid going to failure and no accentuated eccentric training)
Cardio intervals
Spin class
Modified strongman—sled pulls, prowler pushes, farmer walks, tire flips, etc.

Play Is the Ultimate Exercise!

When we were younger, most of us loved exercise, even if we didn't know it.

Why?

Because exercise was disguised as "play."

As children, play was our reward, not our punishment. Ask a child what his or her favorite subject in school is, and you'll likely get the reply, "Recess." My son sure loves it. Sadly, it's rare that I speak with adults who tell me their favorite part of the day is their exercise. Most loathe going to the gym, but force themselves to do it, because they think it will help them look and feel better.

As we age, we view play as childish and frown upon it. Many have forgotten how to play. That's so sad, especially when you start reading the research on the impact play can have on adults' lives. Avoid play if you want to be less effective at work, depressed, unhappy, unmotivated, lack creativity, and a poor problem solver. However, play has been shown to be one of the most powerful tools for an enhanced life. Research continually validates play as a powerful tool to boost our mood, motivation, creativity, and problem-solving skills and even help reduce our weight.

At a Driven for Life leadership retreat I attended, one of the core areas of focus was the power of play. Earlier in the day we had completed a team challenge that took my group 11 minutes. After the challenge the retreat trainers had us play a really fun game unrelated to the challenge. There was lots of laughing and activity during the game. Once the game ended, which I can proudly say my team won, we were allowed to strategize as a group about the earlier challenge with the option of redoing it. The creative juices flowing through the group were amazing. After rethinking our strategy, we were able to complete the challenge in 16 seconds. This exercise taught me that play is a powerful tool for creativity that few of us take advantage of.

> We do not stop playing because we grow old;
> we grow old because we stop playing.
> —GEORGE BERNARD SHAW

Over the years I have found ways to get creative with exercise to keep me motivated. Since I spend most of my days in the gym, sometimes the last thing I want to do is spend even more time in the gym, away from my wife and kids, to get in a personal workout.

My solution? I play with my kids! They are little Energizer bunnies and have the stamina to play until daddy has to give up. I love this kind of time together so much that I have set up our home life around creative, fun play.

One of my favorite games is freeze tag with Nerf guns. The game works like this. We start by opening all the doors and gates around the house. We even open the windows. The goal is for me to chase the kids and their friends and try to shoot them with a Nerf dart. Talk about insane conditioning—I am dripping with sweat by the time we finish playing. The best part is hearing my kids scream with joy and laugh as I am in hot pursuit. We play for hours at a time, getting lost in the fun.

It's so rewarding for me in my relationship with my kids. It's exercise that is as far from punishment as you can get, yet it's super-beneficial for my body and my children's bodies. We also play all forms of sports together. I have even tried to mimic their acrobatics training on the grass with them. When was the last time you tried to do a cartwheel? They're so much fun, but wow, they're a lot tougher to do at forty! Yet another reason to keep trying!

Play can be tough at first, so here are some fun ideas to get you started:

Go bowling.

Throw a Frisbee at the park.

Shoot baskets.

Play on the playground at a park.

Go paintballing.

Go paddle boarding (warning: start in a bay or lake; it's tough on the open ocean).

Hike in nature.

Play tag with your kids.

Host a game night at your house. I recommend Hedbanz, as it gets really animated.

Twirl hula hoops.

Go to Chuck E. Cheese's to play games (not eat the pizza!).

Build a fort.

Have a dance party.

One of the greatest tips I received on playing with my children came from one of my clients, Dr. Daniel G. Amen, the "Brain Doctor" and *New York Times* bestselling author of *Change Your Brain, Change Your Life*. He taught me the most powerful thing I can do with my kids is to play with them every week *on their terms*. The structure is simple. I give them my undivided attention, and they take the lead. I simply become part of their game and don't dictate or correct anything. It's so much fun to be absorbed into your child's creativity and imaginary worlds. The connection you experience during these times with your kids is unbelievable. Over the years I've been everything from a pirate at sea, to a ninja in training, to a frog jumping lily pads.

I believe in the power of fun so much that I've even incorporated it into my live training seminars, where I use the game Smack Fu to engage play and wake up my audiences. Smack Fu uses a simple toy that is shaped like a dart with feathers on it. You hit it back and forth to each other, trying to keep it in the air rather than letting it hit the floor. Think volleyball without a net. It's so much fun to watch a group of serious CEOs lighten up by playing Smack Fu in the boardroom.

Creative play is a vital part of a healthy life. Stop taking life so seriously and start adding some fun back in. If you hate the gym, don't go. Replace it with play. People will notice. One of my clients, a professional NFL player I hadn't seen for a while, texted me after a training session asking what I had been doing different, because I looked younger, happier, leaner, and stronger than I had in the past two years. He said he wanted some of my "new secret sauce." I texted him back, "I stopped beating myself up in the gym and started focusing on relaxing more and engaging more in the ultimate form of exercise—*play.*"

> Reduce intense exercise during the Reset. You need an off-season!

10

Tap into Your Ninja Motivation and Stark Naked Mindset

L ET'S FACE IT, we all want to look better, have more energy, or spend more time with family, yet year after year we continually fail at our attempts to stick with and obtain these goals.

I get it! Change is tough. In fact, dealing with change is, I believe, one of our greatest internal struggles. A lot of you already know the changes you need to make to reach that new level of health and wellness, but you can't seem to make a dent in getting there, or you attempt it for a short time, but then fall right back into your former ways. It's true that old habits die hard.

Sadly, most people don't understand what stimulates permanent change. You might think it has to do with willpower, but science has proven willpower is like a muscle. After a while, it fatigues, leaving you vulnerable, especially later in the day. (Hint: that's why most people blow their diets in the evening. I will teach you how to use that to your advantage later in this program.)

Here's some interesting news. When it comes to change, willpower is not the solution. The answer for change lies much deeper inside you.

I have spent a lot of time studying change and have come to the realization that the most powerful creator of change is something I unknowingly used on my father when I was just three years old. My dad was a smoker. For the first few years of my young life, he fought hard to quit. He was constantly trying new strategies, but they never created lasting change. He tried everything from the patch to hypnotization, but nothing was successful in helping my father quit for good. That is, until one day I came across a pack of my dad's cigarettes and, wanting to be just like my dad, I put one in my mouth and pretended I was smoking. When my dad walked into the room and saw the cigarette hanging from my lips, his heart sank. That's all it took to keep my father from ever smoking again.

From that point on, my parents decided to focus on being healthy examples for their children. I remember sitting next to my mom's exercise mat at the community center while she did Jazzercise and being mesmerized watching my dad and his buddies lift weights at the gym. I have been hooked on exercise ever since.

When it comes to change, it's not enough to commit to making the change for yourself, because you will almost always fail. To be lasting, change must be made for those you love the most.

Just as my father witnessed me as a three-year-old with a cigarette hanging out my little mouth, you are doing things right now that those you love the most are picking up as habits. You are not talking about them, but it's sinking into their consciousness, and they are more than likely slowly developing the same unhealthy habits you're struggling with. If you currently have children, take a few minutes and observe their behavior. You might be surprised at what you see. For most of you, it will be a scary realization, but one you can start to do something about right now.

By the way, if you don't have children, you're not off the hook.

Look around at those you love the most. Do you notice any similarities in habits?

It's amazing how powerful our influence is when we do things for those we love—whether positive or negative. We will move mountains for our families, yet when it comes to doing something positive for ourselves, something as simple as eating more vegetables, that thing becomes our immovable mountain. Most of us who are caring for others tend to put those others first in our lives, leaving our own needs for last. We feel as though we just don't have the time to take care of ourselves, especially with so many demands being placed on us today.

A CEO client who has lost over 60 pounds and has totally rejuvenated his life following the Stark Naked 21-Day Metabolic Reset asked me to speak to his executive team about this concept. When I finished the talk, he came up to me with a look of absolute sadness on his face.

"My nineteen-year-old daughter is home visiting from college, and I was really bothered watching her rifle through the pantry looking for unhealthy snacks every night before she went to bed. After hearing you speak, I now realize she learned that from me! That was my comfort blanket to help me deal with stress. I can't believe I caused that," he said.

"I know how hard it is to realize this, but you should be proud that you have changed your messaging. She now sees how great you look, how much energy you have, and how happy you are. She's subconsciously watching the new you. It's critical to just keep walking your path. It will rub off on her! I promise," I assured him.

My client was amazed how his habits had influenced hers, because they had never spoken about it. She just seemed to pick them up. Unfortunately that's how it works; our actions speak so much louder than our words.

Don't think you can live one way, but tell your loved ones to live another. You must live your example!

Ninja Motivation

Every year I sit down with each of my kids to help them set individual goals and dreams to pursue. I started them with this type of goal setting at the youngest possible age as a way of helping them set up their year with something to strive for. You can never be too young for that. Two years ago, my daughter, Isabel, who was just five at the time, hit me with a left hook on the chin with her reality.

The night before we did her goals, I took her with me to sit in on a talk I was doing with a basketball team about health and performance. I downloaded a new game on my iPad to keep her occupied while I spoke. During my talk she sat in the corner, appearing to be fully engaged in the new game, so I figured, like most kids, she probably heard nothing that came out of her father's mouth.

The next morning Isabel and I sat down to work on her goals. We write them out together, but I always make it a point to let my children choose their own goals, as I want them to pursue what they want, not what I want for them. Her first two goals were great:

Goal 1: I can read a book.

Goal 2: I can do a handstand.

I loved how she innately wrote them in a form that seemed to say she had already accomplished them. Goal 3, however, threw me for a bit of a loop.

Goal 3: I drink more water.

Huh? Where did that come from? When I saw that on her list, my initial response as a sometimes oblivious father was to think she was being a little lazy and not really putting a great deal of thought into her third goal.

"Honey, your goals are great. I really like goals 1 and 2. We can really track your progress and work toward reaching them, but I am a little confused by goal number 3. Why did you decide that drinking more water should be your third major goal this year?"

"Daddy, I heard you talk to that basketball team last night, and you told them if they wanted to be better athletes and healthier, they needed to drink more water. Well, I want to be a ninja when I grow up. That means I need to be a better athlete and healthier, so I need to drink more water like those basketball players. I also see you and Mommy drinking water all the time, so it must be really important."

Her response was beautiful. Admittedly, I was floored at first, because I couldn't believe she heard me speaking to the basketball team. I also couldn't believe she was taking her father's advice. Isabel proceeded to quote all of my major talking points from the night before. I had almost missed an amazing opportunity to realize that I am a living example for my daughter—in a positive way. Not only had she heard my advice; she was paying close attention to and watching the actions of her mother and me. I have saved that year's list of goals as a constant reminder of what I now call *ninja motivation.*

Ninjas are lethal, yet you never see them coming. They're similar to our lifestyle habits, because they can silently enhance or destroy the lives of those we love the most. How is your ninja motivation affecting those around you whom you love the most?

If, like my father, you're not happy with how you are silently affecting the lives of your loved ones, now is the perfect time to change. It was my dad's ninja motivation that led me to write this book. Without it, I wouldn't have had the exposure to health and fitness or the desire to dedicate my life to helping others find their inner ninja!

The greatest gift you can give those around you is to live the change you want to see in them. Live the lifestyle habits you want them to pick up and enjoy in their lives. I can't imagine anyone who would want their loved ones to require a constant intake of caffeine to have enough energy to survive their days or push their children into a pattern of not sleeping enough by constantly telling them sleep is for the weak.

The majority of my referrals don't come from people who have

Ninja Motivation Exercise for Success

To truly be successful and create lasting change, you must take a good look at how your ninja motivation is affecting those you love the most. Get a pen and piece of paper and take some time to answer these few questions. Do not think you are doing this for yourself and no one else. That may be enough to get you started, but it won't keep you in the change game long-term.

1. Whom do I love the most in this world? List three to five people for whom you want to be a powerful positive ninja motivator.
2. How is my lifestyle currently affecting these people? List five things you are doing that make you a positive ninja motivator. List five things you are doing that make you a negative ninja motivator.
3. What does my new lifestyle look like? List three lifestyle goals associated with your new ninja motivation that will enhance the lives of those you love the most. (Example: Sleeping 7 hours a night for great natural energy, leading to a more youthful and energetic me all day long.)

been told by my happy and satisfied clients how great the program is, but rather from people who have witnessed the positive changes in those people and asked about how those changes came about. They then come to me to get those results for themselves.

My clients are using their ninja motivation to improve the lives of their family and friends. Trust me—they are watching!

Change Is Hard!

In 2013 I had the incredible opportunity to work with my first SWAT team, providing nutrition and supplementation strategies to help optimize their energy, sleep, and performance. It was such an honor and a challenge, because these are some tough-minded individuals who are resistant to things they don't know or aren't familiar with. I met with them at their regular training grounds. In between testing and working with them, I sometimes got to watch them do their SWAT training exercises, clearing mock houses, practicing target shooting, and so on. Sometimes I got to play the bad guy they were hunting down!

One situation took place in a huge studio with different movie sets. I was the bad guy hiding in an office setting, while the SWAT team came to find me. I was hiding behind a door and remember looking through the crack, right into the eyes of an ex-Navy SEAL as he had me locked in his rifles sites. The intense, focused look in his eyes genuinely scared me.

After several months of training together, they decided that if I wanted to stick around, it was time for me to experience one of their physical workouts with them. I needed to keep their respect, so naturally I accepted their invitation, knowing I was in for an ass kicking. The 1½-hour drive to the workout site was gut-wrenching. I had no idea what to expect, but there was one certainty: it was going to be hell. I went into the physical challenge with two major goals. First, no matter what challenges I faced, I was going to finish. Second, I was not going to come in last place.

Eleven reps into the workout I knew I was in serious trouble. The workout started with 25 pull-ups. The first 10 had to be strict, but after that you could move into CrossFit-style kipping pull-ups that generated a lot of momentum in the movement, making them a lot easier. The only problem was that I had never done a kipping pull-up.

I was able to keep up for the first 10 reps, but then the team took off flying through kipping reps while I struggled to finish. Right out of the gate I fell into last place.

We moved on to what felt like endless repetitions of full-body exercises using heavy sandbags as weights combined with long runs carrying the sandbags on our shoulders. Halfway through these combos, my world started closing in on me. My whole body and mind screamed, *"Stop!"*

My legs were becoming numb. With every step I took, I felt as though I was one step shy of crumbling to the ground. My lungs were burning, and nausea had set in and taken over my body. I had never experienced anything like this.

I had so much respect for these guys coming into this. I didn't want to fail them; if I quit, they would never look at me the same again. I dug deep and repeated my personal motto, "Just keep going. It will eventually end. All pain ends sooner or later."

At the 14th minute of the nonstop high-intensity exercise, I faced two options: to finish or pass out. Those were the only two options I would consider to make the pain stop.

I wanted to maintain my honor with these men I looked up to so much. I pushed myself and completed the sandbag exercise, remaining runs, and 25 more agonizing pull-ups before I finally crossed the finish line. It took every last ounce of my energy to complete that 25th pull-up, but I found a way to finish.

Okay, I'll admit that I finished 10 minutes behind the top guy, but hey, I still finished! And as promised, I didn't finish last.

This 24 minutes of straight high-intensity exercise almost ended my life, but once the pain was over, I was so proud of myself for digging deep and pushing myself beyond what I believed I was ever capable of.

One thing I have learned over the years is that we are capable of far more than we believe. Too many of us set up mental boundaries and give up early on things without ever really trying. We give up before we even attempt them, because we convince ourselves we don't have what it takes.

One common area I see people hold themselves back in is their health and fitness. I hear the craziest excuses about why people won't try to eat healthier or exercise. Most of them are basically bullsh-t. You can do whatever you set your mind to.

Here are some strategies like those I used during my workout with the SWAT team to help you *thrive* when you have to push through tough times.

Thrive Strategy 1: Focus on small things.

At times, focusing on the big picture can be daunting and overwhelming. How do you overcome this kind of challenge? Merely break it down and focus on one small step at a time. During the workout with the SWAT team, I focused on simply taking each next step. Life is all about one baby step at a time, and that strategy got me to the finish line.

When it comes to the Stark Naked 21-Day Metabolic Reset, you might find yourself dealing with hunger the first 3 to 5 days on the plan. Instead of thinking about how many days you have left on the plan or on the foods you can't eat, focus on reaching your next meal without cheating! Set a goal that you will not contemplate giving up until after you have eaten your next meal. It's that simple. Surviving and thriving come from taking small continuous steps, not one huge leap.

Thrive Strategy 2: Never forget your ninja motivation.

Who are you doing this for? When times get tough, picture those people in your mind. They will give you the deep motivation to take another step forward. There have been many times in my life that I have had to close my eyes and picture my wife and children to help motivate me.

Recently, I have been given the opportunity to create a full-immersion destination retreat focused on the Stark Naked 21-Day Metabolic Reset in Belize. During the 5-to-7-day getaway, people will be disconnected from the world, so they can focus on dramatically enhancing their health. They say this location is the closest thing to the Garden of Eden on earth. It's such an amazing opportunity for me, my business, the people whose lives I want to enhance, and my family. The drawback is that my investors want the plan formulated and launched ASAP!

This is a huge opportunity and dream come true, but it's creating enormous stress in my life, because it means I have to take time away from the things I love and need the most for balance and well-being. To help keep me centered and focused, I keep pictures of my wife and kids all over, on my desk, the wallpaper on my phone, iPad, laptop, and so on. Seeing their smiling faces helps to keep me going when I am tired and frustrated, as I know this retreat will bring life-changing experiences for all of us.

I am the kind of guy who needs and enjoys constant reminders of those I love, especially when the pressure builds up. Sometimes, I will admit, I'm tempted to throw in the towel and give up. But when I see my family, even if it's just in my mind, it helps me look past the current obstacles and push forward.

Thrive Strategy 3: The pain will eventually come to an end.

In the movie *Unbroken*, the main character, Louie, suffers being lost at sea and the horrors of prisoner-of-war camps, but has a resiliency that is incredibly inspirational. He represents the epitome of what we as humans are capable of enduring. His brother gave him the best advice for survival, "If you can take it, you can make it."

That is exactly how I have chosen to live my life too. Although I haven't endured the kind of hardship he did as a prisoner of war, I understand that as long as I don't give up, the pain eventually ends—and it always does.

This way of thinking helped me survive my freshman year of college. I grew up loving sports. I especially excelled at baseball, eventually earning a spot on a college baseball team. My freshman year, the coach at the four-year college I was attending decided it would be a better idea if I played at a junior college for the year and then come back, instead of sitting on the bench for the year as a red-shirt freshman.

I agreed. I would much rather have played than sat.

That decision was one of the worst choices I ever made. However, it was also one of the best character-building experiences I have endured. The coach of the junior college I attended was young and, for reasons I will never understand, had it in for me. It was his mission to break me. I played baseball because I loved the game; he viewed baseball as a way to prove you're a man. Every day I had to deal with his negativity. One day he actually challenged me to a fight after I questioned him about what it was going to take for me to get more playing time.

We all experience people like this in life at one time or another—a horrible boss, a negative friend, the wrong girlfriend or boyfriend. Many of you have even known a coach like this as well.

People like this eventually fizzle out. One day, you will no longer have to deal with them, and the pain goes away. No matter what, you have to keep getting out of bed every morning, and you can't let them beat you. Knowing the pain would eventually end helped push me forward, forcing me to keep going.

When I opened my first gym in 2004, I was so financially strapped I had to sleep on a buddy's couch and shower at the gym, because I couldn't afford to pay the bills for the gym *and* rent my own living space. I believed in my training philosophies and wanted to share them with the world my way, but, man, it was a struggle to establish myself in Southern California, where there are gyms on every street corner. So early on, there were many days when I had no idea how I was going to find the money to pay the rent on the gym and keep the lights on. But as long as I didn't give up, I knew that pain would eventually go away—and eventually it did.

Those early struggles have given me the resiliency and character to fight through tough times whenever they arise. And believe me, they do. Tough times are a part of everyone's life. Understanding that the pain will eventually end is where we should focus, not on how bad it hurts. This belief system still gets me out of bed even today when

I am mentally and physically fatigued and I am second-guessing myself and my ability to be an agent of change.

Here's the bottom line: *the start of the Reset is tough.* There is no doubt about it. But you have survived much worse things than this in your life. For the next 21 days I want you to step up for yourself and everyone you love and simply be *all in* all the time!

When I was a kid, my father used to tell me every morning, "Every day you are either getting better or getting worse, but you are never staying the same, so do something today that makes you better." I pass that same advice on to you, but I want to add one more thing: "Change your life and you literally change the world." You will never understand the true power of your ninja motivation, but your simple change will have a ripple effect for generations to come.

> For the next 21 days, I want you to step up for yourself and everyone you love and simply be *all in* all the time!

PART FOUR

THE STARK NAKED 21-DAY METABOLIC RESET

11

Phase 1

The Stark Naked 21-Day Metabolic Reset

IME TO RESET AND REBOOT!

By now I hope you understand that it's not been your lack of effort or something you've been consciously doing wrong that got you where you are today.

You've put in the right amount of effort. You've had enough will-power! You've exercised—likely more than you needed to. You've probably deprived yourself of the foods you needed. You've certainly done all of the right things, hoping to look, feel, and perform better—and despite everything, you don't!

Honestly, it's not your fault!

Your metabolism is simply b-r-o-k-e-n! You need to bring it back online—hit the reset button. Shut down the system and reboot, so you can feel great, look amazing, and finally perform with the boundless energy you've been looking for.

As you have finally discovered, it has likely been your overzealous quest for health, your ignorance about your liver, and eating the wrong foods for you, even *healthy* foods, that have left you looking and feeling the way you do.

As of today, there will be no more trying to force change. There will only be your acceptance that your body needs a break and your willingness to give it one.

Oh, hey. Check your cell phone.

What?

It's frozen?

You can't check your messages?

Get your e-mails?

Texts?

Sh-t!

What would you do if that really happened?

C'mon, be honest.

If you're like most people, you'd likely turn the thing off and reboot it.

It's called a *reset*.

Get it?

Why would you panic over your phone and not do the same over your health?

Imagine it this way. You and I are racing cars against each other in a 500-mile race. You can choose whatever car you want for our race. My favorite car is the 1967 Ford Mustang Shelby GT500 Fastback, the same car that is Nicholas Cage's nemesis in the movie *Gone in 60 Seconds*. The race we are in is all about performance, so make sure you choose a seriously high-performing car.

Got it?

Okay.

Here we go!

We are off!

Everything is going smoothly! We're neck in neck in the early stages. We spend the first few hundred miles fairly even, until suddenly a light starts flashing on my dashboard.

Uh-oh. It's the gas light warning me that I am running out of fuel. I am forced to make a pit stop to refuel my car.

My momentary lapse gives you a chance to pull ahead, until you notice your fuel light blinking. That little voice in your head begins telling you that you can't stop now. If you pull off, I will catch up to you. You convince yourself to push through and just ignore the warning sign. Despite the obvious flashing light, you push the pedal to the metal and go flying right past the pit row. You are brimming with excitement because your lead has grown so much. You believe there is no way I will ever catch up until . . . *clunk!* Your car jerks hard a few times, and then your engine dies. You're out of gas!

The smart solution would be to refuel, but you pride yourself on working harder than everyone else, and that little voice in your head continues to tell you that you cannot afford to circle back, so you jump out and start pushing your car as hard as you can toward the finish line, believing your hard work and perseverance will overcome the lack of gas in your tank and, somehow, you will still win this race. Obviously you have no chance. The reality is you will never even finish the race.

It's a silly story, but that's exactly what we are doing with our bodies when we ignore the warning signs that something is broken and needs to be fixed. We think we are invincible or can sacrifice in ways others can't, because we are high achievers. But we can't. No one can. Eventually, that tank runs out of gas. And no matter how hard you push the car, it will never cross the finish line.

Professional athletes are experts at this, because the majority of them take downtime during the off-season to recover from all the hard work and stress they put their body through during the regular season. The professional athletes I work with aren't allowed to intensely train in the gym when they are on mandatory rest. They are only allowed to do recovery exercises (as discussed earlier, in Chapter 9). They can get massages, spend quality time with their families, get physical therapy for the beat-up areas of their bodies, and give themselves a much-needed break. When they do this, they come back with renewed energy and find themselves ready to train harder and with the chance of less injury. As a result, their progress preparing for the new season is always amazing.

As busy high achievers, most of us never take a break—from anything! Maybe, just maybe, you'll take a vacation, but a recent poll showed that Americans take the least amount of vacation time compared to people in all the other countries in the world.

Everyone needs a break from time to time. If you want the stamina to finish life strong, you will treat this advice as if your life depends on it—because it does.

I recently started working with a client who is a senior PR executive for a major corporation. In some instances, being a public-relations executive can be as stressful as being an emergency-room doctor! To reach the position of senior executive in a large organization, you must be a serious high achiever.

When I first met my client, it was obvious her body had fought the good fight until age forty. But all of a sudden her body started giving out on her. Over the course of the next five years, during which she lived her life exactly the same way she always had, stress began to win the battle. Her body weight began to increase as her energy tanked and lethargy kicked in. She just couldn't keep up the same pace, even though she was doing all of the same things she had done throughout the years to stay in shape and look great. Intuitively she quickly realized something wasn't right. She understood if she didn't make some changes, not only would she not have the stamina to finish out her career; she could get very sick.

This client was very open and honest about her health and future. She had heard a talk I gave to a group of overachieving executives on how fitness masks health. Like most of my clients, she was someone who believed if 30 minutes of exercise was good for her, 90 minutes was better.

Sound like anyone you know? She was the driver unwilling to pull off the track for gas.

This woman pulled into the Brad Davidson repair shop out of gas, with two flat tires, the emergency brake stuck on, and a dragging muffler. She had been pushing her car around for years, believing she was performing at her highest level. After years of taking, the time had come to give back to her body. Leadership consultant Robin Sharma said it best: "Peak performance without strategic refueling leads to enduring depletion."

The Stark Naked 21-Day Metabolic Reset is my gift to you and your metabolism. It's the strategic refueling your metabolism and body are in dire need of.

I want to help you have this breakthrough, but it's time for a new strategy. It's *recovery*—not a willingness to work harder than the next person—that enables the highest performers long-term. Recovery is the true art that enhances performance at the highest level. I know this is hard to believe, and that is why I am challenging you to take only 21 of your (on average) 27,375 days here on earth to test this theory.

So instead of hitting the gym every day, you're going to do things to relax along with following the program, and for some of you that will be harder than giving up some of your favorite foods for three weeks. You're going to cut back on your exercise. You are only allowed two 45-minute high-intensity exercise sessions a week max during the first 21 days. You can do recovery exercise like leisurely walking every day, but you will need to dramatically reduce your high-intensity exercise, and that's going to feel strange at first. If you are really tired, I would highly recommend doing only the recovery exercise discussed in Chapter 9.

Believe it or not, cutting out the self-imposed demand to do and be busy all the time will have a profound impact on your body and well-being. I'm giving you the green light to sit on the couch and relax. Your metabolism, appearance, sex drive, performance level, and general well-being all need this. In fact, they're crying out for it. This is your free pass, so take it.

Why the Stark Naked 21-Day Metabolic Reset Works

Having worked with thousands of clients on this very program, I have witnessed firsthand the challenges they faced on a daily basis to make it through, both mentally and physically. Although the eating portion of the plan isn't necessarily "hard," the general mindset of most people going into it is that it's going to be. To overcome that immediate perception, the program is designed to help improve your likelihood of success. Willpower is like a muscle: *the more it's used, the more it fatigues.* It has been scientifically proven that a person loses willpower and becomes more likely to make poor decisions as the day goes on. I've watched this happen with my private clients. Who hasn't grabbed a midnight snack or something at the airport late in the day that they later regretted?

To combat declining willpower, the Stark Naked 21-Day Metabolic Reset places the toughest choices, like avoiding carbs, early in the day, when your willpower is strongest, and the easier choices later in the day, when your willpower is weakening, dramatically increasing the likelihood of success. By loosening the noose at night and allowing you the freedom of carbohydrates at dinner and a bedtime snack, this plan virtually ensures success. You won't fall prey to weak willpower.

The Eleven Lifestyle Modifications for the Stark Naked 21-Day Metabolic Reset

Now that you know why you're here, it's time to understand the outline of the game for the next 21 days. The following are the eleven core lifestyle strategies of the Reset. Follow these strategies and stick with the plan, and I promise you will see remarkable results. You can't cheat on *any* of these, or it will impact your results. Any deviation will mean the difference between success or failure. Hey, I'm just the messenger. If you don't like what you see in the mirror, don't break the mirror. Change the reflection!

The first four modifications include strategies to reduce your stress load and get better control of your cortisol, the next three include removing all of the unneeded sources of stress on your liver, and the final four are to help you get the most from your diet.

1. Hydrate. For the next 21 days, water is going to be your new BFF. You will need to drink one-half of your body weight in ounces of water a day. For example, if you weigh 150 pounds, you will need to drink 75 ounces of water every day. It won't be easy, but it will be worth it. Water, vitally important to the human body, helps reduce cortisol and really aids in the detoxification process. Yes, you will be going to the bathroom more than usual in the beginning, but the frequency ought to slow down after the first few days.

If it doesn't you, can try adding minerals to your water to help improve your body's ability to absorb the water into your cells. A high-stress lifestyle can severely deplete these minerals, preventing your body from absorbing the water, which creates a flushing effect. What this means is that you drink water and it essentially flushes right out in your urine without doing its job, leaving you dehydrated. It's a very common reason so many people complain of constantly having to go to the bathroom after drinking more water. I personally like adding ConcenTrace minerals to my water. You can find those at most health-food and supplement stores or online.

2. Sleep 7 to 9 hours a night every night. Remember, almost all animals on earth need sleep. The only exceptions are those lacking complex mental functions like jellyfish and flatworms. The more complicated the brain, the more sleep a creature needs. That is why you are going to aim for 7 to 9 hours of sleep every night. I want you in bed by no later than 11:00 P.M. Sleep recharges your battery, and it's when your body goes into healing mode! If you have trouble sleeping, try some of the sleep suggestions in Chapter 8.

3. Drastically reduce your intense exercise. You can train hard for a maximum of 45 minutes 2 days per week, but it is not mandatory. Remember, less is more during your reset. You can do other forms of training, such as the recovery exercise we talked about, but it is critical that your perceived exertion during these workouts stays at 4/10. That is the level that allows you to carry on a full conversation during the workout without feeling winded or breathless. Those of you who don't adhere to this advice, who think you will outsmart me, or who *need* to hit it hard are in for a real awakening. You will *not* get the full benefit of this program. Intense exercise elevates cortisol and bogs the liver down. It will have an impact *opposite* to the one you're seeking.

4. Commit to daily acts of relaxation. Research shows that as little as 10 minutes of relaxation a day has major benefits for your body. All I am asking for is at least 10 minutes of focused relaxation each day. Anything that you find relaxing works. Some examples are meditation, focused deep breathing, reading a book, or simply taking a 10-minute catnap in the afternoon. Trust me, on days 2 and 3 it won't take much persuasion to get you to take a nap. If you have trouble meditating, try one of the apps I mentioned in Chapter 6 (also see the Resource Guide for these).

5. No coffee. Ugh! I know I am ruthless! I am a giver though, because you can have green tea for a little caffeine if you need it. Green tea is loaded with great metabolism and liver support. If you do cut out coffee and caffeine altogether, the headache and energy crash you may feel will only last for the first 3 to 5 days, after which your natural energy will emerge and every day you will feel better and better. *Push through!* It is worth it to feel that natural energy and clarity come back. It's been years since you've had it, and you might just like it.

6. No alcohol. Before your throw this book at someone or across the room, remember, it's only 21 days! Rehab is 28! If you seriously can't give up booze for 21 days, maybe you ought to be looking at

Betty Ford instead of Brad Davidson. Okay, just kidding. Here's some good news! After 21 days, I'll let you put alcohol back in your routine—if you still want it.

Truthfully, so many of my clients tell me once that they get past the first 5 days, they are amazed at how great they feel. Their energy and clarity, especially in the morning, are fantastic. People who drink alcohol, even one to three drinks a night, are impacting their sleep, sometimes wake with a slight hangover, and can be foggy the next day—often without realizing it. Habits are formed. You learn to live as if this is feeling "normal," when in fact you are impaired. Twenty-one days will shed some light on this for you as well as help you shed some pounds. I can't think of a better reason to give it up or give it a try. Stop hyperventilating! You'll be okay going 21 days without alcohol.

7. Remove refined sugar from your diet—all sources of refined sugar. If you have a sweet tooth, this may be the hardest part of the plan for you, especially for the first few days. Believe it or not, on average, most Americans consume 136 pounds of sugar a year, and about 20 percent of their calories come from sugar. That's 25 teaspoons a day! Kids are eating even more than that! Yikes!

Sugar is nothing but empty calories that are adding pounds and causing more harm than good. Worse, for some, it's as addictive as any illicit drug. The brain depends on blood glucose for its energy. Eating anything with sucrose in it can cause a variation in blood-glucose levels. If you want to stabilize those levels, eliminate, or at the very least cut way down on, your total sugar intake. For this program, eliminate all added sugars and foods that are high in refined sugar. Getting off the sugar treadmill isn't easy, but it's totally worth it.

I had a client text me 10 days into his metabolic reset that he felt as if he was getting out of an abusive relationship, because he had no idea how bad his addiction to sugar had become until he was away from it. Halfway through his reset, he suddenly realized how damaging his nutrition and stressful lifestyle were. It was crushing him.

When he finished, he said he'd never recommit to that bad relationship with his food or way of life ever again.

I want you to have the same kind of breakthrough, whether it's with sugar or the things mentioned in any of the other ten lifestyle modifications. One amazing side effect of giving up sugar is you'll begin to notice how good and flavorful other foods taste. It's not that the food tastes better; it's your taste buds coming alive! Cool, huh?

One other important note about sugar is that other sugars and sugar substitutes, such as brown sugar, saccharin, aspartame, cane juice, lactose, fruit juice sweeteners, and fructose, are not great alternatives when eliminating sugar, because they are all chemically processed sweeteners. If you must use a sweetener during the first 21 days, stevia is the only approved option.

8. Follow the list of approved foods. There are no exceptions! For the next 21 days you are going to experience my exclusive elimination-based diet that removes the most common foods people are sensitive to from your diet, based on information gathered from thousands of clients I've worked with over the years. The list of approved foods was created by finding food-induced inflammation commonalities in over 350 food-sensitivity tests (MRTs) done on high performers I personally train or trained.

If you stick with this list, your gut and allergies will thank me, and ultimately you will too. The only time I let people deviate from this is if they have an actual sensitivity lab test done—so if you know something on or off this list is specific to you, adjust accordingly. Otherwise, no cheating! Remember what you're momma always said, "Cheaters never prosper!"

9. Maximize protein and vegetable intake. This is not a deprivation diet, so don't starve yourself. The protein and vegetable serving sizes are the minimums you are allowed to eat. *You can eat as much protein and as many vegetables as you want at lunch and dinner.* (But, remember, everything has its limits, so don't go eating a 40-ounce cowboy steak thinking you aren't going to pay the price.) These foods possess the ultimate rebuilding blocks for your metabolism, so don't be shy.

10. Follow carbohydrate and fat servings exactly. This modification will mean one of two things for you: it will be either a drastic reduction or a major increase in carbohydrates for you. If it's a drastic reduction, your fatigue may last a while longer, as your body will need more time to figure out how to rely on fats rather than glucose for energy. On the other hand, if this is a drastic increase in carbs for you and you're a person who exercises all the time, then you will notice your energy will become elevated rather quickly. You will also see a nice boost in your sex drive sooner too. Lucky you!

I created this plan based on nutrient-timing philosophies, in which carbohydrates and fats really help with energy and focus during the day and then aid in improving sleep at night. Remember, recent research shows that those who eat 80 percent or more of their carbs at dinner or later actually lose more weight, specifically more fat. Although it took a lot of convincing to get my clients to eat carbs at night, those who have gone on the Stark Naked 21-Day Metabolic Reset have validated that as solid fact too.

11. Stick to three meals a day. I know this modification is still a shocker after so many years of hearing that five to six small meals a day is ideal, but I hope after reading Chapter 7, on nutritional confusion, we've built some trust and you'll be on board with me. Eating more small meals a day is actually not any better for your metabolism than eating fewer meals. There have been multiple studies substantiating it has worse results than fewer feedings each day. Try it. You might like it!

But wait . . . there's one more!

Optional Bonus Modification: Clean the toxic solvents out of your house. If you're really feeling ready to hop on the Reset train, I highly recommend taking a look at the products you are using around your house and for your personal hygiene. This is an expensive proposition, one you don't have to take on all at one time, but become aware of what you're using, breathing in, lathering up with, and slathering on and decide what you can and cannot live with. Use the SkinDeep app or www.ewg.org website to help you clean your house of toxic solvents like hygiene products, beauty products, and cleaners. Restock with safe, friendly products. Once you get the toxins out of your life, you will never want to go back to living with them again.

We Took Out the Guesswork for You

For the initial 21 days, make the commitment to stick to the following list of foods at all costs. I know it looks limited, but this elimination-style nutrition plan is one of the most powerful diet protocols I have ever seen. That's why it's at the core of this program. By removing the most common foods found to cause intolerance, the Stark Naked 21-Day Metabolic Reset helps you avoid adverse reactions to the wrong foods and is the best way to break the cycle of food addiction that is causing unnecessary stress on your body.

This plan allows you to completely remove the trigger foods, so that your body has no reason to form antibodies or develop inflammation. I know you may think you don't have issues with any foods, but trust me, you have just gotten use to the symptoms. You have become numbed to your body's response to your trigger foods. If you remove any one of these trigger foods for a while and then reintroduce that food, guess what? It will rock you!

After you have completed the initial Reset, I will teach you how to reintroduce foods back into your diet to make sure they are safe in Phase 2.

Warning! Once you've successfully completed the Reset, your energy will skyrocket and you will want to take on the world.

Understand one thing. All high achievers have a tendency to overdo things. It is a constant and sometimes vicious cycle we can fall into.

Once you start to feel better—and I promise that if you follow this plan, you are going to feel *amazing*—you will inevitably start overdoing and overachieving again. Before you know it, if you aren't careful, you will feel miserable again.

Once you fix what's broken, meaning you've successfully reset your metabolism, you must commit to taking care of yourself like the high achiever you genuinely are, so you can stay in peak condition for the rest of your life.

Are you ready to rock?

Prepare for Success

By failing to prepare, you are preparing to fail.
—BENJAMIN FRANKLIN

I am the kind of guy who needs to force myself to focus to be truly prepared. Lack of preparation is the death of success in anything. I have done the 21-Day Reset many times and have discovered some simple preparation strategies to ensure success. Above all, prep meals as much as you can ahead of time to avoid any bumps in the road and keep stress to a minimum. Breakfast and lunch are my most challenging meals, so I always make sure to prep those over the weekend and have them ready to go for the week. I'm able to prepare a Reset-friendly dinner at mealtime, but if your evenings are harried and the time when you're most likely to slip, go ahead and prep those too. Here are my favorite strategies.

Weekly Prep Strategies

Shopping and prep day: Choose one day each week to go grocery shopping and prep meals. My wife and I chose Sundays, since neither of us works on that day. It's not only quality time together; it helps set up our week for Reset success. Prep time: 1 hour to shop and 75 minutes to prep.

Breakfast prep, Stark Naked detox smoothies: Cut and divide all of the fruits and vegetables for your daily morning smoothies. Store them in small zip-top bags in your refrigerator. Each morning, all you'll need to add to your blender are the contents of a zip-top bag, your fats, and a small amount of water. It's that simple. Quick and easy, and no excuses! Prep time: 15 minutes.

Lunch prep: After preparing your detox smoothie bags, cook up a selection of meat for lunchtime. My wife and I usually cook chicken breasts, turkey patties, bison steaks, and ground wild meats. We store them in lidded glass containers in the refrigerator. We also cut up vegetables to use on salads. Prep time: 60 minutes.

Dinner prep: If you feel you need to prep dinners as well, plan on adding another 30 minutes to your total prep time.

Daily Prep Strategies

Do these at night before going to bed, so you're ready for the next day.

Warm lemon water prep: You'll begin each morning with warm lemon water. I fill the tea kettle and put in on the stove (I do it the old-fashioned way!), set out my mug, and make sure I have half of a lemon in the fridge. All I have to do when I walk out to the kitchen in the morning is turn on the stove, warm up the water, pour it into the mug, and squeeze the lemon in. Prep time: 2 minutes.

Cranberry juice cocktail prep: In a 32-ounce water bottle, combine 4 ounces of unsweetened cranberry juice (not from concentrate) and 28 ounces of water. Store in the fridge until your midmorning cocktail. Prep time: 3 minutes.

Lunch prep: To a lidded glass container, add a large bed of salad greens and any precut vegetables from your weekly prep day. Place your choice of meat from your weekly prep day on top of the salad. For the required serving of fat, dress the salad with olive oil or add avocado. Season to taste. Store in the refrigerator overnight. Prep time: 5 minutes.

A Typical Morning

Okay! It's as simple as that!

By preparing for a little over an hour each week and 10 minutes before bed each night, you can be completely ready for the week and start each day stress free. You can get out the door each morning in just five easy steps:

Step 1: Wake up.

Step 2: Heat water for your lemon water and drink.

Step 3: Get ready for work or the rest of your day.

Step 4: Throw your zip-top smoothie produce, water, and approved fats into the blender, blend, and drink.

Step 5: Grab your lunch and cranberry juice cocktail from the fridge on the way out the door.

Approved Foods

Okay, enough with the success strategies! Let's get to what you've been waiting for. Without further ado—drumroll, please—here are your approved foods for the next 21 days.

PHASE 1 APPROVED FOODS
Proteins
Eggs
Poultry (chicken, turkey, duck, ostrich, Cornish game hen)
Pork
All fish except salmon and shellfish

Wild game meats (buffalo, bison, boar, venison, antelope, duck)
Full-fat cottage cheese (only allowed as the before-bed snack)
Fats
Coconut oil
Olive oil
Macadamia nut oil
Walnut oil
Avocado oil
Seeds (sesame, flax, chia, hemp, pumpkin, and sunflower seeds)
Heavy whipping cream
Organic butter and ghee
Avocado
Unsweetened canned coconut milk
Unsweetened almond milk (only allowed in the morning smoothie)
Cashews and pecans (only allowed as the before-bed snack)
Carbohydrates
Rice (all types)
All potatoes except white potatoes (sweet potatoes, yams, red potatoes, purple potatoes)
Quinoa
Gluten-free pasta (no cornstarch)
Gluten-free oats
Vegetables
All vegetables except carrots, beets, peas, corn, and broccoli
Fruits
All fruits except bananas, grapes, blueberries, and grapefruit
Herbs and Spices
All herbs and spices
Beverages
Water
Green tea
Herbal teas
Unsweetened cranberry juice (not from concentrate)

Meals and Serving Sizes

Now let's take a look at what each day will look like for the next 21 days.

PHASE 1 DAILY OUTLINE		
Hydration		
Number of ounces of water that equals half your body weight throughout the day (includes cranberry juice cocktails)		
Upon Waking		
6 ounces warm water with juice from ½ lemon		
Breakfast (within 1 hour of waking)		
Stark Naked detox smoothie (see recipes, pp. 222–29)		
Green tea (in addition to the smoothie)		
Mid-Morning Snack		
As much of the cranberry juice cocktail (4 ounces unsweetened cranberry juice, not from concentrate, mixed with 28 ounces water) as you'd like now; finish the rest between meals throughout the day		
Lunch		
Men	2 servings protein, 2 servings vegetables, 2 servings fat*	
Women	1 serving protein, 2 servings vegetables, 1 serving fat*	
Mid-Afternoon Snack		
Green tea		
Dinner		
Men	2 servings protein, 2 servings vegetables, 2 servings fat, 2 servings carbs*	
Women	1 serving protein, 2 servings vegetables, 1 serving fat, 1 serving carbs*	
Before-Bed Snack		
1 serving fruit and ½ cup full-fat cottage cheese, or a handful of cashews or pecans		
*Note: Portions of protein and vegetables are the minimum requirements for each meal. You can consume as much protein and vegetables as needed at each meal to keep you satiated. Portions of fats, carbohydrates, and fruits cannot be changed.		

PHASE 1 SERVING SIZES	
Protein	1 serving = 3 ounces uncooked meat (about the size of a deck of cards), 2 whole eggs
Vegetables	1 serving = 1 cup raw
Fat	1 serving = 1 tablespoon oil, butter, or heavy whipping cream, ½ avocado, ¼ cup seeds
Carbohydrates	1 serving = 1 cup *cooked*
Fruit	1 serving = ½ cup

Daily Steps for Success

Here are the six daily steps in the program that help ensure your success and create long-term change.

Step 1: Warm Lemon Water

You will start your day by drinking warm lemon water to enhance liver detoxification and improve digestion. Warm lemon water also helps increase energy, strengthen the immune system, and improve the quality of the skin.

Step 2: Stark Naked Detox Smoothie

My exclusive detox green smoothies are a favorite among my clients for breakfast. They are a great way to get a lot of nutrients into the body fast. Plus, they are superfilling and taste great.

We all know the importance of fruits and vegetables, but very few of us consume anywhere near the recommended 9 servings a day. Blending the fruits and vegetables into a smoothie makes them easier to digest, preventing the bloating and intestinal irritation that usually accompanies increased fruit and vegetable intake. I prefer blending to juicing, because the fiber is not removed from the fruits and vegetables when you blend. Fiber improves the quality and regularity of bowel movements, removes toxins from the body, stabilizes blood sugar, and lowers cholesterol.

Green vegetable-based smoothies also have an alkalizing effect on the body, neutralizing and eliminating excess acid that can cause indigestion and other digestive issues. The most rewarding benefit of these green smoothies is improved blood flow. Better blood circulation leads to more action in the bedroom. As Dr. Daniel Amen says, "What's good for the heart, is good for the brain, is good for the genitals."

Step 3: Unsweetened Cranberry Juice

I will confess that developing a taste for unsweetened cranberry juice may not be pleasant at first, but you do get used to it. It is very important to stay away from cranberry juice from concentrate, as it is loaded with high-fructose corn syrup. This type of sugar places a heavy burden on the liver, and we are trying to reduce the stress on the liver, not add to it. I learned about the power of cranberry juice from Ann Louise Gittleman, a health pioneer and detox expert. In her book *The Fat Flush Plan* she explains that cranberry juice cleanses the lymphatic system, responsible for carrying toxins away from the cells and body tissues, which can help eliminate stubborn fat. Cranberry juice is rich in phytonutrients (anthocyanins, catechins, luteins, and quercetin), which help to keep your liver's detoxification pathways open, so they aren't jammed up by environmental pollutants, trans fats, sugars, and other toxins. In other words, cranberry juice helps "take out the trash."

Steps 4, 5, and 6: Lunch, Dinner, and Bedtime Snack

The nutritional components of lunch and dinner are based on what your body needs most at midday and in the evening to help you perform at your peak. Both meals include protein, as it is vital for complete detoxification. Remember, I suggest *minimal* requirements of protein for each of these meals and *no maximum*. Why is protein so important? The liver uses amino acids such as glycine and cysteine to transport toxins out of the body. These amino acids are found in protein. I do not like juice or fasting cleanses, because they deprive the body of these amino acids. The body prepares toxins for removal, but when the amino acids needed to transport them never show up, the liver is forced to reprocess and store these toxins once again. Do not be afraid of protein; it's essential to complete detoxification.

In addition to protein, lunch includes good fats and vegetables to stabilize blood sugar, enhancing fat loss and keeping stress hormones at bay. This combination also enhances brain function by stimulating dopamine and acetylcholine, brain neurotransmitters that enhance drive, focus, and memory. At dinnertime, it's time to calm your body down and prepare it for good sleep. I've introduced carbs at dinner to enhance this process.

Don't freak! Remember, eating carbs at night *will not make you fat*. But they will help you get a good night's sleep. Carbs stimulate the brain to produce serotonin, a chemical that promotes relaxation and sleep. This means you can kiss your Xanax, Ambien, or Sleep-Eze good-bye once and for all; you no longer need them and you will be eliminating another toxin that's putting stress on your body.

You will cap the night off with a snack that includes a protein containing the amino acid tryptophan, the precursor to serotonin. This snack replicates post–Thanksgiving dinner drowsiness. The benefit? A better night's sleep. When was the last time you had one of those?

Phase 1: 7-Day Sample Meal Plan

Below is a sample 7-day meal plan for the Reset. As you'll see, meals can be supersimple and basic or, if you're a foodie, you can really dial up some fantastic dishes. As long as you stick with the approved foods and the nutritional requirements for each meal, you can get as creative as you like. My wife loves trying out new dishes during our Reset periods. I've included a few of our favorites in the meal plan. You'll find the recipes in Chapter 12.

Pay attention to the servings of fats, carbs, and fruits in each recipe and adjust as needed to fit your requirements. Remember, you can eat as much protein and vegetables as you want.

PHASE 1 SAMPLE MEAL PLAN						
	Breakfast	**Morning Snack**	**Lunch**	**Afternoon Snack**	**Dinner**	**Bedtime**
Day 1	Detox Smoothie: The CEO	Cranberry Juice Cocktail	Fajita Bowl with Pico de Gallo	Green Tea	Yam, Chicken, and Kale Stir-Fry	Pineapple Cottage Cheese
Day 2	Detox Smoothie: Mr. Clean	Cranberry Juice Cocktail	Asian Meatballs Raw Kale and Brussels Sprout Salad	Green Tea	Moussaka	Mango Pecans
Day 3	Detox Smoothie: Hello Mojo	Cranberry Juice Cocktail	Shredded Pork Lettuce Wraps with Avocado Dressing	Green Tea	Hearty Bison Stew	Blackberries Cashews
Day 4	Detox Smoothie: The Energizer Bunny	Cranberry Juice Cocktail	Kabobs with Chimichurri Sauce Salad with Greek Vinaigrette Dressing	Green Tea	Halibut Tacos with Jicama Shells and Cilantro Slaw	Cherries Cottage Cheese
Day 5	Detox Smoothie: Gut Be Gone	Cranberry Juice Cocktail	Mini Meatloaf Roasted Vegetables	Green Tea	Fajita Bowl with Pico de Gallo Kicked-Up Quinoa Salad	Pineapple Cashews
Day 6	Detox Smoothie: The Graduate	Cranberry Juice Cocktail	Ground Chicken Lettuce Wraps Creamed Veggie Soup	Green Tea	Kabobs with Chimichurri Sauce Smashed and Fried Red Potatoes	Orange Slices Pecans
Day 7	Detox Smoothie: Chillaxin'	Cranberry Juice Cocktail	Sea Bass with Garlic, Ginger, and Coconut Oil Roasted Vegetables	Green Tea	Turkey Sliders with Pickled Red Onions Yam or Sweet Potato Fries	Plum Cottage Cheese

12

The Stark Naked 21-Day Metabolic Reset Recipes

Breakfast

All of the following smoothies are approved for use during the Reset. Each smoothie supports the foundational needs required at breakfast for you to succeed on this program. If you would like extra support in a specific area, try the smoothie targeted to your needs. For more ideas and how to create your own smoothie, visit my website.

Also, if a cold smoothie upsets your stomach or causes diarrhea, try drinking a room-temperature smoothie instead.

Each recipe makes one smoothie, unless otherwise noted.

Note: If you have been diagnosed with gout or hypothyroidism, use the Safe Detox Smoothie (p. 228) during the Reset. With these conditions, you need to limit the amount of cruciferous greens you consume and should eat kale, spinach, and Swiss chard only once in a while. You also have the option of replacing kale, spinach, and chard with romaine lettuce in the other smoothies.

The Beginner

(A Safe Place to Start)

If you are new to green smoothies, this is the safest place to start.
My clients consistently rank this as one of their favorites.

- 1 handful kale
- 1 handful spinach
- 1 cup papaya or mango
- 1 green apple with peel, seeded, cored, and chopped
- 2 tablespoons heavy whipping cream
- 1 cup water

Blend ingredients until smooth, adding more water and/or ice to
reach the desired consistency.

The CEO

(Enhanced Brain Performance)

Life as a CEO requires high cognitive ability to be successful. Stress
can negatively affect brain function, leading to foggy thinking,
reduced memory, poor judgment, and reduced capacity to learn.
Packed with powerful brain-enhancing ingredients, this smoothie is
for you if you feel you need a CEO-level boost of brain power.

- 2 handfuls spinach
- 2 celery stalks
- ½ cup mixed berries (no blueberries)
- ⅓ cup unsweetened canned coconut milk
- 1 tablespoon coconut oil
- 6 ounces yerba mate tea
- Optional: 1 sprig fresh rosemary, leaves removed and
  finely chopped

Blend ingredients until smooth, adding water and/or ice to reach
the desired consistency.

The Energizer Bunny

(Energy Boost)

If you have a tough time finding the energy to get going in the mornings, then this smoothie is for you. These ingredients will wake you up, get you moving, and keep you going until lunch with stable, long-lasting energy.

- **1 handful kale**
- **1 handful spinach**
- **¼ avocado**
- **½ cup pineapple**
- **⅓ cup unsweetened canned coconut milk**
- **6 ounces room-temperature green tea**
- **1 teaspoon cinnamon**
- **Optional: 1 teaspoon maca powder**

Blend ingredients until smooth, adding water and/or ice to reach the desired consistency.

Mama's Little Helper

(Calm, Cool, and Collected)

I remember being a young trainer and listening to mothers talk about their "mama's little helpers." When I asked what that meant, they laughed and told me it was what they used to keep stress and anxiety at bay, such as Xanax. This anti-anxiety smoothie is a great, natural "mama's little helper." Built to fight high stress and anxiety, it is guaranteed to keep you calm, cool, and collected.

- **2 handfuls kale**
- **½ cup diced mango**
- **½ cup diced peaches**
- **1 cup unsweetened almond milk**

¼ cup mint
1 teaspoon chia seeds
1 tablespoon cocoa powder

Blend ingredients until smooth, adding water and/or ice to reach the desired consistency.

Mr. Clean

(Loving Your Liver)

If you struggle with waking between 1:00 and 3:00 A.M. most nights or you have horrible morning energy, this is the smoothie for you. Your liver needs extra support, and this smoothie is packed with known natural liver aids that help detoxification. It will improve your quality of sleep and boost your morning energy.

2 handfuls kale
½ cup pineapple
½ cup mango
⅓ cup unsweetened canned coconut milk
2–3 dandelion leaves
¼ teaspoon ground turmeric

Blend ingredients until smooth, adding water and/or ice to reach the desired consistency.

Hello Mojo

(The Power to Shag)

If your mojo is so low you would rather sleep than shag, this is the smoothie for you. A natural aphrodisiac in a glass for both men and women, it is packed full of natural ingredients to boost sex drive and enhance blood flow. Life's more fun when it's flowing with mojo! Warning: only drink if you desire more action in the bedroom.

- **1 handful spinach**
- **1 handful Swiss chard**
- **2 celery stalks**
- **½ avocado**
- **½ cup blackberries or strawberries**
- **½ cup chopped watermelon**
- **1 tablespoon maca powder**
- **1 teaspoon cinnamon**

Blend ingredients until smooth, adding water and/or ice to reach the desired consistency.

Svelte

(A Gracefully Slender Figure)

This smoothie is great if you're looking for added fat-burning capabilities to enhance your figure. Packed full of foods that contain known fat-burning nutrients, this smoothie will add extra firepower to attack your waistline.

- **2 handfuls spinach**
- **1 small cucumber, chopped**
- **1 green apple with peel, seeded, cored, and chopped**
- **⅓ cup unsweetened canned coconut milk**
- **6 ounces green tea, chilled**
- **1 teaspoon cinnamon**
- **Optional: 1 jalapeño, stem removed**

Blend ingredients until smooth, adding water and/or ice to reach the desired consistency.

Gut Be Gone

(Better Digestion)

If you suffer from digestive problems like bloating, gas, and acid reflux, this is the smoothie for you. Packed full of gut aids, this smoothie replenishes good gut bacteria and digestive enzymes and reduces gut inflammation.

2 handfuls spinach
½ avocado
1 cup pineapple
⅓ cup unsweetened canned coconut milk
½-inch slice fresh ginger
1 tablespoon chia seeds
Optional: 1 serving probiotic powder

Blend ingredients until smooth, adding water and/or ice to reach the desired consistency.

Chillaxin'

(A Little Chillin' Plus a Little Relaxin')

If you live a highly driven life that's full of stress, then this is the smoothie for you. Packed full of foods that naturally fight stress, this smoothie will offset the damage a high-stress day causes your body. Chillaxin' at breakfast is a great way to start the day.

1 handful spinach
1 handful Swiss chard
½ avocado
1 cup blackberries
1 cup unsweetened almond milk
1 tablespoon cocoa powder
Optional: 1 serving probiotic powder

Blend ingredients until smooth, adding water and/or ice to reach the desired consistency.

Pretty Hot and Tempting

(Some Like It Hot!)

Want a little spice in your life? This smoothie turns up the heat, enhancing blood flow, reducing inflammation, and helping to burn stubborn belly fat.

2 handfuls kale
½ cucumber, chopped
1 bell pepper, cored and chopped
1 cup mango
⅓ cup unsweetened canned coconut milk
½-inch piece of jalapeño (remove seeds to reduce heat)
Optional: ½-inch slice fresh ginger

Blend ingredients until smooth, adding water and/or ice to reach the desired consistency.

The Graduate

(Love Me Some Veggies)

If you love veggies, you'll love this smoothie, but be warned: it tastes supergreen. It's crazy healthy, but this smoothie is definitely for the advanced green-smoothie drinker.

1 handful kale
1 handful spinach
2 celery stalks, chopped
1 small cucumber, chopped
1 apple with peel, seeded, cored, and chopped

1 cup unsweetened almond milk
½ lime, peeled

Blend ingredients until smooth, adding water and/or ice to reach the desired consistency.

Headache No More

(Stop the Pounding)

In the first 3 to 5 days of the Reset you may experience headaches, especially if you're coming off coffee. It's normal and only lasts a few days, but this smoothie is a blessing.

2 handfuls spinach
1 small cucumber
1 apple with peel, seeded, cored, and chopped
½ cup pineapple
⅓ cup unsweetened canned coconut milk
1 teaspoon cinnamon
½-inch slice fresh ginger

Blend ingredients until smooth, adding water and/or ice to reach the desired consistency.

Safe Detox Smoothie

(Good for Gout and Hypothyroidism)

If you have been diagnosed with gout or hypothyroidism, this is the only smoothie you should use during the Reset, as you need to limit the amount of cruciferous greens you consume. Romaine lettuce is a safe choice.

2 handfuls romaine lettuce
½ cup parsley

¼ **cucumber**
½ **cup mango or pineapple chunks**
6 ounces water
1 tablespoon coconut oil

Blend ingredients until smooth, adding water and/or ice to reach the desired consistency.

Lunch and Dinner

When my clients go on the Stark Naked 21-Day Metabolic Reset, their biggest worry is whether they can stick with the eating plan. No matter how many times I tell them it's easier than they think to eat the right foods for their body, they still panic.

Although I am a master at the grill, I will admit I am no chef in the kitchen. My criteria for every recipe in this book was that it had to be so easy to follow, prepare, and cook that even a klutz in the kitchen like me could make it!

Since I am not a master in the kitchen, I decided to ask my friend and chef extraordinaire Rebecca Clubb, owner of Whole Health Everyday, to step in. Based on my guidelines, Rebecca provided these amazing and delicious recipes to use throughout your 21-day reset and beyond.

Rebecca is the private chef for many of my clients and a favorite chef of many of my professional athletes. Not only is Rebecca an incredibly talented chef, she is also someone who suffered from many common food sensitivities. She understands how hard it can be to remove typical food triggers, while still finding a way to keep your nutrition choices interesting and enjoyable. As a result of her own struggles, she has now committed her life to providing safe and incredible healthy meals for people with food sensitivities without having to cut the flavor and comfort we all crave from our food.

Serving sizes for protein, vegetables, fat, carbs, and fruit are listed for each recipe, except where the amount included does not equal one complete serving. Pay particular attention to the amounts of fats, carbs, and fruits and adjust as needed to stay within your serving requirements. There is no limit to the amounts of protein and vegetables you can eat during the Reset. We've designed these recipes to be very flexible and forgiving if you need to dial back the fat or carbs.

Note: For chicken and vegetable broth, choose organic, if possible, and brands that do not add sugar, corn syrup, or thickeners such as wheat.

Bon appetit!

Lunch and Dinner Protein-Based Mains

Bison Meatballs with San Marzano Sauce

2 servings of protein
2½ servings of fat (2 in meatballs and ½ in 1 cup sauce)

For the meatballs
 2 tablespoons extra virgin olive oil
 3 tablespoons finely diced onion
 1 clove garlic, minced
 6 ounces ground bison
 1 tablespoon finely chopped parsley
 Salt and pepper, to taste

For the sauce
 2 tablespoons extra virgin olive oil
 1 small onion, roughly chopped
 3 cloves garlic, chopped
 1 28-ounce can organic San Marzano tomatoes
 ¼ cup chiffonade fresh basil
 Salt and pepper, to taste

Preheat the oven to 350°F.

To make the meatballs: Heat the oil in a small sauté pan and add the onions. Sauté over medium-low heat until the onions caramelize. Add the garlic and continue to cook for another minute. Remove from the heat.

In a large bowl, combine the onions (with all the oil from the pan) with the ground bison and parsley. Season with salt and pepper.

Form a small amount of the mixture into a test patty and cook in the sauté pan. Adjust seasonings to taste.

Form the remaining mixture into 4 small balls. Place the meatballs on a parchment-lined baking sheet and bake 15 minutes.

To make the sauce: Heat the oil in a small sauce pot and sauté the onion and garlic until just opaque. Add the basil and continue to cook for 1 minute. Add the tomatoes and stir. Let simmer for 30 minutes, then blend with an immersion blender or in a conventional blender until the desired consistency and return the mixture to the pot. Add salt and pepper to taste.

To serve: Serve meatballs with 1 cup of sauce. Freeze the remaining sauce in 1-cup portions for later use.

Turkey Sliders with Pickled Red Onions

2 servings of protein
2 servings of fat

½ red onion, thinly sliced
Red wine vinegar
2 drops stevia
2 tablespoons extra virgin olive oil
¼ cup finely chopped onion
1 garlic clove, finely chopped
6 ounces ground turkey
1 teaspoon dried marjoram

2 pinches salt, divided
Pinch of white pepper
4 lettuce leaves
2 slices tomato

Place the red onion slices in a small bowl and cover with red wine vinegar. Stir in 2 drops stevia and a pinch of salt. Let sit for at least 30 minutes.

Heat the oil in a sauté pan and sauté the onions until they are a light caramel color. Add the garlic and cook another minute. Remove from the heat.

In a bowl, combine the onions (with all the oil from the pan), turkey, marjoram, a pinch of salt, and a pinch of white pepper.

Place the sauté pan over medium heat. Form a small amount of the turkey mixture into a small test patty and cook on each side until the turkey is cooked through (white with no pink). Taste and adjust seasoning.

Form the meat into 2 small patties and cook in the sauté pan for about 2 to 3 minutes on each side, until lightly browned and cooked through.

Serve the patties on the lettuce leaves topped with pickled red onions and tomato slices.

Ground Chicken Lettuce Wraps

2 servings of protein
4 servings of vegetables
1 serving of fat

1 tablespoon sesame oil
1 garlic clove, roughly chopped
1 tablespoon roughly chopped ginger
2 green onions, sliced, white and green parts separated

6 ounces ground chicken

4 cups finely chopped water chestnuts

1–2 tablespoons coconut aminos (great alternative to soy sauce)

Pepper, to taste

4 butter lettuce leaves

Cilantro leaves, for garnish

Heat the sesame oil in a sauté pan and add the garlic, ginger, and white part of the green onions. After the garlic and ginger become fragrant, add the ground chicken. Make sure to break up the chicken and cook until lightly browned. Add the water chestnuts and season with coconut aminos, pepper, and additional sesame oil to taste.

Spoon the mixture into the centers of the four lettuce leaves, dividing evenly, and garnish with cilantro and green onions.

Fajita Bowl with Pico de Gallo

2 servings of protein
2 servings of vegetables
2 servings of fat

For the fajita bowl

6 ounces chicken, bison, or buffalo, sliced into strips

Salt and pepper, to taste

Cumin, to taste

Chipotle pepper, to taste (optional)

2 tablespoons coconut oil, extra virgin olive oil, or ghee, divided

1 onion (any kind), sliced into thin strips

1 clove garlic, chopped

1½ cups thinly sliced bell pepper, any color

½ jalapeño, seeded and sliced into thin strips

Paprika, to taste

For the pico de gallo

   1 Roma tomato, chopped
   1 tablespoon finely chopped onion
   1 clove garlic, chopped
   ½ jalapeño, seeded and chopped
   Juice of ½ lime
   Salt and pepper, to taste

Sprinkle the strips of meat with salt, pepper, cumin, and chipotle pepper.

Heat 1 tablespoon coconut oil in a sauté pan and add the meat. Let the meat sear until it is browned and crisp on one side, then flip and sear the other side. Remove the meat from the pan and place in a large bowl.

Add the remaining oil and onions to the pan and sauté until they become golden brown. Add the garlic, peppers, and jalapeños. Once the peppers are nearly cooked through, season with salt, pepper, cumin, chipotle, and paprika to taste. Sauté until the peppers are cooked through. Remove to the bowl with the meat and toss.

To make the pico de gallo: In a small bowl combine all the ingredients. Season to taste.

To serve: Top the meat and peppers with pico de gallo.

Kabobs with Chimichurri Sauce

2 servings of protein
2 servings of vegetables
2 servings of fat (in ¼ cup sauce)

For the kabobs

   6 ounces chicken, buffalo, or bison, cut into 1-inch cubes
   2 cups veggies, such as mushrooms, zucchini, bell peppers,
      or onions, cut into 1-inch cubes

Skewers, wooden or metal (if using wooden skewers and grilling
the kabobs over an open flame, soak them in water for at least an
hour before using)

For the chimichurri sauce

½ cup extra virgin olive oil

¼ bunch (½ cup) fresh Italian parsley, most of the stems removed

1 bunch (2 cups) fresh cilantro, most of the stems removed

1 tablespoon fresh oregano or 2 teaspoons dried

2–4 garlic cloves, peeled

2 tablespoons chopped red onion

2–3 tablespoons red wine vinegar

½ teaspoon ground cumin

Pinch of red pepper flakes (optional)

Sea salt and white pepper, to taste

Place the meat and vegetables on skewers, alternating meat and
vegetables or making separate meat and vegetable skewers.

To make the sauce: In a food processor or blender, add ¼ cup of
olive oil and the rest of the ingredients. Blend until well combined.
Slowly add the remaining oil until at the desired consistency. Taste
for seasoning and adjust salt, cumin, vinegar, and pepper as desired.

Coat the skewered meat and veggies with 1 tablespoon of the
sauce and let marinate at least 30 minutes or overnight. Set aside
3 tablespoons for serving, and reserve the remaining ¾ cup sauce
for another use.

Skewers may be grilled on an outdoor grill, in a grill pan, or
seared in a sauté pan. Grill over medium-high heat until browned
on all sides and cooked through.

Mini Meatloaf

2 servings of protein
2 servings of fat

2 tablespoons extra virgin olive oil
3 tablespoons finely diced onion (any kind)
1 clove garlic, minced
6 ounces ground bison
1 tablespoon finely chopped parsley
Salt and white pepper, to taste
1 Roma tomato, chopped
2 leaves of fresh basil, chopped
Pinch of red pepper flakes

Preheat the oven to 350°F.

Heat the oil in a small sauté pan over medium-low heat and add the onion. Sauté until the onion caramelizes. Add the garlic and continue to cook for another minute. Remove from the heat.

In a bowl, combine the onions (with all the oil from the pan), bison, parsley, a pinch of salt, and a pinch of white pepper.

Place the sauté pan over medium-low heat. Form a small amount of the bison mixture into a small test patty and cook on each side until the meat is cooked through. Taste and adjust seasoning as desired.

On a parchment-lined baking sheet, form the bison mixture into a loaf shape with a well down the middle.

In a small bowl, combine the tomato, basil, red pepper flakes, salt, and pepper and spoon the mixture into the well. Bake the meatloaf for 25 minutes. Slice and serve.

Shredded Pork Lettuce Wraps

2 servings of protein

6 ounces pork loin, cut into 1-inch pieces
1 garlic clove, roughly chopped
1 tablespoon roughly chopped ginger
2 tablespoons coconut aminos (great alternative to soy sauce)
1 star anise
4 drops stevia
½ cup vegetable broth
¼ teaspoon pepper
4 romaine lettuce leaves
2 green onions, sliced
Bean sprouts, for garnish
Cilantro leaves, for garnish
Sriracha sauce, for garnish
1 lime wedge

In a small sauce pot, combine the pork, garlic, ginger, coconut aminos, star anise, stevia, vegetable broth, and pepper. Cover and simmer over low heat about 30 minutes or until the meat is cooked through. Shred the pork. Strain and discard the excess liquid.

Serve the shredded pork on the lettuce leaves and garnish with green onions, bean sprouts, cilantro, and sriracha. Squeeze lime over the top.

Sea Bass with Garlic, Ginger, and Coconut Oil

2 servings of protein
1 serving of fat

Zest of ½ lemon
1 clove garlic, minced

1 teaspoon grated ginger

1 tablespoon coconut oil, divided

6 ounces wild sea bass

Salt and white pepper, to taste

Lemon wedges, for serving

Preheat the oven to 400°F.

In a small bowl, combine the lemon zest, garlic, ginger, and 1½ teaspoons coconut oil. Rub the mixture onto the top of the sea bass. Let sit in refrigerator for 30 minutes to 2 hours.

Season sea bass with salt and pepper.

Heat a nonstick sauté pan over medium-high heat and add remaining 1½ teaspoons coconut oil. When the oil is hot, place the sea bass face down (presentation side), skin side up. Let the fish sear without disturbing it for about 2 minutes. When it is a little more than golden brown, flip the sea bass over and sear for another 2 minutes.

To finish cooking the fish, place the pan in the oven for 2 to 4 minutes or until the thickest part of the fish flakes easily.

Remove from the oven and let sit 5 minutes before serving. Serve with lemon wedges.

Asian Meatballs

5+ servings of protein

2 servings of fat

1 pound ground turkey

2 tablespoons ground flax mixed with 4 tablespoons water (let sit for 5 minutes)

1½ tablespoons minced ginger

¼ teaspoon white pepper

½ cup finely chopped cilantro

4 green onions, white and green parts, finely chopped

1½ tablespoons coconut aminos or soy sauce

1 tablespoon sesame oil

1 teaspoon toasted sesame oil

Preheat the oven to 400°F.

In a large bowl, combine all the ingredients.

Form the mixture into 16 balls and place on a parchment-lined baking sheet. Bake for 25 minutes.

Dinner-Only Protein-Based Mains

(Containing Approved Complex Carbs)

Halibut Tacos with Jicama Shells and Cilantro Slaw

2 servings of protein

2 servings of fat

1 serving of carbohydrates (or more, depending on the size of jicama)

This recipe can be adjusted in many ways for your own tastes by using ground or sliced meat instead of fish. You can use any meat on the approved-foods list such as duck, chicken, bison, or even turkey! To create jicama taco shells, you will need a basic mandolin slicer.

1 jicama

1 lime, zested and juiced

1 clove garlic, finely chopped

½ teaspoon ground cumin

½ bunch cilantro, stems removed and finely chopped (reserve some for garnish, if desired)

2 green onions, green and white parts, finely chopped

1 tablespoon extra virgin olive oil or avocado oil

Sea salt and white pepper, to taste

6 ounces wild halibut
½ cup thinly sliced or shredded savoy cabbage
1 tablespoon coconut oil
1 Roma tomato, diced and sprinkled with sea salt and black pepper
1 teaspoon finely diced jalapeño

Use a sharp knife to cut off one end of the jicama and then, working around the bulb, cut off the rough skin. Use a knife or vegetable peeler to make a smooth surface around the jicama. Slice the jicama on a mandolin into thin rounds. The slices should look like taco shells.

Combine the lime zest, juice, garlic, cumin, cilantro, greens onions, olive or avocado oil, salt, and pepper in a medium-size bowl, mashing with the back of a fork. Coat the halibut with 1 tablespoon of the sauce and let it marinate for 10 to 15 minutes.

Toss the remaining sauce with the cabbage, adjusting seasoning to taste.

Heat the coconut oil in a small nonstick sauté pan over medium-high heat. Cook the halibut until the fish is just opaque and flakes easily with a fork, about 2 to 3 minutes per side. Transfer the fish to a plate and cut into pieces.

Serve the fish inside jicama taco shells with slaw, tomato, and jalapeño. Garnish with extra cilantro.

Hearty Bison Stew

2 servings of protein
2 servings of fat
3 servings of carbohydrates

6 ounces bison, cubed
2 tablespoons organic butter, ghee, or extra virgin olive oil
1 yellow onion, roughly chopped

2 garlic cloves, roughly chopped

2 cups vegetable broth

1 cup peeled and cubed parsnip

1 cup peeled and cubed yam or sweet potato

1 cup peeled and cubed rutabaga

Salt and white pepper, to taste

1 bay leaf

Pinch of thyme

Sprinkle the bison cubes with a little salt and pepper.

Heat the butter, ghee, or oil in a medium saucepan. Add the bison cubes, and sear them on all sides. Remove them to a small bowl.

Add the onions to the same saucepan used to cook the bison and sauté over medium heat, stirring often until they start to caramelize and become slightly browned. Add the garlic and continue to cook for another minute.

Add the broth, the rest of the ingredients, and the bison. Bring to a simmer, then lower heat, and cook for about 1 hour or until veggies are tender. The length of time will depend on the size of vegetables.

Remove the bay leaf. Adjust salt, pepper, and thyme to taste.

Moussaka

5+ servings of protein

15 servings of vegetables

6 servings of fat

1 serving of carbohydrates

1 large eggplant (about 2 pounds), peeled and cut into 1-inch cubes
   (choose one that is heavy for its size)

6 tablespoons extra virgin olive oil, divided

3 cups vegetable or chicken broth

1 medium red potato, cut unto 1-inch pieces

1 head cauliflower, cored and cut into florets

2 yellow onions, chopped

4 garlic cloves, chopped

1 pound ground lamb, bison, or turkey

1 28-ounce can San Marzano tomatoes, drained and crushed

1 tablespoon tomato paste

½ cup chopped parsley

2 teaspoons dried (or 1 tablespoon fresh) oregano

1 teaspoon cinnamon

Salt and white pepper, to taste

Preheat the oven to 400°F.

Sprinkle the eggplant cubes with a little salt and set them aside in a strainer to drain for about 30 minutes. Once they have let go of some moisture, toss them with 4 tablespoons of olive oil and pepper. Bake them in a 9 x 13-inch baking dish for 20 to 30 minutes or until golden. Remove from the oven.

Heat the broth in a small saucepan over medium heat and add the potato and cauliflower. Simmer over medium heat until they are soft, but not mushy. Remove the potato and cauliflower pieces to a blender or food processor and whip until they reach the consistency of mashed potatoes. Add some of the broth from the pot as needed to get to the desired consistency. Taste for seasoning and add salt and pepper if needed.

In a large sauté pan add the remaining 2 tablespoons oil and onions. Sauté the onions over medium heat, stirring often, until they become slightly browned. Add the garlic and continue to cook for another minute. Add the ground meat and continue to cook, breaking up the meat, until cooked through. Stir in the tomatoes, tomato paste, parsley, oregano, and cinnamon. Taste for seasoning and add salt and pepper to taste.

Spread the meat mixture over the eggplant. Top with whipped cauliflower, spreading evenly over the meat.

Broil 3 to 5 minutes, or until the top is browned.

Yam, Chicken, and Kale Stir-Fry

2 servings of protein
2 servings of vegetables
3 servings of fat
1 serving of carbohydrates

6 ounces chicken breast
1 tablespoon extra virgin olive oil
1 cup cubed sweet potato or yam
2 tablespoons coconut oil
1 tablespoon finely chopped garlic
1 tablespoon finely chopped ginger
1 tablespoon turmeric
2 cups thinly sliced and destemmed kale
Salt and pepper, to taste

Preheat the oven to 400°F. Line a baking sheet with parchment paper.

Place the chicken breast on the sheet. Drizzle with olive oil and sprinkle with salt and pepper. Add the cubed sweet potato or yam on the sheet pan.

Bake for 30 minutes or until the chicken is cooked through and juices run clear. Cool and shred chicken. Once the yam is soft, remove it. It may take only 20 minutes.

Heat the coconut oil in a wok or sauté pan over medium heat. Add garlic and ginger and sauté for just a minute or two, then add the yams, chicken, and turmeric. Once the kale is wilted, season with salt and pepper to taste.

Vegetable Sides

Creamed Veggie Soup

4 servings of vegetables
1 serving of fat

Make this a complete meal by adding protein such as baked, cubed, or shredded chicken.

- **1 tablespoon extra virgin olive oil, coconut oil, or ghee**
- **½ yellow or white onion, chopped**
- **1 clove garlic, chopped**
- **4 cups chopped asparagus, cauliflower, or other approved vegetable of your choice**
- **4 cups vegetable broth**
- **Salt and pepper, to taste**

In a medium-size pot, heat the oil over medium heat and sauté the onion and garlic until tender. Add the vegetables and broth and bring to a boil. Lower the heat to a simmer and cook until vegetables are tender.

Remove the vegetables to a blender with just enough of the broth to help it blend. Puree the vegetables until they reach the desired consistency, adding more broth as needed. Taste for seasoning, and add salt and pepper as desired.

Raw Kale and Brussels Sprout Salad

2 servings of vegetables
2 servings of fat (in 3 tablespoons of dressing)

For the salad
- **1½ cups destemmed kale, cut into thin strips**
- **½ cup thinly sliced Brussels sprouts**

For the dressing
- ¼ cup lemon juice
- 1 tablespoon Dijon mustard
- 1 tablespoon finely chopped shallot
- ½ cup extra virgin olive oil
- Salt and pepper, to taste
- Fresh thyme leaves, to taste
- Chives, to taste
- Lemon zest, to taste

Combine all dressing ingredients in a jar with tight-fitting lid and shake. Taste. Adjust seasoning to your taste.

Toss kale and Brussels sprouts with 3 tablespoons of dressing. Reserve remaining dressing for another use.

Serve topped with chives, thyme, and lemon zest.

Roasted Vegetables

Varies

Need to add more vegetables to a meal? It's easy to makes as many servings as you need by roasting them. The potential flavor combinations are endless!

The fat content will depend on how much oil you add to the vegetables before roasting. A little goes a long way!

- **Extra virgin olive oil (about 1 tablespoon per 2 cups of vegetables)**
- **Sea salt and white pepper, to taste**

Any combination of these vegetables
- Acorn squash, peeled, seeded, and cut into 1-inch wedges
- Butternut squash, peeled, seeded, and cut into 1-inch pieces
- Parsnips, peeled, and cut into 1-inch pieces
- Brussels sprouts, halved
- Asparagus, rough ends cut off

Green beans, ends trimmed

Cabbage, cut into 1-inch rounds

Cauliflower, cut into florets

Accents to add for additional flavor

Garlic	Chives	Lime zest
Rosemary	Balsamic vinegar	Curry powder
Sage	Dijon mustard	Paprika
Thyme	Sesame oil	Cumin
Tarragon	Soy sauce	Cinnamon
Mint	Lemon zest	Nutmeg
Parsley	Orange zest	

Suggested accent matchings

Acorn squash: cinnamon, sage, or nutmeg

Butternut squash: sage

Parsnips: curry powder, lemon, nutmeg, or tarragon

Brussels sprouts: drizzle with balsamic vinegar when they come out of the oven and top with rosemary, Dijon mustard, or thyme

Asparagus: garlic, lime, mint, balsamic vinegar, or orange zest

Green beans: soy sauce, sesame oil, or garlic

Cabbage: paprika, parsley, or garlic

Cauliflower: chives, parsley, curry powder, or lemon zest

Preheat the oven to 450°F. Line a baking sheet with parchment paper.

In a large bowl, toss the vegetables with extra virgin olive oil, sea salt, and white pepper until coated. Add accents for more flavor.

Spread the vegetables on the baking sheet. Make sure veggies are in a single layer and not piled up, which will result in steaming them rather than roasting.

Roast green beans and asparagus about 15 minutes and other veggies up to 45 minutes. Toss and stir the veggies halfway through anticipated cooking time. When the veggies are browned, they are done! Be careful not to char them.

Complex Carbohydrate Sides

Coconut-Ginger Rice

8+ servings of fat
2 servings of carbohydrates

1 cup jasmine rice
1 teaspoon coconut oil
3 tablespoons diced shallots
2 teaspoons minced ginger
½ cup unsweetened canned coconut milk
1 cup vegetable broth
¼ teaspoon salt
2 tablespoons chopped chives
Zest of 1 lime

Rinse the rice in cool water.

Heat the oil in a small pot over medium heat. Add the shallots and sauté for about 2 minutes. Add the ginger and continue to cook about 1 more minute. Add the rice and continue to stir for another 2 minutes until the rice gives off a nutty aroma.

Add the coconut milk, broth, and salt and bring to a simmer. Reduce the heat to low, cover, and simmer until all the liquid is absorbed, about 15 minutes.

Toss the rice with chives and serve topped with lime zest.

Kicked-Up Quinoa Salad

6 servings of vegetables
3 servings of carbohydrates
2 servings of fat

1 cup quinoa
2 cups water or chicken or vegetable broth

4 green onions, white and green parts, sliced

2 tablespoons diced white onion

1 jalapeño, finely diced

1 cup cherry tomatoes, quartered

1 yellow bell pepper, diced

½ bunch cilantro, stems removed and finely chopped (about ½ cup)

1 avocado, diced (about 1 cup)

Zest and juice of 1 lime

1 tablespoon adobo sauce or to taste

Sea salt and black pepper, to taste

4 cups spinach, roughly chopped

Rinse the quinoa under cool water.

Bring the water or broth to a boil, add the quinoa, reduce the heat, and cover. Let simmer until all the broth is absorbed, about 11 minutes. Remove from the heat. Remove the cover, lay a few paper towels over the pot, and place the cover back on. Let this sit for another 5 minutes. Remove the cover and towels, fluff with a fork, and let cool. If you want it to cool quickly, you can spread it out on a sheet pan.

Toss cooled quinoa with remaining ingredients, green onions through salt and pepper. Adjust seasoning to taste. Serve over spinach.

Smashed and Fried Red Potatoes

2 servings of fat

2 servings of carbohydrates

1 pound (7–9) red potatoes

1 teaspoon salt, plus more to taste

Pepper, to taste

Garlic powder, to taste
2 tablespoons extra virgin olive oil, ghee, or coconut oil
2 tablespoons chopped parsley

Wash the potatoes and add to a pot with 1 teaspoon of salt and enough water to cover. Bring to a boil and simmer until the potatoes are tender, about 20 minutes. Remove the potatoes and let cool.

With the back of a spatula press down on each potato and flatten it. Sprinkle with salt, pepper, and garlic powder.

Heat the oil or ghee in a pan and fry each potato until golden brown. Flip and brown the other side. Remove and serve topped with parsley.

Yam or Sweet Potato Fries

3 servings of fat
6 servings of carbohydrates (depending on the size of the potatoes or yams)

3 medium sweet potatoes or yams
3 tablespoons extra virgin olive oil
Sea salt and white or black pepper, to taste
Garlic powder (optional)
Paprika (optional)

Preheat the oven to 450°F. Line a baking sheet with parchment paper.

Wash and peel the sweet potatoes or yams. Cut them into thick steak fries or ¼-inch thick strips.

In a bowl, toss the potatoes with extra virgin olive oil and sprinkle with sea salt and white or black pepper. Sprinkle with garlic powder and paprika, if using. Toss until coated.

Spread the potatoes on baking sheet. Make sure the fries are in a single layer and not piled up, which will result in steaming rather than roasting them. Roast for 20 to 40 minutes, tossing occasionally, until golden brown. Roasting time depends on the size and thickness of the fries.

Salad Dressings

Greek Vinaigrette Dressing

8–12 servings of fat

¼ cup red wine vinegar
½ teaspoon salt
¼ teaspoon white pepper
½ teaspoon dried oregano
¼ teaspoon dried mint
½–¾ cup extra virgin olive oil

In a small bowl whisk the vinegar and salt. Add the pepper, oregano, and mint. Slowly drizzle in ½ cup of olive oil while continuing to whisk. Taste and add more olive oil and seasonings as desired. You may also combine all ingredients in a tightly sealed jar and shake vigorously to emulsify.

Avocado Dressing

4 servings of fat

Juice of 1 lemon or lime, divided
2 tablespoons water
1 ripe avocado, flesh removed
2 tablespoons avocado oil or olive oil

1 small clove garlic
½ cup cilantro leaves
Salt and white pepper, to taste
Stevia (optional)

In a blender or food processor, combine 1 tablespoon of the lemon juice with the rest of the ingredients (start with a pinch of salt and pepper). Blend until smooth. Taste and add more lemon juice and adjust seasoning as desired. Thin with additional water as needed to reach a dressing consistency. If using stevia to sweeten, start with one drop and taste before adding more.

▶ PART FIVE

YOU'VE RESET, NOW OPTIMIZE

13

Phase 2

The Stark Naked High-Performance
Optimized Nutrition Plan

ONGRATULATIONS!
Now that you have completed Phase 1, the Stark Naked 21-Day Metabolic Reset, and healed your metabolism, it's time to optimize it with Phase 2, the Stark Naked High-Performance Optimized Nutrition Plan.

During the past three weeks, your metabolism has recovered from all of the damage your stress has caused. You feel great, don't you? You should be able to look in the mirror and say, "I don't ever remember *feeling* or *looking* this good!" Let's keep it that way!

The Stark Naked High-Performance Optimized Nutrition Plan is an easy way to sustain a long-term program that provides you with our exclusive nutritional strategies, which are currently being used only with a small population of really healthy and truly resilient high achievers in the world. These strategies create a resiliency to high levels of stress, protecting the body from falling back into the Metabolic Breakdown Cycle, which you were in before you started your reset.

The Optimized Nutrition Plan generates exceptional energy to meet your daily demands, enhances your fitness levels, and creates that ideal body you've been dreaming about. Are you ready to go the next level?

If so, then it's important to understand that long-term compliance is critical for success in this phase. The program is sustainable for true long-term progress, and if you follow it, you will reap the rewards for your efforts year after year, constantly reaching new heights.

The Optimized Nutrition Plan should be your year-round nutrition plan except for 3 weeks each year when I recommend you do the 21-Day Reset. If you fall off the program after spending a long weekend in Vegas or taking a vacation, I've created a 7-day reboot to get you back on track.

How High-Performance Optimized Nutrition Works

Reintroduction of Eliminated Foods

During the Reset, I know you may have started to miss or crave foods that were not on the approved-foods list. Hey, I get it. Food tastes good, especially the foods you're fond of. That's why now I'm giving you the option of reintroducing some of those foods to see if they can fit back into your diet without causing food-induced inflammation, intolerance, and discomfort or leading you back into the Metabolic Breakdown Cycle. You don't really want to go back to feeling like that, do you?

Look, if you are feeling great by sticking with the current approved-foods list, then there is no need to reintroduce anything. "If it ain't broke, don't fix it!"

However, if you find yourself craving foods that are not on the approved-foods list, go ahead and make a list of the foods you miss most. Reintroduce the foods *one by one,* following this simple re-introduction protocol:

- Choose *one* food to reintroduce.

- Consume significant servings of the reintroduced food on day 1 (for example, if you want to reintroduce dairy, have yogurt and a glass of milk at breakfast and large glasses of milk at lunch and dinner). Then abstain from the food for at least 2 days following to allow time for delayed-response symptoms to appear. Without this time period, you might miss sensitivity signs.

- During days 2 and 3, mark any of the following symptoms that occur:

  ☐ *Insomnia*   ☐ *Itching in the roof*
  ☐ *Bloating*   *of your mouth*
  ☐ *Constipation*   ☐ *Gas or belching*
  ☐ *Acid reflux*   ☐ *Diarrhea*
  ☐ *Allergies*   ☐ *Joint pain*
  ☐ *Wired at night*   ☐ *Sneezing*
  ☐ *Foggy thinking*   ☐ *Fatigue*
  ☐ *Loss of libido*   ☐ *Wheezing*
  ☐ *Ringing in ears*   ☐ *Runny nose*
  ☐ *Headaches*   ☐ *Intense cravings*
  ☐ *Puffy, watery, or itchy eyes*

- If you experience any of these symptoms, you need to eliminate that food from your diet again.

- If on days 2 and 3 you experienced no symptoms, you can occasionally include the trial food back into your diet.

You must follow this protocol on all the nonapproved foods you miss to make sure you do not reintroduce a food that causes inflammation back into your diet.

Optimized Eating

Next, we want to make sure you are eating foods that enhance and maintain *optimized metabolic resiliency, high energy, charged sex drive,* and *deep, regenerative sleep.*

Eat protein and vegetables at every meal. Protein and vegetables are the core of the Optimized Nutrition Plan. They must be consumed at every meal. They provide the building blocks for all the chemical reactions, hormones, neurotransmitters, and tissues within the body that make up the metabolism; without them health is compromised and true metabolic resiliency cannot be developed.

Eat ample amounts of healthy fats. Healthy fats enhance brain function and provide support for hormone development. Eating fat earlier in the day stabilizes blood sugar, controls food cravings, and improves your ability to lose body fat. Fat is also a great way to wake the brain up and support drive and focus, helping you to become a production machine. Fat helps us look good, generates our mojo, and keeps us focused to make smart decisions, and it's essential to your long-term success.

Consume complex carbohydrates. Skip the carbs, and your metabolism will stall out quickly and your results will quickly diminish. Furthermore, *the more you exercise, the more carbohydrates you need.*

When you exercise, you deplete muscle glycogen. Glycogen comes from carbohydrates. When glycogen starts running low and isn't being replaced from carbohydrate consumption, you will experience fatigue, lack of motivation, and a noticeable decrease in performance. Not good!

I am not proposing that you become a carboholic, as that can lead to a whole cascade of different health problems, but you do need to recognize that carbohydrates are a serious piece of the Optimized Nutrition protocol and must be included in your diet if you want to maintain and optimize your progress.

Research shows that if you follow a calorie-restricted or low-carbohydrate diet for too long, your metabolism begins to slow down. The human body is a highly adaptive organism and eventually responds to these restrictions by downregulating a hormone called leptin. Reduced leptin levels increase hunger and cravings while slowing the metabolic rate and reducing energy expenditure—not a good combo. In addition, leptin is a master control hormone, meaning its levels have an effect on other hormones such as testosterone, growth hormone, and thyroid hormones. Lower levels of these hormones cause your metabolism to be sluggish and leave you looking and feeling lousy and hungry.

So what's the answer?

Here it comes.

It's called *carbohydrate cycling.*

Carbohydrate cycling is a method of eating carbohydrates that enhances performance and does not increase the risk of type 2 diabetes, heart disease, or other health problems associated with high levels of carb intake. Carbohydrate cycling means consuming a modest amount of carbs daily for 6 days a week and then on the 7th day including a Metabolic Boost high-carb cheat meal (200–300 grams; for ready-made foods you can check the label for number of grams of carbs). Think of it as a cheat meal that improves how you look, recover, and perform.

For example, for most of the week I consume 80–120 grams of carbs daily, about 2 cups of complex carbs like rice or sweet potatoes. Then on the 7th day a typical Metabolic Boost meal for me consists of 3 gluten-free pancakes with 4–5 tablespoons of blueberry syrup, followed by 3–5 ounces of gluten- and dairy-free frozen yogurt. Notice that I stay gluten-free and dairy-free for my Metabolic Boost meal. When I reintroduced gluten and dairy, they caused me lots of problems, so I leave them out. If you have reintroduced either of those and not had a negative response, you can include gluten- and dairy-based foods in this meal.

Carb cycling has been around for years in the body-transformation and body-building realms. It's one of the reasons body builders can get their body-fat levels down so low. They learned early on that low-carb or no-carb diets will only reduce body fat for a very short time and lead to lethargy. But by carb cycling with a Metabolic Boost high-carb meal, they not only burn fat, but feel great.

Having a larger than normal meal with lots of carbohydrates causes leptin and other hormones to spike, kick-starting your metabolism back into high gear, so you can continue to feel great, look great, and perform great. These simple Metabolic Boost meals once a week are the key to keeping your metabolism supercharged and resilient. They also give you an opportunity to eat and enjoy the foods you love, but aren't able to include during the rest of the week.

The outcome of eating to optimize your metabolism is a resilient, energetic, lean, sexy, incredibly motivated *you*!

> Athletes and lean people (can-see-your-abs lean) who exercise at a high intensity more than 4 days a week will need to consume even more carbohydrates during the Metabolic Boost meal. Aim for 400–600 grams of carbs during the Metabolic Boost meal. Your carbohydrate intake during the week can also increase. I have found 200 grams a day to be more ideal. If your body fat is below 8 percent, you will want to have the Metabolic Boost meal twice a week.

The Twelve Lifestyle Modifications for the Stark Naked High-Performance Optimized Nutrition Plan

1. Coffee is back. Yeah!!! Yes, you read that right! You can have coffee again. I personally love coffee. I like to pretend I am a coffee connoisseur and roast my own beans. I love every part of coffee—the smell, the taste, the experience—so removing coffee is the toughest part of the 21-Day Reset for me. So of course I have figured out how to work it back into our lives. If you are enjoying the green tea you've been drinking, you do not have to switch back to coffee, but if you miss coffee as much as I do during the Reset, please feel free to reintroduce it and pray it doesn't make you feel bad. However, you need to make sure you control your intake. Limit coffee to 1 12-ounce cup a day, and I highly recommend you get the best-quality coffee you can find. Coffee crops are heavily sprayed with pesticides, so go organic whenever possible.

2. It's okay to enjoy up to 4 glasses of wine throughout the week.

Wow! Brad is recommending coffee and alcohol? I love this guy, but what's the catch?

Hey, I enjoy a glass of wine with my wife. I love the alone time to reconnect with her, and of course what usually follows wine consumption. Thanks to my increased mojo, so does she! I would rather have you enjoy a glass of wine and decompress from all the stimulation of the world than stare at your TV or computer. We need more connection with other human beings as much as we need more sleep. Enjoying a glass of wine together is one way to create that connection. So if you drink, go ahead and enjoy wine with friends or loved ones a couple of times a week.

I prefer red wine as the optimal choice, because the resveratrol found in red wine enhances insulin sensitivity, making it less likely you will get fat from the increased carbohydrate intake. Just keep it to a max of 2 glasses in a day. The key here is control. Less is always more.

3. Continue to keep refined sugar to a minimum.

It's okay to enjoy a little refined sugar during your Metabolic Boost meal, but try to keep it to a minimum the rest of the week. Sugar is essentially empty calories that do nothing good for the body and have actually been shown to lead to nutrient deficiencies. Sugar in the form of fructose is needed by the liver in small amounts to replenish liver glycogen but too much consumption of it just adds extra unneeded work for your already stressed and overloaded liver. You can get enough natural fructose from a couple of servings of fruit daily.

Sugar consumption in the form of glucose causes elevations in insulin and can potentially lead to type 2 diabetes, making it almost impossible to lose weight. And if that's not enough to deter you, sugar has also been linked to cancer. There is nothing beneficial to consuming sugar outside of a little natural fructose from fruit to refill liver glycogen.

4. Avoid complex carbohydrates for breakfast. In the morning, after a night of sleeping and fasting, our insulin levels (the hormone that tells the body to store energy) are low and our muscles are full of glycogen. If you want to prevent your body from storing fat, this is not the time to eat carbs. Eating carbs at breakfast will cause an insulin spike telling your body to stop burning fat and start storing it instead. We do not want to start our day storing fat. Instead, have some fat at breakfast and your body will consume that as fuel.

According to research by Molly S. Bray, of the University of Alabama at Birmingham, mice fed a high-fat meal at the beginning of the day were able to burn fat more efficiently throughout the day, suggesting that what you eat for breakfast may dictate which energy source your body will use for the rest of the day. They were also better able to breakdown and utilize the components of a mixed diet, including carbohydrates, fats, and protein throughout the day. It is critical that you avoid complex carbohydrates for your breakfast for optimal health, performance, and fat loss.

5. Hydrate. Continue to drink half your body weight in ounces of water every day. Your trips to the bathroom should have slowed to a manageable number. If you are still taking more trips than you would like, you should really try adding ConcenTrace Trace Mineral Drops to your water.

6. Sleep 7 to 9 hours a night every night. Remember, the more complicated the brain, the more sleep you need. That is why you are going to continue to sleep for 7 to 9 hours every night. I want you in bed by no later than 11:00 P.M. if you can. Sleep recharges your battery, and it's when your body goes into healing mode! At this point sleep is critical for your long-term success and resiliency. *Do not cheat sleep!*

7. Exercise. Phase 2 is built to support a high volume of exercise, so you finally have the green light to hit it hard again. Your body is primed and ready for it, but please remember to include at least two recovery workouts a week in your program. Also unless you're a professional athlete or training for a big event like a marathon, keep your high-intensity workouts to a maximum of 4 times a week. Research has shown that training hard for a maximum of 45 minutes is ideal. If your workout takes longer than that, you're spending too much time socializing, not training.

8. Commit to daily acts of relaxation. Continue to find time to take small relaxation breaks during your day. Again, anything you find relaxing works, and it can continue to be for as little as 10 minutes. Examples are meditation, focused deep breathing, reading a book, or a 10-minute nap in the afternoon. If you haven't tried the meditation apps I discussed in Phase 1 (also see the Resource Guide), now may be a great time to experiment. Both are voice guided and do a phenomenal job of calming you down with zero effort on your part. Just sit back and let the voice lead you.

9. You're allowed to reintroduce foods. Just follow the reintroduction process laid out earlier in this chapter and pay attention to your body's response. You'll also note that there are more foods on the Phase 2 approved-foods list for you to enjoy. These foods do not require you to go through the reintroduction process.

10. Maximize protein and vegetable intake. This rule stays in effect. This is not a deprivation diet, so don't starve yourself. The protein and vegetable serving sizes are the minimums you are allowed to eat. *You can eat as much protein and as many vegetables as you want* *for lunch and dinner.* Remember, these foods possess the ultimate rebuilding blocks for your metabolism, so don't be shy.

11. Follow carbohydrate and fat servings exactly. Continue to follow these guidelines exactly as laid out. They will help you drop body fat and obtain that great-looking body you're searching for without wiping out your metabolism.

12. Stick to three meals a day, but add snacks if needed. I have added a couple of snacks to Phase 2. They are completely optional, and if you are having great success with only three meals a day, then there is no need to make any changes. However, if as your exercise volume increases your hunger increases, you may want to add a couple of small snacks to keep hunger under control, so you don't become irritable and no fun to be around.

Are you ready to take your metabolism and life to the next level?

Let's do this!

Approved Foods

PHASE 2 APPROVED FOODS
Note: If you have successfully reintroduced foods that were disallowed during Phase 1, for example, gluten, dairy, shellfish, or beans, you may add them back to the list.
Proteins
Eggs
Poultry (chicken, turkey, duck, ostrich, Cornish game hen)
Pork
Free-range beef
All fish
Wild game meats (buffalo, bison, boar, venison, antelope, duck)
Fats
Coconut oil
Olive oil

Macadamia nut oil
Walnut oil
Avocado oil
Seeds (sesame, flax, chia, hemp, pumpkin, and sunflower seeds)
Heavy whipping cream
Organic butter and ghee
Avocado
Unsweetened canned coconut milk
Unsweetened almond milk
All nuts except peanuts
Carbohydrates for Regular Meals
Rice (all types)
Potatoes (all types)
Sweet Potatoes
Yams
Quinoa
Gluten-Free Oats
Additional Carbohydrates for the Metabolic Boost Cheat Meal
Gluten-free pasta
Gluten-free pancakes and waffles
Gluten-free desserts and treats
Gluten- and dairy-free ice cream or frozen yogurt
Bananas
Grapes
Vegetables
All vegetables except carrots, beets, peas, and corn
Fruits
All fruits except bananas and grapes
Herbs and Spices
All herbs and spices
Beverages
Water
Green tea
Herbal teas
Coffee (1 12-ounce cup max daily)

Meals and Serving Sizes

PHASE 2 DAILY OUTLINE	
Hydration	
Number of ounces of water that equals half your body weight throughout the day	
Upon Waking	
6 ounces warm water with juice from ½ lemon (optional)	
Breakfast (within 1 hour of waking)	
Men	2 servings protein, 2 servings fat, 1 serving coffee*
Women	1 serving protein, 1 serving fat, 1 serving coffee*
Mid-Morning Snack	
1 serving fruit, 1 serving nuts or other fat, or 1 detox smoothie (optional)	
Lunch	
Men	2 servings protein, 2 servings vegetables, 2 servings fat*
Women	1 serving protein, 2 servings vegetables, 1 serving fat*
Mid-Afternoon Snack	
1 serving fruit or 1 serving nuts or other fat (optional)	
Dinner	
Men	2 servings protein, 2 servings vegetables, 2 servings fat, 3 servings carbs*
Women	1 serving protein, 2 servings vegetables, 1 serving fat, 2 servings carbs*
Before-Bed Snack	
1 serving tryptophan-enhancing food: ½ cup full-fat cottage cheese, a handful of cashews, a handful of pecans, 1 scoop whey protein powder, dark chocolate	
Weekly Carbohydrate Cycling Instructions	
One night a week consume a high-carbohydrate cheat meal that includes 200–300 grams of carbohydrates. Red wine is allowed with this meal (2 glasses max).	
Note: Just as in Phase 1, protein and vegetable servings are minimums with no maximums.	

SERVING SIZES	
Protein	1 serving = 3 ounces uncooked meat (about the size of a deck of cards), 2 whole eggs
Vegetables	1 serving = 1 cup raw
Fat	1 serving = 1 tablespoon oil, butter, heavy whipping cream, ½ avocado, ¼ cup seeds, ¼ cup nuts
Carbohydrates	1 serving = 1 cup *cooked*
Fruit	1 serving = ½ cup

Phase 2: 7-Day Sample Meal Plan

Below is a sample 7-day meal plan for Phase 2. As in the Reset, as long as you stick with the approved foods and nutritional requirements, meals can be as basic or as gourmet as you like. Use the recipes from Chapter 12 as a starting point. Pay attention to the servings of fats, carbs, and fruits in each recipe and adjust as needed to fit your requirements. Remember, you can eat as much protein and vegetables as you want.

PHASE 2 SAMPLE MEAL PLAN						
	Breakfast	Morning Snack	Lunch	Afternoon Snack	Dinner	Bedtime
Day 1	Eggs Cooked in Coconut Oil Avocado	Apple Cashews	Mini Meatloaf Raw Kale and Brussels Sprout Salad	Apple Cashews Green Tea	Halibut Tacos with Jicama Shells and Cilantro Slaw	Cottage Cheese
Day 2	Create Your Own Protein Shake	Raspberries Almonds	Shredded Pork Lettuce Wraps	Raspberries Almonds Green Tea	Hearty Bison Stew	Cashews
Day 3	Sautéed Ground Buffalo Macadamia Nuts	Mixed Berries Heavy Cream	Kabobs with Chimichurri Sauce Roasted Vegetables	Mixed Berries Heavy Cream Green Tea	Yam, Chicken, and Kale Stir-Fry	Pecans

	Breakfast	Morning Snack	Lunch	Afternoon Snack	Dinner	Bedtime
Day 4	Eggs cooked in Coconut Oil Avocado	Plum Walnuts	Fajita Bowl with Pico de Gallo Salad with Avocado Dressing	Plums Walnuts Green Tea	Turkey Sliders with Pickled Red Onions Yam or Sweet Potato Fries	Dark Chocolate
Day 5	Sautéed Ground Beef Avocado	Pineapple Cashews	Ground Chicken Lettuce Wraps Creamed Veggie Soup	Pineapple Cashews Green Tea	Asian Meatballs Kicked-Up Quinoa Salad	Cherries
Day 6	Create Your Own Protein Shake	Apple Almonds	Bison Meatballs with San Marzano Sauce Roasted Vegetables	Apple Almonds Green Tea	Sea Bass with Garlic, Ginger, and Coconut Oil Coconut-Ginger Rice	Cottage Cheese
Day 7	Sautéed Ground Turkey Nitrate-Free Bacon	Mixed Berries Heavy Cream	Mini Meatloaf Creamed Veggie Soup	Mixed Berries Heavy Cream Green Tea	Moussaka	Cashews

You can have up to 2 protein smoothies for breakfast each week during Phase 2. Make sure to follow these steps. Follow the serving-size guidelines for the appropriate amount of each ingredient to add.

PHASE 2 SHAKES: CREATE YOUR OWN	
Choose a Protein Powder	
Serving size: 1 scoop for women, 2 scoops for men	
Whey protein	Vegan protein (rice, pea, hemp)
Choose a Green	
Serving size: approximately 2 handfuls	
Kale	Spinach
Romaine	Arugula
Cabbage	Lettuce
Chard	Collard greens
Choose a Fruit	
Serving size: 1 cup max	
Pineapple	Mango

Papaya	Green apple
Lemon	Lime
Berries (any type except blueberries)	
Choose a Healthy Fat	
Serving size: Amounts listed are for women. Double for men.	
½ avocado	Coconut oil, 1 tablespoon
Organic butter, 1 tablespoon	Heavy whipping cream, 1 tablespoon
Unsweetened canned coconut milk, ½ cup	Olive oil, 1 tablespoon
Choose a Veggie Boost for Taste (Optional)	
Serving size: as desired	
Celery	Cucumber
Bell pepper	Parsley
Mint	Ginger root (use a small amount)
Dandelion root (use a small amount)	Jalapeños (use a small amount)
Choose a Superfood (Optional)	
Serving size: 1 teaspoon (or follow package directions)	
Cinnamon: Enhances insulin sensitivity and supports healthy blood sugar	
Maca: A natural adaptogen helping the body to adapt to stress; also a natural hormone balancer; increases energy and promotes a healthy sex drive	
Cacao: One of the foods richest in magnesium (supports mood, muscles, sleep, and bowel movements) and in antioxidants; the original form of chocolate, no added sugars or milk	
Probiotics: Enhance gut health	
Blend	
Blend ingredients until smooth, adding water and/or ice to reach the desired consistency.	

The 7-Day Reboot

I totally understand how life gets in the way at times or we make choices that negatively affect our metabolism. I recently volunteered to help Joseph, our eleven-year-old son, with his sixth-grade science-fair project. I was so proud that he wanted to do his project on how food affects the human body. He recruited a trainer I work with at

Stark to eat home-cooked meals for 5 days, and I agreed to be the fast-food test subject eating nothing but fast food and drinking soda for 5 days.

At first glance, it sounded like a fun cheat week, but after the second day of Joseph's experiment, my body started to rebel. I couldn't sleep, my brain felt as if it had stopped working, I was severely constipated, and every time I tried to workout I ended up throwing up. I threw in the towel after 4 days, because the food I was eating was wreaking havoc on my work and family life, not to mention my body.

I was far from a fun person to be around when I was feeling that gross. A 7-Day Reboot was the answer. I followed the Phase 1 Reset for 7 days, got back on track, and then went back to the Phase 2 Optimized Nutrition Plan. I can proudly say that after the dust settled, Joseph's experiment was definitely worth the sacrifice. He ended up being the only kid in his class to get an A+ on his science project— and it confirmed for me just how important it is to eat to support a healthy metabolism.

If you drink a little too much wine on a vacation to Napa Valley or enjoy a few too many desserts over the holidays, don't stress! Reboot when you get home. Crazy bachelor or bachelorette party in Vegas? No sweat! Enjoy the party, but come home and commit to doing the Reboot.

Life should be lived, not just endured. Have fun when you get the opportunity, and then reboot to bring your metabolism back online.

Don't beat yourself up for enjoying the finer things in life. I give you permission to fully enjoy your vacations and special occasions with friends and family. Reboot and pick right back up where you left off. If you've done the 21-Day Reset and been following the Optimized Nutrition Plan, your healthy metabolism has the resiliency to survive some fun.

The Stark Naked 21-Day
Metabolic Reset Resource Guide

Safe Hygiene Products

In Chapters 3 and 5 we explored how the products that come into contact with our skin on a daily basis might be wreaking havoc on our livers and disrupting our hormones. To help you find some alternatives to the products you are currently using, I've put together a list of my favorite and safest products, including personal-care products, sunscreens, household solvents, and cleaners. If you don't find what you're looking for here, you can expand your own search at www.ewg.org.

Adult Body Wash

Dr. Bronner's 18 in 1 Hemp Pure Castile Liquid Soap
(www.drbronner.com)
Be Green Bath and Body Bath and Shower Gel
(www.begreenbathandbody.com)
Lion Bear Naked Soap Head to Toe Wash (www.lionbearnaked.com)

Kid's Body Wash

Dr. Robin for Kids Body Wash and Shampoo (www.dermstore.com; search "Dr. Robin")
Healing Scents Just for Kids, Shampoo/Bath/Shower Soap (www.healing-scents.com)

Baby Needs

Ava Anderson (www.avaandersonnontoxic.com)
Be Green Bath and Body (www.begreenbathandbody.com)
Nurture My Body (www.nurturemybody.com)

Lotion

Be Green Day Face and Hand Cream (www.begreenbathandbody.com)
Nurture My Body Moisturizer (www.nurturemybody.com)

Adult Shampoo/Conditioner

Nurture My Body Shampoo and Conditioner (www.nurturemybody.com)
Penny Lane Organics Shampoo with Conditioner (www.pennylaneorganics.com)

Kid's Shampoo

Dr. Robin for Kids Body Wash and Shampoo (www.dermstore.com; search "Dr. Robin")
Healing Scents Just for Kids, Shampoo/Bath/Shower Soap (www.healing-scents.com)

Deodorant

Jungle Man Deodorant (www.junglemannaturals.com)
Jungle Woman Deodorant (www.junglemannaturals.com)
(Trust me on these, I searched endlessly for a safe, quality deodorant that actually worked, and this one is amazing for both men and women!)

Adult Sunscreen

All Terrain AquaSport SPF 30 (www.allterrainco.com)
Aubrey Organics Natural Sun Sunscreen
  (www.aubrey-organics.com)

Kid's Sunscreen

Dr. Robin for Kids Sunscreen (www.dermstore.com;
  search "Dr. Robin")
Thinkbaby Sunscreen (www.gothinkbaby.com)

Household Cleaners

Green Shield Organic (www.greenshieldorganic.com)
Sun & Earth (www.sunandearth.com)
Earth Friendly Products (www.ecos.com)

Air Fresheners

Earth Friendly Products Uni-Fresh Air Freshener (www.ecos.com)
Aussan Natural Room Odor Eliminator (www.aussannatural.com)

Bulletproof Mindset Training

In Chapters 1 and 6 we explored stress and how it can lead to adrenal
burnout. Below are my favorite resources, the ones I have personally
used to conquer my response to mental/emotional stress, and I know
they can help you battle this aspect of stress too. This collection of
books, tools, and seminars has helped me reign in my inner Hulk
and control my emotional response to nondangerous stressors that
can literally wipe out my energy, desire for life, and sex drive.

Books

Brené Brown, *Daring Greatly: How the Courage to Be Vulnerable
  Transforms the Way We Live, Love, Parent, and Lead*

Mark Divine, *The Way of the SEAL: Think Like an Elite Warrior to Lead and Succeed*

Brian Klemmer, *The Compassionate Samurai: Being Extraordinary in an Ordinary World*

Bruce McEwen, with Elizabeth Norton Lasley, *The End of Stress as We Know It*

Robert Sapolsky, *Why Zebras Don't Get Ulcers*

Hans Selye, *The Stress of Life*

James L. Wilson, *Adrenal Fatigue: The 21st Century Stress Syndrome*

Tools

HeartMath Inner Balance App or emWave2 (www.heartmath.com)
These are an incredible tools using biofeedback to help you take control of your emotional states. You will learn how to transform feelings of anger, anxiety, or frustration into feelings that are more peaceful and relaxed and discover what it feels like to shut down your inner Hulk. I spent a lot of my time early on dealing with stress by using the emWave2. I literally had to reteach my brain how to calm down; I was stuck in a constant state of high stress even when I was trying to relax.

Calm App (www.calm.com)
This app for your smartphone is a great tool to relax your body, especially when you are feeling tense from stress. You can also access the Calm program on the website if you don't have a smartphone. Just plug a pair of headphones into your computer and calm away. The program is voice-guided and does a phenomenal job getting the mind settled and quiet with minimal effort; all you have to do is just sit back and let the voice take you there. I personally use this app two to three times a day to keep my inner Hulk from emerging. (I won't lie. Every once in a while he still shows up, but I have found a way to control him 95 percent of the time, and this is one of my secrets.)

Headspace App (www.headspace.com)

This is another app for your smartphone that is a great tool for meditation. By walking you through 10 minutes a day of meditation, Andy Puddicombe helps you create a mindful meditation practice. I prefer to do the headspace program first thing every morning. I have found that starting my day with just 10 minutes of meditation clears my mind and makes me so much more effective, especially when speaking.

Seminars

Driven for Life (www.drivenforlife.com)

Driven for Life has a special place in my heart. I have attended multiple full-immersion retreats with this group, and the impact it has had on my life has been amazing. Sometimes the way to become more resilient to stress is to get out of your comfort zone and break through whatever is holding you back from living at your ultimate level. The courses offered by this group are full-immersion, detached from the rest of the world, and they really dig deep to help you grow from the inside out. Awesome life-changing experiences!

Klemmer and Associates (www.klemmer.com)

The Klemmer and Associates workshops are incredible for helping you to strip away self-doubt and the destructive belief systems that are holding you back in life and replace them with productive, beneficial, and supportive beliefs. It's amazing how much easier life is when you remove limiting beliefs. So much of the mental/emotional stress in our lives is produced by our own self-created negative belief systems.

Acknowledgments

I WANT TO START by thanking Tom Ferry for taking four hours out of his busy life two years ago to coach me into thinking bigger. Your introduction to Laura Morton has forever changed the trajectory of my life. I owe a huge thank-you to my writing partner, Laura, for believing in my message, pushing me beyond my limits, and always having my back. You have been an amazing rock of stability through this process and your ability to add sizzle to my words has been amazing to witness.

Thanks to my agent, Mel Berger at William Morris Endeavor, for taking a risk with me and seeing the possibility in my work, and to Nancy Hancock, who first saw something special in my ideas and made my dream of writing a book a reality at HarperOne.

A huge shout-out and thank-you to my incredible publishing team at HarperOne, including my publisher, Mark Tauber, my amazing editor, Julia Pastore, and the entire production, marketing, publicity, and sales staff. Thank you so much for your amazing support and patience. I wish to also thank Tina Andreadis, SVP of Publicity at Harper-Collins, for all her wonderful support and belief in my program.

I am grateful for Heidi Krupp and Darren Lisiten from Krupp Kommunications for their guidance in getting my message out to the world.

Thank you to my clients, who have put their faith and trust in my program, and thank you to all those courageous souls who willingly tested the Stark Naked 21-Day Metabolic Reset. Your experiences helped me to shape and perfect this program; I could not have completed this without your bravery.

Deep gratitude goes to all of the mentors I have had through the years who have taken the time to offer me guidance, counsel, and support on my journey.

Thank you to my amazing friends who have always been there for me throughout the years, with an extra special thank-you to three of the greatest friends a guy could ask for, Jason Von, Jeff Stover, and Chris Panaia. Thank you for being there through thick and thin—your friendships I will always cherish.

To my family: I am forever grateful for your support and belief in me. Maria and my kiddos, you have given my life incredible meaning.

Mom and Dad, thank you for always being there to pick me up, brush me off, and kick me in my fanny to keep moving forward.

Jake and Katie, life growing up with you was amazing. I so cherish the times our families get together. To my extended family, thank you for all your support, and to my wife's family here in California, thank you so much for the support during the writing of this book. Without your help with our kids, this book would never have reached completion!

Bibliography

Afaghi, Ahmad, Helen O'Connor, and Chin Moi Chow. "High-glycemic-index Carbohydrate Meals Shorten Sleep Onset." *American Journal of Clinical Nutrition* 85(2) (February 2007): 426–30. http://ajcn.nutrition.org/content/85/2/426.full.pdf.

Alter, Charlotte. "Going Off the Pill Could Affect Who You're Attracted to, Study Finds." *Time*. November 20, 2014. http://time.com/3596014/attraction-sex-birth-control/.

Amen, Daniel G. *Change Your Brain, Change Your Life: The Breakthrough Program for Conquering Anxiety, Depression, Obsessiveness, Anger, and Impulsiveness.* New York: Three Rivers, 1998.

American College of Cardiology. "Low LDL Cholesterol Is Related to Cancer Risk." *ScienceDaily*. March 26, 2012. www.sciencedaily.com/releases/2012/03/120326113713.htm.

"Androgen Deficiency in Women." *Better Health Channel*. October 22, 2014. www.betterhealth.vic.gov.au/bhcv2/bhcarticles.nsf/pages/Androgen_deficiency_in_women.

Angelilli, Jonathan. "The Massive Fitness Trend That's Not Actually Healthy at All." *Greatist*. September 29, 2014. http://greatist.com/connect/militarization-fitness.

Anwar, Yasmin. "Sleep Deprivation Linked to Junk Food Cravings." *UC Berkeley NewsCenter*. August 6, 2013. http://newscenter.berkeley.edu/2013/08/06/poor-sleep-junk-food/.

Aude, Y. Wady, et al. "The National Cholesterol Education Program Diet vs. a Diet Lower in Carbohydrates and Higher in Protein and Monounsaturated Fat." *Archives of Internal Medicine* 164(19) (October 25, 2004): 2141–46. http://archinte.jamanetwork.com/article.aspx?articleid=217514.

Bannai, Makoto, and Nobuhiro Kawai. "New Therapeutic Strategy for Amino Acid Medicine: Glycine Improves the Quality of Sleep." *Journal of Pharmacological Sciences* 118(2) (2012): 145–48. www.ncbi.nlm.nih.gov/pubmed/22293292.

Barrett-Connor, Elizabeth, et al. "The Association of Testosterone Levels with Overall Sleep Quality, Sleep Architecture, and Sleep-Disordered Breathing." *Journal of Clinical Endocrinology and Metabolism* 93(7) (July 2008): 2602–9. www.ncbi.nlm.nih.gov/pmc/articles/PMC2453053/.

Belluck, Pam. "In Study, Fatherhood Leads to Drop in Testosterone." *New York Times.* September 12, 2011. www.nytimes.com/2011/09/13/health/research/13testosterone.html ?_r=0.

Bennington, Vanessa. "How Sleep Deprivation Fries Your Hormones, Your Immune System, and Your Brain." *Breaking Muscle.* http://breakingmuscle.com/health-medicine /how-sleep-deprivation-fries-your-hormones-your-immune-system-and-your-brain.

Berardi, John. "The Get Shredded Diet." *T Nation.* July 10, 2006. http://www.t-nation.com /diet-fat-loss/the-get-shredded-diet.

"The Best Foods for Your Brain." *Prevention.* March 28, 2014. www.prevention.com/food /healthy-eating-tips/best-foods-your-brain.

"Bisphenol A (BPA)." *Breast Cancer Fund.* www.breastcancerfund.org/clear-science /radiation-chemicals-and-breast-cancer/bisphenol-a.html.

Blank, M. C., et al. "Total Body Na-depletion without Hyponatraemia Can Trigger Overtraining-like Symptoms with Sleeping Disorders and Increasing Blood Pressure: Explorative Case and Literature Study." *Medical Hypotheses* 79(6) (2012): 799–804. www.ncbi.nlm.nih.gov/pubmed/23234732.

Bledzka, Dorota, Jolanta Gromadzinska, and Wojciech Wasowicz. "Parabens: From Environmental Studies to Human Health." *Environment International* 67 (2014): 27–42. www.ncbi.nlm.nih.gov/pubmed/24657492.

"Body Burden: The Pollution in Newborns." *Environmental Working Group.* July 14, 2005. www.ewg.org/research/body-burden-pollution-newborns.

Boyles, Salynn. "Estrogen Is Involved in Stress Response." *WebMD.* December 3, 2003. www.webmd.com/depression/news/20031203/estrogen-is-involved-in-stress-response.

Brehm, Bonnie, et al. "A Randomized Trial Comparing a Very Low Carbohydrate Diet and a Calorie-Restricted Low Fat Diet on Body Weight and Cardiovascular Risk Factors in Healthy Women." *Journal of Clinical Endocrinology and Metabolism* 88(4) (2013): 1617–23. http://press.endocrine.org/doi/citedby/10.1210/jc.2002-021480.

Breus, Michael. "Early Bird or Night Owl? It's in Your Genes." December 14, 2012. www .psychologytoday.com/blog/sleep-newzzz/201212/early-bird-or-night-owl-it-s-in-your -genes.

———. "Mind-body Therapies to Ease Insomnia." Insomnia Blog. *Sleep Doctor.* November 6, 2014. www.theinsomniablog.com/the_insomnia_blog/2014/11/mind-body-therapies -to-ease-insomnia.html.

———. "Sports' Secret Weapon: Sleep." Insomnia Blog. *Sleep Doctor.* November 19, 2012. www.theinsomniablog.com/the_insomnia_blog/2012/11/sports-secret-weapon-sleep .html.

Burke, Leo. "Quotations About Sleep." www.quotegarden.com/sleep.html.

"Can't Sleep? Neither Can 60 Million Other Americans." *NPR.* May 20, 2008. www.npr.org /templates/story/story.php?storyId=90638364.

Chapman, Karina (AlohaKarina). "The Importance of Play . . . for Adults." *The Positive Page.* March 7, 2012. http://thepositivepage.com/2012/03/07/the-importance-of-play -for-adults/.

Chaput, J. P., and A. Tremblay. "Sleeping Habits Predict the Magnitude of Fat Loss in Adults

Exposed to Moderate Caloric Restriction." *Obesity Facts* 5(4) (2012): 561–66. www.ncbi
.nlm.nih.gov/pubmed/22854682.

Clark, Kevin. "Sleeping Your Way to the Top." *Wall Street Journal*. November 14, 2012.
www.wsj.com/articles/SB10001424127887324556304578117112742606502.

Conger, Cristen. "5 Ways Birth Control Can Trip Up Your Love Life." *HowStuffWorks*. February 6, 2012. http://health.howstuffworks.com/sexual-health/contraception/5-ways
-birth-control-affects-love-life.htm#page=0.

Craig, B. W., R. Brown, and J. Everhart. "Effects of Progressive Resistance Training on
Growth Hormone and Testosterone Levels in Young and Elderly Subjects." *Mechanisms of Ageing and Development* 49(2) (1989): 159–69. www.ncbi.nlm.nih.gov
/pubmed/2796409.

Croson, Eastan. "Increasing Sleep Deprivation Rates Harm Students' Health." *SMU Daily
Campus*. May 4, 2014. www.smudailycampus.com/lifestyle/health/increasing-sleep
-deprivation-rates-harm-students-health.

Dean, Carolyn. "Just Say No to Birth Control Pills." *Mercola.com*. October 27, 2004. http://
articles.mercola.com/sites/articles/archive/2004/10/27/birth-control-part-two.aspx.

Dement, William C., and Charles Vaughan. *The Promise of Sleep: A Pioneer in Sleep Medicine Explores the Vital Connection Between Health, Happiness, and a Good Night's Sleep*.
New York: Delacorte, 1999.

Dingfelder, Sadie. "4 of Play's Lesser-Known Benefits." *Huffington Post*. www.huffington
post.com/sadie-dingfelder/play-health-benefits_b_2010275.html.

Divine, Mark. *The Way of the SEAL: Think Like an Elite Warrior to Lead and Succeed*. White
Plains, NY: Reader's Digest Association, 2013.

Durmer, Jeffrey, and David Dinges. "Neurocognitive Consequences of Sleep Deprivation."
Seminars in Neurology 25(1) (March 2005): 117–29. http://faculty.vet.upenn.edu/uep
/user_documents/dfd3.pdf.

Elias, Nina. "Drink This, Sleep 90 More Minutes a Night." *Prevention*. www.prevention
.com/health/sleep-energy/tart-cherry-juice-increases-sleep-time.

Epel, E. S., et al. "Stress and Body Shape: Stress-induced Cortisol Secretion Is Consistently
Greater Among Women with Central Fat." *Psychosomatic Medicine* 62(5) (September–
October 2000): 623–32. www.ncbi.nlm.nih.gov/pubmed/11020091.

"Erectile Dysfunction Drugs Market Is Expected to Reach USD 3.4 Billion Globally in 2019:
Transparency Market Research." *PR Newswire*. October 21, 2013. www.prnewswire
.com/news-releases/erectile-dysfunction-drugs-market-is-expected-to-reach-usd-34
-billion-globally-in-2019-transparency-market-research-228593931.html.

Ericsson, K. A., R. Th. Krampe, and C. Tesch-Romer. "The Role of Deliberate Practice in
the Acquisition of Expert Performance." *Psychological Review* 100(3) (1993): 363–406.

Fleet, Anna. "10 Signs of Low Testosterone in Women." *ActiveBeat*. December 30, 2013.
http://m.activebeat.com/your-health/women/10-signs-of-low-testosterone-in-women/.

FPS Team. "High Cholesterol and Metabolism." *Functional Performance Systems*. December
28, 2012. www.functionalps.com/blog/2010/12/28/high-cholesterol-and-metabolism/.

Frangoul, Anmar. "The World's 10 Leading Causes of Death." *CNBC*. February 6, 2014.
www.cnbc.com/id/101388499/page/11.

Gittleman, Ann Louise. *The Fat Flush Plan*. New York: McGraw-Hill, 2002.

Gold, Lois, Bruce Ames, and Thomas Slone. "Misconceptions About the Causes of Cancer." In Dennis J. Paustenbach, ed., *Human and Environmental Risk Assessment: Theory and Practice*. New York: Wiley, 2002. Pp. 1415–60.

Gregoire, Carolyn. "Taking a Walk in Nature Could Be the Best Thing You Do for Your Mood All Day." *Huffington Post*. September 23, 2014. www.huffingtonpost .com/2014/09/23/walk-nature-depression_n_5870134.html.

———. "10 Ways Stress Affects Women's Health." *Huffington Post*. February 6, 2013. www .huffingtonpost.com/2013/01/30/health-effects-of-stress-women_n_2585625.html.

Grossman, Richard. "Healing Points." 1994. www.acudoc.com/exercise.html.

Gunnars, Kris. "Debunking the Calorie Myth—Why 'Calories In, Calories Out' Is Wrong." *Authority Nutrition*. http://authoritynutrition.com/debunking-the-calorie-myth/.

Halyburton, Angela, et al. "Low- and High-carbohydrate Weight-loss Diets Have Similar Effects on Mood but Not Cognitive Performance." *American Journal of Clinical Nutrition* 86(3) (September 2007): 580–87. http://ajcn.nutrition.org/content/86/3/580.long.

Hellmich, Nanci. "Sleep Loss May Equal Weight Gain." *USA Today*. December 6, 2004. http://usatoday30.usatoday.com/news/health/2004-12-06-sleep-weight-gain_x.htm.

"How Do Birth Control Pills Work?" *Go Ask Alice*. April 18, 2014. http://goaskalice .columbia.edu/how-do-birth-control-pills-work.

Hsu, Christine. "Nearly a Third of Americans Are Sleep Deprived." *Medical Daily*. April 27, 2012. www.medicaldaily.com/nearly-third-americans-are-sleep-deprived-240273.

"The Importance of Play for Adults." *First Things First*. http://firstthings.org/the-importance -of-play-for-adults.

"Insufficient Sleep Is a Public Health Epidemic." *Centers for Disease Control and Prevention*. January 13, 2014. www.cdc.gov/features/dssleep/.

Jones, Rachel. "Beyond Birth Control: The Overlooked Benefits of Oral Contraceptive Pills." *Guttmacher Institute*. www.guttmacher.org/pubs/Beyond-Birth-Control.pdf.

Kadey, Matthew. "The 11 Best Foods for Your Brain." *Shape Magazine*. www.shape.com /healthy-eating/diet-tips/11-best-foods-your-brain.

Kay, Vanessa, Michael Bloom, and Warren Foster. "Reproductive and Developmental Effects of Phthalate Diesters in Males." *Critical Reviews in Toxicology* 44(6) (2014): 467–98. www.ncbi.nlm.nih.gov/pubmed/24903855.

Kharrazian, Datis. *Why Isn't My Brain Working? A Revolutionary Understanding of Brain Decline and Effective Strategies to Recover Your Brain's Health*. Carlsbad, CA: Elephant Press, 2013.

Khoo, Joan, et al. "Comparing Effects of Low- and High-Volume Moderate-Intensity Exercise on Sexual Function and Testosterone in Obese Men." *Journal of Sexual Medicine* 10(7) (2013): 1823–32. www.ncbi.nlm.nih.gov/pubmed/23635309.

Kirby, Elizabeth, et al. "Stress Increases Putative Gonadotropin Inhibitory Hormone and Decreases Luteinizing Hormone in Male Rats." *Proceedings of the National Academy of Sciences* 106(27) (2009): 11324–29. www.pnas.org/content/106/27/11324.full.

Kirchhof, Mark, and Gillian De Gannes. "The Health Controversies of Parabens." *Skin Therapy Letter* 18(2) (2013): 5–7. www.ncbi.nlm.nih.gov/pubmed/23508773.

Klingmuller, D., and A. Allera. "Endocrine Disruptors: Hormone-active Chemicals from the Environment: A Risk to Humans?" *Deutsche Medizinische Wochenschrift* 136(18) (2011): 967–72. www.ncbi.nlm.nih.gov/pubmed/21526461.

Knutson, Kristen, et al. "The Metabolic Consequences of Sleep Deprivation." *Sleep Medicine Reviews* 11(3) (2007): 163–78. www.ncbi.nlm.nih.gov/pmc/articles/PMC1991337/.

Koebler, Jason. "The New Moneyball? It's Major League Sleep." *US News.* June 15, 2012. www.usnews.com/news/articles/2012/06/15/the-new-moneyball-its-major-league-sleep.

Konduracka, Ewa, Krzysztof Krzemieniecki, and Grzegorz Gajos. "Relationship Between Everyday Use Cosmetics and Female Breast Cancer." *Polskie Archiwum Medycyny Wewnetrznej* 124(5) (2012): 264–69. www.ncbi.nlm.nih.gov/pubmed/24694726.

Kuoppala, Ali. "Sleep and Testosterone: Each Hour Means 15 percent More T." *Anabolic Men.* December 14, 2014. http://anabolicmen.com/sleep-testosterone/.

"Lack of Sleep Tied to Teen Sports Injuries." *American Academy of Pediatrics.* October 21, 2012. www.aap.org/en-us/about-the-aap/aap-press-room/pages/Lack-of-Sleep-Tied-to -Teen-Sports-Injuries.aspx.

Lam, Michael. "Estrogen Dominance—Part 2." *DrLam.com.* www.drlam.com/blog /estrogen-dominance-part-2/1781/.

Lange, Claudia, Bertram Kuch, and Jorg Metzger. "Estrogenic Activity of Constituents of Underarm Deodorants Determined by E-Screen Assay." *Chemosphere* 108 (2014): 101–6. www.ncbi.nlm.nih.gov/pubmed/24875918.

Larsen, Amber. "The Role of Testosterone for the Female Athlete." *Breaking Muscle.* http:// breakingmuscle.com/womens-fitness/the-role-of-testosterone-for-the-female-athlete.

LaValle, James B., with Stacy Lundin Yale. *Cracking the Metabolic Code: 9 Keys to Optimal Health.* North Bergen, NJ: Basic Health Publications, 2004.

Laverne, Lauren. "Why Play Is Important to Us All." *The Guardian.* www.theguardian.com /lifeandstyle/2014/oct/05/why-play-is-important-to-us-all-lauren-laverne.

Leosdottir, M., et al. "Dietary Fat Intake and Early Mortality Patterns—Data from the Malmö Diet and Cancer Study." *Journal of Internal Medicine* 258(2) (2005): 153–65. www.ncbi.nlm.nih.gov/pubmed/16018792.

Leproult, Rachel, et al. "Sleep Loss Results in an Elevation of Cortisol Levels the Next Evening." *Sleep* 20(10) (October 1997): 865–70. www.journalsleep.org/ViewAbstract .aspx?pid=24246

Lerchbaum, Elisabeth, et al. "Combination of Low Free Testosterone and Low Vitamin D Predicts Mortality in Older Men Referred for Coronary Angiography." *Clinical Endocrinology* 77(3) (2012): 475–83.

Lorgeril, Michel, et al. "Mediterranean Diet, Traditional Risk Factors, and the Rate of Cardiovascular Complications After Myocardial Infarction: Final Report of the Lyon Diet Heart Study." *Circulation* 99(6) (1999): 779–85. www.ncbi.nlm.nih.gov /pubmed/9989963.

"Luteinising Hormone." *You & Your Hormones.* January 7, 2015. www.yourhormones.info /hormones/luteinising_hormone.aspx.

MacLean, Christopher, et al. "Effect of the Transcendental Meditation Program on Adaptive Mechanisms: Changes in Hormone Levels and Responses to Stress After Four

Months of Practice." *Psychoneuroendocrinology* 22(4) (May 1997): 277–95. www.ncbi
.nlm.nih.gov/pubmed/9226731.

Maglione-Garves, Christine, Len Kravitz, and Suzanne Schneider. "Cortisol Connection: Tips
on Managing Stress and Weight." *Stress Cortisol Connection.* www.unm.edu/~lkravitz
/Article folder/stresscortisol.html.

Marcantel, Tina. "Hormones and How They Interact." *Dr. Tina Marcantel.* February 21,
2014. www.drmarcantel.com/hormones-and-how-they-interact/.

McEvoy, Michael. "Cholesterol: Your Body Is Incapable of Making Hormones Without It."
Metabolic Healing. April 11, 2011. http://metabolichealing.com/cholesterol-your-body
-is-incapable-of-making-hormones-without-it/.

McTiernan, Anne, et al. "Effect of Exercise on Serum Estrogens in Postmenopausal Women:
A 12-Month Randomized Clinical Trial." *Cancer Research* 64 (2004): 2923–28. http://
cancerres.aacrjournals.org/content/64/8/2923.full.pdf.

Mercola, Joseph. "9 Healthy Foods to Boost Your Brain Health." *Mercola.com.* October
31, 2013. http://articles.mercola.com/sites/articles/archive/2013/10/31/9-foods-brain
-health.aspx.

———. "Research Again Confirms Links Between Poor Sleep, Weight Gain, and Cancer."
Mercola.com. July 11, 2013. http://articles.mercola.com/sites/articles/archive/2013/07/11
/poor-sleep.aspx.

Michalsen, A., et al. "Effects of Short-Term Modified Fasting on Sleep Patterns and Daytime Vigilance in Non-Obese Subjects: Results of a Pilot Study." *Annals of Nutrition and
Metabolism* 47(5) (2003): 194–200. www.ncbi.nlm.nih.gov/pubmed/12748412.

Munsters, Marjet J. M., Wim H. M. Saris, and Anita Magdalena Hennige. "Effects of Meal
Frequency on Metabolic Profiles and Substrate Partitioning in Lean Healthy Males."
PLoS One 7(6) (2012): e38632. www.ncbi.nlm.nih.gov/pubmed/22719910.

Nagendra, Ravindra, Nirmala Maruthai, and Bindu Kutty. "Meditation and Its Regulatory
Role on Sleep." *Frontiers in Neurology* 3 (April 18, 2012): 54. www.ncbi.nlm.nih.gov
/pubmed/22529834.

Nago, Naoki, et al. "Low Cholesterol Is Associated with Mortality from Stroke, Heart Disease, and Cancer: The Jichi Medical School Cohort Study." *Japan Epidemiological Association* 21(1) (2011): 67–74. www.ncbi.nlm.nih.gov/pubmed/21160131.

Nakamura, Daichi, et al. "Bisphenol A May Cause Testosterone Reduction by Adversely
Affecting Both Testis and Pituitary Systems Similar to Estradiol." *Toxicology Letters*
194(1) (2010): 16–25. www.ncbi.nlm.nih.gov/pubmed/20144698.

National Sleep Foundation. "Facts and Stats." *DrowsyDriving.org.* http://drowsydriving.org
/about/facts-and-stats/.

Neckelmann, Dag, Arnstein Mykletun, and Alv A. Dahl. "Chronic Insomnia as a Risk Factor
for Developing Anxiety and Depression." *Sleep* 30(6) (2007): 873–80. www.journalsleep
.org/ViewAbstract.aspx?pid=26880.

Owens, Paula. "Your Hormones and Where You Store Fat." *PaulaOwens.com.* http://
thepowerof4-paula.blogspot.com/2010/10/your-hormones-where-you-store-fat.html.

Park, Alice. "Tip for Insomniacs: Cool Your Head to Fall Asleep." *Time.* June 17, 2011. http://
healthland.time.com/2011/06/17/tip-for-insomniacs-cool-your-head-to-fall-asleep/.

Penev, P. D. "Association Between Sleep and Morning Testosterone Levels in Older Men." *Sleep* 30 (4) (April 2007): 427–32. www.ncbi.nlm.nih.gov/pubmed/17520786.

"Phthalates." *Breast Cancer Fund.* www.breastcancerfund.org/clear-science/radiation-chemicals-and-breast-cancer/phthalates.html.

"Progesterone." *You & Your Hormones.* www.yourhormones.info/hormones/progesterone.aspx.

Pulsipher, Charlie. "15 Foods to Improve Your Memory Naturally and Boost Brain Power." *Sunwarrior News RSS.* October 21, 2013. www.sunwarrior.com/news/brain-foods/.

Radcliffe, Shawn. "Birth Control Pills Affect Long-Term Relationships." *Men's Fitness.* www.mensfitness.com/women/sex-tips/birth-control-pills-affect-long-term-relationships.

Reinberg, Steven. "Low Testosterone Could Increase Death Risk." *Consumer Health-Day.* August 15, 2006. http://consumer.healthday.com/general-health-information-16/endocrinology-news-231/low-testosterone-could-increase-death-risk–534396.html.

Reynolds, Amy, et al. "Impact of Five Nights of Sleep Restriction on Glucose Metabolism, Leptin, and Testosterone in Young Adult Men." *PLOS One* 7(7) (July 23, 2012): e41218. http://journals.plos.org/plosone/article?id=10.1371/journal.pone.0041218.

Richards, Byron. "Unclog Your Liver and Lose Abdominal Fat—Leptin Diet Weight Loss Challenge #6." *Wellness Resources.* May 7, 2012. www.wellnessresources.com/weight/articles/unclog_your_liver_lose_your_abdominal_fat_leptin_diet_weight_loss_challenge/.

Ruper, Stefani. "Low on Progesterone? Why Stress Reduction Might Be the Only Way to Hack It." *Paleo for Women.* March 19, 2013. http://paleoforwomen.com/low-on-progesterone-stress-reduction-might-be-the-only-one-way-to-hack-it/.

Sapolsky, Robert. "Sex and Reproduction." In *Why Zebras Don't Get Ulcers.* 3rd ed. New York: Holt, 1994. Pp. 120–143.

Schackne, Elliott. "Fix Your Breakfast." *Orion Lifestyle.* January 15, 2015. www.orionlifestyle.com/#!Fix-Your-Breakfast/clfr/3827CC11-72A3-41EB-9F92-59F8FBDF40F1.

Schatz, Irwin, et al. "Cholesterol and All-cause Mortality in Elderly People from the Hono-lulu Heart Program: A Cohort Study." *Lancet* 358(9279) (August 4, 2001): 351–55. www.ncbi.nlm.nih.gov/pubmed/11502313.

Schauss, Mark. *Achieving Victory Over a Toxic World.* Bloomington, IN: Author House, 2008.

Schwarzbein, Diana, and Nancy Deville. *The Schwarzbein Principle: The Truth About Losing Weight, Being Healthy, and Feeling Younger.* Deerfield Beach, FL: Health Communica-tions, 1999.

Scott, S. J. "How Good Habits Can Decrease Stress on Multiple Levels." *Develop Good Hab-its.* December 18, 2014. www.developgoodhabits.com/decreases-stress-habits/.

Seaman, Greg. "The Healing Power of a Walk in the Woods." *Eartheasy Blog.* July 5, 2011. http://eartheasy.com/blog/2011/07/the-healing-power-of-a-walk-in-the-woods/.

Shankar, Anoop, Srinivas Teppala, and Charumathi Sabanayagam. "Urinary BPA Lev-els and Measures of Obesity: Results from the NHANES." *ISRN Endocrinology* 2012(965423) (2012). www.ncbi.nlm.nih.gov/pubmed/22852093.

Siri-Tarino, Patty, et al. "Saturated Fat, Carbohydrate, and Cardiovascular Disease."

American Journal of Clinical Nutrition 91(3) (2010): 502–09. http://ajcn.nutrition.org /content/91/3/502.abstract.

Sisson, Mark. "Chronotypes: Are You an Early Bird or a Night Owl?" *Mark's Daily Apple*. November 5, 2013. www.marksdailyapple.com/chronotypes-are-you-an-early-bird-or -a-night-owl/#axzz2jp0zMfUI.

———. "How to Manufacture the Best Night of Sleep in Your Life." *Mark's Daily Apple*. November 6, 2013. http://www.marksdailyapple.com/how-to-manufacture-the-best -night-of-sleep-in-your-life/#axzz3NLMVL9Ti.

———. "Testosterone: Not So Manly After All?" *Mark's Daily Apple*. June 29, 2010. www .marksdailyapple.com/testosterone-women/#axzz3NDAXfiul.

———. "Your Heart Is Telling You to Sleep." *Mark's Daily Apple*. December 27, 2008. www .marksdailyapple.com/link-between-sleep-heart-health/#axzz3NLMVL9Ti.

"Sleep and Mood." *Healthy Sleep*. Division of Sleep Medicine at Harvard Medical School. http://healthysleep.med.harvard.edu/need-sleep/whats-in-it-for-you/mood.

Smith, Pamela. "A Comprehensive Look at Hormones and the Effects of Hormone Replacement." *American Academy of Anti-Aging Medicine*. www.a4m.com/assets/pdf/bookstore /aamt_vol7_41_smith.pdf.

Sondike, Stephan, Nancy Copperman, and Marc Jacobson. "Effects of a Low-carbohydrate Diet on Weight Loss and Cardiovascular Risk Factor in Overweight Adolescents." *Journal of Pediatrics* 142(3) (2003): 253–58. www.sciencedirect.com/science/article/pii /S0022347602402065.

Sprague, Brian, et al. "Circulating Serum Xenoestrogens and Mammographic Breast Density." *Breast Cancer Research* 15(3) (2013): R45. www.ncbi.nlm.nih.gov/pubmed /23710608.

Strandberg, Timo, et al. "Long-term Mortality After 5-Year Multifactorial Primary Prevention of Cardiovascular Diseases in Middle-aged Men." *Journal of the American Medical Association* 266(9) (1991): 1225–29. http://jama.jamanetwork.com/article .aspx?articleid=391550.

"Stress Effects on the Body." *American Psychological Association*. http://www.apa.org/help center/stress-body.aspx.

"Survey: Americans Know How to Get Better Sleep—but Don't Act on It." *Better Sleep Council*. http://bettersleep.org/better-sleep/the-science-of-sleep/sleep-statistics -research/better-sleep-survey.

Taubes, Gary. *Why We Get Fat and What to Do About It*. New York: Knopf, 2011.

"Ten Rules for Raising Testosterone for a Stronger, Leaner Body." *Poliquin Group*. February 28, 2014. www.poliquingroup.com/ArticlesMultimedia/Articles/Article/1129/Ten _Rules_For_Raising_Testosterone_for_a_Stronger_.aspx.

Teta, Jade. "Female Belly Fat: Stress, Menopause and Other Causes." *Metabolic Effect*. June 28, 2013. www.metaboliceffect.com/female-belly-fat/.

———. "Female Hormones: Estrogen (Oestrogen) and Weight Loss." *Metabolic Effect*. June 10, 2013. www.metaboliceffect.com/female-hormones-estrogen/.

———. "Female Hormones and Weight Loss." *Metabolic Effect*. February 23, 2012. www .metaboliceffect.com/female-effect-hormones-determine-female-fat-patterns/.

———. "Hormones and Stress: Cortisol." *Metabolic Effect.* April 2, 2013. www.metabolic effect.com/hormones-stress-cortisol/.

———. "Want to Lose Fat? Count Your Hormones, Not Your Calories (Part 2)." *Huffington Post.* August 8, 2012. www.huffingtonpost.com/dr-jade-teta/weight-loss_b_1703931 .html.

Teta, Jade, and Keoni Teta. "The Calorie Trap. Why Some Will Never Win the Weight Loss Game." *Metabolic Effect.* March 1, 2012. www.metaboliceffect.com/calorie-trap-win -weight-loss-game/.

"Tip 172: Add Tart Cherries to Your Diet for Better Sleep, Better and Faster Recovery." *Poliquin Group.* September 15, 2011. www.poliquingroup.com/Tips/tabid/130 /entryid/641/Tip-172-Add-Tart-Cherries-to-Your-Diet-for-Better-Sleep-Better-and -Faster-Recovery.aspx.

"Toxin Exposure Among Children." *Unite for Sight.* www.uniteforsight.org/environmental -health/module2.

"Triazine Herbicides (Atrazine)." *Breast Cancer Fund.* www.breastcancerfund.org/clear -science/radiation-chemicals-and-breast-cancer/pesticides.html.

"The Truth About Tart Cherry Juice and Sleep." *Valley Sleep Center.* December 6, 2012. http://valleysleepcenter.com/blog/the-truth-about-tart-cherry-juice-and-sleep/.

Turner, Natasha. *The Hormone Diet: A 3-Step Program to Help You Lose Weight, Gain Strength, and Live Younger Longer.* New York: Rodale, 2010. Pp. 204–5.

Ulmer, Hanno, et al. "Why Eve Is Not Adam: Prospective Follow-up in 149,650 Women and Men of Cholesterol and Other Risk Factors Related to Cardiovascular and All-cause Mortality." *Journal of Women's Health* 13(1) (January–February 2004): 41–53. www.ncbi .nlm.nih.gov/pubmed/15006277.

Vann, Madeline. "One in Four Men Over 30 Has Low Testosterone." *ABC News.* March 23, 2015. http://abcnews.go.com/Health/Healthday/story?id=4508669.

"Vitamins and Minerals—What Do They Do?" *Netdoctor.* www.netdoctor.co.uk/health _advice/facts/vitamins_which.htm.

Volek, Jeff, Stephen Phinney, et al. "Carbohydrate Restriction Has a More Favorable Impact on the Metabolic Syndrome Than a Low-Fat Diet." *Lipids* 44(4) (2008): 297–309. http:// link.springer.com/article/10.1007/s11745-008-3274-2.

Volek, J., M. Sharman, et al. "Comparison of Energy-restricted Very Low-carbohydrate and Low-fat Diets on Weight Loss and Body Composition in Overweight Men and Women." *Nutrition and Metabolism* 1(13) (2004). www.ncbi.nlm.nih.gov/pmc/articles /PMC538279/.

Wachob, Colleen. "14 Things I Wish All Women Knew About the Pill." *MindBodyGreen.* September 13, 2013. www.mindbodygreen.com/0-10932/14-things-i-wish-all-women -knew-about-the-pill.html.

Wada, Kai, et al. "A Tryptophan-rich Breakfast and Exposure to Light with Low Color Temperature at Night Improve Sleep and Salivary Melatonin Level in Japanese Students." *Journal of Circadian Rhythms* 11(4) (May 25, 2013).

Whitman, Jessie. "The Overnight Diet: Lose Weight While You Sleep, No Exercise Required." *Fitness Watch MD.* April 18, 2013. http://fitnesswatch-md.com/2013/04/overnight-diet -lose-weight-while-you-sleep-no-exercise-required/.

Wolf, Robb. *The Paleo Solution: The Original Human Diet.* Las Vegas, NV: Victory Belt, 2010.

Wrobel, Anna, and Ewa Gregoraszczuk. "Actions of Methyl-, Propyl- and Butylparaben on Estrogen Receptor-á and -â and the Progesterone Receptor in MCF-7 Cancer Cells and Non-cancerous MCF–10A Cells." *Toxicology Letters* 230(3) (2014): 375–81. www.ncbi .nlm.nih.gov/pubmed/25128701.

Yi, S., et al. "Short Sleep Duration in Association with CT-scanned Abdominal Fat Areas: The Hitachi Health Study." *International Journal of Obesity* 37(1) (2012): 129–34. www .ncbi.nlm.nih.gov/pubmed/22349574.

"Zeranol." *Breast Cancer Fund.* www.breastcancerfund.org/clear-science/radiation -chemicals-and-breast-cancer/zeranol.html.

Zhao, Hong-yan, et al. "The Effects of Bisphenol A (BPA) Exposure on Fat Mass and Serum Leptin Concentrations Have No Impact on Bone Mineral Densities in Non-obese Pre-menopausal Women." *Clinical Biochemistry* 45(18) (December 2012): 1602–6.

Zinczenko, David. "10 Superfoods Healthier Than Kale." *Huffington Post.* December 25, 2014. www.huffingtonpost.com/david-zinczenko/10-superfoods-healthier-t_b_6213842 .html.

Index

About the Author

Brad Davidson is an author, speaker, and performance coach from Orange County, CA. He is a highly-respected nutrition and fitness expert, a world-renowned strength coach, and a highly sought-after international speaker on the topic of metabolism and performance enhancement. Brad grew up in McMinnville, a small town in Oregon, and moved to California in 1998 to pursue his passion for health and fitness. Today, he has become a leading authority in helping high-achieving executives, professional athletes, tactical athletes, and highly-driven individuals to offset and optimize their insatiable need to push themselves beyond physical limits. In the last 3 years, Brad has consulted for over 450 CEOs; athletes from 28 professional teams; 6 First Round NFL Draft picks; 4 Miss California contestants; 9 athletes from the Crossfit Games (including the top 3 most fit women at the 2013 Games); and active members from SWAT, SEB, and the Navy Seals. He serves clients from as far away as Dubai and New Zealand, as well as throughout the United States and Canada, and he also hosts a weekly Podcast, *Relax and Conquer Radio*.

Brad has trained with some of the world's leading experts in such areas as stress resiliency, cellular physiology, performance nutrition, recovery methodology, behavioral sciences, brain optimization, and hormonal regulation, leading to his development of Stark's cutting-edge protocols. He has been featured on Dr. Daniel Amen's PBS special and in his bestselling book *The Amen Solution* as the program's fitness coach and wrote the workouts for Tana Amen's bestselling book *The Omni Diet*. He was a monthly contributor to *TapOut Magazine* and *MMA Worldwide* for two years and also hosts a weekly podcast, *Stark Naked Radio*. He has also been a featured guest on the Robb Wolf Podcast and Wodcast Podcast.

www.braddavidson.com

Laura Morton is the coauthor of more than forty books and twenty *New York Times* bestsellers, including work with Joan Lunden, Al Roker, Melissa Etheridge, Susan Lucci, John Maxwell, Danica Patrick, Sandra Lee, Marilu Henner, Justin Bieber, and Duane "Dog" Chapman, among many others. She lives in New York.